1

———

SPECIAL AGENT MITCHELL PARKER TRIED TO KEEP HIS heart rate steady. He breathed in deeply, exhaled slowly and applied techniques that were second nature to him in stressful situations, except when he was on the water. His six-foot-two frame and diving gear took up one corner of the 42-foot Duffy boat in which he sat and waited.

"OK?" his teammate Ellen Beetson asked from port side.

He looked over at Ellen, petite and blonde, and a divemaster.

"Unlike you, I prefer my feet on land or in the air," he said.

She laughed breaking the tension.

"You've got to agree this is beautiful," their

skipper called back as he navigated over the endless stretch of blue ocean.

Mitch turned his gaze to the water streaming by him. He looked over the edge and scoped the surface of the area they were approaching. He knew what to expect and beauty didn't come into it on this fly-in, fly-out assignment; he'd be home late tonight like nothing happened.

"We're almost at the coordinates," the skipper called, "and there's about an hour of light left."

"Let's get to it," Ellen said. She zipped up her wetsuit and Mitch followed suit. Ellen checked their gear again before shrugging on the air tank that Mitch held up for her. He slipped his own tank over his shoulders.

The boat stopped and dropped anchor. A minute later the skipper joined them.

"Right above where you need to be," he said.

Mitch and Ellen put on their masks and sitting on the edge of the boat, flipped back into the water with one easy push. Mitch was struck by the silence as he glided through the depths following Ellen. The only sound he could hear was his own breathing ... in and out. He reeled as a large black-spotted eel zipped past his mask. He followed Ellen towards the wreck on the floor of Cape Hatteras. She pointed to a shark following a large school of fish.

Mitch didn't notice. He was looking to a flat area on the bottom of the ocean not far from the wreck where a bundle lay.

He swam towards it; dreading what he knew to expect. Tangled with cable, their masks and tanks still on, two drowned men stared blankly at him.

———

TWO DAYS EARLIER

The middle-aged Asian man stood on the shoreline of Cape Hatteras lighthouse beach and looked out to sea. Remnants of sand castles were dotted around the water's edge. Several families braved the cool weather to wade knee-deep into the water.

He knew this beach.

The Graveyard of the Atlantic; strong tides and rip currents, home to hundreds of ships lost at sea. The definition ran through his head.

And well located for navigation along the eastern seaboard of North America.

He raised the binoculars to his eyes. Water engulfed his shoes; he didn't notice. He lowered the binoculars. Panic swept through him as he stared out to sea; he had been waiting for hours now. The sun was beginning to dip lower on the horizon.

Where are they? He clenched his teeth. They're an hour late. No instruction to abort.

An elderly couple stopped near him.

"Give it a few more weeks ... the herons are migrating now but soon the ducks and geese will be here for the winter." The man tipped his hat.

The Asian man smiled and nodded. "Thank you, thank you," he said.

As the couple passed, he glanced at his watch, turned and walked towards a sandy ledge. He climbed and stood atop.

Another glance through the binoculars; nothing.

He sank down, discarded the binoculars and rubbed his hands over his face.

What's gone wrong this time?

William decided then that he would not report the extent of the failure up the line; this project had to work, there was no going back and he wouldn't tolerate someone higher up getting cold feet and calling it off.

After a few moments, he rose, stumbled down from the dune and disappeared behind it.

2

NOW

MITCH FOLLOWED THE BLACK LINE.

He winced from the strain in his shoulders and promised himself he could quit after four more laps. Mitch was a running man. He liked to put on his runners and head out the door, any day, any time. Swimming required organization—fitting around pool opening times, packing gear and carrying cash —planning he couldn't be bothered with most days, not to mention sharing lanes with fellow swimmers who had to be competitive. He would have liked to have counted the dive yesterday as water time but he knew that was cheating. Besides he spent more time on the flight to and from Cape Hatteras than he did in the water... no exercise in that.

Once a week, he told himself as he followed the black line, lap after lap. Once a week to give the joints a break and keep up my swimming fitness.

He was a capable swimmer and with his athletic build, he made it look easy. He turned mechanically at the end of the lane, kicked out against the wall and propelled through the water for another round of freestyle. In the water his time was his own; he couldn't carry a pager or be tracked down. A thousand thoughts ran through his mind—what happened to those men? Why were they there? Where did they come from? Where is their ship now?

Mitch hit something in the water. He stopped mid-lane to see a flipper floating in front of him. He looked up and through his goggles saw a tall, blond man standing pool side with hands on hips. It was one of his team, Nicholas Everett.

"Nick! What?" He threw the flipper back and pushed the goggles up on his forehead.

"We're wanted." Nick held up his pager.

"I'm not here," Mitch said.

"I've seen you!"

"Can't you see me in about half an hour?"

Nick frowned.

"Right." Mitch sighed and sank back into the blue surroundings of the pool. He debated not coming up but his lungs demanded it. Nick was gone, and he finished the twenty yards to the end of the pool and hoisted himself out.

Mitch grabbed his towel and wrapped it around his shoulders to cover the scars running the length of his back. He glanced around; no one had noticed.

The adrenaline began to course through him. It was not uncommon to work twenty-four-seven when on a case, but after retrieving the bodies yesterday, it was normally just a waiting game.

Not anymore!

———

Mitch raced up from the parking lot to his office in the J. Edgar Hoover Building, the headquarters of the Federal Bureau of Investigation's field office in Washington D.C. Inside, he took the stairs two at a time to his department's floor and glanced towards John Windsor's office—the Executive Director for the Trans-national Crime Unit. John was on the phone and Mitch's team gathered in the coffee station outside his office, waiting.

"Hey," he announced his arrival.

"Mitch, thanks for coming," Nick, the newest

member of the team and Mitch's oldest friend, ragged him.

"Wanted to make an entrance." Mitch grinned at Nick, who except for being the same height was a perfect contrast to Mitch's dark hair and blue eyes.

Ellen flicked through the newspaper as she sat on the desk next to Nick. Her blonde hair was tied back and the odd splatter of paint featured around her face and on her arms.

Mitch smiled at her. "Nice shade."

Ellen looked at the patch of blue paint on her arm. "Yeah, yeah, I've heard it already. What do you expect if you call me in on a Sunday? At this rate, it will never be finished. It's taken me two weeks to do one wall of the bathroom."

"I hear that is in now," Nick offered. "It's called a feature wall."

Ellen shook her head. "It's featured all right because the other walls now look drab."

"Well I just got out of bed," Samantha Moore boasted as she pushed the plunger down on a fresh pot of coffee.

"Yeah, we didn't want to say anything but the pajama pants and messy hair gave it away," Nick teased.

"Hmph." She poured a hot mug of dark coffee, before handing it to Mitch. "You smell of chlorine. No prize for guessing where you were."

"Thanks," he took a few mouthfuls of coffee, feeling the warmth permeate through him. "I was swimming at the uni. By myself I might add."

Nick cleared his throat. "Yeah, sorry about that ... I intended to come but, uh, I got caught up."

"Where? In the sheets?" Mitch asked.

"No, actually. There was a housemate-wanted notice on the hallway corkboard on Friday and I grabbed it, called up the damsel wanting a house-mate and moved in this morning."

"Who is she?" Ellen asked.

"Amy Callaghan, know her?" Nick asked.

"No," Ellen and Samantha answered in unison. Mitch avoided the question; he knew her, had even dated her once and was pretty sure she didn't want to know him.

"I hate swimming," Samantha continued.

"I know, but you're going to have to get better at it." Mitch turned to her.

"Why?" Samantha looked alarmed.

John Windsor hung up and beckoned them in.

"I'll explain later," Mitch told her.

"Mitch..." John diverted his attention from the computer screen to look at him. "Where were you?"

"At the pool." Mitch's voice was laced with exasperation. "For an hour."

"Remind me to get you a waterproof, vibrating pager." John made a note.

9

"And where do I wear that?" Mitch asked.

"You'll find somewhere."

Mitch observed that even on a Sunday, John was dressed in a navy suit, his tidily cropped gray hair groomed to perfection. He had compromised—wearing a T-shirt under his jacket instead of a business shirt.

Nick collapsed into a chair near the door. "I was hoping when we couldn't reach you, Mitch, that you might have been getting some action."

"I expect you to respond to the pager even if you are getting some ... action," John responded.

Mitch rolled his eyes and kick started the brief. "What have you got?"

John pressed a button on his desk that lowered a screen from the ceiling. He dimmed the lights. "Close the door please."

Nick looked around; the outside offices were empty. He closed the door.

John tapped some keys on his keyboard to call up a photo; a head shot of an Asian man.

"Ying Shan, known to us as William Ying, Chinese ambassador to D.C.," John began. "He applied for permanent residency for himself, his wife and child when he finished his tenure last year and it was granted. On his last day in office, at a function, he disappeared. His wife reported him missing. It's been twelve months and still no sign of him."

John clicked to the next photo; a grainy shot of a figure on a beach, standing at the water's edge. Beside him, a family could be seen wading in the water.

"This photo was sent in by Andrew Gunston, one of our agents. He returned yesterday from holidaying with his family at Cape Hatteras. Gunston worked for a short time on William's case before it was marked unsolved and put on ice." John began to pace around the room. "Gunston didn't notice anything on the day this was photo was taken, but when he looked through his holiday photos last night, he found three successive photos of this man on the beach looking out to sea. In one shot, the man is using binoculars." John returned to the computer and flicked through the shots that had been doctored to feature only the Asian man on the shoreline.

Mitch leaned in and squinted at the shot. "Is it William Ying?"

"Gunston seems to think so." He continued through the photos.

"So when exactly on his holidays were these taken?" Mitch asked.

"On Thursday. Gunston's wife took the shots."

"Any shots out to sea?"

"No, and Gunston doesn't recall seeing anything unusual—no boats, no other swimmers. But he said he can't be certain ... he wasn't looking for anything unusual," John concluded.

"Did this Asian guy, William Ying, take photos or just use binoculars?" Mitch continued.

"Gunston can't recall."

"Geez, when he goes on holidays, he really goes on holidays." Mitch frowned. "So, what's the hook?"

John smiled.

"The binoculars. When Gunston was packing up his family's gear at the beach, one of his kids found the binoculars on a rock. Gunston said there was no sign of an owner so he let his son have them."

Mitch's eyes widened. "And?"

"After he saw the photos, Gunston brought the binoculars straight to the lab when he arrived back from holidays. The lab found William Ying's fingerprints are all over them."

"So why not hand it over to missing persons?" Samantha asked. "They can declare William Ying not-missing!"

"Because we're thinking this is connected to the two drowned Asian divers we retrieved yesterday near the stretch of water where the binoculars were found?" Mitch asked

"Yes," John said, and then played his trump card. "There was another set of fingerprints on the binoculars belonging to a Chinese dissident with a criminal record a mile long—Huang 'Danny' Ming. Note the Asian surname goes first."

"Why do they take a western name?" Samantha asked.

"Probably because when they come here we can't get their name right," Mitch suggested.

John continued. "He goes by the western name of Danny Huang. And Danny Huang, according to our records, isn't even in the country."

Mitch took the fingerprint report from John, had a look, and passed it around.

"Are both prints fresh?" Mitch asked.

"Good question," John said. "If Danny Huang is not in the country, they might be old prints. You can check that out."

"What have we got on Danny then?" Mitch asked.

"Glad you asked." John picked up a manila file the size of the phone book and dropped it into Mitch's lap.

"Good!" Mitch sized it up with dismay. "Some light reading."

"So, where do you want to begin?" John asked.

Mitch stood up. "We need the area under surveillance immediately. Nick, that's your specialty... or it used to be," he said, referring to their time in the Air Force when Nick specialized in reconnaissance, surveillance, search and rescue. "Sam, you look like more of a beachgoer than Ellie, best you go with Nick." He turned to Ellen, noting her almost translucent white skin.

Ellen glanced at her white arms. "I guess it has been a while since I've seen the sun."

"When do you want us to go?" Nick asked.

"On the next flight."

"We could drive down," Nick suggested.

"No, we need someone there now. If there are no flights then yeah, drive, but it's just over a six hour road trip from memory," Mitch said.

"Six-and-a-half hours, if you are doing the speed limit," John said with a glance to Mitch. John turned to his computer and tapped into the company's travel page.

Mitch continued. "Ellie and I will get started on some ground work here."

"There's a flight leaving in ninety minutes, I'll get you both onto it," John said. "It will get you to Norfolk International in an hour and then it's only three hours drive." He picked up the phone to call administration to book the flights.

Mitch continued, "Nick, Sam, follow in Gunston's footsteps; rent a place, play the tourist couple, swim, photograph each other, fish, surf, whatever it takes. Go at sunrise, sunset, different times of the day and observe activity in the area. Get some shots out to sea ... who knows what he's looking for. Photograph everything. If William was there once, he may come back again."

"And I'll put in a courtesy call to the Dare County Sheriff's Office, just in case he notices you two looking suspicious," John added.

"Just stick to the budget," Mitch warned.

"We'd better share a room if we're a couple, just to keep the cover authentic," Nick suggested.

Mitch shot Samantha a look.

"What?" she said defensively. "I sleep with one agent on an overseas job and now I'm branded for life!"

"Don't worry, if we sleep together we won't tell you, problem solved," Nick said.

"Nick, you're not helping." Samantha hit his arm. "Shut up!"

"Nicholas, Samantha ..." Mitch began.

Samantha began to laugh at his fatherly tone.

"You're killing me," Mitch sighed. "Go home and pack."

Nick and Samantha moved to the door.

"Hey, before you go ..." Mitch stopped them. "I've been thinking ... we have got to address our skills shortage."

"What skills shortage?" Samantha dropped back into a chair.

"You're not addressing it if it means more man-power." John shut down the laptop. "Sorry, can't help you there."

"No, not people, prowess," Mitch emphasized. "You know, fill the skills we are short of in our team or need to refresh. That last assignment brought home to me the fact that we can't cover each other."

Mitch saw their blank stares.

"Ellie, if you and Nick had to abort from that plane last assignment, you wouldn't have known how to."

"I could have done a tandem parachute jump," Nick said.

"You could have. But what if you are not around, Nick? How does Ellie get out of the plane? Ever parachuted?" He didn't wait for an answer. "Sam, you've said yourself a thousand times you're a hope-less swimmer; what if you had to swim to save your-self or tow one of us in to shore?"

"I passed the fifty yard freestyle test at high school," Samantha declared. "Besides, there was no swimming requirement when I joined the FBI."

"Sam, you're not in the Information Technology department anymore. You will get water-based as-signments. Besides, fifty yards is the length of the bathtub!" Mitch exaggerated.

Nick laughed out loud and attracted Mitch's attention.

"And Nick..."

"Ah, here we go..." Nick frowned.

"Given you've just finished your course at Quantico, your skills should be the most up-to-date, even though we've been carrying the load while you've been off playing."

"Poor you!" Nick sympathized.

"So, we've got to skill-up. Samantha, the Lifeguard Association offers a certification program—lifeguard with first aid. I want you to complete it."

"Can't practice that in the bathtub," Nick smiled.

Samantha scowled at him.

Mitch continued. "Ellie, there's a parachuting course for the military at Fairchild Air Force Base. It goes for about five weeks, but I can't spare you for that long, so do the basics. John can you pull a few favors and get Ellie in sooner rather than later? There's a hefty waiting list."

"Should be doable." John nodded.

Ellen looked at Mitch as though the sky had fallen on her. "You know I don't like heights."

Mitch didn't wait for her to finish the protest. "We need to work out the dates. Don't all go in the same week and leave me and Nick to hold the fort. Having said that, I want all certificates by the end of the year if possible, any questions?"

"That's only three months away!" Samantha looked alarmed.

Mitch thought for a moment. "That's right."

"But," Samantha protested, "it is way too cold to do swimming training now."

"They heat the pool, Sam."

"And what course, pray tell, will you do?" Nick asked.

"Finance skills for managers," John piped in. He moved to his in-tray and withdrew a wad of paper and handed it to Mitch. "How anyone can ace the mathematics and physics required to become a pilot, but not be able to manage a balance sheet is beyond me."

Mitch glanced at the paperwork with the column in red indicating his budget for the year had long ago been depleted.

"If you increase my budget, then it will balance."

John continued. "Nice try. One of the college's has a six-week external Financial Skills for Managers course that starts next month. I'm prepared to spend a grand from my budget to put you through it."

Mitch looked up at him. "You're not serious?"

He noticed his team doing their best to suppress their smiles.

"Signed you up for two subjects; your textbook is in the mail." John rose. "All right, I'll go see to these flights and accommodation. I'll email them to you Nick and Sam if you want to grab your gear and head straight to the airport." He walked out of his office.

Mitch followed John. "John, wait up."

3

DANNY HUANG WAITED IN LINE AT THE WASHINGTON-Dulles International Airport to officially enter onto American soil. Behind him three of his male colleagues, aged between nineteen and thirty-five, stood motionless, accustomed to the discipline of standing at attention for long periods.

Their visas indicated they were from the Beijing Armed Police Force; trainers and guests of the United States for three weeks to take part in a training course with the former G20 security command team and to complete the Diploma in Professional English offered by the International College of English in D.C. in preparation for the G20 to be staged in Beijing next year.

Danny Huang glanced at his passport and when

the time came, stepped up to the yellow line and handed it over the counter to the ageing, overweight customs officer. He did not anticipate any trouble passing through customs; after all, he was a police officer and invited guest. The customs officer looked at the photo of police officer Ip Shi and back at Danny Huang. Stamping the book, he nodded for him to pass through.

Danny Huang suppressed a smile.

Not even my photo or my name. Yes, we all look alike to you westerners.

He waited as each of his colleagues were stamped and cleared.

Too easy. The hardest part of the operation is over, he mused.

On the way to their hotel, Danny Huang looked out the window at the city passing by him. His mission had been many years in the planning and now the time to act was drawing near. The excitement coursed through him. He was tired of the wait; like being a solider never sent to war. The world would be surprised, shocked and critical, but he would be proud.

He looked around at his team of three; each man trustworthy and hand-picked to get the American VIP out of the country. Danny squinted as he looked at Kiang Hai; he was the best at his game but the man had leadership aspirations. Better not try to flex his muscles on this mission. As he stared, Kiang Hai looked up and made eye contact. Danny nodded and looked away.

Fan Wen was different; a foot soldier ... keen to please and impress, good at what he did and a very capable frogman. Give me two more of him and I'd be happy, Danny thought, watching the young man. Behind the driver sat young Pan Ru. Wet behind the ears but a whiz at communications, he could wiretap or shut down any technology known to man.

The bus pulled up. Alighting, the men nodded their thanks to the driver. An Asian representative from the university waited to greet them. Danny looked around at the campus where he and his colleagues would spend the next three weeks while undertaking their studies. A pleasant enough place, he thought. He turned his attention back to the university guide who was working with the bus driver to unload the luggage. Danny recognized his bag and grabbed it. Nodding their thanks again to the driver, Danny and his men followed the guide up the stairs of the university and through the entrance hall.

———

"Just for the record," said Samantha, turning to Nick in the cab on the way to the airport, "I don't sleep around ... usually. What happened in London was just one of those things."

Nick saw the taxi driver's eyes flicker to Samantha in the mirror and momentarily back to him as if to say 'bad luck, buddy'.

"That's OK," he assured her. "Just for the record, I'm not asking you to and I need this job, so I'd rather we stayed work friends."

"I didn't mean to imply that you wanted to sleep with me, I mean for all I know I might be nothing like your type, but I didn't want you to think I ... you know what I mean." Samantha sat back in the seat.

Nick smiled at her. "I get it. How long is the flight?"

"Just under an hour. Do you think that's long enough for them to serve lunch?"

"Nuh, a bag of nuts and a can of Coke if you're lucky," Nick opened his camera bag for the second time since they had departed from headquarters. He checked the equipment.

"Everything OK?" Samantha asked him.

"Fine." He zipped the bag up and sat back.

"You know you do that a lot." Samantha watched him.

"What?"

"Check and recheck gear. I saw you do it on the last assignment too."

Nick shrugged. "Old habits." He glanced impatiently at his watch.

"Rather be flying the plane than a passenger?" Samantha asked.

"Any day."

————

The VIP looked out his office window to the manicured lawns outside. He wished it was over; the waiting and the tension from waiting was doing his head in.

He turned back to his desk, pulled a cigarette from a gold case in the top drawer, and retreated to the balcony before lighting it. He leaned on the balcony rails and thought about where his next office would be located. He had always had a thing for Asia: those beautiful Chinese princesses, the energy of the city, the untapped opportunities and all that cheap labor. He liked their work ethic, that the country, not the individual, came first. He couldn't help but smile as he thought about a government with abundant labor at its disposal and a desire for the common good. He was going to lead an unimaginable life. And at last, he thought, my experience and skills will be appreciated.

He finished his cigarette, stubbed it out and reached into his pocket for a mint. Stepping back inside, he pulled a comb from his coat jacket and groomed his salt and pepper hair and moustache.

Not too much longer and the plan begins; the sooner, the better.

4

DANNY HUANG CALLED HIS TEAM INTO HIS DORM room. He spoke in rapid Chinese.

"We have three weeks to put our plan in action and in that time, you must remember that at all times you are masquerading as members of the Armed Police Force, in training to guarantee the successful fulfillment of the G20 security mission. You have limited or no English, hence we are here to learn. One slip and you will jeopardize the mission."

They nodded their understanding.

"That includes accidentally using our real names and not those of the officers we are meant to be. From now onwards, we will use our given names, not family names."

"But they won't match the given names of the

officers we are replacing." Kiang Hai stated the obvious.

"No," Danny Huang agreed, "but we can say they are nicknames if they ask. Westerners love their nicknames and there's less chance we'll slip up. Besides, our names mean something. Your name, Kiang Hai—Hai means sea."

"That fits," Fan Wen said, "being a naval man."

"I get it, named as such because of my love of the sea," Hai agreed. "Good thinking—at least we are not learning new names."

Danny Huang nodded and continued. "Fan Wen shall be Wen, a nickname meaning?"

"Cultured," Fan Wen replied. "Yes, that's me, a cultured frogman." The small, compact man laughed at the prospect of being cultured given his poor upbringing.

"We could call you Froggy... because you take to the water like a frog and have a love of diving," Hai suggested.

The men laughed. Danny Huang nodded. "I like that. Froggy you will be."

Fan Wen grinned. "My mother would be so proud."

Danny looked at the two navy men. "Right, Hai and Froggy, it is."

He turned to the young communication whiz, Pan Ru.

"Ru means scholar, does it not?" Danny asked.

Pan Ru nodded.

"Then as you are here as a scholar to learn, Ru it is. The Americans will 'rue' the day you came to their shores." Danny smirked. "And you can call me Danny or Sir depending on where we are. Danny can't be traced to either my name or the police officer I'm supposed to be. We'll say I selected it after a Western pen friend from my childhood. Understood?"

The men nodded.

Danny went to the fridge in the dorm room and opened it. It was stocked with water and Coke. He offered drinks to the men, then sat down with a bottle of water. He continued. "We have three days of classes from eight in the morning to midday Monday to Wednesday in English. Afternoons are for training with the US squad, Thursday, Friday and the weekend are ours to assimilate and practice, in theory. In this time block, we will follow a strict routine to get our work finished. You are to keep no written evidence of your work or findings; nothing that can be connected to us. Understood?"

Again, there was a general murmur of assent. Danny looked around the room.

"Hai and Froggy, you are responsible for the lifting of the VIP. With the help of young Ru on communications, you are to work closely with our

Beijing team, know their every move, check and double-check when is the easiest time to perform the lift, remembering we need a clear window of ten hours to move the VIP before taking him offshore." Danny moved to stand right in front of the two naval agents as they sat on the furniture around his dorm room. "Be prepared in case this should change. On Thursday morning, I want you to get down to Cape Hatteras and case the area. Check our tidal readings are correct and that the area our Beijing crew expects to access is workable and has the visibility we need. I want you to also prepare the VIP house."

"What shall we say if we are asked why we chose to go there?" Froggy asked.

"We will say that a friend of Hai's family once visited there and spoke highly of its history. Being keen divers, you wanted to dive around the wrecks. While in Cape Hatteras, monitor everything going on but stay below the radar. When we come down with the VIP, he needs to remain invisible while we wait for the connection. If you know the lay of the land, there should be no reason for anything to go wrong."

Froggy and Hai nodded.

"And you will be practicing your English with the locals," Danny said. "Remember it is broken English; you are here to learn, so don't speak well. I doubt anyone will care too much about us moving around the tourist areas, we are cops after all."

The group smiled at the irony of their new status.

"Ru," Danny began, "I want everything the VIP says recorded and anything of note reported to me. It might be best to bug his phone as he'll always have that with him. I will be meeting with him Wednesday night so give me whatever you need planted and instructions. I want summarized daily dialogue."

"Yes, sir," Ru nodded.

"I need to be sure the VIP does not get cold feet at the last moment," Danny said.

5

NICK STARED OUT THE WINDOW OF THE PLANE AS THE flight attendants went through the safety drill. He was pretty sure if the plane went down whether he was in the brace position or not wouldn't matter. Minutes later, he closed his eyes as the plane took off skywards.

"Don't tell me you hate take-offs? You're a pilot!" Samantha exclaimed.

He opened his eyes to find Samantha watching him. "No, I was just going through the process; pays to keep up the practice."

"Really? I've never noticed Mitch doing that."

"It's just something I do. Besides, Wonder Boy probably never forgets a thing."

Samantha smiled. "You're on his case a lot."

"I'm his best friend, it's my job," Nick said.

"Someone's got to keep him grounded. But I've got his back too."

"Mm. You've known Mitch a long time, so what is the deal with his scars? Especially the ones on his back; he's pretty cloak-and-dagger about it."

Nick shrugged and looked away. "It's not a big deal. He's just not into talking about it."

"But, how did he get them?" Samantha persisted.

Nick hesitated. "You know, best to ask him. Or maybe he will spill it one day."

Samantha smirked at him. "Mm, loyalty will get you a long way, with Mitch anyway."

Nick tried to hide his smile. He changed the subject. "So what do you think we'll find at Cape Hatteras?"

Samantha flicked open the newspaper. "Some kelp," she snapped.

———

Mitch led the way down the stairs to the parking lot.

"At least working on a Sunday there's plenty of parking, unless you've got an allocated park seven days a week," Ellen gave Mitch a glance and grinned.

"True. We should work more Sundays just for

you then," he teased her. "I'll drop you back for your car later."

Mitch unlocked his black Audi and slid into the cream leather interior. Ellen opened the back passenger door and threw her folder and bag on the backseat. Mitch's phone rang and the car's Bluetooth speakerphone projected John's voice.

"Are you still in the office?" John asked.

"No, we're off to follow up the few witnesses to William Ying's disappearance a year ago. Want to come?" Mitch joked. "I can swing by and pick you up at home."

"Mm, love to but I've got to do that … thing. Heard from Sam and Nick?"

"Yep, they've landed and got the car hire and accommodation details."

"OK, keep me in the loop," John said, and hung up.

Mitch started the car. "First address?"

Ellen read out the address of the first witness on her list. "Want me to put it in the TomTom?"

"No, I've got a rough idea of where that is." Mitch turned the car out of the car park and headed right.

"What did you find on William or the witnesses?" he asked.

"From what I could gather in the few hours you gave me, there was surveillance footage at the function that William Ying disappeared at a year ago; it's in our library and I'm yet to see it. But according to the file notes at the time, it had nothing incriminating in it."

"Mm, I guess that depends on what the cops were looking for and what we're looking for now," Mitch interrupted. "Let's try and finish the witnesses this afternoon and then we'll visit William Ying's wife or widow tomorrow."

Ellen nodded. "The witnesses' accounts were vague then, and we're asking them a year later to recall the night of his disappearance."

"I know but anything might help—like who did William Ying speak to that night at the art exhibition, how did he look—happy, stressed, scared? Which direction did he leave in? Did he use his phone during the night or take any calls? Tomorrow we'll try the buildings surrounding the gallery; I'm not holding out hope that they'll have kept their surveillance tapes or remember anything from a year ago, but you never know, someone might be anal about security."

They drove in silence as Ellen looked up the addresses for the other witnesses and Mitch frowned in concentration.

"They all live nearby," Ellen said. "I guess they wanted to be close to work or study."

Mitch swung the car into the street of the first

witness. It was a sterile street, neat with small brick houses.

"Keep an eye out for the house number, Ellie."

Ellen ruffled back through her paperwork to check the number. She looked to the nearest house to her left. "It should be on your side about half way up the street."

Mitch spotted it first and pulled up out front of a barren home. The house next door had a well-tended garden, but number fifteen simply had a mown lawn and a concrete path to the door. The curtains were closed.

They exited the car and Mitch followed Ellen up the path. She knocked on the door. Adjusting his tie, Mitch flipped through the brief information on the first witness on the list: a Chinese student who was at the photographic exhibition that evening and was one of the last to be seen talking with William Ying.

Ellen stood beside Mitch in her jeans and jacket, trying to keep warm. Mitch eyed the paperwork again, noticing the witness was a second-year student at the time, so would now be in her third and final year of her degree. He hoped she was still in the country.

He glanced to Ellen as she watched the door impatiently. She knocked again.

Mitch was just about to leave when the door

opened a few inches. A tiny, elderly Asian lady peered out through the slit in the door.

"Sorry to disturb you," Mitch began, "but we were hoping to speak with Jessica Wu." He read her nominated English name from a list.

"She not here."

Mitch showed his identification. "We're with the Federal Police and we need to speak with Jessica about a statement she gave last year about the disappearance of William Ying."

"She gone."

"Will she be back?"

"No, she gone," she answered bluntly.

Mitch glanced at Ellen.

Like extracting teeth.

"Are you related to Jessica, uh, Ms. Wu?" he persisted.

"Yes," she answered in a staccato fashion.

Mitch frowned, as the elderly lady was giving nothing away. "Do you have a contact number where we could reach her please?"

"She dead." The old lady closed the door abruptly leaving Mitch staring at it with a surprised look.

Mitch turned to Ellen. "Well, that can't be good," he whispered.

Ellen nodded, equally surprised. "I didn't think to search death records."

"Well you wouldn't," Mitch agreed.

They headed to the car. Once inside, Mitch made a note to check on the date and means of Jessica Wu's death.

Ellen typed the next witness' address into the navigation system. Mitch started the car and followed the directions voiced by the articulate navigator to the next location. He pulled the car to the curb and double checked the address. A vacant block of land was all that existed at that street number.

"That was the address of Rodney Lam." He looked at Ellen. "Starting to see a trend here?"

"I think so," she agreed. "Let's try the next name; he's a lecturer at the university, lives at Harcourt Street." She typed the address in the navigator and Mitch followed the directions as voiced.

Ten minutes later he drove down Harcourt Street.

"It is on your side again," Ellen said.

Mitch scanned the house numbers until he found it and pulled over to the curb.

"Third time lucky." He exited the car. They walked to the front of the two-story dark brick home with a 'For Sale' sign out the front.

"I hope they haven't moved yet," Ellen said under her breath, doing up her jacket against the cold.

Mitch tried the doorbell. He heard it echo.

"Sounds empty." He tried again.

"They've gone, dear," a voice called.

Mitch and Ellen turned to find an elderly woman standing on the stairs of the house next door.

"Hello, we were looking for Joseph Kinaird." Ellen walked towards the neighbor, who remained on the stairs in her pink sweater and blue-gray pants.

Mitch noticed her hair was a similar color. He let Ellen approach and listened from afar.

"No dear, Mrs. Kinaird and her daughter have moved. She's in the eleventh grade now. I've known her since she was a baby. They came here when Mr. Kinaird got a job at the university. It was nice and close."

"And Mr. Kinaird didn't move with them?" Ellen asked.

"Oh no dear, Mr. Kinaird died last year. Terrible thing. On his way home from work one night, he lost control of the car, the police said. It was a wet night. The family was devastated of course. He was only fifty-three."

"Terrible," Ellen agreed. "Thank you Mrs. ...?"

"Stapelton, Pamela Stapelton."

"Thank you Mrs. Stapelton. I don't suppose you know where Mrs. Kinaird and her daughter moved to? We're from the police." Ellen stopped to show her badge. "We're looking for a university friend of Mr. Kinaird's who has gone missing. His family is very worried, as you can imagine. Mrs. Kinaird might remember some small detail about him which could help. You never know."

"Of course. I have a forwarding address, so just give me a moment and I'll write it out for you." She turned and shuffled inside.

Ellen waited on the lawn, while Mitch returned to the car and updated his notes... he now needed details on the death of Joseph Kinaird.

Our first lead, he thought. Something odd happened to the last three people to see William Ying before he disappeared.

6

DANNY HUANG SIGNALED FOR SILENCE. HE CHECKED no one was outside their dormitory, closed the door and returned to the group.

"We will be working undercover, and closely with our expert on the ground, William Ying."

The men's eyes widened with surprise.

"Yes, William has been missing for twelve months, but we know exactly where he is and what he is doing."

Murmurs of laughter bubbled around the room.

Danny Huang continued, "William has been working between Washington and Cape Hatteras now for the past few months. He will be second-in-charge for this mission. In my absence, everything is to go through him. Understood?"

The men agreed. Danny moved to the window to make a call.

"Hello old friend," he said. "I am putting you on speaker phone."

Danny put the phone on the table and pressed the speaker.

"Present are our extraction divers Hai and Froggy and Ru on communications."

William welcomed the men to the United States.

"How did the first trial go off shore on Thursday?" Danny asked.

"Not good," William replied. "I waited on the shore for two hours longer than the planned liaison time ..."

"A mistake, William," Danny broke in. "You might have been seen by someone or looked suspicious."

"I was bird watching; that's my cover," William explained. "Fooled a few including an elderly couple," he continued. "But the sub did not give the required signal. I understand the coordinates were wrong, but we have fixed that situation."

"Not good," Danny said.

"It is worse than that. The two men got trapped; I don't know what happened but there was an accident," William said.

"And?" Danny pushed.

"Two dead," William withheld that the bodies were left behind.

"This is bad," Danny paced. "How did they die?"

"Problems with the air tanks and line extraction. Let's hope the next drill goes better."

"Were they seen?" Danny persisted.

"To the best of our knowledge the sub wasn't, but the men's bodies ... they might have been seen by divers in the area, it's unclear," William said.

"We may have to move the mission forward," Danny said.

There was a delayed silence. Eventually William spoke.

"Your men are coming here?" William asked.

"Yes, Hai and Froggy will be there. And the premises?" Danny asked.

"The premises are secured for the overnight storage of the VIP on the last day of the month," William continued, "and the pickup will be at 0400 hours."

"I want to visit the premises later this week," Danny advised.

"We'll be expecting you," William agreed. "But I will see you before then, with the VIP on Wednesday?"

"Of course. Until then..." Danny cut off the call. He looked around at the group. "Questions?"

No one spoke.

"Let's formulate an extraction plan in case we need to move faster," Danny Huang ordered.

———

"It's really nice here ... about sixty-eight degrees. The sun is out, and Norfolk is such a pretty place," Samantha informed Mitch.

"Lovely; what a shame you haven't got time to stop and enjoy it," he said, speaking with his two agents through their car's speakerphone.

"We're almost at Cape Hatteras," Nick said.

"So what's your plan?" Mitch asked.

"When we get there, we are going to swing by the Visitors' Centre if it is still open and see if they have tidal charts, and then we'll go straight to the beach and check it out," Nick said.

"A sunset walk on the beach," Mitch sighed, "how nice. Ellie and I are still door-knocking in suburbia. Stay in touch."

Mitch disconnected as Ellen rejoined him in the warmth of the car.

"You disappeared quickly." She shivered.

"I figured an elderly lady would feel safer talking to another woman."

"Mm, rather than a tall, dark, handsome man? You might have made her day."

"Think we might have got a cup of tea and a cookie?" Mitch teased.

"Who would knock that back? Or apple tea cake, don't old ladies always make that? Instead, all I got was a forwarding address in Boston," Ellen said.

"Boston! Great." Mitch sighed. "Why couldn't they move across town? Any phone number?"

"No, just an address, but I'll hunt a phone number down."

Mitch started the engine and turned the car back to headquarters.

"OK, let's call it a day while we can. You might get some painting done."

"Ha, I don't like to paint unless I have at least three guaranteed, uninterrupted hours ... the clean-up is such a pain in the butt."

"I can't say I've ever done it."

"Really? Haven't you ever wanted to buy and renovate?" asked Ellen.

"I've thought about it and once I actually did a calculation of the number of days I spent at home in my own bed. It worked out to about three months in a year. So I bought an investment property instead, rented that out and now I just rent a room somewhere."

"Why didn't you move into your own property and rent out its rooms?" Ellen asked.

"Because the last thing I need if I'm away on a

job is a housemate calling because the plumbing has packed it in and I'm supposed to do something about it. Nah, this way, the realtor manages it and I'm just a tenant."

"Way too sensible," Ellen said. "You'll never be able to own a cat if you think like that."

Mitch laughed. "Yeah, feeling that loss. Tomorrow, I'll leave you to follow up on the surveillance footage. I'm going to make a start on the fingerprints and their history, and we'll pay a visit to Mrs. Ying."

———

"So what are we going to do about sleeping arrangements?" Samantha asked as she entered the room of their B&B and closed the door.

Nick sat in a white cane chair near the door and pulled off his boots. "I'm going to put my head on a pillow and sleep. What do you mean?"

"I am not sure if you have noticed, but there is only one bed." Samantha stared at the large four poster bed.

"No couch either," Nick noted. He dumped his bag on a small timber table under the window and fished for a pair of sport socks in his black-issued knapsack.

"Why don't we take it in turns?" she suggested.

"I'll take the bed tonight, and then tomorrow night, I'll take the floor."

"It's no big deal; why don't we both share the bed. I'll wear clothes. It is work after all."

Samantha shrugged. "Suit yourself, but if you snore or sleep with your mouth open, I'm telling your next girlfriend that and all other secrets that I gather."

"I don't date, so that's just fine."

"Come on, everyone dates eventually." She opened her bag and began to stuff her socks and underwear into the chest of three drawers on one side of the bed.

"Not me. I'm on the wagon, practicing abstinence, so not interested … "

"Why?" Samantha looked at him.

Nick shrugged. "I just want to focus on work and fitness for a while."

"You know, Nick, no matter how bad your last break up was, you're going to have to get back on the horse eventually." She watched him as he pulled on his runners.

Nick rose. "We didn't break up, she died. I'm going for a run to check out the lay of the land. I'll be back in an hour. Then we can find something to eat if you like."

He closed the door behind him.

———

As he ran, Nick thought about the mission, Mitch, life, work, Samantha, Ellen—trying to stay in the present. To slip back would mean revisiting the death of his fiancée. A car accident; he had been the driver. He had that filed away, so it only returned when he let his mind wander.

He looked around; the area was pretty much deserted now. Bet the locals like the downtime, he thought. He turned to run along the empty beachfront and looked out to the farthest point.

I could tip off the edge of the world out there.

Tempting. So what's out there, and what are these guys expecting to come over the horizon?

Or what might be coming on the seabed?

When Nick returned, Samantha was on her iPad going through emails.

"Anything new?" he asked.

"Mitch rang again," she answered. "I'll give you an update over dinner. Go shower, you're sweaty."

Nick rolled his eyes. "Yes, Mom."

7

"DAY TWO OF OUR WONDERFUL BEACH HOLIDAY," NICK said as he finished his coffee and rose from the small table in the B&B breakfast dining area. He stretched from left to right. Samantha frowned at him as she grabbed her beach bag from the chair beside her.

"I'm stiff from trying to stay on my own side of the bed," Nick said. "I was too scared to stretch out."

"And so you should be," she said with a glance out of the window to the beach. "C'mon let's go. It's far too cold for swimming and sun baking; no one in their right mind would strip off in this weather."

They called their thanks to the B&B owner and Samantha followed Nick across the road and onto the sand. Finding a good spot to view the entire area, she placed her towel down as Nick dropped beside her on the beach.

"Look at those people." She pointed to a family arriving with a ball, buckets and spades. "They're dressed warmly. Why would you take a beach holiday in this weather?" she continued to grumble.

"So leave your gear on," Nick suggested. "It's October! There's still a few weeks of warm weather left at least. We could have been here next month, then you would have something to complain about."

"We probably still will be here at this rate," she said. "I'll look a bit odd just sitting here for hours on end half dressed. I'm sure we can come up with a better cover than this. Besides, I was hoping to work on my tan."

"I was hoping you would too," Nick agreed. "Do you want me to rub some suntan lotion on you?"

Samantha turned to look at him. "You wish."

"Yeah, I do actually."

"Maybe we should take up fishing or something." She looked out past the rocks where the waves were coming into shore. A couple of keen surfers wearing wetsuits paddled out towards the waves.

"Surfing ..." Nick thought out loud. "Now there's a good idea. Then I can have a view back to shore. Just need to hire a board."

Late Monday, Marcus the Caribbean Casanova and former boyfriend of Samantha printed off the report and frowned. He sat down and doubled checked the information again. Picking up the phone, he rang Mitch.

"Mitch my man, I've got some information for you that you might want to see, like now."

He hung up and waited. Within a minute Mitchell Parker appeared at the door.

"You've I.D. the two dead divers?" Mitch asked expectantly.

"Did you take the steps or fly here?" Marcus asked.

Mitch grinned. "I've been sweating on this info. Looking very mute today, for you."

Marcus looked down at his pale blue shirt. "All my best shirts are at the dry cleaners."

"I hear you," Mitch said dropping into the seat next to him and looking at the screen.

"The divers we found are two ex-marines," Marcus began. He looked around ensuring no one was nearby and continued. They are identified as navy officers from the People's Liberation Army Navy." He watched as Mitch's eyes squinted as he ran through a million scenarios in his head.

"Are they in the country?" Mitch asked.

"No. There's no record of them entering the country, not now, not ever."

"Christ," Mitch swore. "Can you print that out for me?"

———

On his way back to his level of the building to see John, Mitch's phone rang. Samantha's name came up.

"Hey, where are you now?" he answered.

"We're still on the beach."

"Surf up?" Mitch asked.

"Well, Nick said it was a decent swell and there's a few surfers out. But we're all work, we haven't really noticed," Samantha answered.

Mitch laughed. "Sure, good answer. So what's next?"

"We're going to give it another half hour then pack up," Samantha said. "The light's fading and it is chilly. No one's on the beach."

"Except us idiots!" Nick piped up in the background.

"Our B&B in the village is cute, not far from the lighthouse," Samantha told him, "but we could do with something closer..."

Mitch heard Samantha surrendering the phone.

"Cute if you like everything having a frill," Nick's voice came down the line. "It would suit you, Mitch."

Samantha grabbed the phone back and put it on speaker. "Don't start you two," she warned. "Besides, it's not that bad."

Mitch cut in. "So did you see anything unusual today at all?"

"Not a thing—and I mean zilch. What are you guys up to?" Nick asked.

"We tried to see William's wife but she couldn't see us until later in the week. So we've been following up witnesses, their families, liaising with missing persons, waiting on results," Mitch said, keeping the identification of the navy officers close to his chest until he reported to John.

"Any luck?" Nick asked.

"We couldn't find any that are still alive," Mitch said.

"Were they all old?" Nick asked.

"No."

"This might be bigger than we thought," Nick said.

"I've got that feeling too," Mitch agreed. "Stay in touch."

He hung up and knocked on John's door at the same time he entered.

"Uh oh," John read Mitch's face.

Mitch closed the door behind him.

"Got some info for you that we better feed up the line now. The two divers ..."

"The ones that you and Ellie collected on Saturday?" John asked.

"The same—they're Chinese navy men that are not officially in the country," Mitch said handing over a printed sheet listing their identifications.

"And now they're not leaving it either," John exhaled. "How did they get on the ocean floor at Cape Hatteras? Washed ashore, fallen off a boat or ship, fell from the air?"

"Well we know they weren't part of the local dive group since they called it in," Mitch said.

"Lucky that group leader had a bit of nouse and noticed they were using equipment that wasn't run of the mill. Imagine if the local police had found them and then the local media got a hold of it," John shook his head.

Mitch continued. "The level of decomposition suggests they've only been there a couple of days. Hell of a wash from China if they got swept away while swimming," Mitch smiled. "Going to ring?"

"No, I'll go in person. But you're right. This is ugly," John rose, taking the print out, he grabbed his phone and diary and headed out of the office.

One hour later he rang Mitch to say the case was

getting attention at the highest levels. Mitch knew what that meant, more reporting, more meetings and plenty of finger pointing.

8

MITCH GLANCED OVER THE SIDE OF THE BOAT. THE water looked dark and cold. God knows what's down there. He heard the Jaws soundtrack music somewhere in the back of his mind. Mm, Steven Spielberg has a lot to answer for, he thought. Turning, he lowered his scuba mask over his face, inserted his mouthpiece, and gave the thumbs up before leaning back and dropping into the water.

So quiet. The ocean was dark and silent. Mitch heard his heart beating way too fast.

Calm down. Breathe ... hold ... let it out. He repeated the mantra to himself as he followed the light from his torch, swimming deeper.

He knew what he was going to see, but that never made it any easier. His instincts were on full alert. The report said a package was some forty feet below the surface. Two amateur divers had called it in.

Shame *they* didn't investigate, he thought. But it was on his turf, right where he had been doing his surveillance. There was no way round it but to make the dive. He knew he wasn't swimming very fast; fear and loathing slowed his pace. The silence of the water was deafening.

Mitch saw it.

Damn. Definitely looks like a body wrapped up. He swallowed his revulsion and swam towards the package. He turned slightly to look around.

There's no one around, he told himself, just get it over with.

The package was wrapped in plastic. He could just make out patches of clothing, a person's features and shoes.

Mitch reached for his switchblade and began hacking at the rope tied around the body and secured to a concrete brick block. His movements were slower in the water, but soon the rope gave way. He grabbed a corner of the package to pull it to the surface and shone his torch over it. Two eyes stared back at him and blinked.

Mitch yelled.

He sat up in bed gasping for air, his T-shirt drenched.

No body. No water.

"Mitch!" Charlotte, his girlfriend of seven months, reached for him.

Mitch pushed her off. "It's fine, it was just a dream."

"Again. You're drenched." She stroked his back. "These night sweats are happening more and more."

"It's nothing, they're not night sweats, it was just a bad dream." He exhaled.

"The third night in a row?" Charlotte's training as a psychologist kicked into gear. She rose and went to get a wet facecloth from the bathroom. Returning, she handed it to him, sliding back into her own side of the bed.

Mitch wiped his face with the cloth.

"Sorry I woke you. Go back to sleep," he said quietly as though expecting that to have a lulling effect.

"You know, Mitch, it might help to talk about it."

"Nothing to talk about, I'm OK." Mitch rose from the bed. "I'm taking a shower."

He headed to the shower knowing he wouldn't get off that lightly. Charlotte was a psychologist after-hours as well and would want to talk about it, and talk about it, and talk about it some more.

He stripped off his T-shirt and boxers, pulled open the glass shower door, adjusted the water temperature and stepped in. He closed his eyes, feeling the stream of water on his face.

Got to get that case out of my head, long time ago now. The Cape Hatteras dive is not helping.

He felt Charlotte step into the shower behind him.

"Mitch, talk to me."

Mitch turned to face her. "Charlie, it's just a bad dream, but nice to have you here."

He pulled her closer.

"I'll tell you what," she bartered. "You tell me about your dream and then I'll help you forget it."

Mitch put his head back under the shower stream and let the water pour over him.

Charlotte pulled him forward.

"I know what you are doing. You're stalling so that you can give me a manufactured version of the dream. Spill it."

Mitch groaned.

"Spill it or that's the only groaning you'll be doing," she said.

9

MITCH PACED. IT WAS JUST AFTER SIX IN THE MORNING and he was alone in the office.

The best time to get things done, even if Charlie's not happy I'm M.I.A from bed so early.

It was so quiet he could hear the clock ticking on his office wall. He knew John Windsor would be in at seven; another early riser. Other floors and departments had random activity going on, but not his.

Mitch logged into his laptop and opened the file from John. He set the images on slideshow and projected them full-size onto the adjacent white wall in his office. He stood up and watched them, concentrating on each shot.

Nothing.

He hit the button and started again. Mitch put

his hands in the pockets of his suit pants and rocked on the soles of his shoes. He ran his eyes over every inch of the wall photo.

Nope.

Picking up the phone, he glanced at the clock and put it down again. He went behind the desk and sat to send an email. He would request anything the Criminal Justice Information Services Division had on the former Chinese Ambassador, William Ying including any press clippings. He shot the email off and then opened the internet search engine. He began his own search on William Ying.

Thirty-six thousand references. Good, had nothing else to do.

Mitch scanned a line each from the first ten listed; it covered William's disappearance, interviews with William's wife, pleas from his family and even a hefty reward offered. Next, Mitch opened the Missing Persons department file that he received late yesterday. He began reading through the material on William Ying.

Last seen almost exactly one year to the day while attending a photographic exhibition at the China Club in association with the university; witnesses place him at the exhibition until eight p.m. He was not seen again and did not return home that evening.

Mitch didn't hear Ellen enter his office until she

was right in front of him. He jumped back in his seat. "Shit, you nearly gave me a heart attack."

"Sorry. I didn't want to interrupt you. How's things?"

Mitch put his hand over his heart. "Once I recover from the heart attack, I should be fine. And you?" He indicated the seat opposite him.

"Excellent." Ellen smiled sitting down. "I got motivated and finished painting the bathroom last night."

"Bravo, blue and white, huh?" Mitch studied her. Strands of paint were visible in her blonde hair. As if to match the paint, she was wearing a white suit with a navy singlet below.

"How did you reach the ceiling?" he asked.

She gave him a wry look. "I stood on a ladder, smarty. Just because you can reach from the ground."

Mitch chuckled.

"But I also got a bit of work done before I picked up the paint brush," she said. "On a hunch, I dropped in on Jessica Wu's grandmother on my way home and yes, it is her grandmother. Her nephew was there and he spoke fluent English. Jessica's phone was not given back to the family and her grandmother never thought to ask for it," Ellen said.

"Where's the mother?"

"Both parents are dead. They died when Jessica was a young girl and her grandmother raised her."

"Any chance the phone is in storage in some police box?"

"Nope, tried that."

"Yeah, big surprise." Mitch rose and began to pace. "Good job, thanks Ellie, but I want that phone."

"I know. What are you doing?" she asked.

"Missing Persons file for William Ying," Mitch said, nodding towards the open file on his desk. "I'm checking if there's anything from the original case files that can give us an insight into why William might have disappeared, or where he is."

"Won't missing persons have flagged that if they found anything?" Ellen asked.

"Yep, but they were looking for a missing person. I'm looking for someone who may not want to be seen."

Ellen studied him. "Right."

"Coffee meeting?" he asked.

"You're on," she agreed.

Ten minutes later, Mitch sat with his latte in the ground floor coffee shop across the road from their building. Ellen sat opposite inhaling the aroma of her skinny cappuccino. Ellen stirred her coffee, took a sip and with a nod of satisfaction, pulled a wad of paperwork out of her bag.

"What have you got?" Mitch looked around and checked no one was in earshot.

"I like that tie." She admired his gold-and-navy-print tie, highlighted on his crisp white shirt and paired with his navy suit.

"That it?" he teased.

"Yep," she said. "Shall we head back?"

Mitch laughed.

"But to business ... no luck with neighboring surveillance footage after the function at the university. I've even tried the streets en route to and from the uni but it's too long ago now, the footage is gone. If we had done that a day or week after, we would have seen the black car, maybe got more witnesses."

"Tell me about it. So, speaking of witnesses ..." Mitch said.

"First up, Jessica Wu. She was hit by a car while returning home from university. According to the police report she had been studying late and was walking home in the dark, didn't use the pedestrian crossing and was hit. A couple walking on the opposite side of the street saw it and called the ambulance. She died before it arrived."

"What happened to the driver?"

"They never caught the driver. It was a hit and run. The witnesses said it was a black sports car but couldn't recall seeing any plates."

"What did Jessica recall about William Ying in the witness statements?"

Ellen thumbed through the file. "Let's see ... she said that she saw William talking with a man. She only saw the back of him, but he was Caucasian and they were walking towards a black limousine parked at the rear of the gallery. She recalled the number plates looked like they were government-issued."

"Mm." Mitch thought. He sat back and looked away. "How long after she was listed as being one of the last people to see William did the accident occur?"

Ellen went back to the accident report and then to the witness report and checked dates. "Two days later."

"So two days after the exhibition, she's cleaned up by a hit and run. Coincidence?"

"You won't think so when you hear this." Ellen stopped to sip her coffee, shuffled a page and continued. "Rodney Lam. Remember the address we had for him was a vacant block of land?"

"Uh huh," Mitch nodded.

"Rodney Lam was the head student of the Asian Commerce and Culture group and editor of its newspaper."

"Was?"

"Was," Ellen nodded. "He was commissioned to

do an article on the exhibition for a national art magazine. According to the police statements, Rodney Lam was the university representative who was to meet and greet William Ying that night and accompany him on the tour. Rodney Lam said in his statement that he saw William leaving the exhibition and remembers it distinctly because he heard the man with William mutter the words, 'my career is on the line'. Lam said in his statement that he turned to look at the speaker but couldn't make out his features in the shadows. But it was definitely William with this man, so he was still alive at that point."

"So what's the connection with the vacant block of land?"

"Well it wasn't vacant then. It had a timber cottage on it which Rodney Lam lived in. Two days after Lam gave his statement to police, the house burned down and Rodney Lam along with it, allegedly."

"Did they find a body?" Mitch asked.

"Yes." Ellen passed him the report on the fire. Mitch glanced over it.

"But this is in keeping with our findings," Ellen continued, "the body was so badly burnt that it was unidentifiable and there were no dental records. So they had to assume it was Rodney Lam, given he was not seen again."

"Surely they must have regarded that as suspicious?" Mitch asked.

"I spoke with the inspector on the case at the time and he said all the boxes were ticked; Rodney Lam was a smoker and it appeared the fire started in his room. There were bottles of alcohol around the bed, evidence of smoking in the bedroom and they believe he fell asleep with the cigarette still burning. The coroner said he died of smoke inhalation. He probably didn't even wake up."

"If you keep this up, I'm going to need another coffee." Mitch shook his head.

"But wait, there's more!" Ellen teased him.

"Give it to me." Mitch drew a large breath.

"I spoke with Mrs. Kinaird. Remember her husband was a lecturer at the university and part of the group that organized the grant for the exhibition?"

"Yep, and he was our last witness." Mitch nodded.

"Right. Well, Mr. Kinaird had to go to the exhibition because of his position, despite not wanting to go, she said. While there, he took some social photos for the university magazine."

"And he might have snapped a photo of William and this unidentified person?"

"He might have," Ellen said. "But this is where it gets tricky ... according to Mrs. Kinaird, her husband had left the camera in his car after the function, so hadn't downloaded the photos yet. She remembered this because it was a couple of days after the event and the event organizer asked him to send through the pics. So he asked his wife to remind him to download them that night at home. He was bringing the camera home to do it there because it was already after six p.m. and he didn't want to spend any longer in the office. Mr. Kinaird had an accident on his way home that night and so did his camera. In fact, it was not in the car at all when the police got to the scene."

"It wasn't in his office, on his desk or anywhere on campus?" Mitch asked.

"It wasn't on any inventory list or with his personal belongings."

Mitch looked out the window again and squinted. "The neighbor said he lost control of the car on a wet night. Is that consistent with the police report?"

"More or less. They think his car might have skidded in the wet. It is the only explanation for him hitting a light pole," Ellen said. "According to the traffic scene report though, he was doing a hell of a speed."

"Guess you would be if someone was chasing you."

10

Nearing mid-morning, Samantha was beach-weary; covered in sand, chilled and tired. She rose and strolled casually along the beach. She waved to Nick as he sat on a surfboard out beyond the breakers, waiting for a ride. She saw it coming—the large wave—but Nick was too busy looking at something to his right. She suppressed a smile as he was dumped by the wave, head over heels—or board over heels, in this case. All the time, she made small motions on the sand with her feet, feeling for anything out of the ordinary; any odd little bit of dropped evidence. Occasionally, she leant down and picked up a small pebble or a shell, examined it and carried on, casually strolling around the area.

There were few on the beach at this hour; several joggers, a family with young children—the parents pressured into going to the beach—and a number of walkers, particularly senior residents taking their daily exercise. Nothing out of the ordinary.

Then, everything changed.

———

Mitch's phone rang and he glanced at the screen. "Nick," he answered, rising from his desk to pace as he talked.

"Something interesting," Nick said. "There's an Asian guy here, don't know if it is the same one that was in Gunston's holiday snaps, but he's sitting pretty much in the same place and he's looking out to sea using a set of binoculars."

"This is good," Mitch said, excited.

"Yeah. We'll try and get pics and send them back ASAP. Hang on ..."

"What's happening?" Mitch asked.

"I'm just posing for Samantha while she takes a photo. It's a lovely happy snap of me with the Asian dude in the background of the shot. Hope she got my best side. What am I saying, they're both good."

"The back of your head's the best," Mitch offered. "So what's he doing now?"

"Wait up, I've got to turn around subtly," Nick said. "Same thing. He just keeps looking at his watch, and then back out to sea, now he's checking his phone again. Anyway, got to go, I'm going to paddle out and do some surfing; see if I can see anything beyond the wave breaks. Sam's going to continue taking snaps and frolicking on the beach, despite the wind factor. We'll keep an eye on him and send the shots now."

"Excellent, thanks Nick. Watch out for sharks and keep me posted."

"Will do," Nick hung up.

———

"Mrs. Ying rang, she can see us at two p.m. today," Ellen stuck her head in the door of Mitch's office. "She still lives in the same house."

"Even better," Mitch said. He glanced at his watch. He had thirty minutes up his sleeve before the conference call. "I'm going down to see Henri. What are you working on?"

Ellen waved a file at him. "I'm still trying for more surveillance tapes from surrounding buildings. A year ago is a big call, but you never know. Plus I'm trying to get the guest list for the gallery exhibition night. Someone must have photos on their cameras."

"Good thought. I wonder if Jessica's grandmother would have any photos of Jessica at uni," Mitch said.

"Maybe. Jessica might have posted some shots to Facebook if I can find an old account," Ellen said, moving out of the way as Mitch exited his office.

"Excellent, thanks Ellie. I'll be back for the conference call at noon," he called as he headed down the stairs to the lab offices below.

———

There wasn't much that Henri Spalter—head of the science division, professor of science and Mitchell Parker's stepdad during his teen years—didn't know. It was Henri that Mitch credited with sparking his interest in his current line of work. He took the stairs two at a time and arrived at the labs to find all hands on deck. Henri's two young lab assistants looked up to greet him as he passed. Henri had his back to Mitch and was studying something on his computer screen.

"Hey Henri, got a minute?" Mitch asked.

Henri turned and beamed at him. "Mitch, my lad, always got time for you. Coffee?"

Henri kept a special brew that he only pulled out for visitors.

"I've only got twenty minutes, but I'm sure I can manage one in that time ... especially your coffee."

Mitch inhaled the aroma as Henri began spooning it into the percolator before Mitch had finished accepting.

Henri offered coffee to his two assistants—the younger, Jared, waved an enormous takeaway coffee back at him and Tom held up a caffeine-loaded can of soda.

Henri turned back to Mitch and shook his head. "These young ones ..."

Mitch grinned and pulled up a stool.

"I want to pick your brains about passport and visa forgeries."

"Mm." Henri shook his head. "Difficult thing these days, particularly since September 11. What's happened?"

"Those binoculars Gunston found ..."

"Yes, the ones with the two sets of fingerprints," Henri said.

"That's them." Mitch accepted the coffee as the first cup dripped through. He inhaled it appreciatively, adding milk and waiting for Henri to fill his own cup. "The prints for William Ying and Danny Huang were on the binoculars. William Ying has been missing for a year and Danny Huang's not even in the country supposedly. Those fingerprints on the binocular casing could be years old, couldn't they?"

Henri nodded. "But they're not," he concluded, sitting opposite with his coffee.

"How do you know?" Mitch sipped the hot brew.

"Well, there are ways to tell. Oddly, the fingerprints of some blood types will disintegrate before others," Henri said. "But, staying on track, fingerprint age is determined by studying a number of factors: physical, chemical, biochemical ..."

Mitch nodded, urging him to continue.

"Because the papillary fingerprints degrade in stages, you can determine the blood group and the age of the fingerprint. You determine this by the varying ridges' thickness in a fingerprint, the width of the valleys, the number of pores." Henri stopped. "Basically, it was easy to compare because the two sets of fingerprints were different ages. William Ying's were recent. My guess would be that he held those binoculars within the last week or so."

"And Danny Huang's?"

"Almost as recent ... probably about three months old."

Mitch stared blankly at his coffee and began talking to himself. "A week or so ... so William Ying and Danny Huang have both touched those binoculars within the last three months. William has disappeared but hasn't left the country and Danny hasn't entered it. William was spotted on the beach with the binoculars, so odds are Danny is here in the country somewhere and is working with William or he's sent them to him ... but why? There's no shortage of binoculars here unless they have a feature that is unique. They could have been given to him from someone else, but then their prints would be on them."

Henri brought him around. "So you're wondering if Danny Huang could be in the country on a false visa."

Mitch nodded.

"Anything and everything is possible," Henri said. "As our technology improves for scanning and protection, so too does the technology for creating forgeries. It's a catch-22. Is Danny Huang currently in his native country, which is ...?"

"China," Mitch informed him. "I'm trying to find out now, just waiting on a call back. And William Ying never left the States, he just went missing."

"I remember his case," Henri said. "Should we be worried about this Danny Huang?"

"He has a criminal record for a range of violent and political crimes."

Henri nodded. "Then if Danny is clever and in the country, he'll find someone who can be him or vouch for him at home in Beijing. Just as importantly, you need to know who he is here because he's obviously not Danny Huang."

Mitch nodded. "If we don't have some date range

of when he might have entered the country it could mean days and days of trawling through airport footage."

Henri nodded sympathetically. "Or you could just get Marcus to run the facial recognition software for the past six months."

Mitch grinned. "Yeah, well there's that. I love technology."

"You're looking thinner, Mitch," Henri said.

Mitch rolled his eyes. "You always say that."

"But seriously, when was the last time you ate?"

"Now," Mitch rose. "Thanks for the coffee and sounding board, Henri."

"Coffee doesn't count as a meal," Henri called after him.

———

Samantha and Nick sat in the very pink and frilly surrounds of their B&B waiting for Mitch's conference call. Samantha pulled on a light knit jumper over her shirt. Nick, oblivious to the cold and wearing only a T-shirt and shorts, concentrated on his chicken and salad sandwich.

"C'mon, it's a lovely sixty-eight degrees out there." Nick gauged the temperature.

"That's right," she agreed, "with a chill factor of

even less. What maniac goes to the beach at this time of the year?"

Nick shrugged. "The water was lovely and warm this morning."

"I think we should change accommodation."

"Too pink?" Nick looked around.

Samantha made a face at him. "I'm pretty sure that Asian man is staying at the motel on the beach. We need to be in a room near or opposite so we can watch his comings and goings."

"You're right. We're going to draw attention to ourselves if we keep spending every hour of every day on the beach."

"It's kind of desperate," Samantha agreed. "That place right on the beach will let us watch all that is going on from our room."

"Yeah," said Nick as he looked around, "what was John thinking?"

The phone rang and Nick leaned forward to press the speaker button. Samantha rose and, bringing her sandwich and tea, came closer to the phone.

"Good morning, Charlie," Nick started, "and Ellie."

Mitch laughed. "Very funny."

"How was your morning?" Ellen asked.

"Cold and windy," Samantha said matter-of-factly. "So, the pics we sent through of the Asian guy...could you identify him?"

They could hear Mitch shuffling paper.

"Well I'm not sure," Mitch said. "There's an ugly guy in the front of the shot ..."

"Nick?" Ellen offered.

"Ah, so it is," Mitch finished. Ellen laughed.

"Now they're a comedy team," Nick said. "Lord help us."

"But seriously," Mitch said, "Marcus is still running the shots. I need more from you. Where is this guy staying?"

Samantha looked to Nick. "We were just discussing that before your call. Nick saw him go into the motel on the beach; might have just been going in for lunch but I'm guessing he's staying there. We need to move out of here and get up there."

"We need to stay at the place right on the beach so we can monitor without attracting attention," Nick summed it up.

"Agreed," Mitch said. "Sam, after this call find out where you want to stay and call it through to John to book."

"OK," she said. "But you want us to break into his room, don't you?"

"Yes, and fast. As soon as you find it and he leaves to go sightseeing, or to dinner, whatever."

Nick exhaled. "We'll get some surveillance

started on him; we haven't seen him since earlier this morning."

"Also try the nosy shop owners, tour groups, slip some notes to the porter at the hotel—and just get a name. If it is William Ying—and the fingerprints seem to suggest he was the last person holding those binoculars—then he has to be using an alias surely."

"Right," Samantha said.

"What about you two, what have you found?" Nick asked.

"Plenty and nothing," Ellen answered.

"Yep, know that feeling," Nick agreed.

11

MITCH TURNED HIS AUDI INTO THE LEAFY STREET IN Rockville. Following Ellen's directions, he pulled up in front of a large white house with a neat garden out the front and a quaint, old-world feel about it.

"Nice," Ellen muttered beside him as she looked past him to the house.

"Mm, must be money in politics," Mitch agreed, "or William Ying had very good life insurance."

"Will you tell Mrs. Ying about her husband's fingerprints on the binoculars?"

"No, not at this stage," Mitch said. "We'll tell her it is normal procedure to follow up a year after a case is closed to ensure nothing new has come up. We'll see if she is oblivious to his whereabouts. Look for signs that there might be a man in the house, assuming she hasn't got a new guy, of course."

On the second floor, he saw a figure move away from the window.

"Let's do it." Mitch alighted. They made their way to the intercom system on the gate, Mitch announced themselves and they were admitted.

Ellen pushed open the gate and they proceeded to the front door, taking the four stairs to the entrance. Waiting for them was a lady in her mid-forties, immaculately groomed and dressed; her pale pink and white woolen suit was cut to perfectly fit her trim figure. Mitch showed his identification and she indicated for them to enter. They sat on the floral couch as instructed. The room was full of furniture—every square inch had a piece of furniture, a photo frame, artificial flowers or a mirror trespassing on it.

Mitch began. "Mrs. Ying, thank you for seeing us. This is just a routine visit, given it is now a year since the disappearance of your husband, William."

She nodded her understanding. Mitch noted how stiff she seemed; she sat with her feet crossed, her back perfectly straight and her hands clasped in her lap.

"Will you be closing the case?" she asked in a calm voice.

"Not yet. Have you learnt or heard anything about your husband or his whereabouts in the past year?" he asked the obvious question.

"Nothing," she said and shook her head.

"Have you heard from any of his colleagues here or in China?"

"No. Only his mother who calls on days of occasion."

Mitch nodded. She gave nothing away.

"Have you returned home since the disappearance of Mr. Ying?" Mitch continued.

"No," she answered firmly. "This is home for me; my daughter is in first grade now."

"Do you know Danny Huang?" Mitch asked. He noted she didn't look surprised or shocked by the name. She frowned slightly.

"I know that name, Huang. But Huang is quite a common name ... I went to school with a Huang and to university with another Huang."

"So you don't know a Danny Huang? Or to use his Asian name, Huang Ming?"

She frowned again. "No. Is he relevant to my husband's disappearance do you think?"

"Just a line of enquiry," Mitch said. He tried to take in as much of the surroundings as he could—the hallway, the bathroom with its open door and the kitchen. He rose and stood near the window, conscious of her eyes upon him.

"Mrs. Ying, are you living here alone?" Ellen asked, distracting Mrs. Ying from watching Mitch.

"My daughter and I, yes."

Ellen continued. "Did Mr. Ying own a pair of binoculars?"

"Binoculars!" she exclaimed surprised. "Why yes. He was given a pair by the company he worked for before we left Taiwan. I remember because I thought it was an odd present. William had been working for him as a negotiator. What did he want with binoculars?"

"Do you still have them by any chance?" Ellen continued.

"I haven't seen them, but I'm sure they are here somewhere. I don't know that William ever used them." She looked up at the ceiling while thinking. "If I still had them, they would probably be in a box in the garage. I can see for you, but I would prefer to get the gardener to look for you."

"You have a gardener, how often does he come?" Mitch asked.

"Once a week," Mrs. Ying answered. "He was here today."

"And what is his name please, just so we don't waste our time if his name comes up as connected to the property," Mitch said.

Mrs. Ying frowned. "His name is Lam Ji."

Mitch made a note. "Thank you. So he could check to see if the binoculars are there for us?"

Mrs. Ying nodded. "If you don't mind waiting?

The garage is dirty and full of ..." She wrinkled her nose as she seemed to be searching for a word.

"Rodents?" Ellen suggested.

"Memories," she concluded.

———

"Rodents. I'm a dill," Ellen laughed as they slipped back into Mitch's Audi.

"I don't know, rats would have kept me out of the garage," Mitch said. "I wonder if she allows the gardener access to the house."

"Why?" Ellen asked.

"I saw through to the bathroom and someone male has been inside recently."

"Two toothbrushes?" Ellen asked.

Mitch shook his head. "Toilet seat up."

"Oh! I wonder how often she uses that bathroom or if someone left not long before we arrived."

"Mm, I suspect the house has few bathrooms. Will you ..."

"I'll find out who the gardener is and if he has connections," Ellen finished Mitch's sentence.

———

Ellen bounded into Mitch's office ten minutes after

they arrived back at work. "You are not going to be-lieve it!"

Mitch groaned. "Probably not ... Mrs. Ying is not really alive, that was her ghost?"

Ellen stood up straight and looked surprised. "Well, almost. Lam Ji, the name Mrs. Ying gave as the gardener, is Mrs. Ying's brother. Her maiden name was Lam. But, he's clearly a gardener in spirit only," Ellen said, "because according to the Registry of Births and Deaths, he died a good ten years ago in Beijing."

"That's a long time to leave the seat up," Mitch agreed. "We really caught her on the hop with that question. She must have come up with the first name that sprang to her mind and didn't think we'd check."

"Especially if it is just a routine report one year after the event, with nothing new to report." Ellen shrugged. "Unless there is another Lam Ji moon-lighting as a gardener."

"So, are we thinking that maybe William Ying had to disappear for some reason, but he's not really gone? And the three people who last saw him and had photo evidence of who he might have left with have died."

Ellen nodded. "That's where we are at. Got any plans tonight? Want to do surveillance at Mrs. Ying's house?" she asked in an alluring voice.

Mitch laughed. "Gee, best offer I've had since lunch. Yeah, we had better. But I can do it on my own, you don't need to suffer beside me."

"I'll bring the thermos," Ellen said and waved a file at him.

———

Nick and Samantha entered the hotel where they had made their new booking. Samantha took the lead as they had planned, and Nick followed her to the reception desk.

Nick tried to read the computer monitor in the mirrored glass. He turned to take in the room, willing the Asian man to make an appearance. *Make my day buddy and walk past.* Nothing happened.

"This will seem an odd question," he heard Samantha start to ask and he turned back to watch her in action. She was using all her charm on the young male receptionist and it appeared to be working.

"My brother and I are here on business but I've lost my diary."

Nick noticed she even blushed appropriately. "We're supposed to be meeting an Asian gentleman whose name escapes me because I'm terrible with names and languages."

"Me too," the young man shared.

"He and his colleague are staying here. I know you probably have hundreds of guests coming and going, but any chance you have an Asian guest or two that checked in about a week ago and is still here?"

"I'll have a look." He smiled at her, then remembered to stop staring at her and looked at the screen. He grabbed a piece of paper and wrote down four names.

"That's the only four guests with Asian names that are checked in. Don't ask me how to pronounce their names though."

Nick noticed he didn't exist; the male receptionist was oblivious to him as he handed over the list.

"You are a sweetie, thank you," Samantha gushed. "I'll know him once I see him, so I'll start practicing names and at least I won't totally embarrass myself."

Nick leant over and took the room key the receptionist was about to hand Samantha for their room.

"Thanks buddy," he said, and strode outside.

"Thank you, again." Samantha lingered a little longer for effect before following Nick.

They walked along the veranda until they found their room number.

"Ooh," Samantha said, "it's actually called an

oceanfront townhouse." She looked around, and added, "and it is oceanfront."

"Yeah, the townhouse description might be a bit liberal." Nick put the key in the door of the room and they entered.

"Nice," he said, impressed. "John's excelled this time."

"Two bedrooms, woo hoo!" Samantha yelled out.

"And a great view of the beach." Nick drew apart the curtains. "We can stake it from our room."

Samantha rejoined Nick, pulled out her phone and placed a call to Mitch.

"I've got four Asian guests' names from the receptionist ... it's Samantha." She stopped to announce herself before continuing, "yep, four names but I don't know if one of them is William or his alias."

"Excellent," Mitch answered. "We can try and match them to the photos you took earlier, if we can find them in any system. Read them to me."

Samantha read out the names and spelled them.

"What now for you two?" Mitch asked.

"We are going to eat soon but we'll keep an eye out. If we see him, we can follow and confirm if he is staying here or elsewhere. How soon can you run those names in case I have a room to bug?"

"I'll get them started now. Sam, separate beds or

tell Nick he has to marry you." Mitch hung up before hearing her reply.

———

Charlotte Curtis was pleased to find their regular sofa free as she slid onto the red velvet cushion opposite her best friend, Sally Downing. She had intended to have after-work drinks with Mitch, but yet again he was still at the office, leaving her alone.

"So where's Mitch the ditcher?" Sally asked, glancing down the wine list.

"Three guesses," Charlotte answered curtly.

"Work?"

"You win. He's joining us later, maybe. He's all work, with only guest appearances at home." She glanced down the wine list. "A Cab Sav?"

"Done," Sally agreed. She sat back and smoothed out her red dress with the flat of her hand. "I'm blending into the couch, no one will see me."

Charlotte laughed and caught the waiter's eye. She ordered and turned at the sound of a cheer from the crowd gathered at the bar. They were watching a football match being broadcast on a large screen.

"So, trouble in paradise?" Sally asked.

Charlotte looked back at Sally. She thought before answering.

"Depends how you define trouble." She brushed her dark shoulder length hair back behind her ears and frowned with concentration. "Since we had plenty of practice as housemates before sharing a room, living together is the easy part. But when it comes to communicating, Mitch is a closed book. When we were just housemates it was no big deal but now ... he just doesn't ever open up. And don't say give it time, it's been seven, almost eight months."

"Are we talking physical or verbal communication?" Sally asked.

Charlotte stopped to take the wine from the waiter. She clinked glasses with Sally and took a sip as though she needed it.

"That's good." She sipped again. "We're talking verbal. Don't get me wrong ... he's gorgeous ... and sweet; and good in bed; you know ..."

"Too much information," Sally cut in.

"And loyal," Charlotte continued. "I know with Mitch, I'll be the only one, he's just that type but ..."

Sally waited.

Charlotte continued. "I can honestly say, I probably don't know him any better than I did when I was just his housemate; except physically of course. He just lives on a day-to-day basis. He doesn't discuss how he feels or how his day was, or his thoughts about his friends or his staff. He's not interested in having them around for dinner or even introducing them to me. I still haven't met his mother or his brother! It's like he is keeping all his worlds separate. Even if he is frustrated, he will go for a run rather than get angry or talk about it."

"Your last boyfriend wasn't the greatest communicator either," Sally reminded her.

"No, but at least Lachlan showed some emotion. He would get pissed off or tell me to get lost. I knew his family, his friends and I knew some things about him. He'd like to show me off … a girl likes that."

Sally shrugged. "I'm not saying you and Mitch are not suited so don't read that into what I'm going to say … I just think you have to find the right personality match for your needs. You do this for a living, you know what I mean."

"I do, but I think we are right, on many levels," Charlotte jumped in.

"Do you, or are you scared of wasting another year and starting over again?" Sally asked.

"Well, of course there is that too." Charlotte sighed.

Sally continued, "I'm quite happy not to deal with a lot of drama and I'm especially not interested in their past relationships or baggage—somewhat impossible to avoid at our age, but I don't mind living in the now." She stopped to sip her wine before continuing. "I'm more likely to tell you my dramas than to tell a boyfriend. Do you think you expect too much from him?"

"Telling me how his day was and if I've pissed him off isn't a big ask though, is it?" Charlotte continued without waiting for Sally to answer. "And, if I ask questions, he says I'm bringing my work home and trying to analyze him. He has been having these regular nightmares." Charlotte leant forward and dropped her voice. "Last night he woke up drenched in sweat and yelling, kind of a fearful yell ... but do you think he will talk to me about it? It's like the night sweats that veterans get. I said that to him but he blew me off and said it was just a bad dream."

"Maybe it is just a bad dream." Sally shrugged.

"Three nights in a row?" Charlotte grabbed a menu. "Let's order a pizza to share. Frustration makes me hungry."

"You don't want to wait another thirty minutes in case he makes it here?" Sally asked.

Charlotte scoffed. "Mitch will never make it here, trust me."

Sally smiled. She placed her drink down on the table and grabbed the second menu. "So what are you going to do? Do you love him?"

"Sure, of course I love him but it is almost one dimensional. He's gorgeous, strong, has the most beautiful smile and those blue eyes, but I can't get into his head. Sex is his only emotional attachment to me. I know that's normal," she added before Sally could speak. "Women connect by communicating, while men on the other hand spend their whole life believing they shouldn't show emotions, so connect through sex. But, I am not sure that connection alone is going to be enough for me."

Sally groaned. "I love the two of you. This is always the problem when friends get it on together."

"Don't say anything to him," Charlotte said.

"God no, I wouldn't dream of it. It is a shame that you are living together, given you're feeling so unsure."

"I know, it just complicates matters further. Sometimes, I wish we had just stayed housemates."

"Yes." Sally twirled a strand of her blonde hair around her finger and cocked her head to the side. "You should have left him for me; I've never liked the clingy types."

"Yep, well he's not that," Charlotte agreed. "More like Teflon."

12

WEDNESDAY AFTERNOON—THE LAST DAY OF THEIR formal classes which had tested Danny Huang's patience; his blood had boiled with frustration as the days not spent directly working on the project dragged for him. He knew he had to keep up the farce, but his mind was working through the job. Nevertheless, he remained calm on the outside—he was a disciplined man. It was difficult not to automatically speak English or fall into defence maneuvers during combat classes; to remember they were only as skilled as the Armed Police Force of their country and not the elite team they actually were.

He looked at the clock and went through the plan: in one hour Hai and Froggy will leave for Cape Hatteras and stay the weekend, while tonight I will catch up with William and the VIP. Tomorrow, young Ru and I will head to Cape Hatteras, meet up with William there and check all is OK. There's a lot to do in the four day break. He looked to the clock again with impatience.

He returned his concentration to the classroom; Froggy was attempting to repeat some difficult English words after the instructor—the real difficulty was pretending not to know the words; Danny nodded at him encouragingly. The teacher was delighted with progress, claiming them all fast learners. They accepted the teacher's praise with great enthusiasm and a smirk meant only for one another.

Danny Huang caught the teacher's attention.

"Yes, Danny?" The middle-aged teacher nodded towards him.

Danny stumbled on the words. "We question how many languages speak?"

"You were wondering how many languages I speak?" the teacher asked, correcting him.

Ru, Froggy and Hai nodded their interest and the teacher smiled in delight. He sat on the edge of his desk and counted them off.

"Mm, I speak English." He held up one finger and the men laughed after an appropriate delay to pretend to translate the joke in their own heads. The teacher nodded and laughed too. He held up a second finger. "German, I speak German. A little

French," he waved his hand side to side and then moved his hands together and said, "just a little Mandarin."

Danny nodded and said in rapid Mandarin, "you are a clever and kind man, but how good is your understanding of our native tongue?"

The teacher shook his head and held up his hands in protest. "No, no, too fast, too advanced for me. I know simple greetings like 'hello, would you like tea?' Perhaps we can learn from each other," he said kindly.

Danny nodded and smiled. Safe, he thought.

The class continued and Danny's phone buzzed. He tried to move his phone into his line of vision without the teacher seeing him. With fifteen minutes remaining he was struggling to stay alert; easier to stand still on parade for hours than this, he thought. Danny looked to the front on hearing his western name, contributed an answer in a stumbling manner and glanced subtly at the phone again. It was his cousin in Beijing. He read the message:

Had call. US Govt rep asking for you. I said you were here but in meeting. Call ASAP.

Danny felt a cold wave pass over him. Too soon. How could they know I'm here? This puts the timeline under pressure.

He looked up impatiently. The teacher was

wrapping up the lesson. *Let's get going here. Work to do.* He ran his hand over his mouth nervously and then began to text back.

Got to cover for me. Get Tai to be me, tell him to call me after. I must be there!

Minutes later, when the class finished for the day Danny stormed to the dormitory and gathered the three men around him. "We've got to get moving. They have found out I am in the country."

"How?" Hai asked.

Danny shook his head. "I don't know how. But now the clock is on. There is a lot to do to get the VIP out of the country and we don't have the luxury of an extension. It must go to plan on the third weekend. I don't need to remind you there is a lot riding on this."

The men nodded. Danny's chest swelled as he thought about his party, in the shadows for so long; now the light was at the end of the tunnel. *And I will be the leader of the change. Nothing is going to stop that.*

————

"He's not staying here... not in this hotel anyway," Samantha told Mitch down the phone line. She ordered another cup of tea from the waiter as she sat in the cafe, watching the beach and the hotel, both in her line of vision.

"Have you seen him today?" Mitch asked.

"Nope, and if we don't see him soon I'm going to explode. How much tea and coffee can any one agent drink?"

"The things you do for the job," Mitch agreed. "So the last time you saw him was when?"

"Around eleven a.m. yesterday. Do you think he's gone?" Samantha asked.

"I don't know, strange he's disappeared from sight though," Mitch said. "What did you find out from local operators?"

"The desk clerk said he had no remaining Asian guests at all, and the porter confirmed it. The lady at the corner store said a charming Asian man came in yesterday morning and bought tea and milk," Samantha said.

"Which he wouldn't need if he was staying in the hotel. So why was he in there?"

"Who knows, maybe having lunch like Nick suggested or meeting someone," Samantha said.

Mitch continued. "Any luck with the tour operators?"

"That's where Nick is now," Samantha said.

"OK, so we can't get any bugs in. Can you try and lift something with a print on it?"

"If I see him, I'll do just that."

"Thanks, Sam," Mitch said.

Samantha was about to ask what they had

found when she realized he had hung up. "Right then, talk later." She put the phone down. She saw Nick pull the hire car into the driveway of the hotel and disappear below into the parking lot. Minutes later he walked across the road and joined her at the cafe.

"I've got something," he said, his voice laced with excitement. "I'll just phone it through to Mitch. Anything?"

"Yes, I can't drink any more tea or coffee."

"Noted," Nick said, and looked at his watch. "In a few hours, it'll be cocktail hour and we can move onto beer for me and sparkling wine for you."

Samantha looked at him and brightened. "Marvelous," she said in her best posh accent. She turned to watch the sidewalk and studied the façade of nearby buildings as Nick called Mitch. They were old hotels that had been given a facelift a few times over the years, which explained the odd décor from the seventies, nineties and now.

"It's gone to message bank, not like Mitch. He must be on the phone." Nick sat back. He nodded to the hotel. "The place is doing a reasonable trade considering it is the off-season. I'm going in."

"Going in where?" Samantha sat upright.

"I'm going in to the hotel. I'm going to follow some of the guests in and ride the lift a bit. See if I can see anything."

"But he's not registered there as a guest, no Asian men are," Samantha said.

"He might be staying with another guest," Nick suggested.

"Maybe." Samantha shrugged. "I'll head down to do a final patrol of the beach for the day. If he is not staying at the hotel, he's got to be staying somewhere and if I see him I can follow. Plus the light will be fading soon."

"Not much else to do," Nick agreed. "Unless he's gone walking in the national park, in which case he's a tourist and we've got the wrong end of the stick completely."

Nick tried Mitch again and got him.

"Mitch, got something. Yesterday an Asian guy —could be our guy—booked a dive for two people with one of the dive groups here. He told the bookings clerk it wasn't for him but his two friends who were experienced divers. The dive booking is for Saturday and..." Nick reached in his jacket for a piece of paper he had scribbled on. "He's booked in one name, that of Ba Hao-cun."

"Excellent," Mitch said, checking the spelling. "Thanks Nick, leave it with me. Call you later tonight."

"Right," Nick said. He pocketed his phone and turned to Samantha. "I'm off to play in the lifts. Ciao."

Samantha sighed as she watched him depart. She rose, paid the bill and headed off to the beach. She turned back to glance towards the hotel and down the tourist strip. Nothing.

————

Mitch hung up from Nick and looked at his phone. He dreaded the call, but knew it had to be made. Charlotte answered, and sounded pleased to hear from him.

"I was just thinking of you," she said.

"And here I am!" Mitch answered. "How's tricks?"

"All good. I've got one appointment left and then I'm heading home. Want to head out for dinner tonight?"

"Um, that's why I'm calling." Mitch heard her groan. "Sorry, I've got to do a bit of surveillance, but I won't be late, probably eight or so."

"So last night you were a no-show at drinks because you had to do surveillance, and tonight you're on surveillance again. Are you sure you're not having an affair?"

Parker scoffed. "Hardly. We can go out when I come home. I'll call you when I'm almost there and we can go out then," Mitch offered.

"Whatever."

"Charlie ..." He looked at his phone, and she was gone. "Well that went well," he muttered. "No wonder most agents are single or divorced."

"This Danny Huang is a public menace." John Windsor waved a piece of paper as he walked into Mitch's office and dropped down into the seat opposite him. He stopped on seeing Mitch's annoyed look. "You all right?"

"What? Oh yeah, fine." Mitch put the phone down.

John continued. "Danny Huang ... he's a founding member of a subversive political agency, the New Red Guard, not to mention he's been associated with a string of illegal and unrecognized political parties in the People's Republic of China over the past decade. He's been arrested on fraud, theft, violence, starting riots, starting new parties, starting a religion, you name it."

"The New Red Guard ... I vaguely remember Mao's Red Army and the Russian Red Army from my history days at school, but the Red Guard—old or new—is new to me," Mitch said.

John read from the sheet. "The New Red Guard strives to provide an enlightened way forward: a selfless community selecting production for use and profit; health and education for all with consolidation of the ruling status of the Party and—here's a twist—opportunities for capitalist advancement in designated industries."

Mitch exhaled. "So are they capitalists or socialists?"

John frowned. "It's anyone's guess ... they're leaning to elements of both. So Ying's widow didn't know Danny Huang?"

"She denied knowing him but I can't tell if she was telling the truth, she didn't give much away." Mitch rose and moved to the window. "She definitely had a male in the house at some time, whether it was her missing husband, a new love or the gardener, we don't know. No-one showed last night at her house, that we could see, but I'm just going to do a quick stakeout again tonight."

"By yourself?"

"Just for a few hours," Mitch said, "I don't need back up."

Mitch reached out his hand for Danny Huang's history and when he finished reading, he looked up at John. "I can't work out why his prints are on the binoculars."

"And what is his connection to William Ying," John added.

"Mrs. Ying said William did own some binoculars and they were a gift from William's old company. I wonder if Danny worked for the same company."

John nodded. "Worth investigating."

Mitch began to pace. "Socialism ... social organization," he thought aloud, "like in Marxist theory—a transition state between capitalism and communism." Mitch continued to pace, as John watched and waited. Mitch turned to him. "If you were going to form a socialist party which combined the best of socialism and capitalism, how would you go about it?"

John crossed his arms over his chest. "I'd get the most powerful, respected or successful representatives of both parties as figureheads for starters."

"Yes," Mitch said. "So is that why Danny Huang is here? Is that why William Ying disappeared? Are they targeting people here? The capitalist?"

John exhaled. "So given the circles that William Ying moved in as Chinese Ambassador to the US, are you thinking that his disappearance is linked to the fact that he might have tried to target the wrong person? Someone in power?"

Mitch shrugged slightly. "William would have made some very powerful allies while he was in the role of ambassador. He needed to stay in the country longer but if he didn't want to become a citizen ... or if he was earmarked for something bigger or wanted to work below the radar ..." Mitch continued to think out loud.

"He'd have to disappear," John confirmed.

"Drastic though. Whatever it was, it must have been important enough to kill all three witnesses who saw him leave the exhibition that night. Plus if William was working on getting someone to be an ally or leader in this New Red Guard party, what would he have to offer them? What protection?"

"And how radical are we talking here? Why couldn't they just 'walk'?" John asked.

"I guess it depends on how high up the person is; if it was a cabinet member, chief of staff or advisor who walked out of government and went to take up a role in a subversive Asian political party that could command millions of people and be privy to secrets of American security, I'd be pretty anxious about that."

John swore under his breath.

"I'm just theorizing," Mitch assured him. "This could be all pipe dream stuff. I need to think it through."

John rose to go. "Mitch, we are talking about a former ambassador who is back on the radar. If there is any credibility in your thought process, this case has just become a huge international security issue and I need to move it up the chain urgently."

Mitch nodded. "Leave it with me just a little longer. We'd wear egg on our face if we created this drama and missed the mark."

John frowned.

"Seriously," Mitch said, "just give me until to-morrow morning. Nick and Sam are making progress—Nick got a name of one of them, assuming it is his real name, so that might help. I've got surveillance tonight, and I'm running facial recognition checks from the international airport of everyone who has entered in the last six months ... hopefully Danny Huang is there because at the moment, he's still not officially in the country."

John looked across the office. "Let's try for William Ying too. See if he has come or gone under some other name. Get young Matt onto it." He nodded towards the officer-in-training. "It'll give him something useful to do while he's spending the month here."

"Great, thanks." Mitch glanced at the young man who was currently filing. He rose and went out to introduce himself to Matt Bennett. The young man, all of twenty, stood a head shorter than Mitch and had the customary short, back and sides haircut of a rookie. He obviously lifted weights; his business shirt bulged at the arms. He shook Mitch's hand with great enthusiasm.

"I need some help," Mitch stated.

"Anything, please," Matt indicated the filing.

Mitch smiled. "Yeah, been there." He sat beside Matt and called up a photo of William Ying.

"This is William Ying," Mitch began. "Former

Chinese Ambassador to the US. He's missing, but I need to be sure he's not coming or going from the country under an alias. Run this image through the facial recognition software and then go back one year on the airport customs footage. The photo is not big on distinguishing marks, but give it a shot and don't sweat it if he is not on there or if you find twenty who could be him, that's all fine."

"No problem," Matt said.

"If I'm not in and you find something, just call my office number; it'll go to my phone. Thanks, Matt," Mitch said.

"Pleasure, really," he said, and smiled, turning to start.

13

As soon as it was dark, Danny Huang hailed a taxi. He asked the driver to drop him a street away and walked the rest. After a quick look around, he was confident no one had seen him arrive at the home of William Ying's wife—or widow, given William was presumed dead. She greeted him warmly and he slipped into the house.

"You look wonderful, Danny." She hugged him.

"It is so good to see you, Mei, you haven't changed, so beautiful." Danny studied her.

"Thank you, you are too kind, come, come." She led him towards the back of the house and opened a door to a large white room with two chocolate brown Chesterfield couches and one wall covered in books. Tea was served on a mahogany table in the middle of the room. Mrs. Ying retreated.

Danny Huang smiled and extended his arms wide as he walked towards the two men standing by the window.

"It's been a long time." Danny smiled, "at last in the flesh."

"Too long. You look well my friend," William Ying said.

The VIP stepped forward and embraced Danny.

"It must be fifteen years, no, more," he said.

"Twenty-two years," Danny Huang told the men.

"No!" The VIP declared.

Both men laughed. "Sadly yes," Danny confirmed. "We were twenty-one at university when you joined us. Now, you might not have aged, but last birthday I had forty-three candles on the cake."

The men embraced again.

"Tea, come." William poured as the men took a seat.

"Life good, Danny?" the VIP asked.

"I can't complain; still working for the cause, aren't we all? But you William, how are you? You look very well for a dead man." Danny turned the conversation to William.

William turned slightly to glance out the window. "It hasn't been easy, disappearing, being away from my wife and child for months at a time. But of course I am happy to do so for the mission."

Danny nodded. "It will pay off. It's beginning to

already. You couldn't have had the university access that you have had under your own name." He squeezed William's shoulder as William leaned in to pass him the tea.

"So good to see you both again. Ah, the things we got up to!" Danny laughed.

"You were a terrible influence on William and me," the VIP agreed.

"What?" Danny laughed. "Never."

"My poor folks thought I was there to study and improve my Mandarin." The VIP shook his head. "Meanwhile you two with your private clubs and pipes," he grinned at the memory.

"Couldn't do it today," William said.

"That makes two of us," Danny agreed.

The three men reminisced for some time. Eventually Danny got down to business.

"So, you are confident the lift will go well, William?" he asked.

"I am very confident."

"What was the hitch?" Danny continued.

"Just a mix-up in bearings. They were supposed to send me a small signal, just a mirror reflection at 1700 hours; nothing that would be picked up by anyone on the beach. But they got the coordinates wrong. It won't happen again. I am driving back to Cape Hatteras late tonight and I will review the whole exercise. I assure you, they will be there for the pick-up," William guaranteed him. "One other thing—I have misplaced the binoculars you sent me for good luck a few months back. I know they were a gift from our Chairman. I apologize and ..."

"It's not important my friend. I am only concerned about the job. I trust that you have it under control." Danny studied his oldest friend as William nodded confidently.

"So, William, have you had contact with your family in Beijing?" the VIP asked.

William shook his head and lied. "No. It was agreed I would walk away. I do my best not to ever think about it; like it was another life and I was another person. It helps that I can see my wife occasionally like today and to know that they will never want for anything. Sometimes, I even feel liberated by my new identity."

"I am looking forward to that," the VIP nodded.

Danny smiled. "I understand. I too am a new man, several times over."

————

Danny Huang got in late to his dorm room, there had been much reminiscing to do. Regardless, he couldn't sleep with the excitement of the plan unfolding before him. He rose early and waited for young Ru to collect the hire car and pick him up. He was pumped not to have class today and to not have to return until Sunday. Gingerly Danny pushed aside the curtain and looked out the window. *Old habits* he told himself, remembering that he was a welcome guest of the country, a respected police office and didn't have to hide. He smiled at the thought.

The occasional car went past. His warm breath fogged the window. He was grateful for the cooler weather. If it had been a warmer time of the year, it would have been impossible to wear long sleeves without attracting attention. They hid the tattoos and scars that might have raised suspicion about his identity as a police officer. At the thought of the scars he felt a slight burn—a phantom pain.

He thought about the mission and how easily it could be blown.

I must remember, at all costs, not to speak in English. After all, we are representatives of the Beijing Armed Police Force here to do a crash course in English and G20 security.

Danny Huang reached for his phone and called Hai.

"Report?" he said when Hai answered.

"We arrived last night about eleven p.m. The VIP house is secure and well-hidden, fully-equipped and ready for the VIP. The communications room is functioning; there are four cameras covering the house perimeters, the tank, beach and the view from the lighthouse," Hai said.

"Have you made contact with Beijing?" Danny asked.

"Yes, and they are on schedule. No changes. They will do a communication drill with Ru when he arrives with you later today."

"Good." Danny saw Ru alight from a blue SUV out the front of the dorm. "We are heading off now. What are your plans for this morning?"

"We will scope the beach and chart the coordinates again just to be sure," Hai answered. "Froggy's going to do a bit of snorkelling today just to check the coordinates, but we've got a dive booked in for Froggy and me on Saturday with a school. William thought it better to join a local dive group rather than hire a boat; fits in with the tourism profile. It will give us another chance to scope the area. Other than that, we'll be checking and re-checking everything we can."

"Good. See you at approximately 1400 hours." Danny hung up, grabbed his bag off the bed and headed to meet Ru. He left his room, closing and checking the door was locked. As he headed down the front stairs of the campus, he noted how empty it was due to the Fall break. Only the stray student wandering around the grounds was to be seen.

"You drive, Ru," Danny ordered the young man

who was leaning against the back of the car, smoking. Ru extinguished the cigarette and raced around to get behind the wheel.

Ru started the engine and handed several pages to Danny. "Here's the latest printouts from the bugs in the VIP's phone, sir."

"Slim pickings," Danny said.

"Yes, nothing to highlight in there, sir," Ru reported.

They drove the entire trip in silence... Danny testing the young man's nerve and Ru not being one for small talk. Eventually Ru turned off the main road, following the directions William had given him. He drove up the forest path to the VIP house; the track was several miles from the main road, with the occasional side street. A few properties dotted the turn-offs, but the area was largely deserted.

"Good," Danny said his first words in hours. "Well away from the road, reasonably isolated."

Ru came to the end of the road and saw the brick house. He drove into the property and put the car into the large garage beside the second vehicle. Danny Huang alighted, studied the area, and, satisfied that it was isolated, grabbed his bag and followed Ru into the house.

He was greeted by his own men, Hai and Froggy and by William Ying, who had arrived earlier despite a very late night with the VIP. He shook the men's hands and accepted a tour of the premises; Ru stopping and staying in the communications room.

"Satisfactory, sir?" Froggy asked.

Danny Huang nodded and smiled. "Very satisfactory."

———

Ellen waited to speak with Amy Callaghan, the team's allocated contact in the Criminal Justice Information Services Division. A young officer having trouble accessing photo files was dominating Amy's time; she sorted him out within minutes and turned to Ellen.

"Two o'clock rush hour," she joked and Ellen laughed.

"Ellen Beetson." Ellen extended her hand. "I don't think we've officially met even though you've been here a while now."

Amy rose and shook hands. "About eight months, and it seems like longer." She smiled. "You're on Nick's team aren't you?"

"Yes, and you have the dubious honor of being his housemate," Ellen said.

Amy sighed. "Yes, it has its challenges and I'm trying to train him."

Ellen laughed. "Mm, good luck with that." She studied the sporty looking blonde. She was about her own height, clearly worked out and had similar length blonde hair. Her eyes were dark brown, unlike Ellen's own green eyes.

"Thanks for helping us out. The surveillance footage has been really disappointing," Ellen said. "But you have something for me?"

"Pull up a seat," Amy offered, logging back into her screen. "If only we had got to this earlier. Not many people keep footage for a year."

Ellen watched as Amy clicked through screens and files. She looked around; half a dozen people wandered about looking for intel.

"So research is the biggest part of your job?" Ellen asked.

"Got it in one. If some of these photos had been catalogued under William Ying as well as the Photo Gallery Exhibition I would have found them earlier. There's about a thousand gallery exhibitions in the greater Washington area every year. Now check this out ..."

Ellen leaned forward just as her phone rang.

"Sorry," Ellen apologized.

"No problem, this is one quiet area where you can have your phone on."

"Mitch?" Ellen answered and listened. "I'm just with Amy; she has something for me but I'll see you there."

Ellen hung up. "Sorry." She glanced at her watch.

Amy continued. "I lifted as many images as I could from the background of the two CCTV footage reels we had. There's not much there, but around William Ying, I've been able to pull out half a dozen images that might be of interest." Amy opened the file. "I've identified these people through funeral notices and tributes that were online as well as the university's obituary."

Amy called up a shot of William Ying walking out of the gallery with a Chinese girl framed in the doorway behind him.

"Is that Jessica Wu?" Ellen asked.

"That is definitely her. Notice how close she is to him, as though seeing him off? Everyone else is still inside mingling," Amy said.

"Yes," Ellen leant forward. "Why? Joseph Kinaird is supposed to be the host. Why is Jessica there at all?"

"She wouldn't have been having an affair with William Ying; or perhaps he was her mentor?" Amy suggested.

"Mm, worth exploring," Ellen said.

"Now check this shot out," Amy continued. "Here's William getting into the backseat of the car, and in the left-hand top of the shot, there's a man with a camera taking photos. I'm fairly confident from the physical build that this is Joseph Kinaird."

"Amy, this is great. I didn't see these before," Ellen said.

"It was pretty hard to see them. I've magnified these and doctored them to try to get some definition," Amy explained.

"But Mr. Kinaird was definitely there snapping away, so he must have photographed something they didn't want to be seen."

"The one that gave me the most grief was trying to find Rodney Lam. It's weird because he is not in the uni's year book, maybe because he didn't show for photo day or didn't like having his photo taken. He's also one of the few students who wasn't in any other clubs aside from the Asian Commerce and Culture group. But nope, before you ask, no pic there either."

Amy pulled up a photo. "I think this is him."

"Wow it is blurry," Ellen agreed. "What makes you think it is him?"

"Well I found a couple of Facebook pages from students in his class and a couple had written about him, but no shots. Really weird; most students are all over social media," Amy explained.

"What's the context of this shot?" Ellen asked looking at the blurry photo.

Amy found the original shot and pulled it up.

"This is William Ying getting into the car." She zoomed in again and again. "That small figure through the open door and the adjacent window ..."

"He's in the back passenger seat with William?" Ellen gasped.

"I think that's Rodney. Where he was going is a bit of a mystery."

"Just like William Ying," Ellen said. "But we know or think Rodney Lam died in a house fire. I wonder where they drove to after the exhibition."

14

MITCH LEFT HIS OFFICE AND TOOK THE STAIRS DOWN to the I.T. department. Marcus was working on a translation, adorned in one of his customary loud shirts. Seeing Mitch, he removed the headphones.

"Marcus, you rang?" Mitch asked.

"Mitch my man, looking resplendent in that suit, but just once, I'd like to see one of these lovely Caribbean shirts beneath that black suit jacket." Marcus frowned.

Mitch laughed. "Yeah, that's on the cards. How is it going?"

"Can't complain so I won't. But I have something for you." Marcus rose and handed Mitch a photo. "The name you gave us to trace, the one Nicholas got of the man registered for the dive ..." Marcus looked at his notes. "Ba Hao-cun, he is one of the four police officers from the Beijing Armed Police Force here to study with our former G20 security team and doing that English course."

Mitch dropped down onto the stool in front of Marcus.

"Ah ha," he said.

"Is that a good 'ah ha' or not-so-good?" Marcus asked.

Mitch frowned, his eyes narrowed as he thought.

"This is very worrying." Mitch ran through the scenario in his head: *I have a missing ambassador whose fingerprints are found on binoculars at the beach at Cape Hatteras, along with the prints of a dissident who is not in the country supposedly. Now I have one of the Beijing Armed Police Force visiting the same location doing a dive.* Mitch rose. "Marcus, I need to know if this Ba Hao-cun is the real thing if you know what I mean?"

"I'm way ahead of you my man. I have photos of the four police men that were due to enter the country last Sunday, their security clearances and their fingerprints as supplied by the Beijing Armed Police Force several months ago. Knowing you were going to ask me to check it out—mind you, there's no reason why we might check it out because Ba Hao-cun is a welcome guest and he's doing some diving—but knowing you, Mitch..." Marcus grinned.

"You're killing me, what did you find?" Mitch groaned.

"I matched the photo of the police officer named Ba Hao-cun against the face of the person who came through the international airport last Sunday on Ba Hao-cun's passport. The facial recognition scanner says 'not a match'."

"Seriously?" Mitch sat down again next to Marcus to view the screen.

"Wait, there's more," Marcus continued. "Glad you're sitting, because the facial recognition software did bring up a match of the man who came through on Ba Hao-cun's passport. Fortunately the young man has been to the States before, mind you he was a teenager travelling with his parents on a holiday, so I have no current information on him, but his name is Fan Wen and he is not a member nor has he ever been a member of the Beijing Armed Police Force. Your on-the-ground person in China can help you out with what he does these days now he is all grown up."

"But where is the real Ba Hao-cun and are the other three police officers that came through security at the same time the real thing?" Mitch said.

"I'm onto that too. I checked security and yes, three other police officers entered the country at the same time as Ba Hao-cun or Fan Wen, or rather, three men entered on the policemen's passports,"

Marcus confirmed. "I've given Justin the photos of the three other Beijing police officers and he is running facial recognition software on everyone who entered the country at that same time as Fan Wen to see if there is a match... he'll know soon enough if the real thing entered the country."

Mitch exhaled. "What we do know for sure however, is that we are training a man who is not a Beijing police officer... I need to get someone in that classroom." He tapped his foot on the stool. Remembering where he was, he stopped and rose. "Thanks Marcus, seriously great work."

"Anytime, my friend. Why only four though?" he asked.

"What do you mean?" Mitch asked.

"Why are only four of them here ... surely they've got a bigger security team than that planned for the event," Marcus said.

"It's train the trainers—we train them, they go home and train their teams," Mitch said.

"Ah, gotcha. That's a relief, I thought we might have lost the rest," Marcus said, with a grin. "Catch Justin before you go, see if he's got any answers yet."

Mitch went down the hallway, entered another department and greeted Justin, another of the young I.T. whizzes with his two-toned hair, earphones dangling from his jacket and a desk surrounded by gadgets. Mitch looked over the tech's shoulder, as a program ran the remaining three policemen's images against people entering the country in a continuous stream of images—it stopped every now and then to consider someone whose face was constructed in a similar manner.

"No connection yet, Mitch," Justin said, "but check with Sophie." Justin nodded to his right. "She's running criminal checks on those four hotel guest names."

"Thanks," Mitch said.

He went to the other side of the room where a young female researcher with the biggest pair of framed glasses he had ever seen was wading through online files.

She pointed to the first one on Mitch's list. "I think you can eliminate the hotel guest Heng Yoo," Sophie said. "He's got one traffic ticket and is about eighty years old. He's an American citizen."

Mitch sat down beside her. "Nice work," he encouraged her.

She opened the files on the second name on the list.

"Kang Nguyen has a criminal record ..." she began.

Mitch sat upright with interest.

"For pornography," she finished. "He is twenty years old and was born in America."

Mitch slumped back in the seat.

"I've got two more to run," she said. "But it'll only take a minute." She put the names in and within a few minutes, had the results.

Sophie frowned, and removing her large glasses, turned to look at Mitch. "I think those names are fake."

"Why?" Mitch asked.

"It is a man and woman, the names are in the system, but the woman has used her maiden name to book in and she is now married. I think maybe ..." Sophie hesitated.

"Yes," Mitch pushed.

"I think they might be having an affair." She blushed.

"Oh, right. Could be. Well I was looking primarily for two men, but thanks," Mitch stood again.

"Got something!" Justin yelled, punching the air.

Mitch grinned at his enthusiasm and returned to Justin's side.

"What is it?" Mitch looked at the two photos frozen on the screen and another two frozen on another screen.

"One match so far... two to go. The guy on the right hand side of the screen came into the country last Sunday with..." Justin stopped to consult his notes, "...along with Fan-Wen who Marcus identified as impersonating the policeman Ba Hao-cun."

"Right, but is he the real policeman?" Mitch pushed.

"His passport says he is Foo Deshi, one of the four members of the Beijing Armed Police Service but I got some other files popping up. His real name is Kiang Hai."

"And Kiang Hai is not a police officer," Mitch said looking at the original four policemen.

"Absolutely not. Check this out," Justin said opening some media files. "This is a story about the four police officers who were coming over for training. The guy on the left is the real thing, Foo Deshi." Justin flicked back to the customs photo. "Now check out the photo of this coming through security who is supposed to be Foo Deshi."

Mitch leaned forward and studying the clipping. "They are two different men."

"Yeah, this guy is impersonating Foo Deshi and we have his name—Kiang Hai—because he was a navy man who has been here with his fleet."

"Great job, Justin, just brilliant," Mitch said.

"I'll keep trying to match the other two men," Justin said.

"Yes, please."

So where are the other two real police officers if these two are impersonating them? Mitch mused. He kept studying the press clipping, then grabbed Justin's desk phone and called upstairs. He waited until the trainee, Matt Bennett, was located. He asked him to come down to the floor below.

"Matt's been looking through customs vision for me," Mitch explained. "He's one of our trainees."

"Poor guy," Justin added.

Matt bound in and Mitch introduced him to Justin.

Mitch continued. "This might impact on your search through the customs vision of William Ying," he explained to Matt. Turning to Justin, he said, "So let me understand this. Two people by the name of Kiang Hai and Fan Wen are in the country at the moment. They entered the country last Sunday. Their occupation is listed as police officer."

Justin nodded.

Mitch continued, "So if Matt is looking at customs entry vision from last Sunday, he should see these two men on the right of the screen enter the country only they entered with passports that said they were Foo Deshi and Ba Hao-cun respectively, who are actually the two men in the photo on the left in the police uniforms?"

"Affirmative," Justin nodded.

"So you might find William Ying has done the same thing—entered as someone else. Or he may never have left the country, but check all other arrivals around the same time as the two Asian officers. OK Matt?"

"Absolutely," Matt nodded his understanding.

"Can you print these out for Matt?" Mitch asked. "And thanks," he said as he tapped Justin on the shoulder, "great work. Not a word of this to anyone guys, you know that I'm sure."

He rang John Windsor.

"Where are you?" Mitch asked.

"I'm just returning to the office, about fifteen minutes away. What's up?"

"I've got something we need to be worried about. I'll set up a conference call for the top of the hour?" Mitch said.

"I'll be there. How worried?" John hesitated to ask.

"Majorly worried," Mitch hung up.

15

MITCH AND ELLEN ENTERED JOHN WINDSOR'S OFFICE on the hour and closed the door. John called Samantha's phone. She answered on the first ring and put it on speaker phone.

"Go ahead, Mitch," John said.

"Right then. Marcus ran the name of the diver that you supplied, Nick, by the name of Ba Hao-cun. He is one of the four men from the Beijing Armed Police Force who are in the country, and now one of two who is on his way to Cape Hatteras supposedly to do a dive on Saturday. Except, when we did a facial scan, Ba Hao-cun is not the real Ba Hao-cun police officer. His name is Fan Wen and we have no more information on him other than he entered the country a few years ago as a minor travelling with his parents on a holiday visa."

"Unbelievable," John muttered and nodded for Mitch to continue.

"Marcus and Justin then found the other three police officers, checked their passports and images against the men who entered the country claiming to be them. So far we have one returned result... a man by the name of Kiang Hai has entered as the policeman Foo Deshi."

"So what is he doing down at Cape Hatteras where—" Samantha started.

"Wait," Mitch said, "let me finish so you can get your head around the big picture." He continued, "We were able to match him because he is a naval man who had come to the States before with his fleet. I've emailed you a press clipping featuring the real Foo Deshi and an original passport photo of Kiang Hai." Mitch put them on the screen for John and Ellen's benefit.

John drew a deep sigh. "There's more isn't there?"

"Oh yeah," Mitch continued. "Everyone with me so far?"

There was a murmur of assent.

"What about the four guest names from the hotel?" Samantha asked.

"No connection and no cause for concern," Mitch said. He stood up and began his customary pacing. "So in summary we have at least two police officers we are teaching English to and sharing our security techniques with, who are not police officers —but we can probably safely assume all four are aliens. We may have four missing Chinese police officers but I won't know for sure until I can get prints from each class member; two of those so called police officers are at Cape Hatteras and have been seen looking out to sea at who knows what, in the very same location where William Ying's fresh fingerprints were found. Danny Huang, a dissident who belongs to a party called the New Red Guard is supposedly not in the country but his fingerprints say differently; Mrs. Ying is receiving male guests and the last three people to see William Ying alive have either vanished or are dead."

John rose. "I need to flag this upstairs. Mitch, have you had time to formulate your next step?"

"Yep, Ellie and I will continue our ground work here; Sam and Nick need to get themselves booked onto that Saturday diving trip and spend the next few days waiting, watching and photographing. I need confirmation of everything I've just said— photo and fingerprint evidence. You're going to have a busy weekend."

"Good," Nick added.

"This will be a ground work weekend," Mitch continued. "John, I need to get someone from the

Language Squad, an Asian-speaking agent in that classroom as a teacher-cum-sympathizer from Monday, can we do it?"

John frowned and headed for the door. "Actually, that I can do, I've got someone in mind."

Thirty minutes later Mitch received a text from John advising Dylan Ting would be in to see him on Friday morning.

———

Mitch was in the good books on Friday morning; he'd managed to get home at a normal hour on Thursday night and have a night in with Charlotte. He called Nick and Sam while Charlotte was in the shower and none the wiser. He didn't start until eight a.m. Friday morning to have breakfast with her; it was killing him. By the time he got in, he was sure his heart rate and blood pressure were soaring from the pressure of trying to look relaxed at home, while his head was exploding with all the things he had to do and the enormity of the case as it opened before him.

Thirty minutes after arriving, Mitch looked up upon hearing a tap on his door. An Asian man in his late twenties, compact, and wearing an expensive dark suit, stood there.

Mitch rose, towering above the man who was at least a foot shorter. He extended his hand.

"I'm Dylan Ting. John Windsor said you needed some help."

Mitch introduced himself. "Have a seat," he said. "What's your background Dylan?"

"Grandparents and parents are Chinese, but my father came here on a university scholarship and never left. Brought my mother over and here I am. We speak English and Mandarin at home and I have been teaching agents both English abroad and Mandarin locally. I've been in the Language Squad here now for about a year," he said.

Mitch looked relieved. "Has John briefed you?"

"He has."

"Have you had a chance to look at the course they are studying and could you slot in?" Mitch asked.

"I have. I got my hands on the training schedule; they only do Monday to Wednesday—the other days are free for them to practice assimilation and language skills, supposedly."

"Ah," Mitch said, "good to know. So they could go anywhere from Thursday to Sunday effectively?"

"Don't see why not," Dylan agreed.

"What about the course?"

"It's an executive Diploma in Professional English—that's like an abridged course. Their current instructor has done a good job at basic skills, but he has limited Mandarin so he can't interpret the cultural differences or anything they may say in their own tongue. For their purposes though, they can be told I've been brought in as an American-Chinese to tell them some of the challenges we had with cultural misunderstandings at our G20. In the meantime, I'll gather prints and listen in as much as I can. I can start Monday."

"What's John going to do with the other teacher?" Mitch asked.

"Sick parent," Dylan answered.

"That's always a good one," Mitch agreed. "But I don't just want you listening in Dylan, I want you to be one of them."

Dylan sat up straight.

"You want me to become an ally?"

Mitch nodded. "More or less. Does that worry you?"

"No, not at all, but it's been a few years since I've done any real undercover work," Dylan said.

"We'll have a full briefing this afternoon and I'll run through exactly what I need from you. If you don't think you can do it, that's fine but you need to tell me now."

"I'll be fine to do it," Dylan said. His eyes widened with enthusiasm. "Just fine."

"Day one in class, I want you just to get fingerprints for me. I need to know if your new students are who they say they are and I know for a fact two aren't. Hand out pencils, keep equipment they touch, whatever it takes, I need every student cross-checked to their passport," Mitch said.

Dylan nodded. "I can do that."

16

FOR MITCH, THE WEEKEND WAS MORE GROUNDHOG than ground work day... it passed in a blur of research; liaising with his team in Cape Hatteras; working with the in-house weekend resources to get photo and face analysis done; trying to keeping Charlotte happy; and, responding to questions fired at John that consequently came down the line for Mitch's response.

He rang Samantha and Nick at eight a.m. Sunday morning. Nick answered.

"Lucky I was up," he growled.

"Given up on beauty sleep? Fair call," Mitch ragged him. "Thanks for the photos from the diving course, the lads are working on them."

"Yeah, can't believe we lost them after the dive though. We followed them and waited while they ate, then, they were gone... giving me the shits, it's not like the place is huge but they've just eluded us," Nick said. "One minute we're following them at a safe distance, the next... they're gone."

"Might be staying at a private residence some-where," Mitch suggested. "Well, we know they need to be back for class tomorrow so they are going to be leaving there today at some point and time. Ellie and I will be watching Mrs Ying's house in case William decides to drop in on his wife."

———

Early Sunday morning, William Ying left the VIP house, Danny Huang and Ru followed about an hour later, Hai and Froggy would make the return to D.C. later that afternoon. Around midday, Danny and Ru converged at William's secured premises on the outskirts of the city. William slid the roller door open and when the men entered, he closed it imme-diately. The warehouse where William had been living and working since disappearing was small and stark with two rooms. Industrial lighting was the only natural light.

William looked anxiously at Danny. "So are you happy with the work in Cape Hatteras?"

"The site is good and we are on track, my friend," Danny said.

William nodded and visibly relaxed. "You'll be equally as pleased with the work done here I believe." He led the two men to the second room where a desk with three laptops sat opened and operating. Ru shivered; the room was temperature-controlled and chilly.

William continued. "I have all the VIP's networks—he's been transferring data to me gradually over time. There is quite a bit of intelligence material there too which I've no doubt will please."

Danny Huang looked at the coded files on the screen. "They look so innocuous, don't they?" he smirked.

"Considering the impact they could have." Ru smiled.

William nodded. "If you broke in here, they would mean nothing to you, but to us, they're invaluable."

————

That evening, the men gathered in Danny Huang's dorm, eating boxed noodles. Froggy was in the corner on the phone, scribbling down notes. He eventually rejoined the group.

"Have you confirmed the site coordinates for the sub?" Danny asked.

"Yes. It will suit us. We can definitely get the VIP

out to the sub without being seen from the mainland."

"Any concerns re access and depth?" Danny asked.

"No, it is deep and accessible. But it is a tough piece of ocean," Froggy said.

"That's OK, the captain will know that," Danny assured him. "I'll confirm with William, then we'll meet with the VIP and confirm the time of the lift. Hai, have everyone on alert and standby."

"Yes sir," Hai snapped. "It doesn't help that the VIP is anxious. I think the sooner we lift him the better in case he gives it away ... even if it means us keeping him in the VIP house for a few extra days to lie low."

Danny Huang swore under his breath. "We can't risk removing him too early, he's too visible; bring it forward one day at this stage and see how that fits with Beijing. We finish the course on a Wednesday, so we'll do the lift Friday instead of Saturday. Just update William, get him to call the VIP regularly, let him know it's moving forward, tell him everything is going perfectly. Don't let him know otherwise."

"And if he asks why we are going earlier?" Hai asked.

"Tell him because we are ahead of schedule with our planning. Do whatever you have to do to keep him confident," Danny ordered. "If you and Froggy are happy with the final pick-up point and have a back-up, send the location bearings to William ASAP. We need one more practice run with the captain."

"What's the story with the new teacher?" Hai asked.

Danny Huang shook his head. "Mr. Jones left me a message to say he has a sick mother, and he's had to fly out over the weekend. So we now have, Ting ... Dylan Ting from tomorrow."

"Know anything about him? With that surname he must be able to speak Chinese," Ru added.

"You would think," Danny agreed. "I'm having him checked out now. Remain alert and cautious regardless." He dialed William Ying's number. "Can we talk in person, tomorrow night?"

"Yes. 2100 hours, same location as before?" William answered.

"Yes." Danny hung up.

————

Mitch picked up his phone.

"Working Sunday evening too?" Charlotte said.

Mitch bristled beside her. "You know what I do, don't you?"

"I sure do, twenty-four-seven," she smirked.

Mitch drew a deep breath. "I've just got to make

a quick call to check on a new agent I'm putting on location tomorrow." It was as much as he could share, but she was become increasingly difficult. Mitch rose and left her momentarily; he didn't need the stress of Charlotte's growing demands on his time, it's not like she was new to this life with him. He placed a call to Dylan Ting.

"Hey Dylan, just checking you were OK about taking the class and hadn't changed your mind overnight?" He turned to see Charlotte had come out behind him. Seriously, did she think he was calling a woman?

17

ON MONDAY MORNING, DYLAN TING HUNG UP THE phone after a final briefing from Mitch. He dressed and arrived at the college an hour before class for his first day in front of his new students. He knew what he had to do and say, he knew the risk. He put his phone on silent, stored it away and entered the building, looking for the room number. He found it, took a deep breath and entered the classroom on the second floor of the city college building.

He had lectured before, that was no big deal, but he had never lectured to a group of cops or worse still, crims. He walked in from the back of the room and checked out the charts on the wall and what they had been learning to date. Simplistic stuff, especially if they're faking they don't know English, he thought, amused. He had time to go for a coffee and toast and headed out to the campus cafe.

An hour later Dylan re-entered the classroom, counting three heads. He turned at the front of the classroom and found all eyes staring at him. He introduced himself in English and the group nodded and mumbled awkward greetings in English. The men present were introduced as Hai, Froggy and Ru.

Dylan switched to Mandarin and got their attention. As he talked about the role he would have for a couple of hours at the start of each day, he reached into his bag and pulled out four sample bags.

"I thought there were four of you in the class?" he asked in Mandarin.

The one identified as Hai spoke up. "Danny, one of our team, has been taken ill."

"Ah, sorry to hear that." Dylan nodded. "How is your English training going?"

Several of the men grinned. One attempted to say 'going good' in English and they all joined in the joke.

Dylan smiled and nodded, sympathizing with them in Mandarin and telling them how fortunate he was to have come from such a strong country as China and to have both parents who spoke Mandarin at home. While he relaxed and bonded with them, he distributed the sample bags and invited them to explore. Inside each was a range of items they would use during their training, including dummy phones, signs and lesson plans. Dylan suggested they unwrap the plastic of the signs to begin with and they would start with that today—he would say a word in English and they would pick a sign that corresponded to the word.

He watched as the three men unwrapped their signage packages and discarded the plastic, which he would collect at the end of the class. Three plastic wraps complete with fingerprints. As soon as class was over and they had left the room, Dylan Ting gathered the plastic and headed to the lab.

———

Instead of spending the day in class, Danny Huang spent Monday with William Ying at his warehouse office—there was too much at stake with the project, and one day out of class wouldn't raise too much suspicion. Even the VIP joined them for one hour; it was a safe house, somewhere they could meet that no one knew about.

He eyed Danny with suspicion.

"I've known you a long time, Danny; you are not moving it forward because we're about to be blown, are you?" the VIP asked.

Danny smiled. "If you know me so well, you know I am not a patient man," he said, walking around the office and looking in at the various laptop screens. "If we finish the last week of the course on a Wednesday, why wait until Saturday to act? There's no reason to and the sooner we get out the better, especially if graduating photos of us are published even on the university's online site."

"I assume you have moved to control that?" the VIP said, alarmed.

"Of course, that is under control, but you can see my point," Danny said.

"Yes, I can. I trust you, I always have."

The two men smiled at each other.

"Brothers," Danny said, extending his hand. The men shook.

"When do you next go to the site?" the VIP asked.

"Most of the team will go after class Wednesday afternoon and will be there by late that night. You and I will have our next briefing meeting Thursday morning as planned, and then I will head there afterwards for the final test early Sunday morning—it's good to be on location where we can control things."

"And our exit the week after?" the VIP asked.

"It will work. It's a beautiful plan, trust us," Danny smiled. William looked up from his work and nodded.

The VIP grinned and shook his head. "Ah you two have led me astray with those words before."

The men laughed.

———

Mitch glanced at his watch. Too soon to hit up Marcus for more intel? I'll go via Henri. He stopped in the stairwell to answer a call.

"Hi Dylan, all OK?" Mitch asked answering his phone.

"Great, I'm with Marcus, can you get here?" Dylan Ting said.

Mitch hung up and raced down the stairwell, bursting in on them. Marcus and Dylan were gathered around a screen.

"That was quick," Marcus said.

"I was loitering in the hallway debating whether it was too early to stalk you."

"Your work is always my priority, Mitchell my man," Marcus crooned. "And you're going to love this. The fingerprints from the class of cops are done ... just give me a minute to do the printouts."

Mitch turned to Dylan Ting. "Well done, first day and you've got prints already."

Dylan nodded. "Yeah that was the easy part. There was only three there. The one called Danny was missing."

"Did they say where he was?" Mitch asked.

"Sick."

"Hmm, sick of being in class," Mitch muttered. "Just give me a minute, guys."

He moved away and made a quick call to Samantha to let her know to keep an eye out in case Danny Huang surfaced in Cape Hatteras early. Or he could be with William Ying, with the VIP or who knows where.

Mitch returned to the desk. "So are they getting a reasonable head start on the language?"

"They said it was going well ... but if they speak good English, they are doing a fine job of faking that they can't speak it," Dylan informed them.

"Did you overhear anything?" Mitch asked.

"No. There was no small talk. But, I think Danny's the boss and in his absence, the one called Hai seems to be the leader. He is the one who talks if I ask a generic question; they all seem to look to him."

"Interesting," Mitch mused.

"Here we go." Marcus handed around the results. Mitch pored over them.

"In the left hand column are the names and fingerprints of the four Beijing police officers who are supposed to be here in the country," Marcus explained, "and on your right are the men who are in Dylan's class."

Mitch dropped onto a stool. "Not one a match."

He flipped to the second page. "So where are the real cops? Four of them are missing."

"Funny, no alarm bells have begun to ring," Dylan Ting said.

"Perhaps no one knows they are missing yet," Marcus said. "They will when the course finishes and they don't return home."

"Yep but we don't want the word out yet or their families finding out." Mitch rose to go, taking the results with him. "Marcus, thanks; Dylan, great job getting these so fast, can you let me know urgently if you pick up anything else in class? Call me anytime."

———

Ellen passed Mitch on the staircase as she headed to see Marcus.

"Ah ha, so this is where you all hang out," she entered the room.

"I've got something for you, Ellie," Marcus said.

Ellen extended her hand and introduced herself to Dylan Ting. "You look familiar. Did you go to Georgetown uni?" she asked.

"No, I studied Law at Howard. I suspect we've crossed paths somewhere," he said. "Well, I've got to get back to the college. Going to hang around the cafe in case someone wants to befriend me," Dylan said, departing after Mitch.

"Actually, I'll be back in a sec Marcus, just got to catch Mitch," Ellen called.

"I'll just carry on here then," Marcus said to their backs.

———

That afternoon, Dylan Ting sat in the cafe at the campus going through his phone messages; he knew he was being watched by two students in his class. While the campus was almost empty, the cafe was doing a reasonable trade from lecturers preparing for next semester or guests from nearby businesses. He put the phone down and looked outside. A few moments later they approached. Dylan addressed them by the names they had supplied in class—Ru and Hai. Dylan smiled and welcomed them to take a seat. They spoke in Mandarin.

"How are you enjoying your time here?" Dylan asked.

"It's interesting and very different from our culture," Hai responded, comfortable in his mother tongue. "Quite an honor to be chosen to do the course and to have a chance to come here."

"That's good of you to say, but I know of the training you go through to be in the Armed Police

Force. Perhaps you can teach us a thing or two," Dylan flattered them.

Hai nodded and smirked.

"And you Mr. Ting?" Ru asked. "Are you enjoying the work you do, especially when you get bad English students like us?"

Dylan laughed. "Please call me Dylan. It is always satisfying to see people progress." He stopped as though he was going to say something more and hesitated. He knew they were watching him. "But I'm ready for a new challenge; I am thinking I might go into a private law practice," Dylan added with a shrug.

"What is your family's heritage?" Hai asked. "If you don't mind me enquiring," he added.

"My family, on my father's side have always worked in the public sector—lawyers, advisors, etc. My father and my grandfather strongly believed in serving the public and duty to country."

Dylan stopped and thought carefully about his next sentence. "I often feel as though they did so much for the cause, for the community they served and I, well I think only of myself."

"The capitalist way," Hai said without hesitation. Dylan noticed he checked himself and continued, "It is not your fault when you have been brought up in a society where the individual comes first," Hai said.

"I want to honor my family name and my country, but I'm not sure what country that is," Dylan said. "I'm boring you, sorry, we should talk about something else."

"It is noble that you studied Chinese law," Ru continued. "I wish I had done law as well as history."

Dylan leaned forward. "So you too question your life choices? I probably should not discuss this with you as your teacher, but I question what I believe in. Maybe I'm just getting old and philosophical. But what is there to fight for when I have everything I need and every opportunity? Sometimes, I wish that I could do just one thing before I die to make a difference. Do you know what I mean or am I being melodramatic?"

Hai leaned back and returned his smile. "I understand more than you know."

The seed was planted.

"Enough from me," Dylan said. "Allow me to buy you a drink as a guest of this country and tell me what sightseeing you have done."

———

Mitch's phone rang and he glanced at the screen. He closed his office door before answering.

"Dylan, all OK?" he asked.

"Yes, I've planted the seed already and I think it went well. They asked for it actually, so it was easier than I thought it would be," Dylan said.

"Run me through it," Mitch said, closing his eyes as he sat back in his office chair and listened to Dylan's report.

"I went back to the cafe and waited. The students were in their afternoon class but I knew they had a half hour break at around three p.m. ..."

Mitch tapped impatiently, trying not to butt in and tell him to get to the point.

Dylan continued ... "Hai and Ru approached me. I think one is senior, the other is the team junior."

"And?" Mitch pushed.

"We got a bit in-depth about what we wanted to do and I mentioned how my ancestors proudly contributed to their country. I said I felt sometimes that I gave nothing back but only thought of myself. Hai said he totally understood how I feel and Ru thought it was patriotic that I had studied Chinese law. They swallowed whole the alias you set up."

"Mm, maybe," Mitch opened his eyes and sat forward at the desk. "Are you up to doing this?"

"You bet ... I'm ready. But they're moving fast."

"They're on the clock," Mitch said. "Dylan, I want you to think about it tonight and call me first thing in the morning, before the next class. You need to think about the danger, what happens if you have to betray your country for this mission, even if it is only a front; can you do that? What if they find out? You could be killed. Sure, we can say we'll have your back and protect you, but I'm not going to sugar-coat it for you. And I will understand if you decide against it. A lot of people would."

"OK," Dylan agreed.

"You've got the fingerprints for me, and it's not too late to pull out, so have a think about it," Mitch said. "But Dylan, great work."

18

Mitch arrived home and unlocked the front door. He called out a greeting to Charlotte. He found her in the kitchen pouring a glass of wine. With one fluid motion he kissed her, grabbed a glass and presented it for pouring.

"What happened to surveillance?" she asked.

"In an hour's time. One drink won't kill me," he added as he saw her looking at the glass. "Good day?" he asked.

"One out, one in," she answered.

Mitch accepted the glass and followed her into the living room where she dropped on the couch and kicked off her shoes.

Sitting beside her, he began to remove his tie. "What does that mean?"

"I finished up one patient ... he's well enough to go back into the world without me."

"Well, congrats," Mitch said.

"And I scored another."

Mitch shook his head. "The endless cycle of the self-analytical."

Charlotte opened her mouth to say something and Mitch jumped in before her. "I know, I know ... I could benefit from some self-analysis."

Charlotte agreed with a curt nod. She pulled the band from her long dark hair and ran her fingers through it, massaging her scalp as she answered. "I'm always here for you Mitch, you can download anytime you want to, and no charge," she reminded him.

Mitch slid down into the couch. "I'm sure I'll pay somehow," he smiled.

They sat in silence for a moment. Charlotte turned to face him.

"You know, you haven't been home before nine o'clock five out of seven nights last week and when you do come home you think about work all night, and now you're not even here tonight. When do we get to talk?"

"You could come with me? Several hours in the car is plenty of time to catch up," he joked.

"Yeah, Mitch, you know how to show a girl a good time," she snapped.

Mitch put his glass down and sidled next to her.

"I'm sorry, Charlie. I can't promise to make it up to you just yet, because I don't know what the next few days hold."

"I spend more time with the television than you!"

Mitch sighed. "It's not like you didn't know the hours I worked before we started this. You saw me coming and going."

"But I thought you threw yourself into your work because you didn't have a relationship," she said. "But obviously work is why you don't have a relationship."

Mitch thought about what to answer. "When we're not on a case, I have more downtime."

"You've been on a case the whole time I've known you."

Mitch rose from the couch. "I'll be home by eight I hope, we can do dinner then or go for a drink. I've just got to drop Ellen home."

"So you're doing surveillance with Ellen? Just forget it, Mitch, really. Your head will be on the job even when you get home."

Charlotte rose and grabbed her phone. Seconds later, Mitch could hear her asking a friend if she had dinner plans.

How did that happen? He thought back over the conversation.

———

Mitch swung by Ellen's house and picked her up on the way to conduct surveillance at Mrs. Ying's house. They pulled into the street and found a park some distance from the house on a rise that looked towards the gated entry at the front and allowed for a partial view of the side and back of the property. A couple of interior lights were on in Mrs. Ying's house; one on the top level, two at ground level.

"Surely, now that we've been to see her, if William Ying was staying there he'd pack up and go," Ellen said.

"You'd think so," Mitch agreed attaching a zoom lens to the camera, "but stranger things have happened. She may genuinely believe we were just doing an annual follow through ... but I probably blew that with the binoculars question."

They sat in the dark making small talk for an hour before a car went past and pulled up in the Ying driveway.

"Here we go." Ellen sat upright.

A petite woman dressed in a suit got out of the car and walked to the front door. The door opened before she had a chance to knock and Mrs. Ying stood in the doorway. They embraced, talked for a few minutes and then the woman turned and left the same way she had come. Mitch snapped a few shots of her as her interior car light illuminated her face. He turned the camera to Mrs. Ying, and took some shots before she closed the door. The lights went off downstairs.

"I wonder what that was about," Ellen mused.

Mitch looked at the photos he had just taken. "I need to get these transferred and blow up the background. I want to see if there's anyone behind her or a shadow checking out who is at the front door. Still it is the most action we've seen here so far."

"Coffee?" Ellen reached for the thermos.

"Thanks, white with none," Mitch said.

"I know. How many times have we been on surveillance?" Ellen sighed.

"Sorry, force of habit. J.J. used to forget every time."

"Do you ever think about J.J.?" Ellen asked, remembering their former team member who betrayed them.

"Sometimes I see him. It's not him of course, but you catch a glimpse of something familiar; hair, stance, you know? I wonder what he's up to."

Ellen put his coffee in the cup holder.

"Thanks. Hey, I brought banana cake." Mitch reached into the backseat.

"No! Really?" Ellen laughed. "You baked?"

"Yeah, in my spare time today." He looked at her

in disbelief. "Mrs. Bell from the cafeteria at work made it for me."

Ellen shook her head.

"What?" he asked, watching her take a slice.

"She made you your own cake? She only started last month and she sees hundreds of staff every day and still you've charmed her already into making a cake for you."

Mitch shrugged. "I didn't ask her to, I just admired it one day ..." He took a piece, stuck the container back behind him and returned his gaze to the house. He took a bite and groaned his appreciation. "So good. More to the point, Mrs. Bell should be a spy. She's already managed to find out my weakness ... imagine what she could do for us. That grey hair and grandmotherly exterior is dangerous."

Ellen laughed. "This is damn good."

Mitch nodded. "I'm telling you ... she's dangerous."

They sat in silence finishing their cake and coffee. A couple of lights went on and off inside.

"Nearly eight-thirty." Ellen looked at her watch. "I reckon another hour at least, up for it?"

"Might as well" he said remembering Charlotte had now gone out without him. "Can I ask you something but you don't have to answer."

"Sure, what?" Ellen reached for Mitch's empty cup.

"How have your partners coped with your work hours?"

Ellen looked at him while Mitch continued to watch the house. "Most were OK with it because they worked in the Bureau in some capacity, so they got it. But the downside of that is that you feel like you both live and talk work, you never get away from it. I think it would be hard to date someone not in our line of business unless they really had their own life. My last ex, Andy, remember him?"

Mitch nodded.

"He was one of the boys so he really loved me having my own life. I'd say I've got to work and he'd be happily heading to the pub or to watch the game with a friend before I'd even finish explaining. Ben and I have only been together a few months, so who knows. We're in that phase where we are really obliging," she said.

"Hmm, I remember it." Mitch nodded. He was pleased Ellen knew better than to ask more.

———

Danny Huang had the taxi drop him a street away from Mei Ying's house as he did last time. He walked the last street in the shadows, staying close to fence lines. Occasionally he stopped, waited and observed.

No one around, no moving cars, no one following.

He rang Mei and the gate was buzzed open before he arrived. He slipped through it and around to the back door.

———

Twenty minutes had passed when Mitch saw a movement in his peripheral vision; he picked up the camera and started snapping. A man came from the shadow of a tree, pushed open the gate and entered the Ying property. He disappeared from sight but Mitch caught a glimpse as the light spilled from a back door.

Mitch checked the car interior light was off. "I'm going to slip down the property boundary. Be ready to roll if we need to," he said.

Ellen shuffled over into the driver's seat while Mitch quietly clicked the car door closed and moved down the side of the property out of Ellen's sight. He found a footing in the high fence, balanced on the edge and snapped the figure entering the house. He then snapped the different backlit windows. Mitch lowered himself and returned to the main gate and hid from sight.

If he goes in, he has to come out. Was that William Ying entering his own property? Is he there for the night?

As he thought this a delivery van pulled up. *At this time of the night?*

On the side was the wording 'Wine to your door'. A driver leant out and pressed the buzzer on the gate.

"Delivery," he announced, and the gate door opened.

Mitch snapped a shot of the driver and waited. The van stopped at the front entrance, a man, not the driver, exited from the side of the van carrying nothing and entered the house. Mitch zoomed in and snapped away. The van turned and drove back through the gate. When it was clear, Mitch returned to the car.

"That's two people that just entered the property. What are the odds we've just found William Ying and Danny Huang?"

"Well we have definitely found the means of entry," Ellen agreed. "Should we wait?"

"No they might not leave tonight and I don't want to do a raid, too much intel to gather yet. I'll send these to the lab now while you drive to your place." Mitch sat in the passenger seat emailing each shot from the camera to Justin. He reached over and called Nick and Samantha, placing the call on loud speaker.

"We haven't seen them since Sunday," Samantha said of the Asian men.

"Not surprising, they seem to be all back here," Mitch said. "Ellie and I have just seen two men entering William Ying's wife's residence. We're guessing it is William Ying and Danny Huang."

"Should we stick around here?" Nick asked.

Ellen pulled the Audi up in front of her house and waited for the call to finish.

"Yeah, I have a feeling based on their school schedule that they'll be back in your turf on Thursday ready to go," Mitch said.

"No wonder you're paid the big bucks," Nick said.

Mitch laughed. "Yep, worth every cent too."

"How did your new teacher go today?" Samantha asked.

"Appears to have nailed it," Mitch said. "Got the fingerprints from the classroom. I need prints from you two as well... not yours, their prints," Mitch clarified.

"Oh, that makes it harder," Samantha took the bait. "We've been working on that. If we could just find out where they've been staying and if they still have it booked—we were going to do the maid or room service trick. I'll knock, and if no one answers I'll pick the lock. But at least I'm in character in case one of them discovers me."

"Do it as soon as you can and be careful," Mitch said.

"Aye, aye, boss," Nick said.

"We're all over it," Samantha promised. "Over them, not each other," she clarified.

"Yeah, sleep well," Mitch said and hung up.

———

Mitch saw Ellen's neighbor move the curtain and glance around.

"Your neighbors are checking out your latest guy," Mitch said to Ellen. "Better come clean with Ben before he gets a report."

"Yeah, next thing Mrs. Carlson will be telling the neighbors that I'm a loose woman."

"So I shouldn't say 'thanks for everything' or hand over a twenty dollar note then?"

"Were you wanting change from that?" Ellen grinned.

They exited the car and Mitch returned to the driver's seat. He waited until Ellen was safely inside and drove home. He crept into the house; the lights were off and Charlotte was in bed. Exhausted and cold, he stripped off and showered, leaving a pile of clothes to collect in the light of day. He quietly slid out a drawer, then threw on a loose T-shirt and a pair of boxers. Ten minutes later, he climbed into bed. Charlotte turned and he reached for her and pulled her closer. He buried his face in her neck and smelt her scent.

"You're late," Charlotte mumbled. "Again ..."

"Again," he agreed. "What time did you get back?"

She ignored the question. "I thought you were only doing a few hours' surveillance." She pulled away. "You're still wet from the shower ... brr. Get off me until you warm up."

"Can't you warm me up?"

"If you were here two hours ago when I went to bed, I might have."

Mitch sighed and closed his eyes. "I could have been home earlier, but I thought you made plans to go out ... I heard you talking on the phone. Sorry."

"Mitch ..."

"Mm?" Mitch opened his eyes to look at her.

"Why are you so late?"

He lifted his head. "I was doing surveillance, and we actually got something. So I dropped Ellie home and returned to the office just to see if the shots could be blown up; that took an extra hour," he mumbled. "Then one of the team called, Nick—he's on a job in North Carolina, and we got talking. Then I started on a plan for tomorrow and look at the time." He yawned as he read just after midnight on the clock.

"So were you in any danger?"

Mitch smiled. "Only of falling asleep or running out of coffee."

"Who were you with?"

Frustration began to play on his face. He closed his eyes.

"I told you, I was with Ellie," he answered. "Let's sleep, it's late."

"But who is the team that you talk about?" Charlotte persisted.

Mitch opened his eyes again to look at her. He began to feel sleep fading away and his defenses rising.

"Ellen is here on the ground with me. I spoke on the phone with Nick, and Sam is with him," he answered precisely and watched as she considered his words.

"And what's Samantha's story?" Charlotte continued.

"Can I tell you tomorrow?"

"You won't, though, you never do."

Mitch moved closer to share her pillow and sighed, exhaustion riding him.

"I'll tell you about the whole team in the morning," he said as he wrapped his arm around her. "I promise. If I forget, you can withhold my visiting rights."

"Is that all men ever think about? Sex?"

"You should know the answer to that one."

"I want to know about your team now." She moved out of his arms and turned onto one side, resting her head on her hand. "Why not now?"

"Come on Charlie, it's late."

"It's early," she corrected him, "and I'm wide awake thanks to you. So why not tell me about the team now?"

"Because I'm wiped out and I've got to be up in five hours," he snapped.

Charlotte looked at him wide-eyed.

"At last, a reaction."

"What?" Mitch asked, confused.

"Nothing," Charlotte muttered.

"Charlie, shh." He pulled her closer again. "Let's sleep." He felt Charlotte pull away. Mitch clenched his jaw.

"I want to talk now, Mitch. You never talk to me; everything else comes before me, so now is as good a time as any. Or have you got something more important to do than talk to me? Sleep? Work? Study?"

Irritated, Mitch raised himself on one elbow.

"Fine, Charlie since you want to punish me."

"Punish you?" she exclaimed.

"Isn't what this is about? So let's talk. I'm all yours. What subject do you want to cover?" He turned, propped his pillow up and sat back, folding his arms across his chest.

"You, my favorite subject," she said. She watched him.

"Of course. Right, let me see; my day with my team. Well, I started the day with Ellen—going through our notes, then I saw Marcus, Justin and Sarah in the I.T. team unit and a couple of our new recruits—like Matt the trainee. I had a conference call with my boss John and the team, then went on surveillance with Ellen. Nothing happened between us. We sat in a car for a few hours. She poured me a coffee at one stage. I handed her the phone a couple of times, we might have had a joke or two, but that's about it. Then I chatted on the phone to Nick and Samantha for a bit, dropped into the office, and here I am."

"What's she like?"

"Who?"

"Samantha!" Charlotte said impatiently.

"She's tough, she's a martial arts black belt and a great skydiver, but a lousy swimmer."

He could read Charlotte's face; the personal details about Samantha annoyed her.

"What's she look like?"

Mitch shrugged. "Tall, long brown hair..."

"And Ellen?"

"Ellie." Mitch sighed, running out of steam. "Ellie's small, blonde, a professional diver, an excellent shot, scared of heights, likes cats and has a new boyfriend who is an architect. Nick on the other hand," he continued, "he's recently single, new to D.C., an old school buddy ..."

"Why don't you partner with Nick? How come you always partner with one of the girls?" Charlotte cut him off.

"I'm not attracted to Sam or Ellie if that is what you're thinking."

"No?"

"No," he affirmed.

Charlotte sighed. "I don't think you are attracted to them. I just want to know who you work with. Most people in normal relationships know that sort of thing about each other. Sometimes they even get to meet work friends!"

Mitch frowned. "I spend all day with them, I don't need to see them after hours. Anything else?"

"Yes, I want to know about your brother."

Here we go, Mitch thought. Only a matter of time until she moved onto my past. She's got to have access to every case file.

He felt Charlotte watching him.

"Of course if I'm not good enough to meet your family, just good enough to sleep with ..."

"Charlie," he sighed, the anger diffusing. "Where does all this stuff come from? You know you're the most important thing in my world," he reassured her. "I love you." He pushed her hair from her face and leaned in to kiss her.

"No," she pushed him off. "If you love me, then share a bit of yourself. Everything in this relationship comes from me; my friends, my family, my work. You're like ... hollow."

Mitch's jaw dropped in disbelief. He looked as though he had been slapped.

Charlotte kept going. "Why is there a file on the Department of Child Welfare database with your name on it?"

"What?" Mitch froze.

She bit her lip. "You have a sealed file—a case file. Something that must have happened to you when you were a kid. I saw it when I was looking for one of my client files."

"Well then, you know what it says," Mitch snapped.

"I can't access it unless you're my patient," Charlotte told him.

Mitch swung his legs over the side of the bed and began to rise. Charlotte grabbed the back of his T-shirt and pulled him back down onto the bed.

"This is what I mean," she exclaimed. "I'm supposed to be the love in your life and you can't talk about something that happened twenty years ago?"

He turned on her angrily. "Why do you need to know that? What difference does it make to us?"

"It's about letting me in."

"Into what? Why can't you feel close to me because we have shared experiences from the day we met? I don't need to know all your history, what you want to share is fine. I don't give a stuff about it as long as you are with me now."

"So, that's you. Why do you have the file?"

"Who cares?"

"I do."

"For fuck's sake."

"Tell me, Mitch."

"It's nothing, an accident, no big deal."

She scoffed. "Seriously, you're an emotional wasteland."

"For chrissake," he yelled at her. He rose from the bed and strode to the window.

Charlotte smiled at him. "At last, Mitch, some real emotion from you."

Mitch turned and looked at her, hurt and disappointment evident in his face. He leaned back on the windowsill.

"It's a child abuse file." He swallowed and took a deep breath. "Because after several teachers reported to the police that I was bruised, my back was bleeding through my school shirt and I flinched when they came near me, the department decided to investigate my family and they opened a case file on me. And when I was admitted to hospital unconscious after being beaten senseless by my father, they had somewhere to store the photos." He stood up and Charlotte went towards him, reaching for his arm. Mitch brushed her away. "Feel closer to me now?"

"I feel like you trust me," she said in a quiet voice.

Mitch continued to look away.

"Mitch."

He heard her hesitate.

"You and I ..." Charlotte continued, "we're not going to make it."

He felt the instant pain.

He turned to her. "Charlie, don't do this."

"It's not because of anything we've said tonight," Charlotte said. "I've been thinking about this for a few weeks. Our needs are ... polar."

"So? Why does it matter if we're not alike? Aren't you happy?" He moved from the windowsill back to the bed, pulling her towards him.

"I'm not sure. I don't feel like I'm really with you." She pulled away.

Mitch put his head between his hands. Regaining his composure, he looked up. "If you've been thinking about this for a few weeks, why didn't you say something?"

"When? Talking isn't really big on your agenda."

"Then let's talk."

She laughed. "We haven't in seven months. You only talked to me tonight because I forced you to speak with me. What is left to say now?"

"Charlie ... you are supposed to be the great communicator; why didn't you tell me earlier that you felt this way instead of just blowing up?"

"When, Mitch? Today, tonight, on the weekend, ... oh no that's right, you were at work."

"Come on, I made time for us on the weekend ... why didn't you say something then?" He began to get angry. "I bet Sally knows, doesn't she?"

Charlotte picked up her pillow and without looking back, she walked out. He heard her returning to the room that used to be hers before they began sharing one bed.

19

Mitch didn't sleep that night. He went after Charlotte and they talked in circles for another hour before he returned to his room after two. At five that morning, he gave up on sleep and headed to the shower.

Mitch arrived at work Tuesday at six to find John Windsor already at his desk. *I wonder if John's wife ever gives him a hard time about his hours.*

With a wave to John, he went straight to his office and opened his emails to see if Justin had enhanced the photos. There was a note saying he was almost done and would be in at seven if Mitch wanted to catch him then. Mitch looked to the clock, five past six. He opened the file with the latest intelligence on Danny Huang.

Need to finish reading this file. He scanned the words, not taking them in.

Mitch sat back and looked at the ceiling. I've just read for ten minutes and can't recall a word.

John appeared at his door.

"Everything all right, Mitch? You look dark around the eyes; what time did you finish surveillance?"

"Not late, I'm fine, how are you?" Mitch diverted the conversation.

"Good."

Mitch felt John continue to stare at him. "Couldn't find the razor this morning? You look like you've had a hard night, what's wrong?"

"Nothing. We might have a win with the surveillance. I'll know when Justin is in at seven."

John persisted. "Are Nick and Samantha alright?"

"They're fine, I would tell you if they weren't," Mitch snapped. He withdrew his anger and took a deep breath. "Sorry. I spoke to them last night after nine or so." He kept his eyes on the computer and hoped John would go away, but he came in and sat down.

Mitch continued to avoid looking at him.

"How's Charlotte?" John asked.

Mitch looked away from the computer towards the window.

"You know," John began, clearing his throat, "our jobs can make it a little tough to have normal relationships. You need to have partners who understand that or are in similar games themselves."

Christ, he has me chipped, seriously.

"So, did Julieann used to be a spy?" Mitch asked curtly. "Sorry," he said just as quickly, "I didn't mean ..."

"She used to be a paramedic actually," John said. "They work odd hours and deal with some amazing stuff. Life's far from normal. But she loved it. That was her and I never asked her to change that, nor did she ask the same of me. She only gave it up a few years ago to move into training. She enjoys that too, working with the young ones coming through."

Mitch nodded. "She is great," he said feeling churlish for his last comment.

"You only say that because she mothers you and cooks for you whenever you drop in."

"Yeah, well there's that." Mitch smiled. He made eye contact with John and looked away quickly.

"What's happened between you and Charlotte?"

There was silence as Mitch drummed his fingers on the desk. Then he said, "It's over." Saying the words out loud took all his energy and to hear it for the first time made it sound official. He swallowed the lump in his throat, and sat back to look at John.

"Do you think I'm ..." Mitch bit his tongue and decided against asking. "Forget it."

"No, what do you want to ask me?"

"Nothing. No big deal." He turned back to the laptop.

"Do I think you're what, Mitch?"

Mitch stared at the laptop.

John waited.

"Hollow," he said not looking at John. "An emotional wasteland, to be exact."

John looked surprised.

"No. Far from it," he answered. "I think you have many dimensions. The way you relate to your team and Henri," he said referring to the closest thing Mitch had to a father. "Those connections stem from having formed strong bonds. Mitch, there is not one person on your team, me included, who wouldn't put themselves on the line for you. You don't get that without having built emotional connections."

Mitch nodded, not looking at John.

I need to drop this discussion now.

"Listen Mitch," John began.

"It's OK." Mitch shrugged, embarrassed.

Great. Wish I'd never open the door to this one.

"Let me finish and then we'll drop it," John said. "Some people need things we can't give them—I've had partners over the years, my first wife was one, who wanted to do everything together, all the time. I couldn't be that person, in retrospect I don't know how we ever came together. Julieann, well she is her own person. She doesn't need to cling to me and she finds me a compatible fit. You will find that person who thinks you are a perfect fit."

Mitch nodded, the dull ache of the separation knotting his stomach.

John rose. "If you want to— "

"I'm fine, thanks," Mitch cut in, not taking his eyes from the computer monitor. "I've got to call Dylan Ting." He picked up his phone and dialed the number. John left his office.

———

"Buddy I'm sorry to hear about your bust up with Charlotte," Nick said via phone as he sat in the car idling, waiting for Samantha.

"How did you know?" Mitch asked.

"John mentioned it earlier. He thought you might need a place to crash. I've called Amy and you can crash in my room while I'm gone. She said call her and she'll let you in, or the spare key's in the top drawer of my desk."

"I never even thought about having to move out. Thanks, I'm might have to take you up on that one ... but Amy ..."

"What's wrong with Amy?" Nick asked.

"Nothing, it's just that, well remember me talking about 'records girl', the girl from the records section that I took on a date and accidentally called her Charlotte and that pretty much ended the evening? That's Amy."

Nick laughed. "Smooth, Mitch."

"Yeah, wasn't my finest hour."

"Well she said staying over wasn't a problem, so don't worry about it. If I was there, I'd take you out to get pissed and laid. Raincheck on that one."

"Yeah, that would be a big help, thanks," Mitch said.

"Guess I'm going to have to be your wing man again," Nick sighed.

"I'm a lucky guy," Mitch said.

"Took the words right out of my mouth," Nick agreed.

20

MITCH WAS SOUND ASLEEP AT FIVE A.M. WEDNESDAY morning when his phone rang. He woke, squinted at the screen and answered. "Hey Dylan, how is it going?"

"Mitch, the students are really starting to trust me. I think I can go all the way. Sorry, did I wake you?"

Mitch couldn't help but smile. He remembered being that excited to get his first location assignment.

"No, yes, doesn't matter. Play it steady now. Prepare to sound a bit concerned if they discuss finding your calling ... you know like, 'am I cut out for it?', 'I'm not as brave as some, but I want to be', you know, that sort of thing."

"Gotcha," Dylan said.

"Keep me posted and good luck today." Mitch hung up, levered himself out of bed and dressed for a run. He crept out, doing his best to avoid the cold front coming from Charlotte's room. He had agreed to move out on the weekend. Until then, separate rooms, early departures and late arrivals were working to his advantage.

———

Ninety minutes later Mitch was in the office when Justin rang from the office several floors down.

"Scored the early shift, huh?" Mitch said.

"Yeah, lucky I'm a morning person," Justin said.

"What have you got?" Mitch listened and exhaled. He looked up as John Windsor arrived at work just before seven a.m. and gave him a casual salute.

"Righto, thanks Justin, appreciate it." Mitch hung up and went to John's office, closing the door behind him.

"Mitch, how are you?" John began taking off his coat.

"Good. Justin just rang ..."

"Yeah good thanks," John interrupted him.

Mitch grinned. "How are you, John?"

"Good of you to ask, Mitch, just fine. Go on be-

Graveyard of the Atlantic

fore you explode," John lowered himself behind his desk.

"The surveillance photos we took reveal we have a very much alive William Ying and Danny Huang both here in the country and visiting Mrs. Ying," Mitch said leaning on one of John's cabinets. "Plus, Justin ran the facial recognition software on Danny Huang, and on the customs arrivals at the international airport, and sure enough, he entered the country without any complications."

"Don't tell me, he's one of the Beijing Armed Police Force?" John said.

"He is indeed. He came in under the name of Ip Shi, one of the most senior ranked police officers of the group."

"Can you believe this?" John asked.

Mitch shook his head. "I need our legat in Beijing to visit the families of the four police officers and see if they have heard from their family member who is training over here."

"Can't Dylan make those calls from here?" John asked.

"No, I think he's a bit rattled already so I want to keep him focused on the task at hand; I'd rather get the legat in Beijing onto it. Besides, it has to be handled carefully. They most likely don't know their police officer son, brother, father, whoever, is missing," Mitch said.

"I understand," John agreed. "Leave it with me and I'll drop in on International Operations and see who they've got in Beijing that we can access," John said with a look to the wall of international clocks. "It's about seven at night there now, but it would be good to talk with someone today."

"Thanks." Mitch opened the door and greeted Ellen as she arrived for work. He felt like he had been there all day, but the day had barely begun.

———

Danny Huang listened to his colleagues' thoughts on the new teacher.

"He's ripe for the picking," Hai said.

"Not too ripe is he? You don't think he's a plant? It's a bit opportune that suddenly he steps in," Danny said.

"Yes and no," Hai countered. "If they were suspicious, why wouldn't they have someone in from day one?"

"Should we put him to the test? Give him a little exercise to see if he wants to be involved?" Danny asked.

"I'm not sure," Froggy said, "I think it is dangerous involving anyone at this stage."

Ru agreed.

"I think we could," Hai said.

"When we return from Cape Hatteras, let's ask Dylan if he would like to go with Ru to organize the drop off of the container."

Danny nodded. "That's a good idea. Don't tell him what is in the container, Ru, just ask him if he would like to come and help you with your English if you need it at the receiving dock. Yes, very good idea," he nodded begrudgingly at Hai. "If the container stays immersed over the next week, we'll know he can be trusted. If it is recovered, he's dead."

"But so will we be," Froggy reminded him.

"If that is the case, we're already dead," Danny said.

21

DANNY HUANG'S CLASS RECEIVED AN EARLY MARK ON Wednesday afternoon, allowing Hai, Ru and Froggy to head straight for Cape Hatteras. It wasn't often Danny Huang was alone and he didn't relish it. He was a man who had spent his life in the company of many; an extended family of elders who adored him, the only child, living in a city packed with life, and then a career in the military constantly in the company of fellow soldiers.

The dorm was eerily quiet. It was three p.m. and he was not due to catch up with William Ying until nine p.m. Then William would head straight to Cape Hatteras that night to work with the team in preparation for the Sunday morning test. Danny would remain, see the VIP in the morning and arrive at Cape Hatteras late Thursday afternoon to oversee matters. He felt trapped like a bird in a cage. Grabbing his coat, he decided to head to Chinatown to get some paid-for company.

Danny Huang wandered the streets anonymously; no one recognized the 'cop' in town for training or knew who he really was, as he blended in with the local population. He allowed himself to be persuaded into a club and paid for the company of a young woman who looked barely legal. He liked them young. He wandered into a restaurant later for a meal. At eight p.m. he hailed a taxi and repeated his routine of being dropped a street away from William Ying's house. William would do the same or organize his courier delivery drop off again. This time, Danny intended to stay the night. Since William is leaving late for Cape Hatteras, Mei might like to have a man in the house, he thought.

———

It was after eleven p.m. when William Ying said goodnight to his old friend Danny and leaving him in the family guest room, he left for Cape Hatteras, driving through the night and arriving at the beach by five-thirty a.m. He waited in his car in the dark. Daybreak was some time away yet. He was frustrated that the last test mission had failed. It was unacceptable. He looked out to sea; the small tide made it look peaceful. If Sunday's conditions could be the same for the test, it should go fine.

William sighed and thought of his family. He had lied to Danny Huang. Had Danny guessed, he wondered. He had regularly spoken with his mother in Beijing and had spent more nights with his family than he should have, but he trusted his mother and his wife more than anyone in the party and he trusted that they would never betray him—not even under duress. They were from good stock.

At six a.m., William grabbed his towel, left the car and walked across the sand to the water's edge. He turned to see a shadow approaching in the dark. As the person got closer he made out Hai's features in the moonlight. Froggy remained a few steps behind carrying a backpack and towels; he was scanning the area. There was no sign of Ru whom he guessed must have remained behind in the VIP house communications room and was probably watching them now. William liked Hai, he was a man of his word. He knew his good friend Danny did not feel the same. The two men shook hands and turned to look out to sea.

"We're ready," Hai said. "Test this Sunday, the lift Friday fortnight?"

"Yes, after you all graduate with honors, especially in English." William grinned. "That gives us time to iron out any issues and this time, it will go like clockwork. Shall we do our test?"

Hai nodded. "Ready Froggy?" he asked.

Froggy pulled out his stopwatch, pen and pad, and got himself organized while the two men stripped off to their swim trunks. He gave them the go ahead, clicking the stopwatch on.

———

Hai and William swam out about thirty yards and disappeared from the surface. Shortly after, they reappeared; Froggy noted the time and how far the tide had carried them. He looked around to gauge visibility but it was a dark morning and the sun was slow to hit the horizon. He noted this information.

The men swam back in and did the same exercise parallel to their last location. Again Froggy timed them, making notes. They drifted further. Coming in, both men shivered with the cold and dressed.

Froggy updated the men. "It is as we calculated. I am concerned about what will be visible when the divers are underwater at this hour ... but we'll know on Sunday after the test."

"We don't want to be using any lights," Hai agreed. "We should do a dive this time tomorrow, Froggy, and see what we can see. We can give them the heads up the day before the test and get an idea what we might need."

Froggy agreed. He was always keen to get below water.

"The timing was correct though?" William asked.

"Yes, perfectly manageable, even allowing for the age of the VIP and his state of fitness," Froggy said.

"I am concerned though," William said. "If the VIP panics ..."

"I will inject him if needed," Hai said. "Then Froggy and I will put the oxygen mask on him and take control. Not ideal, but doable."

"Good, good. So, let's head to the VIP's premises," William said.

"Of course." Hai led the way to the car and Froggy and William followed.

"I'll drive your rental, William, and you travel with Hai," Froggy offered.

"Good idea, then you can get me up to speed, Hai," William said, giving his keys to Froggy. "But breakfast first? We'll find somewhere open early around here."

William nodded. "An even better idea."

As the two vehicles drove out of the parking lot, the sun began to turn the horizon pink and they saw two board riders arriving for a morning surf. They did not see Nick waiting in the parking lot to follow them or Samantha watching from her beachside hotel room window.

———

Ru had waited at the VIP house watching on one of the screens as Hai, Froggy and William stood on the beach, looking out to sea and checking coordinates.

Ru looked at his phone and up at the screen again. Hai was calling from the beach parking lot. He took the call and made some notes, before hanging up and making contact with his network in Beijing. He glanced at his watch—seven a.m., it was seven p.m. in Beijing but all hands were on deck. He gave the updated coordinates and information phoned in by Hai on the beach only moments earlier. He waited until the communicator in Beijing confirmed he received and understood the information. Ru confirmed the date and time of the test in local and Beijing time, and the coordinates based on the tidal charts.

"All good, we are fine to proceed with the test this time on Sunday," he informed Beijing.

Again he waited for confirmation before disconnecting and then called Danny Huang to advise him.

Danny answered on the first ring and sounded

satisfied. "Good. When we return to class on Monday, we want to know everything has worked perfectly, because next week will be our last and the plan will be in action."

"Yes sir," Ru agreed.

Ru then called Hai and advised him that all was confirmed with Beijing. He declined the offer to join them for breakfast, preferring to have some time away from authority. He put his feet up on the console and watched Hai, William and Froggy as they drove away from the beach.

———

"They were just here," Samantha said with excitement, "they must have come late last night because they were on the beach; I watched them from our room. There's three of them." She stopped for breath. "Mitch?"

"I'm here, just couldn't get a word in," he teased.

"That's a relief; I want to know where they are staying. Who's there?"

"The same two as before and a third party."

"Is the new addition William Ying?" Mitch asked.

"I think so, given I've only seen Gunston's original photo. I'd say it is a fair bet it's him. He arrived about ninety minutes ago, sat in the car until six a.m., then went straight to the beach and looked out to sea. The other two came down to meet him."

"Where's Nick?"

"In the car," she said. "He's just left and is following them. I'm handy in case they park in the village for breakfast; I can try for prints if you still need more clarification?"

"I have prints from the classroom, but wouldn't hurt to have them of the men on location, just to prove they were definitely in Cape Hatteras. I don't want to give them an inch to find an alibi," Mitch said. "Keep me posted, Sam."

"Sure. So exciting, the waiting was killing us." She hung up and glanced at her watch—just after seven. The phone rang and she answered it, then hung up. Nick had given the signal—Hai, William and Froggy were heading into the village.

Samantha grabbed her bag, locked the room and raced out to the sidewalk. She entered the hire car. Nick spun the car out and down the street, following the Asian men.

———

"We have some fingerprints for you and they're not mine," Nick assured Mitch as he sat in the car, watching the three Asian men. "Sam got their water glasses. They've just left the cafe and are standing out the front talking, Sam's paying our bill then she'll scan these and get them to you."

"What next?" Mitch asked.

"I'm waiting to follow these guys; they're in two vehicles: a navy RAV4 and a white Toyota Camry."

"Hire cars?" Mitch asked. "I can find out what name they used to sign it out."

"Yep hire cars. The Camry has a Budget sticker on it," Nick read out the registration number. "Can't see the RAV's rego yet."

"Has Sam got her bug kit?" Mitch asked.

"Yeah, it's in the backseat," Nick said without taking his eyes off the men. "OK here they come now and here comes Sam. They are getting into a car and we're about to follow. Hey, why don't you come down here for a stint, swap with me or Sam? Change of scenery will clear your head."

"Only if I need to, but thanks. Be smart, don't take any risk with these guys. If they've bumped off four cops, two more of ours won't bother them."

"Cheery thought, but I hear you. Got to go." Nick hung up.

———

"So?" Ellen leaned forward.

"It's coming, little lady," Marcus calmed Ellen. He relayed the scanned print to the fingerprint data base. "In the old days," he continued, "you would have had to commit this fingerprint to memory and look at photo card after photo card. Hours and hours of work," he crooned.

Ellen watched as the computer ran through hundreds of fingerprints in a matter of seconds looking for a match.

"Where is it from?" Marcus asked.

"Nick transferred them to me just now," she tried to explain without mentioning Samantha's name.

"Mm," Marcus nodded. "Nick who would be on assignment with Samantha in Cape Hatteras?"

Ellen reddened. "Yes, that Nick."

Marcus grinned. "You don't have to protect my feelings, Ellie. Samantha and I were only ever a short-lived couple. If she prefers flings with pale English men to me, what can I do? There's no accounting for a lady's taste."

"No accounting indeed." Ellen shook her head.

Mitch bounded into Marcus's lab room with a manila folder under his arm. "Hey Marcus, anything yet? I need to confirm that the fingerprints that Nick sent match the classroom prints."

Marcus looked up at him and then to Ellen. "What did they teach you at Quantico? Clearly not patience."

Mitch grinned. "It's just you're so good, we knew you'd have results."

"And that, Ellie, is how you do it. Flattery will get you everywhere!" Marcus announced as the scanner stopped and flashed the word 'match'.

They all leant forward. Marcus read the name. "I can confirm that the two men's fingerprints match those from the classroom and are Kiang Hai and Fan Wen. And yes, they are impersonating the cops, consider it a match.

Mitch muttered as he looked at the printout. He headed towards the doorway with Ellen in pursuit. "Thanks Marcus. By the way, nice shirt," Mitch said with a backward glance. "That green is very becoming," he joked.

Marcus smiled and stroked his green linen Caribbean shirt.

"Thanks Mitchell, my man," he called after him. "It was a present from my mother."

22

As Mitch and Ellen walked by his office, John Windsor motioned them in.

"What have you got?"

Ellen sat in a chair in front of John's desk as Mitch paced.

"Confirmation." Mitch handed him the paper.

John motioned for him to sit down. "Stop pacing."

Mitch dropped into a chair next to Ellen.

"Good." John handed the paper back to Mitch. "What else?"

Mitch looked at his phone. "Sam and Nick are following the three men now to find out where they are staying so we can bug their accommodation. I need the dialog translated daily ASAP. There's also a hell of a lot of sea gazing go on so I need to keep Nick and Sam on observation."

John nodded and jotted down a few words.

Mitch kept thinking out loud. "I need someone on the water looking back, looking around, trying to see what they are looking at ... I'd like to keep surveillance going at Mrs. Ying's house to see who else might be coming and going but we don't have the resources. Mrs. Kinaird—she's the widow of Joseph Kinaird who died a day after the gallery event—rang to say she has his diary if we wanted to look at it. I'm keen to get that before someone else hears about it, but she's in Boston. And since half of the class is either in Cape Hatteras or on their way there until class resumes for their final week on Monday, I wouldn't mind getting there to do some serious surveillance on them."

Mitch stopped.

"So, a bit on?" John said.

Mitch smiled. "Yeah, why? Did you want your car washed?"

"Please!" John grinned.

"I've got some interesting surveillance photos from the night William Ying disappeared," Ellen added. "I haven't had time to show you, they're pretty grainy but Amy did a good job sourcing them from CCTV footage. You can see Jessica Wu and Joseph Kinaird watching William Ying leave and there is someone in the car with William. Hard to make it out but if we knew what Rodney Lam looked like, it could be him," Ellen said.

"Rodney Lam's the other victim who disappeared that night," Mitch reminded John, "the head of the student paper."

"It can't be a coincidence that the last three people to see William Ying alive are all dead or missing," John said.

"And what did Jessica and Joseph see or photograph that was enough to get them killed? What the hell is William Ying up to? What are the chances of getting the Ying household phone tapped?" Mitch asked.

John sighed. "Can you provide me probable cause that the wiretap will provide evidence of a felony? Remember he was an ambassador with immunity and it is officially his widow's house. On what grounds ... because we think we've seen him or a person who shouldn't be in the country going there?"

"Works for me," Mitch said.

John gave him a wry look. "It was hard enough getting permission for Sam to bug their rooms, when she finds them in Cape Hatteras, so don't push it."

"Right then." Mitch rose. "Ellie, come walk with

me and let's brainstorm," he said, heading to the door.

"Good luck." John smiled at Ellen.

————

Mitch's phone rang. "Nick?"

"We've lost them," Nick told Mitch as Mitch and Ellen brainstormed on the roof garden of the work cafeteria.

"No, really?" Mitch stopped, closed his eyes and put his head back, feeling the sun on his face.

"They are definitely not staying near the beach. We were following at a safe distance and then they were just gone," Nick said.

"Right." Mitch sighed. "OK, well stay on it. Back to square one. Head to the beach and the village because they might come back for another test or supplies." Mitch hung up and looked at Ellen. "Boston would be nice this time of year," he said.

It was after ten p.m. when Mitch left Mrs. Ying's house that evening and began the drive home to where he still lived with Charlotte, not sure what he would find there. He chose to do surveillance by himself, keen to see if anything was happening at the Ying household and even keener not to be in the house with Charlotte. They hadn't spoken since she made it quite clear it was over and she wanted him gone by the weekend if he could manage it. His phone rang and he glanced with trepidation at the screen.

"Sam," he said with relief.

"Hey Mitch, we're really sorry about before ... about losing them."

"It happens," he said. "Any sighting since?"

"No," she said.

"What are you doing now?"

"We've been hanging around the pub, having dinner, talking to locals, waiting to see or overhear anything. We will begin on the beach again first thing in the morning," she said.

"Thanks, talk tomorrow then," Mitch said.

"Are you all right? You sound flat; where are you?" Samantha asked.

"Just heading home from surveillance. No action tonight at the Ying household, but yeah, I'm fine."

"What about this water surveillance—did you want one of us to start it?"

"No, I need you two on the ground and I need to work out how we do the water surveillance without drawing attention to ourselves. Leave it with me. I'll call you first thing in the morning with our next step. Thanks for checking in." He hung up and turned his Audi into the driveway of his and Charlotte's residence. The lights were on and Charlotte's car was there. He turned off the ignition, took a deep breath and went in.

Sally and Charlotte were sitting on the couch with empty tea cups in front of them. He hadn't noticed Sally's car. Charlotte had been crying.

"Hi Mitch, well look at the time, I must be off," Sally said, jumping up. She grabbed her bag and squeezed his arm as she passed.

He watched Sally get to her car safely before closing the door. Turning, he studied Charlotte huddled in the corner of the couch in her sweat pants and top. Her hair was tied up in a high ponytail and she looked vulnerable, good enough to hold, he thought.

"Charlie," he greeted her.

"Mitch, I was wondering when you would show up."

"Here I am," he said removing his already loose tie. "I was on surveillance."

"Of course you were," she said.

Mitch continued, "I've got some fallback accommodation organized. Nick's away and he is fine with me crashing at his place. I'll take that up from tomorrow rather than wait for the weekend if that works for you? Might be better for both of us."

Charlotte didn't respond.

"Just let me know what I owe you for power etc when you get the bills," Mitch said.

"You know some people give up jobs, more across the country, make sacrifices for love ..." she started.

Mitch nodded. "Some people love their partner enough not to ask sacrifices of them."

She studied him. "So that's it?"

Exhausted from lack of sleep and the day's dramas, he leaned on the door frame to his room and looked at her. A thousand scenarios ran through his head ... do I want to fight for this relationship? Would it change? Do I want to be like her last ex, Lachlan, always on-and-off? How long until she'd be asking me to give up my work? Do I need someone more easy-going? Do I need anyone? I love her, don't I? Could I give her what she needs if I'm an 'emotional wasteland'? I waited all that time for her and now ...

"Nothing to say?" she prodded.

Mitch shook his head. "No, that's it." He turned, walked into his room and closed the door.

23

EARLY NEXT MORNING, SAMANTHA AND NICK WAITED and watched, peering over the top of the car's dashboard. When the Asian men were far enough away, Samantha and Nick pulled themselves up in their seats, turned on the car and, leaving the lights off followed the white Toyota Camry at a safe distance.

Nick made a call to Mitch and put it on loudspeaker. He looked at his watch.

"Mitch, sorry about the wake-up call," Nick said.

"I was awake," Mitch said.

"Yeah, I figured that. The three of them have been on the beach again. They did the same exercise as yesterday ... very interesting. Two of them swam out a distance while the third looked like he was timing them and now they're in the car again and we're following."

Nick kept a safe distance behind; the road was free of traffic except for the two vehicles.

"We weren't going to let them get away today, so we've been in the parking lot, ready to roll before sun up," Samantha said.

"Which way are they heading?" Mitch asked.

"Out of town," Samantha said. "Mitch, I think something's about to happen here given three of them have arrived; I think we might need back up this weekend," Samantha said.

"I was thinking the same and according to Dylan they were all heading to Cape Hatteras this weekend. They have to be back on Monday for class, then their course is almost done; whatever is happening has to happen soon. I need that bug in now and I need to work out what they are going to do at sea."

"I'm hoping we'll get it in today, if we can find out where they are staying," Samantha said.

"OK. I have to detour via Boston this morning, but I was planning on bringing Ellen and driving down later today. We could do the water surveillance tomorrow."

"Should we organize a boat hire?" Samantha said.

"Thanks, but John's done that, he's hired it for a week under Nick's name. I was thinking of a spot of diving—you drive the boat Nick, Ellie can dive, it's her specialty."

"So when do you think you'll be here and should we book you both a room?" Nick asked.

"Late tonight so we can hit the ground running this weekend. Don't worry about the room, John's covered that too."

Samantha interrupted, "They're turning off. We'll have to stop and wait a bit."

"Fine, thanks for the update. Be careful, you know all the usual warnings."

Samantha hung up as Nick pulled over. They watched the car disappear up a road into the forest.

"Perhaps we should go on foot," Samantha suggested.

Nick leant forward and squinted at the track. "They could be going for miles."

"We can't risk going in there in case it only leads to one place, then we're going to meet them there with no room for escape," Samantha said.

"I think we have to leave now, and come back later when it is light or when we see all three back at the beach and we know the area is clear. We should turn around before they come out and see us sitting here like stuffed turkeys," Nick said.

"Speak for yourself, turkey. Speaking of stuffed, let's eat."

Professor Henri Spalter hung up the phone when he saw Mitch approaching.

"Hi son," he greeted him. "Good timing, I was just about to take off to deliver some blood samples upstairs. John told me about ... are you OK?"

"Man, if you want something broadcast," Mitch shook his head.

"He only told Nicholas and me because he knew you wouldn't reach out to us and he was worried about you. You could do worse for a boss."

"I know, I know." Mitch ran his hand over his mouth.

"So are you all right?"

"Yep, it's over. I don't want to talk about it. Henri, can we have a coffee? I've got to head off to Cape Hatteras later today and I remember you dived there once, didn't you? Amongst the wrecks?"

"The Graveyard of the Atlantic," Henri confirmed, "and there's no shortage of wrecks there. It's a perilous piece of coast, wonderful to dive though. Walk with me while I make these deliveries and we can have a coffee at the cafeteria for a change. Won't be as good as mine, but it will make you appreciate mine. Have you eaten?"

"When?" Mitch asked.

Henri shook his head. "Any time in the last twenty-four hours?"

Mitch thought about it. "I must have ..."

"I'll tell you about the tides and diving if you eat something?"

Mitch looked at his watch. "Deal."

———

"What the ...? There's four of them now," Samantha said as the blue RAV4 went past their hotel window. She rose from her window-side chair, grabbed the camera and went out on the veranda. Hiding behind the post she watched as four men alighted from the vehicle. She snapped a few photos as they went into a local diner. She recognized several of the men from the beach, plus the one they knew as William Ying although he wore a hat and glasses.

"Let's go," Nick called from the doorway.

She re-entered the room, grabbed the camera and bug kit and, locking the room, ran with Nick to their hire car. Nick drove away from the village at break neck speed, back onto the main road.

"I can't believe they walk around so blatantly," Samantha said.

Nick shrugged. "Why wouldn't they? They are guests of the country here to do training and seriously, who would recognize them anyway? How many tourists from all over the country or overseas come here every year and no one blinks an eye. William Ying might be taking a risk but again, you'd have to know him to know he was missing or to recognize him."

"Maybe," Samantha hesitantly agreed.

"Come on, could you tell me what the current Chinese Ambassador looks like or his name?" Nick asked.

"Point taken," she conceded.

Within minutes they were close to the area where the men turned off at dawn.

"Slow down, you'll miss it," Samantha told Nick. "It's just up here to the right."

Nick turned down the winding road, through the forest.

"I still think we should have come later, at dusk, or tonight and parked on the road," Samantha said. "What if someone identifies us as being here?"

"Full light is better," Nick tried to convince her. "We can play the lost tourists and still see where we are going. Tonight our car headlights and torches would really stand out."

"So who are we looking for if we are tourists?" Samantha asked.

"How about your aunty?" Nick suggested, "Aunty Carol on your mother's side. She said her house was about a mile off the main road."

"Aunty Carol it is," Samantha agreed. "There's a road to the right."

They both glanced down it.

"I don't think that's it," Samantha said. "That looks like a family property ... there's swings and a horse."

Nick drove on another half a mile.

"Small road to your left coming up," Samantha said. "I think you're right. It would have been difficult to find this at night and a hell of a long jog from the main road."

"What was that?" Nick asked.

"I think you're ..." She hit him on the arm. Nick laughed.

They turned into the small sandy lane and drove another half mile roofed in by large trees on either side. The road came to a dead end; a small dark brick house sat looking deserted.

"Wow, this really is off the beaten track; no one would come here," Nick said.

"This is it," Samantha said. "In the carport, look, the white Toyota is in there."

Nick and Samantha alighted.

"Let's knock on the door." Samantha shrugged. "We are lost tourists after all."

"Why not?" Nick agreed.

Samantha tapped on the timber door and they waited. She tried the door knob and found it locked.

They moved around looking through the windows. The rooms were sparsely decorated. Samantha returned to the front door and picked the lock, then called for Nick to follow her.

"You mean all those times I've been locking the bathroom door in our hotel room..." He sighed.

"Waste of time," she agreed. "If you had anything I wanted to see, I'd have been in there by now."

Samantha checked the kitchen. "There's fresh supplies and canned goods here. Plenty of them, like they are going to be feeding an army."

"Mm, it's a fair way off the beaten track too, so clearly they need space or don't want to mingle," Nick said.

Nick made his way around the rest of the house, calling out to Samantha. "Two bedrooms, large bathroom and look at this ... a room full of comms equipment."

Samantha raced in. "Wow. They're set up." She flicked on a few monitors; the images were live from different camera locations. "There's the beach where we were—the view looking out to sea." She pointed to another screen. "That view is from the lighthouse, they must have a camera there or are tapping into one and on this screen is the perimeter of this building." She studied the fourth screen. "What is this? A view of ... some room, two adjoining rooms?" Samantha left the communications room and toured the house again.

"Am I coming up on the screen?" she called.

"Nope, the camera's not in any room you've entered yet," Nick answered.

She rejoined Nick. "That room on the screen must be somewhere else. Hang on, I'll check the garage and yard. Watch the screen," she ordered.

"Yes ma'am." Nick saluted.

He watched the screens but she did not appear. Five minutes later, Samantha joined him.

"There's no storage area or other rooms outside. I didn't appear on TV?"

"Nope," Nick said. "I know this is a bit out there, but do you think it is a room in a hotel in the village? They are spending a lot of time on the beach, maybe they're watching what's going on there too."

Samantha shrugged. "I doubt it, there's no windows ... it looks like a classroom."

Nick shook his head. "Not their classroom at the English Academy though. There's no screens, no board or posters around the wall or windows, but we'll check just in case."

"Most strange," Samantha said, turning the screens off. "OK, I've got a few bugs to place."

"I'll snap some pics and then let's get out of here," Nick said.

Samantha placed a bug out of sight on the back

of the computer monitor and two in the main living area. She returned through the house scoping the area to ensure they had not left anything behind and joined Nick outside. "Ready?"

"We're out of here," he said, "thanks for having us, Aunty Carol."

Driving back through the forest, Samantha pointed to a small lane on the left. "Let's go down there to see if we could hide the car there if we needed to," she suggested.

"Good thinking. It's called Maple Lane." Nick read the sign, swung the car left and followed the road. They could see the house through the trees and soon the road came to a dead end.

"This would do," Samantha said. "You can't see the car from the road and you can easily run through the scrub to the house." She rang Mitch to fill him in. "He'll be a happy man now he can listen to his bugs," she said, and grinned at Nick.

24

MITCH SLID INTO A CAB AT THE BOSTON AIRPORT AND threw his jacket on the seat beside him. He had jumped on a mid-morning flight, had a few hours in Boston to meet Mrs. Kinaird, get the diary and be back at the airport for a return flight to D.C. before driving to Cape Hatteras late that afternoon. He gave the driver the address and sat back to watch Boston go by.

Mitch's phone rang. He looked at the phone screen and felt a stab of pain. Charlotte. Why is she calling? He let the call go to message bank.

"Coming home?" the older driver asked. He was a big man in his late sixties who smelled of tobacco.

"Just here on business for a few hours," Mitch said.

"A few hours! Geez. You want a lift back to the

airport, here's my number." He handed over a card. "Edward Egan," he said, "just ask for Ted."

"Thanks, Ted, Mitch," he said, and introduced himself. "I will need a lift in about forty minutes."

"That'll work. I was going to have a break. I'll drop you off, go have my smoke and pick you up again," the driver said.

He swung into a small street, took a right and pulled up in front of a small white house with an enormous beech tree on the footpath.

"You know your way around," Mitch said, handing over the taxi fare.

"Lived here all my life. Even dated a young lady who lived a few streets away from here in my younger years," he chuckled.

Mitch looked at his watch. "See you in forty minutes then?"

"Done."

Mitch watched Ted drive off and as he reached to unlock the gate, his phone rang. Charlotte again. He took a deep breath and answered.

"Charlie, hi," he said.

"Hi Mitch, how are you?"

"I'm keeping busy, and you?" he asked.

"The same. I think we need to talk," she said.

"What about?"

"Us," Charlotte said. "We haven't spoken about the break-up and if it is what we both want."

Anger boiled inside Mitch. "Charlie, you told me it was over, that I couldn't meet your needs. I spend an hour sitting at the edge of your bed asking you to talk it out, think it through, and you wanted out. We've talked, it's done."

"But I was angry. We should talk now that we're calm. We are good together. I don't think we should throw it out after just one fight."

Something caught his eye and Mitch glanced to Mrs. Kinaird's house. A grey cat jumped through the cat door and disappeared inside.

"Mitch?"

"Charlie, I'm not like Lachlan, I don't do the on-again, off-again stuff. I don't get off on the drama."

"I know that now, so let's try and work it out," she pleaded. "You haven't given it any real thought, I just landed it on you."

"No, I've given it way too much thought. I've had hours and hours of surveillance time ... sitting by myself in my own headspace, running through the scenarios. We've been going out seven months and you have been unhappy with me more times than I can remember."

"I will be more understanding, I've been thinking about it and— "

Mitch stopped her. "Charlie, we're both in pain and nothing would be better than to take that away and pick up again. God I'd love to, but I'm not going to. You're right, I'm hollow, I'm not for you."

"I'm so sorry I said that," she said and began to cry.

"Don't cry, Charlie," he said, and sighed. "Please. I'm sorry about a lot of things I did too; I know I was never around and didn't tell you things. We never took that trip to meet my family, I didn't introduce you to Henri and my work team. But you know, that's not going to change anytime soon." He walked along the footpath. "I leave tonight for about a week on an assignment."

"But you could turn it down," she said.

"I can't turn it down and I don't want to turn it down," he said. "This is what I do and I want to do it. I'm sorry if that's selfish."

"Well I hope the job is worth it when you end up a lonely old man," she snapped.

"Me too," he agreed. "I'll take my gear with me tonight and the room will be empty from tomorrow if you want to get another housemate."

"So you came with one suitcase and will leave the same way ... how about the emotional baggage?" she asked.

"Bye, Charlie."

Mitch hung up, and exhaled. He tried to focus on the job, but his chest ached; he felt alone in the world. He ran through the relationship in his head.

It would be great just to get back with her, he thought, get that part of my life back in order but I can't and won't stay home on this case to keep Charlie happy. Let it go.

He rang Henri.

"Mitch, hello."

"Henri." Mitch was breathing too fast. He couldn't think of anything to say now that he had called.

"Are you OK?" Henri waited.

"Yep ... I just ..." His voice trailed off.

There was silence on the line. "Are you in Boston yet?" Henri asked.

"Yes ... I just talked to Charlotte."

"I gathered. You know this time next week you'll feel better," Henri said in a quiet voice.

"Yeah."

"And it will get easier each day as you go on," Henri continued, "you know that."

"I know, I just thought ..."

Neither spoke for a few moments.

"Are you off to Cape Hatteras tonight?" Henri asked.

"Leaving about five," Mitch said.

"Want to drop your bags into the guest wing before you go?"

"It's only a suitcase and a few suits. But thanks, I'll do that before I pick up Ellie."

Henri waited and then changed the subject. "Just the other day, I was thinking of the number of times that you and Ellie have done surveillance together. Remember that time you were both on surveillance at the zoo?"

Mitch leaned against the beech tree, closed his eyes and smiled.

"What was it that snuck up on Ellie and scared the hell out of her?" Henri asked.

"A giraffe." Mitch laughed remembering Ellen's horror. "It licked her head, plastered her hair down to the side of her face."

They both laughed and Henri continued. "That's right. She just didn't see it coming; she was so cranky I thought she was going to arrest it."

Mitch laughed and ran his hand over his eyes. "I must remind her of that, what a classic."

"Well it is not every day you do surveillance at a zoo." Henri chuckled. He waited in shared silence.

"I'd better go in, I'm here for a meeting," Mitch said.

"All right son, call anytime. Safe travels."

"Thanks." Mitch waited for him to hang up then turned to enter Mrs. Kinaird's property. As he unlocked the gate, he thought about how much pain Mrs. Kinaird must have been in when she lost her love of many years.

———

The VIP recognized the ring tone; it was Danny Huang. He moved quickly to his office door, closed it and answered the phone.

"Clear," he said.

"Morning," Danny said.

"I'm sorry I couldn't meet you in person this morning," the VIP said. "I got called in to work early but the issue is resolved now."

"That's fine. I could have gone to Cape Hatteras last night but I assume it couldn't be helped," Danny said, his voice laced with frustration.

"My apologies, Danny." The VIP tried to be conciliatory. "Can we meet later today?"

"I was going to meet the team, but I have time on my side ..."

"I think we have a lot to cover," the VIP reminded him.

"Yes that will be fine," Danny conceded. "A quick summary until then: this morning, Hai and Froggy timed the route and tide, Ru was happy with it and phoned Beijing with the results. William is confident that the second test will go well."

"So do you think we have enough resources? Will anyone be suspicious?" the VIP asked.

"No, there's still other tourists around, we blend

in. Hai and Froggy are having another morning dive tomorrow, but there is no need for them to hide."

"Of course, I forgot their welcomed guests of the country," the VIP said.

"As for your residence, it is stocked and ready. Once collected, transferred and delivered, you will be taken to your new office and residence in the heart of the capital. They are ready for you now," Danny said, ensuring the VIP knew plans had not changed. "The next day you will meet the party, and we will be ready to begin. We serve at your pleasure."

The VIP's chest swelled. The thought of his own party at his disposal, the thought of being a modern-day 'emperor' excited and exhilarated him. What I could do, he mused.

Danny continued. "The facilities at the pick-up site are modest, but when we arrive in Beijing ..."

"I understand. We are on a mission, every man makes sacrifices."

Danny continued. "After Sunday's test run, we will continue our studies for the remaining time, graduate and collect the certificates, and then we will collect you at 0400 hours on the Thursday for the Friday lift. We are sticking with the day earlier plan."

"Right, I will be ready," the VIP said.

"Ru will collect you. Then on the day of action,

Hai and Froggy will depart with you to the beach on the Friday morning for the lift. Ru, William and I will fly back to Beijing on the false passports. William will use one of the fake ones that Hai and Froggy won't need."

"But that leaves one passport. It will arouse suspicion if one of the cops doesn't return when the visa expires," the VIP said.

"Don't worry, I have a stand-in ready to use it," Danny assured him.

"Of course you've thought of that, excellent. Nothing else?"

"You will have the final information and cash ready a day in advance?" Danny asked.

"Definitely," the VIP assured him.

"Then nothing else to report. William will call with his usual updates as required. Don't worry, all is on track and will be fine. It will be like the old days again only this time, our dream will be a reality."

"Who would have thought? Thank you Danny." The VIP hung up. He moved to the window and looked out over the city. Soon, this will be behind me; my name will be part of history, I will be in school textbooks, I will open the East.

25

LATER THAT AFTERNOON, ELLEN LOCKED HER DOOR and ran down the front steps. Mitch stood in jeans and a black sweatshirt, leaning against the back of the car with the trunk lid up. She threw her backpack in next to his.

"Want me to drive?" she teased as he closed the trunk.

"Yeah, likely." He slid behind the wheel as she entered the passenger seat.

She settled into the cream leather seat. "Can we eat soon? A burger and latte would be great," she said.

"We haven't even gotten to the end of your street yet."

Ellen laughed. "I'm getting in early. You know

you hate to stop when you're on the road. I have to fake I need a bathroom stop most of the time."

"Ah ha, no more bathroom breaks for you from now on. It's just that you overtake every slow Joe and then they catch up with you again the moment you stop," Mitch said.

"Not necessarily, because they have to stop at some point and time too," she reasoned.

"Let's get two hours under our belts then I'll get you your coffee and burger, although a sandwich would be less messy. Can you lean out while you are eating it?" he joked.

Ellen rolled her eyes. "I'll try and spill it on myself not your car." She looked down at her own jeans and sweatshirt. She turned her attention to her watch. "Check, that will be seven p.m. then."

Mitch smiled. "Yes ma'am, make sure you alert me."

"Oh I will. How was Boston?"

"Lovely, and I got the diary," Mitch confirmed. "I started reading it on the plane but nothing revolutionary yet."

"I hope there's some gem in there to make that effort worthwhile. Did you get the diving gear?" Ellen asked.

"Yep. Boat is booked and gear is on it already, supposedly."

Mitch's phone rang and Dylan Ting's name came up.

"Hey Dylan," Mitch answered. "We're driving so you're on speaker. Ellen's with me."

"Hey Mitch and Ellen, you said you wanted to chat, Mitch?"

"Yeah thanks. I just wanted to check you weren't getting too freaked out. Given what you've told me, I'm expecting they might make you an offer to change sides," Mitch said.

"Yeah, I've been wondering if they will test me with something," Dylan said.

"If it happens, you can get us some significant intel," Mitch said.

"It can't be too hard, given I'm the same nationality as them, to convince them I'm disgruntled with my life, culture, whatever."

"Maybe, but these guys aren't amateurs. They've been together for some time, following the same party politics, and they trust each other. I need you to understand more about them. Do some research on a group called The New Red Guard," Mitch instructed. "John Windsor can help you with what we've got so far and Amy Callaghan is our contact in the Criminal Justice Information Services Division. She can help you find more background info. Some of these guys, maybe all, have an affiliation to this group. Read up on what they stand for. I want you to subtly start dropping a few lines to show you might be sympathetic. Be clever how you do it—don't be textbook. Try a look, a comment, have a quiet phone conversation that can be overhead by one of them, make a disgruntled remark about your work ... anything that might make them think you are not only unhappy but could be turned. You're getting into dangerous territory here, Dylan."

"I'll do the research," Dylan said. "I'm keen to do it, Mitch, but I want it in writing that you want me to play for the other side and a copy given to John Windsor, so on my record there's no question ever about my loyalty. Is that OK?"

"Yes," Mitch said. "But why?"

"I'm American born, but an Asian by appearance. There's still a lot of prejudice in the world. I really would feel better if I had the orders in writing," Dylan said.

"I'll talk with John. Dylan, this case is highly classified, you understand?"

"Of course," Dylan said.

"There's four cops missing, bear that in mind and be careful. These guys know how to get rid of someone," Mitch said. "Stay in touch." Mitch disconnected Dylan, put in a quick call to John Windsor and briefed him on what Dylan wanted. He hung up.

"I wonder where that paranoia comes from,"

Mitch mused.

Ellen shrugged. "We haven't had the multicultural upbringing he's had and maybe he's always had to take a side or he remembers his history lessons; you know, how American citizens born overseas but living here were interned during the war."

"Don't mention the war," Mitch joked.

"I think it's very clever that he has asked for that, to cover his ass," Ellen said. "I'm going to do that from now on. Can you talk into this tape recorder and confirm we will stop for food at nineteen hundred hours?"

"If I talk into that recorder I won't be saying anything about a food order," Mitch warned her with a grin.

———

Mitch and Ellen arrived just after eleven p.m. in Cape Hatteras and while Ellen checked them into their two-bedroom suite next to Samantha and Nick, Mitch paced out the front of the hotel talking with John on his phone.

"Are you worried he's not up to it?" Mitch asked.

"No, Dylan's bright and keen. I'm worried he hasn't had sufficient training," John said.

"Well he's only teaching in-class for a few hours

each morning, can't he do a crash course in the afternoon on covert operations and procedures?"

John sighed. "Sure Mitch, I'll call the Covert ops-R-Us unit and get them onto it."

Mitch chuckled. "Excellent, thanks John. Nick and Ellie are going out in the boat in the morning, and Sam and I will be trailing the three men. Have you got anything for me yet from the bugs Sam planted?"

"Getting translated as we speak. Marcus will email them to you when he gets them back," John said. "Did you have an I.D. on the fourth person down there with them yet? The one Sam sent the pic of?"

"Not yet. Marcus and Justin are a little overworked," Mitch said. "I want to talk VIP with you."

"Just hang on," John said, "I'll move into the study."

"Is Julieann still up?" Mitch looked at his watch.

"She's reading in bed."

Mitch heard John close the door. While he waited, he pulled his jacket tighter as the chill set in.

"All clear," John said, "VIP. So we can assume this VIP is someone of some value to a group of men who are prepared to knock off four police officers to get here and get the VIP out of the country."

"Precisely. What they are doing may have nothing to do with the G20, it may have just been that those four spots provided easy access to the US for four people," Mitch said.

"Agreed. So looking at this from the other end, they finish the course, get the VIP out and head back to Beijing where it will be noted that four police officers returned, even if they were not the four that were supposed to leave," John said.

"Yes, they will have returned in the names on their stolen passports. But if they wanted trouble with us, surely they would dump the four bodies here and made it look like we were responsible ... but then how do they re-enter Beijing and as who?" Mitch said.

"We can't rule out that they still might dump the bodies here," John said.

"We know from the images we have now that the four policemen men didn't go through customs here, but they must have in Beijing ... unless they were eliminated somewhere between being dropped at the airport and boarding the plane. Or did they die somewhere on the flight between Beijing and landing in the US? Where are their bodies?" Mitch stroked his forehead. "Sorry, I'm thinking out loud."

"That's fine," John said, "that's what I'm here for."

"Anyway, we're digressing, I want to come back to the VIP," Mitch said. "Why do they need the VIP?

What is he or she giving them that they need to sneak the VIP out of the country and what value is that person to them?"

John continued. "What security secrets could be exposed or already have and how does William Ying fit in? And we know for sure now he's connected to them."

"Which brings me back to the missing and deceased people at the university," Mitch said. "They must have seen something ... there must be a connection with the university and the VIP."

They both thought silently.

"Did you get the diary?" John asked.

"I did. I got through half of it on the flight back, nothing of any significance yet."

"Hold on Mitch, incoming call from the office," John said.

Mitch walked around the parking lot waiting. He looked up and saw Ellen unpacking in one of the rooms.

"Mitch," John's voice cut into his thoughts.

"I'm here," Mitch said.

"I have some info for you. The translator has dialog from the bug ... nothing worth noting, most of it just banter except for one line which is interesting." John read it out. "'After the test this Sunday, we'll know more.' It was said to Danny Huang."

"This Sunday! It's a good thing we're here then.

Nothing else? No time or what the test is?" Mitch asked.

"No, but the full transcript is in your email inbox now."

————

Mitch checked out his hotel room with the ocean view. Better than most, he thought. Across the hallway were Nick and Samantha. Ellen shared his lounge, kitchenette and bathroom, but the two bedrooms were adjoining. Mitch had two single beds, how appropriate. He didn't look to see what Ellen had.

She knocked on the door.

"Come in," Mitch said.

"I'm going to keep this locked on my side," she said, "not that I don't trust you or anything because I do, it's just that I might be wearing a face mask or ..."

Mitch held up his hand. "Enough said, really. That's fine."

A knock came on the other door. Mitch opened it and Samantha and Nick came in.

"Isn't this nice, we're all here," Nick said.

Mitch grinned. "Yes, my ideal holiday, really."

Samantha jumped on Mitch's bed. "It's the same as ours," she reported to Nick.

"Hard as a rock," Nick answered.

"Let's plan. I want to get a few things done so I can go through my emails," Mitch said as he stood by the window.

"It's nearly midnight," Ellen said.

Mitch looked at his watch. "So it is." Mitch dropped beside Samantha on the bed. "Good work on getting the bugs in. I've already got the first translation and Sunday is the test day."

"Do we know for what, where or what time?" Nick asked, sinking to the floor as Ellen sat on the other single bed.

"Nope, that's all we have so far." Mitch looked around the bedroom. "We could go into the living room."

"We're here now." Samantha stretched out on his bed.

"So we'll expect to see them on the beach doing lord knows what at whatever time," Mitch said. "Nick, Ellie, you two need to be at sea tomorrow morning before sunrise, casually fishing or diving depending on the time of day just to see if there's any preparations going on for Sunday. Sam, you and I will be on the beach or here and ..."

"I was thinking," Nick interrupted.

"Yeah?"

"There's a scenic flight that goes around the islands to spot the wrecks from the air twice a day.

We've seen it around ten a.m. and two p.m. daily. I was thinking I could take a ride with the pilot."

"Yes, brilliant," Mitch jumped in. "But it won't work with the pilot and passengers, you won't get a chance to do rounds if you need to. We'll have to hire it for a bit of joyriding in the other times. Get John on to it first thing tomorrow... great idea."

"So tomorrow, you and Sam will be on the beach from five a.m. onwards and Ellie and I will take the boat out around the same time?" Nick asked.

"Yep, that's it." Mitch grabbed his folder and pulled out some paperwork. "That's where the boat is harbored and where to find the key." He handed it to Nick. "Ellie's dive gear should be on board. I've got to go through the translation report, so all of you get out of here, go to bed."

The team filed out.

Twenty minutes later, Mitch heard a knock at his bedroom door and Nick entered with two beers. Nick opened the doors in Mitch's room that led out onto a worn timber balcony. He handed a beer to Mitch and dropped onto the adjacent single bed. Mitch closed his laptop and sat back against the wall. The men sat in silence with their beers as the breeze moved through the doors, blowing the curtains and the ocean crashed on the beach out the front.

26

IT WAS DARK AND DEATHLY QUIET ON SATURDAY morning when Ellen and Nick steered the boat out of the Hatteras Harbor Marina towards the deeper waters, making their way parallel to where William Ying first stood on the beach the day FBI agent Gunston took the photo. Reaching their destination, Nick turned off the engine and looked to shore.

"Out far enough do you think?" Ellen asked.

"This will do it," he answered. "So they could be looking for a boat or ship to come in or, I know this will sound a bit out there, but a submarine to rise."

"You're right, it's out there. But hey, never say never. I'll have a look if there's anything untoward below, other than a couple of wrecks."

"Isn't it too dark to go down yet?" Nick said.

"Maybe, but it's another hour until sunrise. I'll

see what I can see; I like watching the underwater world wake up," Ellen said. She put on her diving gear and Nick casually opened a fishing box, pulled out the bait and grabbed a fishing rod, then went through the process of baiting it and throwing it overboard.

"I hate fishing," he whined. "Seriously who could sit still, just waiting... waiting."

"I think that's the point," Ellen said, "normal people can sit still. It's supposed to be good for you. Besides Henri told me it's a great spot for fishing, supposedly lots of king mackerel and red drum ... that's a fish."

Nick gave Ellen a wry look. "Really? Don't be long."

"I won't. I'll just have a cursory look around." With that Ellen sat on the side of the boat and flipped over into the water. He watched the surface of the water still after she disappeared into it and he looked at his watch. He felt a tug on the line.

"Already?" he said aloud with increased interest. "Or is that you Ellie being funny?" He reeled it in and felt it tug some more. I guess I'm fishing then, he thought. He continued to reel it in and pulled up an empty line. The bait was missing. I hate fishing, he thought again.

In the quiet and still of the morning, Nick sat back and studied the area, steadying himself as the boat rocked with the tide and rising wind. He took the binoculars and scoped the area, including the lighthouse. He couldn't see Mitch or Samantha—as it should be, he thought—nor could he see anything out of the ordinary. Nick mused on the best area to bring a boat to shore if he was collecting someone; it was near where William Ying kept watch the day Gunston saw him.

He considered the best place to liaise with a boat, if they were taking a person out to sea, taking on board visibility areas and access. Nick checked his watch again, keeping track of how long Ellen had been underwater.

———

Mitch left Samantha watching from the darkened hotel room and jogged to the lighthouse. Dressed in black, he kept to the shadows. He arrived and was not surprised to find the entry door to the light-house was locked. He grabbed a thin hook pick from the kit in his jacket, inserted it, clicked the lock and entered, closing the door behind him. Mitch took the stairs two at a time toward the top, counting automatically.

Two-hundred-sixty-eight, he exhaled victori-ously on reaching the top. The area was clear.

He moved to the side frame of the glass window,

out of sight, and looked below.

No sight of anyone yet.

He looked out to sea and could make out Nick's figure fishing on the boat; he appeared to be alone. He glanced at his watch. Nearing six a.m., still dark. Surely they'll do this test before the sun rises ... if they are true to their usual activity, they should be here soon, he thought.

He looked towards the parking lot and saw a blue RAV4 pull up. The lights were off. Four car doors opened and the men alighted. Mitch watched and looked out to sea again but could see nothing unusual.

———

Nick glanced to the waters below, but no sign of Ellen yet. His phone vibrated and Mitch's name came up.

"What's happening?" Nick asked.

"I've got four in sight; they're about to head down the beach your way so try and look convincing while you're fishing."

Nick chuckled. "Yeah sure, I'll slouch. How far off are they?"

"Less than a minute," Mitch said. "Can't see anything else strange happening inland or out. Anything out there?"

"Not a thing."

"OK, remember, if you see us, you don't know us," Mitch said.

"Done." Nick hung up. "C'mon Ellie." No sooner had he said it, than she appeared. Nick helped pull her in.

"What did you find?" Nick asked not taking his eyes off the shore.

"It's amazing down there, even in the dark," Ellen said, with a shiver. "But my scanner didn't pick up any active devices. There's plenty of room and depth for marine equipment to enter the area, but nothing out of the ordinary."

She removed her tank and wrapped a large towel around herself. They sat in the boat watching the shore.

"Here we go," Nick said, seeing the men on the beach. "The same test as yesterday, two in the water ... disappearing underwater ... one of them timing ... where's the fourth one?"

"He's heading back to the car," Ellen said. "Call Mitch."

———

"Already seen him, thanks," Mitch whispered to Nick. "Not a thing happening out at sea that I can see from here. And there?"

"Same, nothing out here. But this is the same exercise they did yesterday."

"Right," Mitch said. "Then I'm guessing this is how the VIP is going to be lifted at sea. Why swim out though, unless he's going underwater ..." Mitch thought aloud.

"A sub?" Nick said. "We were just talking about how far-fetched that would be."

"That would be something. Talk later." Mitch hung up and began the descent. Half way down the stairs, he heard someone coming up.

Is that the fourth man? Damn, he's driven here to look out to sea too. Mitch leaned forward, identifying that it was definitely one of the Asian party. He turned and silently began the run back up the iron stairs. He stopped and listened; the man continued upwards, puffing loudly. Mitch looked around; there was no choice but to keep going up, nowhere else to go unless he swung underneath the stairs. In daylight, there would be no chance of hiding with the design of the spiral staircase, but wearing black and in the dark pre-dawn, he might just get away with it.

Mitch looked down. The man had stopped ascending. Mitch waited and a few moments later the Asian man began to climb again. Mitch swung over the rail, and locked himself in under the stairs. His black gloved fingers would be visible on the edges of the stair rail only. He was just over halfway up; it would be a hell of a fall.

Christ, hope he doesn't stop for breath and look down through the stairs. Mitch waited. He could hear the footsteps getting closer now. Suddenly a flashlight shone up the spiral stairwell and Mitch turned his face to the wall. The flashlight continued above. He's seeing how much further he has to go, Mitch thought. A cell phone rang and the man stopped to answer. He was no more than ten steps below where Mitch waited suspended. The man was talking in Mandarin, and began to take the steps upwards again. He climbed over where Mitch hung underneath him, stopping three steps further on.

Mitch tried to breathe steadily; his muscles aching with gripping on. Hurry the fuck up, he swore to himself, willing the man to leave. The man continued to talk, not moving from the stair he stood on. Mitch gritted his teeth and held on. Finally he heard the man turn and descend the stairs. He walked over Mitch and down to the entrance.

Mitch sighed with relief and pulled himself back over the rails. He shook himself out, squatted and waited until he heard the door to the lighthouse close. Mitch bolted down the remaining stairs. He heard a car start outside, pulling out of the lighthouse parking lot.

———

After counting off the four men on the beach, Samantha raced to the parking lot and drove out of town. There were no cars on the road and she dimmed her lights as she turned off the main road and into the forest area towards the house where the men were staying, keen to do another sweep while the premises were clear. She parked in Maple Lane, left the car unlocked and ran through the bush to the house, stopping far enough away to observe there was no one around, no lights on and no change in the house surroundings. The slightly graying dawn light was enough to help her find her way.

So if all four are on the beach, she mused, I should be able to get the print of the fourth person and maybe even photograph a few files. Maybe even a print from the VIP! I wonder where that room is that can be seen through the camera. She went to the back of the house this time, picking the lock and entering. It was deathly quiet and dark. She waited for her eyes to adjust.

Samantha began scanning furniture for hairs and bagging fibers. She quickly moved from room to room. The house was spotless, as though uninhabited. She kept getting the eerie feeling that someone was watching her but every time she turned, she was alone. She went to the film room, turned on the monitors and saw the four areas again. Samantha looked around; the vision wasn't being taped, just feeding in real time. Where is that room that the monitor is focused on? Wish I knew. Ha! She could see the boat that Nick and Ellen were in but could not make them out; it was just another boat floating offshore. She couldn't see Mitch but she saw the men coming in from the shore ... What are you three up to? Crap, only three of them, where is the fourth? Better move in case he's on his way back.

That feeling again ... she turned around, no one there. She shuddered. Samantha swiped the keyboard and desks for more prints and hairs. She turned off the monitors as she had found them and headed for the door. With one final look to check she had left it as she found it, Samantha locked herself out. She began the jog back to the car. Driving out, she kept her lights off but did not pass anyone; on the main road, she saw the blue car at the gas station, where the Asian man was getting gas. She returned to the hotel, swinging her car into the parking lot.

———

Mitch ran the distance to the beach. In the rising

light, he took cover and watched the three men finish the test, dry off and wait on the beach. Minutes later, the fourth member returned and collected them.

Where did he go after the lighthouse? Mitch wondered. Samantha might have seen.

He waited until the men departed and went to the water's edge. Mitch stripped to his trunks and followed their exact exercise—swimming out the same distance, staying underwater for the same time and allowing himself to drift. He came back to shore, grabbed his clothes, and, shivering, headed for the hotel room.

He jumped into the shower, changed into dry clothes and then logged into his laptop for the latest intel. Marcus had not been able to identify the fourth member of the Asian party from Samantha's photograph. He had not entered the US before under his own name, he had no fingerprints on file, but the facial recognition software had him entering the country with the other Beijing Armed Police Forces' officers and after comparing him with the press clippings, it was clear he wasn't Zhou Ta, the police officer whose passport he entered the country with. Mitch shot him back an email to say thanks.

He opened the file with the translation of last night's dialog from the house where the Asian men were staying; the house that Samantha bugged. He read the summary that Justin had put together: they're calling it the VIP house, Mitch mused and they've referred to the VIP as a 'he'. So is the VIP there yet? The test is definitely happening on Sunday morning ... the storage area *'is suitable'* ... for what? He read the translation that said the VIP was nervous ... hmm, interesting ... some interesting names mentioned here too - Froggy, unusual, must be a frogman ... an underwater tactical combat man, that's a worry ... Hai, Ru, William ... yep, got you William Ying.

He looked up as Ellen entered the room.

"OK?" he asked.

"Good, are we meeting?"

"Yeah, how about the cafe for breakfast in twenty?" Mitch suggested.

"Perfect, I'll let the others know. Sam's just back now."

Mitch looked up. "Back from where? She was supposed to stay at the window."

"Right, forget I said anything." Ellen backed out.

Mitch shook his head. She's killing me ... got to do something about Sam.

He sent Justin an email and then pulled Joseph Kinaird's diary onto his lap. He looked at his watch. Ten minutes until we meet; time for some more riveting reading in the life of Joseph. He sighed.

27

WHILE THEY WAITED FOR BREAKFAST, MITCH READ HIS team the information sent from Marcus.

"A VIP house for a male VIP," Nick repeated, "so when do we see the VIP?"

"I suspect not for the test if he is that important. So if the lift is the following Friday, they'd want to bring him down late Wednesday or Thursday I'm guessing," Mitch said.

"I think we need to consider what might be going on underwater," Ellen said. "Unless he looks like a frog, I'm guessing Froggy is a navy man, a frog-man. If they are lifting the VIP off that beach, then they are swimming out and going under, like we've seen them practicing."

"Which means something is picking them up,"

Mitch said. "And they are going to need to breathe underwater from that point to the pickup point."

"They're factoring tidal drift too," Ellen said. "Let me investigate what could be used for the lift, Mitch."

"Please." Mitch nodded. "And underwater this morning?"

"It was fantastic," Ellen said. "But if you are just talking work, then my gear didn't detect anything new or active. There's plenty of room to bring in a sub if that's what you're asking?"

"That's what I'm asking," Mitch said, looking around to check they were still alone.

"How could they get that into these waters?" Samantha asked.

"In 2006 no-one heard a Chinese Song-class attack submarine enter our waters until it surfaced about nine miles away from the USS Kitty Hawk. They could have technology we don't even know about," Mitch said. "And I remember there was a Chinese research vessel disguised as a fishing trawler near an island in India as well."

"Who the hell is this VIP if they need to get that person and whatever they are providing out like this?" Ellen said.

"That's what's keeping me awake at night," Mitch agreed. "Sam, your report ..." Mitch sat back and sipped his coffee.

"I dashed back to the house since all four were on the beach just to see if I could get any new intel, you know additional fingerprints, maybe even of this VIP. The place was spotless, but I swiped it anyway. There might be something from the monitors and keyboard. I'll scan it to the lads after breakfast."

Mitch sighed. "Your orders were to observe. What if I needed you and you're off in the car somewhere? Nick rang to say one of them was leaving the group; it would have been really handy if you could have told me he had got in his car and was heading my way!"

"But Mitch, it was an ideal opportunity ..."

"What if there were more of them at the VIP house? You could have blown it for us." Mitch took a deep breath. "Sam, I appreciate the initiative, but check in with me. I've got you there for a reason, not just window dressing."

"Yes boss," she agreed. "Anyway, I saw them on their monitors in the communications room, when they were on the beach and I could see the boat but not you two in it."

"Wait up ..." Mitch froze.

"It wasn't recording, it's just a live feed, I checked," Samantha added.

Mitch hit his chest. "You nearly gave me a heart attack. We could have all been on it. God, I need another coffee. Nick, what have you got?"

"I hate fishing, but besides that, the exercise they did today was identical to yesterday. So if tomorrow is the test, I think we can expect something under-water or at least they'll run it with the appropriate breathing gear surely. John has organized for me to take the tour plane up later today and tomorrow at nine a.m. I've got to have it back by ten o'clock for their ten-thirty tour."

"Excellent," Mitch said. He looked across the road and out to the beach. He began tapping his fin-gers as he thought. "I'm going back first thing after the test tomorrow."

"Home?" Samantha asked.

"Yeah, I've got to run this angle on the VIP and the university," Mitch said. "But Nick and Sam, you need to stay on the ground until the lift, or until we prevent the lift. Ellie ..."

"I'll come back with you after the test if that's OK? I need to speak with the SEALs, they'll point me in the right direction and I've got a few angles to cover with the uni leads as well."

Mitch agreed. "For the test, Ellie and I will be on the boat. Ellie will dive, I'll watch the shore, Nick you'll take the beach so you can get away quicker to take to the air if needed and Sam, you'll stay in the room and observe the beach from there. Un-derstood?"

The group nodded their understanding.

Mitch continued. "Also from three-thirty Sunday morning, I want the translator at our headquarters in your ear telling you anything they say before they leave the VIP house. I'll get John to roster someone on. Sam, you need to phone me through anything that is relevant. Everyone happy?"

They agreed, then stopped talking as the waitress dropped off their meals. She smiled at Nick as she left.

Samantha rolled her eyes.

"The girl's only human," Nick said, reaching for the salt.

"Or desperate," Mitch added. He studied his scramble eggs. "Two hundred and sixty-eight steps to the top of that lighthouse, plus a half a mile jog there and back to the beach. I've earned breakfast."

"That's nothing," Nick scoffed. "You're getting soft; in the old days that would have been your warm up."

"That was my warm up. You and I are going for a run later."

Ellen laughed. "That'll teach you." She punched Nick's arm.

"That was a trap I walked straight into." Nick shook his head.

———

Sally didn't want to make the call, but out of loyalty to Charlotte, she agreed to. She rang Mitch's phone number.

"Parker," he answered.

"Mitch, it's Sally," she said.

She heard him draw a breath. "Sally, how are you?"

"Oh, I'm good, how are you?"

"Yep, been better, but I have my health," Mitch answered.

Sally laughed. "Where are you? Can you talk?"

"Just away on business for the weekend," he replied. "I'm stepping out onto the veranda of the hotel room, hang on."

Sally waited a minute until he spoke again.

"And where are you?" Mitch asked.

"I'm at home, about to go and meet ... you know why I'm calling, and I think you know this is not my idea."

She waited but Mitch didn't say anything.

"It's just that she's miserable and feels she's made a mistake and ..." Sally stopped.

"Sal, do you think we're good together?" Mitch asked. "Be honest."

"No, I don't. I love Charlie but she's too needy for you and you need someone low maintenance," Sally said. She closed the window she was looking out and turned to face her living room where her gray Persian cat lay curled up.

"I want her but not the relationship if that makes sense?" Mitch said. "We had seven months and they weren't great. I just want to deal with it and move on. Can you tell her that? It is over, move on."

"I can tell her that. Good luck, Mitch," Sally said, feeling she was losing a friend.

"See you Sal, I'll miss you," Mitch said.

"Really?" Sally asked. "I bet you say that to all the friends of ex-girlfriends. Well, if you ever need a stand-in for the FBI ball, remember me."

———

Mitch hung up and moved inside. He sat on the couch and went into his text inbox. He deleted all the texts from Charlotte and all in his sent folder. He looked up as Samantha entered his apartment room and dropped onto the couch opposite.

"Anything to report?" Mitch asked.

"Yes, the latest translations haven't given anything up, except ..." she stopped.

Mitch looked up from his phone and gave Samantha his full attention.

"Except that there seems to be a little leadership tension," Samantha said.

Mitch put his phone down and leaned forward. "Really, that's interesting. Between whom?"

"Well the one called Hai and Danny Huang have been snappy with each other. I think Danny and William might be the bosses, but from the way Hai talks to Danny I suspect he thinks he should be."

"Can you run a more detailed background check on Hai, see what you can find on him beyond what was on file?" Mitch asked.

"Sure. Where's Nick?" Samantha pulled her hair back and tied it up.

"Out at sea with Ellie, then they're going to the lighthouse, then Ellie has a phoner with someone from the SEALs and Nick's on one of the plane joyrides, thought it might be worthwhile to have a quick look around this afternoon from the air before he takes it up himself tomorrow," Mitch said.

"What are you doing?" Samantha asked.

"You'd make a good interrogator," he teased. "I just finished Kinaird's diary." Mitch rose again, went to the window and stretched his back. "He wrote something interesting ... he said that William Ying was in the science block talking to one of the young scientists and was angry when Kinaird came to take him to the Photography Gallery Exhibition. William snapped at him that he would meet him outside. Kinaird wrote that he was disappointed given he was not William's servant, but the head of that department there as a courtesy to escort him."

"What was he doing talking to a young scientist?" Samantha asked.

"Kinaird didn't get the chance to find out, but we will," Mitch said.

28

IT WAS DARK WHEN THE ASIAN MEN ROSE AT THE VIP House. Ru went straight to the communications room. It was three-thirty in the morning local time, three-thirty p.m. in Beijing. He heard William, Froggy, Hai and Danny leave the premises and start the cars for the trip to the beach. While yawning and stretching, Ru chatted with his counterpart in Beijing. He watched and waited and within fifteen minutes, he could see his four colleagues on the beach.

Ru leant forward, detecting a movement on the beach, but could not see it on the monitor again. He confirmed Beijing was picking up the signal from the four men, then called Danny Huang to report Beijing was happy, the cameras were working and there appeared to be nothing suspicious at any of the locations.

"In place, all clear," Ru said. He waited for confirmation and the words "Code blue" and then hung up.

"Now we wait," he said to himself.

———

Mitch and Ellen sat in the boat, awake, watchful at four a.m. on Sunday. Sam remained in the room and listened to the translator as he reported what was being said in the VIP house. Nick waited in the car in the beach parking lot, partially hidden by another car and lying low. There was no action yet.

"It's so quiet and still," Ellen whispered.

"I sometimes jog over the Memorial Bridge at first light and there's a time in the morning when the river is unbroken, if you know what I mean, before the day and the traffic kicks in," Mitch said.

"I know exactly what you mean, when it's like glass. It will be beautiful here when the sun rises over the water." She waved her hand over the surface of the water. "So romantic," Ellen teased.

Mitch laughed. "Yes, just the two of us, out here watching the sun rise, waiting for baddies."

"You do know how to show a girl a good time," Ellen agreed.

"Yep," Mitch nodded, "they all say that."

He looked down into the water.

"What are you thinking?" she asked him after a while.

"What's below. It doesn't freak you out?" Mitch asked.

"What?"

"The depth, what lies beneath ..."

"No, it never has, but I grew up on the water, it's second nature to me," Ellen said.

"Yeah, I grew up swimming in Nick's pool."

"Not quite the same." Ellen laughed. "I'm more scared on land than on the water, especially in closed in places ... I could never be a miner."

"I remember you weren't really at home when we were in Broad Arrow." Mitch recalled one of their earlier missions. He looked at his watch again and exhaled.

"What happened to you in the water?" Ellen asked.

"What do you mean?" Mitch turned to her.

"There's a reason people have reservations. I mean you don't have to tell me, but for me, when I was a kid our school class went on this excursion ... we went into this cave, and we kept going down further and further and it was getting really dark. We were studying stalagmites and stalactites. You know, one goes up, the other comes down ... I can't remember which way ..."

"There's a 'c' in stalactite so it comes from the ceiling and a 'g' in stalagmite so it rises from the ground," Mitch responded automatically.

Ellen stared at him.

"Sorry, I don't know which geography lesson in my head that came from. You were saying ..."

"Ah yeah, so we were in this dark tunnel and the tour guide said if he turned off the torch, it would be pitch black but that's the environment they grow in. And he did. It was so black, it was terrifyingly black, there was no outlines, no glimmer and it was only for a minute but I panicked. I've never experienced real black before. I didn't know what I would do if he didn't turned the light on again or if I found I was suddenly there alone. I know that wouldn't be the case, but I dreamt that for months and months after ... I'd be calling out but the tour guide and all my classmates were gone and I was in this blackness." She shuddered. "The water, on the other hand is different. You just head up towards the light."

"I have a friend who hit his head underwater and thought up was down," Mitch said. "Took three of us to get him to the surface."

"Is that why you don't trust it?" Ellen asked.

"No." Mitch glanced at his watch again. He

cleared his throat. "I had a case once, in my first few years with the bureau. I was the young blood and for a while I was attached to the Underwater Search and Evidence Response Team. We went to investigate the report of a package tied underwater to a bridge pier. The boss and I went to cut it off and when I got level with it, these two eyes were staring at me through the plastic. It was a woman and her face was locked in this scream. Sorry, I shouldn't have put that image in your head. It gets worse, but enough said."

"Creepy," Ellen agreed.

"Yep, you never know what's down there."

They sat in silence listening to the sounds of the water and morning, waiting for first light to tinge the horizon.

Mitch's phone vibrated.

"Sam?" he answered.

"According to the translator, one of the Asian men has given the all clear—'Code Blue' he called it. They're at the beach now," she reported.

"Thanks, got them. Keep them in sight. Nothing else?"

"Nothing we didn't know," Samantha said.

"OK, didn't think they'd be talking much at this hour. I'll let Nick know."

Mitch rang Nick. "We're on, they've declared 'Code Blue' for all clear to go," he said.

"Roger that," Nick answered.

Mitch hung up and scanned the area. "A test run," he muttered, looking across the line of water to the horizon and extending his gaze skyward.

29

Nick grabbed his binoculars and scanned the skies. He moved his gaze down along the coastline and the surface of the water. He saw just a ripple in his peripheral vision and returned to the spot. Nothing ... he held the position, watching and waiting. There it was again, a ripple; there's something there—and again ...

Nick rang Mitch.

"At your ten o'clock," he said giving the approximate location, "there's something underwater and it's moving."

Mitch hung up and swung around. "Nick's got something."

"I'm going in." Ellen zipped up her wetsuit.

"What's your radius Ellie? I don't want you going too far."

Ellen gave Mitch an exasperated look.

"I know you are a divemaster," Mitch said, "but I'm not if anything goes wrong and I have to rescue you. Visibility is crap at this hour."

"Trust me Mitch, I won't take any risks, I assure you, I know what I'm doing."

"OK," he reluctantly agreed.

Ellen slid quietly into the water and Mitch watched her disappear. He glanced to the beach, expecting the Asian party any moment now. Then he saw the ripple. It was increasing; something was moving near them, parallel but not heading into the shore. A midget sub maybe, but where's the mother ship and is there one? he thought, excited.

Mitch glanced to the shore and saw the party of four men walking down the beach. He glanced around but couldn't see Samantha or Nick. *Good.* He felt his phone vibrate and answered it.

"There's a signal, looks like it's a mirror reflection," Nick told him. "I've noted the location."

"What's the depth there at a guess?" Mitch asked.

"About forty feet. What's a midget submarine need?"

"About fifteen to thirty-five feet," Mitch said.

"So it's possible," Nick said.

"Sure is. What are they doing?" Mitch asked watching them on the shoreline from afar.

"William Ying is returning the signal," Nick informed him. "The other three are on watch by the looks of it."

"I can see it now, the signal," Mitch said.

"Two of them are stripping off again and going in. One's doing the timing. Danny Huang by the look of it," Nick reported.

Mitch looked to the side of the boat. No sign of Ellen. He kept the phone line open, grabbed his binoculars, slid down low in the boat so he couldn't be seen from land and watched the men enter the water. After they disappeared below the surface, he saw something that almost made him dive underwater himself ... bubbles, a massive spray of bubbles.

"Did you see that?" he whispered down the line to Nick.

"You bet."

"I think the test has worked," Mitch said. "There's an air vacuum by the looks of it and I'm guessing that's how they'll do the real thing."

"But next time with the VIP," Nick said, keeping his voice low. "Take him out, get him in the air bubble or onto an air supply and walk him to the midget sub."

"Why aren't we picking that sub up for chrissake?" Mitch said.

"OK the men have surfaced and are coming in, they've drifted a bit again," Nick said.

"Right, signing off, got to call Sam. Nick, take the plane out as soon as you can. See if you can spot anything unusual ... anything."

"Aye, aye, Major," Nick said.

"Thanks." Mitch hung up.

The two men swam towards shore just as the sun began to tip the horizon. They wiped themselves down and with Danny and William moved to the vehicle.

Mitch rang Samantha. "Anything?"

"Yep, just heard in my ear from the translator the words, 'mission successful'!"

————

Samantha snapped shots of the men on the beach. She zoomed in to get the man closest to the waterline doing the timing. The other two men looked around.

Hard to be subtle, boys, when you are on the beach with a folder and stopwatch at this hour, Samantha thought. She watched them return to one of the cars in the beach parking lot, enter it and sit. They sat and talked. Then one man alighted, went to the second car and drove off by himself. The others followed not long after in the second car. She received another message from the translator and rang Mitch. It went to his message bank. He must be on the phone to Nick, she thought.

She left a message: "Mitch, I just got another message from the translator. One of the men rang the four in the car and reminded them to pick up what they needed for stage two before they head back to D.C. So I'm just going to follow to see where they stop to do that and what they need for stage two. Let me know if you don't want me to, otherwise I'm on the road now." She hung up and ran to the car.

———

Ellen surfaced and Mitch helped pull her into the boat. He answered a call from Nick before speaking with Ellen.

"OK, thanks," Mitch hung up. "Nick's confirmed they've driven off."

Ellen grinned from ear-to-ear. "It was dark but there was no doubt it was a midget sub. You should have seen it. Clever, very clever and extreme."

"This is amazing," Mitch said, as he ran his hands over his face. Frowning, he looked at Ellen.

"Tell me it's not an American sub?"

"Impossible to tell," she said. "It had no visible markings that I could see. But if it is an American sub, that would explain why it hasn't been picked up because it's one of ours. It means the crew is going to defect too, I'm guessing."

"Doing my head in, this case." Mitch rose and grabbed Ellen a towel while she stripped off the wetsuit.

Ellen shivered. "So did it work? The test?"

"Yes, the translator confirmed they said it passed." Mitch ran through his air bubble theory.

"I could see the mass of bubbles heading to the surface—bizarre," Ellen agreed. "I'll see what the SEALs think, but to me, it looked like a small diving bell. They moved it from a sealed section in the sub, it gave off this huge spray of air and then they put it back in."

"Where is the sub when it is not here I wonder?" Mitch thought aloud.

"I'm just thinking ..." Ellen began.

"Go ahead," Mitch encouraged her.

"Any chance it could be a privately-owned sub ... is there any such thing?" she asked.

"Good question—and who would be funding that? Let's get in, get back home and find out. We've got our work cut out for us," Mitch said. He turned the boat towards the shore as Ellen dressed.

30

THE ASIAN DRIVER TURNED THE BLUE RAV DOWN THE long tree-lined road towards the VIP house. Samantha drove a reasonable distance behind and saw him take his usual turn-off. She waited a while, deciding what to do.

He hasn't stopped to pick anything up, did he change his mind? So much for that! What is stage two of the plan? Well I'm here now; I'll just go as far as the first turn-off.

Once the driver was out of sight, Samantha drove down the road and turned her vehicle off the road into Maple Lane. She checked her phone, and saw no call back message from Mitch. She made sure it was still on silent and vibrate. Samantha alighted and walked the rest of the way. Dressed in black from head to toe, she moved quickly and quietly through the underbrush. As she neared the house from the rear, she saw the parked car.

Samantha moved out into the open, and staying along the tree line, ran in close to the house. She sidled up to a window and glanced in. No one was in sight. She saw a shadow and dropped below the windowsill, waiting. After a while, she moved to the other side of the house and, ducking below a windowsill, glanced through the few centimeters between blind and window frame. She could make out two people in the room. Samantha dropped out of sight.

Two in the room, three on the beach, if only I could get a photo. Better get out of here. Maybe the bugs will pick up more about stage two.

————

Mitch and Ellen returned to their hotel room; Nick was waiting.

"Anything?" Mitch asked.

"No, but I'm not surprised," Nick said. "Once the test was done, it wouldn't take much for that midget sub to drop below out of sight. Pretty amazing."

"Unbelievable," Mitch agreed, his eyes wide with excitement.

"You should have seen it from below the surface," Ellen told Nick. "Surreal."

"Where's Sam?" Mitch asked. "Ellie and I are heading back to D.C., we've got a few leads to follow," he continued, not waiting for an answer.

Nick rose, checked their room and returned. "She's not there."

Mitch grabbed his phone to call and noticed the message. He listened and shook his head.

"For chrissake," Mitch muttered, "why does she always have to be a maverick? She's followed them. They're going to see her for sure. It's seven in the morning; how many cars are going to be heading up that road besides them and Sam at this hour?"

He rang her phone and it went to message bank.

"Want me to follow her?" Nick asked.

"No, we need to get a brief through. Can you call John with an update and the coordinates you took? Can you get in the air earlier?"

"I'll try it on... I've got it for nine a.m. worse case scenario."

"Good thanks. Ellie, I need you listening in with the translator while they debrief, which Sam should be doing. We need that intel now, not later. Call in on Marcus's line and find out who is scheduled and operating on that line."

"I'm onto it." Ellen rose, grabbed her phone and rang the office.

"Nick, tell me how to get to the VIP house," Mitch said.

Mitch was there within ten minutes. He drove off the main road and up the dirt path until he saw the first turn off. Not it, he thought, following Nick's instructions. He found the next lane—Maple Lane—and turned in. He drove to the end and found Samantha's hire car.

Mitch left his car beside the hire car and ran fast through the bush until he saw the house in the woods. The two cars were in the garage—the blue RAV4 and the white Camry and then a movement caught his eye; Samantha was ducking below the windowsill. She began to move away. Behind her, from the side of the house, a man emerged.

The man Mitch knew as Hai moved towards Samantha who was completely unaware of his presence. Mitch slowly pulled the gun from under his sweatshirt. His finger automatically flicked off the safety switch, the gun molding into his hand as though it was a natural extension. He stood silently, hardly breathing, as his eyes roamed around the area taking everything in, his concentration almost palpable.

Only the one, which means three or four inside ... but at least one of them knew someone or something was on the perimeter. This could blow the mission.

———

Samantha caught sight of a movement, and spun around.

The Asian man's fist connected with her jaw and she hit the ground. Samantha fought back and defended herself using her training in martial arts. He matched her move for move. She wrapped her feet around his legs, and tripped him, but as she rose, he kicked out, his foot knocking her backwards. She gasped in pain.

Rolling over, she saw Mitch sprint from across the yard, his steely gaze fixed on the Asian. Then everything went black.

31

THE THREE MEN—HAI, FROGGY AND RU—DID NOT stay to celebrate the test mission's success. Hai assisted Danny Huang to get the white male intruder into the room they called the cell, and returned immediately with his colleagues to prepare for Monday's classes. The men drove back in the RAV4, arriving back to the college dorm in D.C. early afternoon. Hai gathered the men in his room for a debrief. He looked at the faces of Froggy and Ru; anticipation was high now the actual date was almost upon them and he was in charge.

As it should be, he thought. He berated Froggy as he entered the room.

"Your tattoo is visible!"

Froggy hurriedly reached to do up his collar.

"Small errors will undermine us," Hai snapped at him.

"Sorry, sir," he said and took a seat.

Hai confirmed that since Danny had remained behind with William to deal with the intruder at the VIP house, he would offer apologies for him in the morning.

"We'll be saying Danny has fallen ill over the weekend, something he ate, but will be back in class as soon as possible. After all, Danny hates to miss out on class and will be studying Ru's notes to catch up." The men all smiled. "Ru, anything from the VIP's office recordings?"

"Nothing that would compromise our mission, sir. It appears to be business as usual. But, if I may sir?"

Hai nodded.

"The VIP did do one thing which I thought was interesting. He rang a travel agent and asked what it would cost to book a one-way flight to Beijing for the end of the month," Ru reported.

Hai's jaw tightened. "Why would he do that when we are getting him out ... he wants to take someone with him. Surely he hasn't told his girlfriend?"

"He hasn't told her in any of our transcripts," Ru said.

"The idiot. Once he arrives in Beijing and his actions become public knowledge he can bring over the whole country for all we care. But not beforehand! I hope we don't have to take him out. Froggy, anything you wish to report?"

Froggy pulled a piece of paper from a navy blue folder and handed it to Hai.

"That's the background report on our new teacher, Dylan Ting," Froggy said. "He seems legitimate. He's been a translator and instructor with the internal security department for five years and was involved with the security detail with their G20 team. He's interesting—Chinese parents and he studied Chinese law at university here in the States."

"He said to me that he was thinking of going to China to learn about his family's history," Ru added.

Hai nodded. "It would be a great advantage to turn him. Glean what you can from him about his loyalties, political beliefs and family. Let's see how easy he would be to own. But be careful, he speaks both languages fluently, so don't slip up in front of him."

———

Samantha's head pounded. She opened her eyes

slightly and saw Ellen coming into focus. She was back in her hotel room, lying on the bed.

"What happened?" She tried to rise but Ellen pushed her back.

"Just lie for a minute," Ellen ordered. "You've taken a hit to the head."

"Where's Mitch?" She looked around.

"We were hoping you could tell us," Nick answered.

"What? No ... yes, I saw him ..." she rubbed her forehead. "What time is it?"

"It's after midday," Nick said. "When we couldn't reach either of you by ten a.m., we were going to drive out to the VIP house. But we found you in the parking lot downstairs, lying over the wheel in the car. You must have driven yourself back before blacking out."

Ellen glanced at her watch. "It's nearly midday and no sign of Mitch. Where is he?"

"Isn't he at the VIP house?" Samantha asked.

"No," Nick said, his voice laced with exasperation, "that was the first place I tried." He sat back on the bed opposite and ran his hands over his face. "The blue car has gone, but the white car is there—otherwise the place is empty. Mitch's car is where he left it in Maple Lane."

"You haven't heard anything on their wire?" Samantha asked.

"I stayed here since we were two down, to listen. I haven't even heard them talking." Ellen began to pace as Mitch did.

"So do you think they've taken him somewhere?" Samantha asked.

"Yes, obviously, but where?" Ellen asked. "We need to move on this."

"Mitch will be fine," Samantha tried to reassure them. "He's always been able to fight back. He was armed."

"Yeah but if he encountered all of them, it isn't the best odds," Nick reminded her.

"Step us through what happened, Sam," Ellen ordered.

Samantha pushed herself up on the bed and propped a spare pillow behind her head. "I was looking through the window of the VIP house and ... one of the Asian guys came up behind me, next thing I was hit and ... Mitch was running towards me ... what was he doing there, how did he get there so fast?"

"He was following you because he didn't want you going out there alone at that time of the morning, so I told him how to find the house and we returned to listen to the debrief."

"Where is he?" Ellen pressed her.

"I don't know." Samantha tentatively touched her jaw. "I saw him running towards me from the other side of the house—the side closest to the road. Then I felt a blinding pain." She felt her ribs. "And ... wait, I remember—I woke for a bit and Mitch was fighting two of the Asian guys ... they were both full on at it, real hand-to-hand combat. You could tell they'd trained ..."

"Sam!" Ellen snapped.

"Sorry, sorry, I'm groggy. Then Mitch yelled to me to get out of there. But I tried to get into the fight to help, but I got another backhander and I—he said it was an order, you know how he gets, so I stumbled back to the car more or less, but he was still fighting, and I got in and locked the doors, and I remember driving but ... how did I get here then?"

Ellen dialed John and put the call on speaker phone.

"How's Samantha?" John asked.

"Conscious but barely remembers anything. She thought it was two against one when she left, but she has no memory of driving back here," Ellen said.

"We need to act fast. Ellie, got a plan?" John asked.

"I'm going to the VIP house, Nick is going to the lighthouse and beach, Sam stays here at base for us listening in case we pick up their voices through the wires or Mitch returns. Any luck tracing the blue car?"

"Yes, it's been returned to the car hire company in D.C., and the three men are back at the dorm. The car is clean, nothing in it, no blood," John said. "Ellie, I want you to report back to me on the hour every hour. Understood? Every minute is crucial."

32

MITCHELL PARKER WAS DRAGGED TO HIS FEET BY A person on each side of his bound arms. His blindfold prevented him from seeing them or where he was going. He tried to listen, to gain his bearings. In the distance he could hear a car engine, and the occasional voice speaking in Chinese, but otherwise the rooms were eerily quiet. Did Sam get away?

Mitch felt his heart pounding in his chest. As he was led into another room, he momentarily felt the sun on his face; it was gone just as quickly, and then he was taken downstairs. He wasn't sure what time of the day it was, or whether he was facing east or west. He was pushed down into a chair, the hands releasing him.

Keep your head, Mitch coached himself, remembering his interrogation training. He braced himself, waiting. For several minutes no one in the room spoke. Someone began to circle the chair, the sound of heels on the floor echoing. He could feel them only inches from his body. Mitch involuntarily tensed, expecting to feel the impact of a hit. He tried to think of something else—of the team, of jogging, of Charlotte... no, not Charlie.

An Asian voice addressed him to his right, making him jump slightly. The male was speaking English.

"We can do this one of two ways," the speaker said. "You can either tell me your name, where you are from and what you were doing near our headquarters, or we can begin the customary process of forcing it from you. We both know that will be tedious, and for you painful, and the end result will be the same, so can I suggest we cut to the chase?"

Before Mitch had a chance to reply he was hit full force in the chest with something that felt like a flat piece of timber. His body wasn't prepared, and the pain was breathtaking. He doubled up in shock, gasping for air, but the two people on either side pulled him upright.

"Shall we begin?" the Asian voice continued.

Mitch could hardly speak for the effort it took him to breathe. His mind was racing.

What can I tell them?

"Name?" the voice rapped out.

Mitch tried to think of what they might believe and he grappled for one of his aliases that were on the system and traceable.

"Owen," the words stumbled out, "James Owen."

There was a silence.

Mitch braced, waiting for the impact, the shock waves coursing through his body.

"Company?"

His body slumped at not getting the beating he expected.

"Innovation Enterprises."

Again the silence. He heard one of the men leave the room, his heels tapping on the tiled floor.

He's going to check it out, he thought, comforted by the fact that the alias would exist. The last use of the credit card would place him at Washington University earlier in the year when he booked a lab.

Mitch could sense someone was still in the room, on the left side of him. He was conscious of his breathing, the rapid increase—he tried to control it but the silence unnerved him.

The next question was issued in a low voice. "Who was the girl?"

"A colleague," Mitch answered.

"Your name?" The Asian man hissed the same question in his ear.

"James Owen."

This time the blow came to the side of his face;

splitting skin near his eyebrow and striking across the bridge of his nose. Mitch felt the blood pouring down his face.

"Who do you work for?"

"Innovative ... Innovative,"... fuck. He had forgotten the company name in the pain that consumed him. His mind froze in fear.

"Who do you work for?" the voice snapped.

This is not good, he thought. He doesn't believe me; we're going to be here for a very long time.

"Company name?"

"Innovative Enterprises," the words stumbled out of Mitch's mouth as he spat out the blood that pooled in his mouth.

"Name?" the Asian voice yelled again. This time the blow was to Mitch's right leg—a direct hit to the side and then to the top of his thigh, the instantaneous sharp and shooting pain shutting down his thoughts.

"Name?" his interrogator demanded.

He answered slowly, knowing he would get another beating after his response.

"James Owen."

Mitch heard the instrument coming towards him, the feel of movement in the air and he braced. He gasped in pain as it made impact and he could hear the crack as it felt like his ribs fracturing.

"Company?" the Asian voice continued to demand, barking the word out military-style.

Mitch gasped, unable to speak.

"Company?"

"Innovative Enterprises." Blood spat from his mouth as he hissed the words.

"What are you doing here?"

"We're a technology company. We picked up signals," he gasped, "on our system," another sharp breath; "we were checking it out, making sure that it was legit ... our cable gets stolen all the time." It was a believable lie, a good one even, he thought, given he had seen the communications room.

No sooner had he finished speaking than the same blunt instrument thumped into the back of the neck. Mitch saw white as pain ran up his neck and down his spine. And again, across the knees. He heard himself yell out from the pain but his mind was scrambling to stay conscious. He knew more was coming.

"What were you looking for?" the Asian voice continued.

Mitch tried to speak, but his chest was racked with pain and breathing was impossible. The delay cost him more pain. This time, he felt the chair falling towards the floor. He couldn't see through the blindfold the boots coming at him—aimed at his throat, his stomach, his ribs. Mitch could feel the blood trickling down the side of his face before blackness engulfed him.

————

Ellen parked her hire car next to Mitch's car in Maple Lane and rang John.

"Anything from his tracer?" she asked.

"Nothing, no signal at all. It's either not on or it has been broken," John said.

"Sam has reported she's not picking up anything from the bugs, so they can't be in the house, but their car is still there ... the white Camry, I can see it from here," Ellen said.

"And Nick and Sam?" John asked.

"Nick has had no sightings at the lighthouse and beach. He's going to pick up Sam and they're on their way to join me. We're going into the communications room to see if the cameras are picking up anything, but I don't want to go in alone."

"Good, wait for them," John agreed.

"Can you get one of the translators to call in if they pick up anything since I'm pulling Sam from it?"

"Done," John agreed. "Ellie, hurry, but be careful."

————

Mitch slowly began to regain consciousness. He didn't know how long he had been out for, but he was lying on his stomach on a concrete floor, blindfolded, hands tied behind his back. For a few minutes he didn't move at all, listening to what was around him. He seemed to be alone. His head was aching and the pain in his chest and knees was made worse by his position. Moving onto his side sent fresh pain waves through his body and he inhaled sharply, running his tongue over his lips. Water—he desperately needed water. He felt the sticky, dry blood on his face and a slight ringing in his ear.

Where are you guys, he thought to his team. He thought about dying there and not being found, but quickly pulled himself out of that spiral. He had to have a plan. He had to get the physical strength to carry out a plan. He tried to loosen his wrist ties, but the skin was raw from the rub of the rope bonds. Mitch debated the wisdom of trying to get the blindfold off. Doing so could be his demise should he see their faces, but there would be no escape if he didn't. He raised his knees to his chest and rubbed the side of his head that wasn't bleeding against his legs. The blindfold began to move up his head. Holding his breath, he continued, until he had pushed it far enough off to see.

He waited until his eyes adjusted to the surroundings and then looked around. He was in a large, empty room. The floor and walls were concrete and the windows had been bricked in. A large metal door looked to be bolted shut from the outside and a small and dirty double-glass square panel in the door allowed for the only source of light. It wasn't much. Unnervingly, he noticed a trail of blood from the wall to the floor in two corners. He obviously wasn't the first guest. A number of bullet holes were also embedded into the concrete.

Mitch pulled himself up to standing position. His black clothing was damp from his own blood and he spat a mouthful of blood and saliva into the corner. He stood, turning slowly around the room, taking in the walls, ceiling and door.

After ten minutes, he realized there was no way out.

I'm truly screwed.

Then he saw it. In a corner, next to a bucket which he hoped was full of water, were several items that had been stripped from him and discarded as worthless. His wallet which never carried any ID, his sunglasses and his watch! His gun and phone were missing. Falling to his knees beside the watch, he silently prayed it wasn't broken. He turned around, leaning down to grab it from behind with his tied hands and feeling along the side of it; he hit the global positioning tracer button. He dropped it, turning around to check the tracer was on, praying the concrete cell would not stop the signal. The "T" on the top right of the screen confirmed it was working. He closed his eyes and breathed a sigh of relief.

Water! His next immediate thought was a need for water. The bucket had something in the bottom, but the stench told him it wasn't water. He looked around but there was nothing else drinkable in the room. It began to distract him. He had to have water.

Enough, he coached himself again. Plan B. There's no way out, so get back in position, conserve energy and face the opposite way to the door.

He pulled himself up again and going back to the pool of blood where he had been dumped originally, slumped down into it again. Pretending to be unconscious, he turned his back to the wall. Using his knees again and lowering his head, he did his best to get the blindfold back over his eyes, then lay in fetal position, not moving, just listening. He knew he had to play weak and defenseless until he could get one of them alone or see a way out. The more fight he put up, the more they would beat it out of him. Mitch closed his eyes, hoping that the signal would get through; that John Windsor would be receiving it right now, before the next question and answer session with his Asian captors.

He knew as soon as they confirmed he was only

James Owen, a tech guy, he was as good as dead. If they believed he was something more, he was dead eventually; but not until they had gathered some more intel from him, and that was not going to be pleasant.

———

John paced the length of his office. Like the old days when he worked as an operative, he picked up the overflow of Mitch's role, coordinating the research team and reports from Ellen who was in charge on the ground. It was nearing three p.m., almost eight hours since Mitch went missing. You can do a lot of damage in eight hours, he knew. John had lost operatives before on the job. His first loss was almost two decades ago now—he hadn't been in the director job for too long himself, when Mark O'Meara, the forty-year-old veteran officer and his team of two, Susan Nicholas and Nelson Robinson, were taken out by a bomb. Nelson had hung on for a few days, but lost his fight. John could still see them as they were then; happy, talented and ambitious.

Nine years later, John lost another one of his leaders, but just the leader—Joe Campbell was shot in crossfire—gone in just seconds. All that energy and experience, wiped out in seconds. The team got a new leader but eventually disbanded; it was never the same.

John knew it was unprofessional, but he would throw the rule book out the window to find Mitchell Parker. He wasn't just an agent under his command; Mitch meant a lot to him. He was the son he would have liked to have had: smart, compassionate, heroic and determined. He knew Mitch, he understood what made him tick, and he was not going to lose this one.

His phone rang and he glanced at the clock—on the hour, every hour as Ellen had agreed.

"We're inside the VIP house," she said quietly. "The lights are on, but it appears empty. The white Camry is still outside. John ..." she took a deep breath, "Mitch, he's on the screen, the monitor in the communications room."

"What?" John exclaimed.

Ellen continued in a low voice. "There are a number of monitors in the communications room; one shows the beach, another is a view from the lighthouse and the external perimeters of the VIP house ... their screens are feeding live. But one of the monitors features a cell and what looks like an interrogation room; they are adjoining but both in shot. The windows are bricked in but there's artificial light coming through the door. Mitch is on the floor of the cell."

"Is he ... " John hesitated.

"We think he's alive." She looked to Nick. "He hasn't moved but I think his chest has risen. He's bound up and blindfolded."

"Where is it?" John asked.

"We don't know, that's the problem. Nick and Sam saw these rooms last time they were here but they're not in this building."

John heard Nick speak beside Ellen.

"What's wrong?" John asked.

"Mitch has moved," Ellen said. "He's alive."

John exhaled with relief. "Then where the hell is he?"

"The room's not here; we've looked in every cupboard, under stairs, every loose floorboard. Nick is on the phone to a local real estate agent to see what has been rented locally in the last six months to a year in case there's a house nearby where he could be," Ellen said in desperation. "I'm going to case the yard, Sam's checking the communication gear to see if it tells us anything. It's all I can think of ... "

"Go to it," John hung up. He needed to think through the next step. Is there any chance Mitch will survive with these guys ... there are four missing police officers, why would they save him?

Where the hell are you, Mitch?

As though reading his thoughts, the tracer on his watch emitted a sharp beeping sound.

33

ELLEN INDICATED TO NICK AND SAMANTHA TO evacuate the house. Outside she waited for Nick to finish his call and then updated them on her discussion with John.

"No luck with the local agents either. The only permanent rentals taken in the last six months have been two families and one aged couple," Nick said.

"We're getting nowhere fast trying to find that room," Ellen said. "We've covered a thirty mile radius from where we left him."

Samantha ran her hands over her face. "This is all my fault ... where is that room, why can't he put his tracer on? Did he have a watch on, could you see?"

"He didn't have it on," Ellen said. "They probably took everything from him. Let's just focus, he's alive, so let's focus."

"We could get a chopper and do thermal imaging. It can come out of John's budget," Nick added as an afterthought.

"Sure, we'll pick up everyone alive in Cape Hatteras," Ellen said.

"Oh, yeah." Nick smirked. "Small oversight."

Ellen's phone rang and she grabbed for it, reading John's name on the screen.

"John?"

"Ellie, he's pressed the tracer, we've got him," John said.

"Thank Christ." Ellen put her hand to her chest, she closed her eyes. "Where is he?"

"I'm sending the coordinates to your phone now," John said. "He's there where you are, at the house. He's at the VIP house," John said.

"What? How?" Ellen opened her eyes.

"I don't know, but he's there."

"On it." Ellen hung up. "His GPS trace has come through, he's here."

Samantha doubled over in relief.

Nick spun around. "Christ, where?"

Ellen grabbed the area scan on her phone and showing it to Nick, turned in the direction of the marker indicating where Mitch's watch was signaling—on the adjoining property sat a concrete water tank.

"Sam, go back to the communications room and watch the monitors; see if you can see me," Ellen ordered.

With Nick, she raced to the tank, climbed the iron ladder and looked in. Nick followed her up the ladder and dropped down on the concrete top.

"Bingo," he whispered. In the center was a large timber door. Nick lifted it, finding a stairwell. Silently they crept down the iron stairs. Ellen could see that underground it spanned out to a number of square rooms and a hallway; one appeared to be a cell, while the other two were tiled rooms.

They climbed out again, down the iron ladder and raced to the VIP house, returning to Samantha.

"I saw you!" Samantha exclaimed. "I saw you on the stairwell."

"We've found our interrogation room," Ellen said. She looked to the screen and saw the two men enter a room in the corner of the monitor screen. "We're all going in, but I want them alive," she said.

"Looks like there's only two," Samantha said.

"That we can see," Ellen answered. "We know three returned to school, so hopefully that's it."

Ellen called John. "We've found the room and are moving in," she said. She listened to him and hung up. "Right." Ellen closed her eyes and gathered her thoughts calmly. She opened her eyes, which burned green.

"There are two of them that we know of, but they have the advantage with Mitch as hostage. We need to create a large explosion, something large enough for them to feel down there. Nick, find whatever you can ... a cylinder, fuel, paper, get it happening. When we're ready and we're talking minutes," Ellen continued, "I'll watch the monitors and give the signal. We'll smoke them out, so to speak."

Nick butted in, "I'll set it off near the trap door so we have some chance of them running out like ants in a nest."

"Yes, ideal," Ellen said. "Sam, wait behind the tank. Nick, you light the explosions and Sam you pick off anyone who runs out. If you need to, shoot to maim and remove their weapon. Nick, tie them up. I expect one of them might remain down with Mitch. I'll be out of sight to the side of the tank and move down the stairs while you two secure above, then come back me up as soon as possible. We'll have to put our watch microphones on since we don't have earpieces. We can hear each other but they can overhear, be mindful of that."

They both nodded and reached for their watches. "Understand?"

"Done," Nick said pressing his watch mic on.

"Go," Ellen said.

Nick raced to the carport where he had seen lighter fluid and a barrel of diesel earlier.

"Hurry!" Samantha exclaimed, watching the monitor. "Mitch is being dragged into that interrogation room."

"Sam, go now, help Nick. I'll be right there, stick to the plan," Ellen ordered, turning her own watch microphone on.

As she moved away from the monitor, she saw Mitch being dragged by two men into a room with one chair in the centre. Her blood boiled as she saw them manhandle him into the next room and pushed him into the chair. The side of his face was covered in blood and he was clearly unable to walk unaided.

———

Mitch gave them his full body weight, making it harder for them as they dragged him into the room and shoved into a chair. This time they undid his blindfold. Mitch squinted, his eyes adjusting to the bright light of the room. He could make out the two figures in front of him, but his head felt concussed and heavy. He began to feel a sense of panic, the anxiety and adrenaline coursing through him. As his vision cleared, he recognized the leader immediately. He was tall for an Asian male, with almost delicate features that could be either cruel or attractive.

Danny Huang with William Ying, Mitch identified them.

"We've checked out your name, Mr. Owen," Danny said. "We might have believed you worked for a local communications company, except for your skills. You single-handedly fought off three of our men before I stepped in. That's pretty good for a telco wouldn't you say? Now where would you learn those skills?"

"School karate club," Mitch suggested.

He received a swift hit in the side of the head from Danny Huang. He momentarily saw black, blinking to stay conscious.

"I've never had a sense of humor, Mr. Owen," Danny said. "I think you might be with security services ... the FBI or SOCA?"

Mitch waited, remembering his training.

Danny moved behind Mitch. "You heard your country was training and sharing their skills with a nation that will inevitably be the world leader and that worries you, doesn't it, Mr. Owen?"

Danny moved back into vision and picked up an object from the corner of the room. Mitch saw it and blood rushed to his head, clearing his mind instantly. Danny was holding a blow torch.

Danny kept talking. "You've stumbled into something bigger than you can imagine and one of your very own is about to join us."

"Who?" Mitch asked, the job overstepping his fear.

"Let's do an exchange of information. I'll tell you what you want to know, if you tell me who you work for? But finding out the truth will kill you." Danny ensured he had Mitch's attention as he squeezed the handle and flicked a lighter to ignite the flame. "I've always loved fire," he said. Danny pulled up his shirt sleeve to show an extensive burn scar. "This was the only time I ever broke," he said looking at the scar. He pulled his sleeve back down over it.

Absolute, sheer terror ran through Mitch. He thought he might pass out before they even started.

At least let me black out quickly, he silently prayed. *Where are you guys? John?*

He watched the naked flame grasped in the hands of the Asian man with the cruel features. He knew what happened in these cases. It was a no-win situation. You told them the truth and they killed you; you didn't tell them the truth, and they killed you. Mitch's eyes roamed around the room, there was no way ... he couldn't think of a way out ... he couldn't even take his own life.

"Now," the voice drifted towards him, "shall we start again." Danny came closer, placing the flame within inches of Mitch's chest. He could feel the heat radiating off it, dangerously close to igniting his clothes.

"Who do you work for and how many of your party are here?" Danny asked in perfect English.

Mitch's mind was racing through scenarios, the heat of the flame overriding his thoughts.

"Too long," Danny said with obvious pleasure and applied the naked flame to the exposed flesh on Mitch's arm.

Mitch yelled, trying to release the pain. He began to retch from the smell of burnt flesh. The pain was excruciatingly raw. Danny stepped away.

"Again, Mr. Owen, who are you working for?" Danny continued.

The room shook as Nick's explosion went off on the outskirts of the building. Heat was felt in the hallway as several pieces of burning timber from the hatch hurtled in. Danny threw down the burner and followed William out of the room and up the cylindrical stairwell.

———

Samantha yelled at the first man to surface, William Ying, ordering him to hit the ground. William drew a gun and she picked him off with a shot to the leg.

He fell to the ground screaming in agony, while Nick felled Danny Huang with a single blow to the head as he surfaced at the top of the ladder.

"Two down," Nick called to Ellen through his watch mic. On cue, she surfaced from the side of the tank and moved, weapon in hand, down the stairs of the tank reserve. She quickly cleared the stairwell and ran into the room where Mitch lay. He looked conscious, the burner was off and she moved out quickly to clear the other rooms.

"All clear," she said into her watch microphone as Nick appeared, running down the stairs.

"Both secured," he reported.

Nick entered the interrogation room and raced to Mitch's side, squatting in front of his chair. Mitch reeled away from him.

"It's me," Nick said. "You're right buddy, you're safe now."

Mitch was breathing too quickly, relief coursing through him, his body involuntarily shaking from the pain.

Samantha appeared behind him. "They're not going anywhere," she assured Ellen while not taking her eyes off Mitch.

Nick moved behind Mitch, reached for a pocket knife in his vest and cut off the binds on Mitch's wrists, peeling them off the skin where the dry blood had sealed them. Mitch winced at the pain from the change in circulation.

"Sam, get some water," Nick ordered her.

Ellen put in a call to John. "John, two alive and secured, Mitch needs medical help. How do you want to handle this?" She waited for instructions. "Thanks John." She hung up. "John's sending back-up by chopper." She moved back to Mitch's side.

Samantha grabbed the water bottle and offered it to him but Mitch could barely raise his arms, the pain of having them tied and immobile made worse by the new movement. Samantha held the water to his lips and he drank thirstily.

Pulling away from her, he leaned forward. "The others? Are there others?" he said, prepared to move if needed.

"Two outside and they're down, three back in D.C. It's OK, take a minute, Mitch," Nick said.

"What's the damage?" Ellen studied Mitch as he seemed to move in slow motion.

"Not sure," Mitch said with a slight tremor in his voice. He breathed quickly, his body reacting to the burn, his skin pale and cold, "but if you had been five minutes later..."

Ellen knelt in front of Mitch and moved his head to the side to check out his wound.

"Sam, run back to the car and get the medical kit

from it, hurry please." Ellen poured water over Mitch's burn. "Nick, get more cold water and check the prisoners, please."

Ellen ran to the kitchen, grabbed a towel, wet it and returned to dab the side of Mitch's head. "Bleeding's stopped," she said.

Nick entered with four bottles of water and poured the contents over the burn. Ellen heard the car pull up and Samantha ran in with the medical kit.

"Thanks." Ellen took it from her and removed two sterile bandages.

"I'm OK." Mitch tried to move away.

"Mitch sit still and sshh!" Ellen ordered.

"You're shaking, Mitch," Samantha said.

"Sam, will you just keep patrol with the captives?" Ellen looked up at her, thinking it best to keep her away from Mitch for now.

Samantha nodded and took to the stairs.

Ellen rolled a sterile gauze bandage around Mitch's burnt arm. Nick felt Mitch's pulse, a look of concern sweeping his face. Ellen looked to him and Nick shook his head.

"You're not going to go into shock on us are you, Mitch?" Nick tried to keep Mitch focused. He took off his windcheater and placed it around Mitch.

"For shock, we shouldn't have given him that water," Ellen muttered. "We need to lay you down Mitch, just for a bit, alright? Can you move?"

"Yeah, I'm fine." He pushed himself up off the chair and as his legs collapsed and the floor rose to meet him, the last thing he saw was Nick diving to reach him before everything went to black.

34

NICK ENTERED THE HOSPITAL ROOM AROUND MIDDAY Monday for the second time that day. His eyes scanned over Mitch who lay sleeping.

As he came within a few feet of the bed, Mitch's eyes shot open and he braced.

"Just me." Nick held up his hands.

"Nick." Mitch sighed and visibly relaxed.

"Brought you a sports mag." Nick tossed it to him.

"Thanks," Mitch caught the magazine. "Good stuff."

"Yeah well, I figure if you can't run, you may as well read about it." Nick shrugged. "How are you feeling?"

"Bit high," Mitch said.

"Yeah? What's in that?" Nick nodded at the IV.

"Demerol I think. Hey, you know last night, when you left ..." Mitch began, readjusting himself to sit up slightly.

"Yeah?" Nick leaned on the edge of the bed.

"Did you see anyone?" Mitch asked.

"Like your ex, Charlotte?" Nick asked.

"Yes."

"She was here, but John told her you couldn't have visitors. Good thing, too. You were raving on about some Asian guy brandishing a blow torch and you beating the crap out of him."

Mitch smiled and pulled himself up further in the bed. "Have Danny or William talked?"

"Not a word, but John's going to keep Danny in solitary until after the lift this week and William, like you suggested will do whatever's necessary so his wife doesn't face accessory charges," Nick answered. "We've got his every move covered."

Mitch nodded. "Except he still hasn't told us who the VIP is."

"We'll know soon enough," Nick said.

"So they bought it?" Mitch asked.

"Seem to have."

"Tell me how it went down," Mitch said, closing his eyes.

Nick sighed. "Don't you want the day off?"

"Nick!"

"Right. As you directed in your blissful state this morning ... you know you're much more pleasant when you're high ..."

"Nick ..."

"Fine. We sent Hai a text from Danny Huang's phone explaining he had been recalled to manage a problem on the ground in Beijing. We added that William was staying at his office premises working on a project until the lift and Hai was to take over and stick to the schedule ... Mitch?"

Mitch opened his eyes. "I'm listening. What response did you get from—"

"Hai?" Nick said, "you are high."

"I'm a bit whacked." Mitch looked to the IV line in his arm.

Nick continued, "He said he was ready for the challenge and all that. He's got a huge ego and thinks he should be leader anyway according to what we've translated."

Mitch's eyes narrowed in his customary fashion when thinking. "We should send an update text in a couple of days from Danny's phone, saying all on schedule, you know," Mitch said. "And Dylan, is he all right?"

"Yes. Ellen rang him but he said he spoke with you this morning."

"He did, that's right." Mitch fought to stay awake.

Nick looked up as his housemate Amy Callaghan entered the hospital room. "Oh yeah," he told Mitch, "I brought you a guest, they let her out of the library." He indicated her with a nod.

"Hey." Mitch smiled at her, "On loan to me!"

Nick rolled his eyes. "He's a bit high."

Amy blushed. "Hi sickie," she said and returned his smile.

Nick noticed how Mitch's eyes lit up and Amy's lingered just that moment longer on Mitch's face. She ran her gaze over his black and blue countenance, forehead stitches and the bandaging on his arm.

"Wow," she said, smiling. "Impressive. You know, there's easier ways to get attention."

"They weren't working," he said drowsily.

Amy laughed. "Ouch, don't make me laugh, it hurts."

Mitch looked at her perplexed. "Isn't that my line?"

"Swimming classes," she said. "I'm learning to swim. Nick tells me it's the same course that Samantha is going to be doing, only not as advanced."

Nick shook his head. "She's got bruises up and down her arms and side from crashing into the plastic lane dividers. We need to find a pool with padded ones."

Mitch laughed, then gritted his teeth with the pain.

"Yes, very funny, laugh at the drowning girl," she said and sat down next to his bed. "So any good presents?"

"Besides my magazine?" Nick reminded him.

"Mm, like chocolate?" Amy looked at his side table.

"No, sorry." Mitch glanced at the bedside table. "No chocolate, flowers, or stuffed toys. I can offer you some hard candy." He indicated the pack that a visitor had left earlier.

"Bet he's said that a few times," Nick warned her.

"When do you get out?" she asked.

"Tomorrow afternoon."

"I'll come back and get you," Nick offered.

"Thanks, but Henri's picking me up."

Nick shrugged. "Probably a better idea. It'll be more comfortable in his Jag than on the back of my bike."

Amy scoffed. "Like he can get on your bike with those." She nodded to the crutches. She turned back to Mitch. "When are you back at work?"

"He hasn't been away," Nick said. "We checked Mitch in here last night and had a team handover here this morning."

"Handover?" Amy asked.

"Yep, Ellie's in charge. She's good, she'll keep Nick in line," Mitch said.

"And she says please after she gives an order," Nick said.

A stern, portly middle-aged nurse entered the room. She glanced at the two guests with a look of impatience.

"Well, I guess it's a short visit today, busy people that we are." Nick rose.

"Thanks for coming," Mitch said with a long glance at Amy.

"Sure," she said. "See you back at work soon."

Nick lingered after she left the room. "So, are you all right?"

Mitch inhaled and thought before answering. "I'm tired of being sore."

Nick nodded. "I get that. Sam wanted to come last night and this morning, she's pretty distraught."

"I don't think I can handle her until I'm out of pain," Mitch said.

"Yeah, that's what John thought. I think you gave him a pretty good scare this time—he's organizing therapy left, right and center. For you, for Sam because she's wracked with guilt, for us because we saw you getting walloped, for the person who reads the report, there was a deer that went by the window ... "

Mitch laughed.

The nurse gave Nick a disapproving look.

"He won't be checking out tomorrow unless he gets some sleep today," she said.

"Get out of here ... please," Mitch said.

Nick grinned. "Yes, sir."

35

On Tuesday morning, Mitch sat propped up in bed with his laptop open. John and Ellen sat by his hospital bedside.

"I need to get out of here, this is getting too close for comfort," he said.

"If you don't stay calm they won't let you out because your blood pressure will be through the roof," John reminded him. "Good to see they've taken the IV out though."

"Yeah, now they're jabbing me instead," Mitch said. "I've got an updated from Dylan Ting... sorry Ellie, he rang in."

"All good," she said, "I'm just holding the fort where I can."

Mitch updated them on Dylan's work.

"He's done well," John agreed. "We've formalized the deal with William Ying. His wife and child will be sent back to China but in return for his cooperation she won't be charged with anything, and I convinced him there was a lot I could think to charge her with."

"Did he tell you who the VIP is?" Mitch asked.

"Says he doesn't know either and won't be told until the last minute by Danny," John said.

"That's crap, he must think we're idiots," Mitch said. "We can't trust him."

"Relax, you're not supposed to get stressed remember," John watched him. Mitch ran his hand over his mouth, frustration riding him.

"We've got William wired," Ellen said, "so he may let it slip. Besides we mentioned that Danny Huang hit on his wife that night William left for Cape Hatteras so he's not feeling too loyal."

"How did we know that?" Mitch asked.

"Danny boasted about it to the VIP and we picked it up in one of their transcripts."

"Right. Ellie, John, there's something happening at the uni I need to sort out," Mitch said.

"I can get Sam onto that," John suggested.

Mitch looked at John and back at his laptop. "It was something Joseph Kinaird said in his diary ... when he went to collect William Ying to take him to the gallery exhibition, he found William in the science lab talking to a young scientist. William snapped at him and told him to wait outside. But William had no reason to be there and Kinaird was angry because he was a head of department, not some junior."

"So what was he doing there and who was he involved with?" John asked.

"Exactly. Seeing William Ying there might have got Kinaird killed. Not Samantha, John, I need this handled really carefully," Mitch said. "Do we know a head of department at the uni we could talk to?"

"Henri will," John said. "I'll ask him to make the call."

"Perfect," Mitch agreed. "There's some more information I need; another angle we've got to explore ... about using midget submarines to infiltrate our shores."

"I'm following that line, Nick's helping," Ellen said.

Mitch nodded. "Thanks. It's more common than I thought ... I read a report this morning that said more than a third of the cocaine smuggled into the U.S. from Colombia travels in midget submarines underwater. They're not submerging, the subs are just skimming the surface."

"So are you thinking this might not be an Asian sub?" John asked.

Mitch winced and leaned forward, moving to ease the pain in his back. "I don't know," he answered. "I think it's an Asian sub because there was something in the translation about the Beijing office wasn't there?"

"There was," Ellen agreed. "But it could be a privately-funded sub, and I suspect this group is funded by a number of important benefactors."

"I agree. These subs—the ones used for drug smuggling—are called submersibles, not submarines, because they don't need a snorkel and periscope above the water," Mitch continued. "They're built for one-way trips and are sunk after. I'm not saying that's the case here, but I want to know all options ... what we might expect. I read there are also robot subs; they don't even have a crew onboard and don't have to surface."

"We saw from the test run on the beach that the sub the Asians are using is not going to surface, it's transferring the VIP using some sort of external oxygenated connection," Ellen told John.

Mitch moved again.

"OK." John rose. "We've got plenty to do, you need a shot and sleep. I'll send the nurse in on our way out. What time are they letting you out?"

"Don't worry about the nurse. Doctor said he'd be here after four, and he'd release me then."

"I'm sending the nurse," John said. "You relax, Ellen will manage all we've discussed."

"I know," Mitch said, leaning back. "Thanks, Ellie."

She held out her hands for his laptop and logging out, put it on the cabinet beside the bed. He was drifting off before Ellen had even left the room.

———

Mitch pushed the seat in Henri's Jaguar all the way back and lowered himself in. He took the crutches from Henri, who closed the door and came around to the driver's side.

"Thanks for picking me up," Mitch said.

"Of course," Henri said as he drove Mitch back to his and Ann's residence late Tuesday afternoon.

"So, what did you find out at the uni, anything?" Mitch asked.

"I'm not talking work with you Mitch, you're in recovery." Henri looked at him then back at the road as he pulled out of the hospital parking lot.

Mitch's jaw locked with frustration as he looked out the window.

"Do I have to call John and ask him?" Mitch said.

"You know why you're tired and can't keep your eyes open? Because your body is trying to recover," Henri explained, "and until you let it, it keeps shutting down, which is why ..."

Mitch tuned out and tapped his fingers on the

arm rest in frustration. When Henri finished, he tried again.

"Henri, please tell me what you found out at the uni," Mitch asked again.

Henri sighed.

Mitch looked at him.

"Fine then," Henri said. "Last year the Chinese government was working on a genetic weapon." He stopped to allow that to sink in.

Mitch waited.

"It is a weapon that if, and I stress the if, it could be developed, is designed to spread an airborne virus that can kill a particular genetic group within a set period of time."

"When you say genetic group, are you suggesting a broad group, like Caucasians?"

"That's exactly what I'm referring to," Henri said. "So if they were successful, they could expose all leaders at the G20 to this virus, which they in turn could carry home to their respective countries, thus potentially eliminating Caucasians, African, African Americans, Hispanic races or whomever they chose."

"Anyone who is not Asian," Mitch finished.

"In theory."

"And can they?"

"No, well not yet, maybe never. We got wind of it actually through MI-5 in London and jointly we were working on both beating them to it and shutting it down," Henri said.

Mitch shook his head. "For chrissake."

"Yes. The university had a sample, that is, has a sample."

"Don't tell me William was trying to get access to it?"

"Yes, trying at the time he was in the role of ambassador, but now that you've discovered him alive, I'd say he's been working underground on it for the last year, but the latter is just my guess," Henri said.

"And the lab person that was working on it with him, the person Kinaird saw William Ying with ... do we know what happened to him?"

"Left not long after William disappeared," Henri said.

"Funny, that," Mitch said.

"We've got it—the prototype—it's not going to happen and it is a long way from happening."

"Has it been tested?" Mitch asked.

"Not to my knowledge, they couldn't advance it to that level," Henri said.

"I wonder if the VIP is connected with the weapon? Does William Ying's team think that the VIP can give them this weapon and whatever else they want to take out of the country?"

"They must know that it hasn't succeeded, but they might want the blueprint. Who's to say a weapon of this nature isn't being developed some-where else in China or in the world—just not here, not now."

"Thanks Henri." Mitch leaned back on the head rest.

Henri nodded, clearly displeased.

Mitch's phone rang.

"Hi John," Mitch answered. He listened. "Thanks, got that, and just got the update from Henri on the uni. I spoke with Dylan and Ellen ear-lier and we need to get back to Cape Hatteras to-morrow. The classmates are going straight there after the certificate ceremony at noon so they'll ar-rive about seven tomorrow night and the lift is still planned for Friday morning."

Mitch listened, finished his conversation and hung up. His phone rang again.

"Ellie, all OK?" Mitch asked. He listened to her update. "Yep, agreed. That all sounds good and thanks for carrying it." Mitch hung up.

Henri shook his head.

"Tell me you're not going to Cape Hatteras, Mitch," Henri said.

Mitch hesitated, anticipating Henri's disap-proval. "We're in the middle of a case; actually we're at the very end of a case that's about to be blown wide open, and I've got to stay on it," he said.

"Mitch, you've got to sit behind a desk for a few days at least. I'll call John," Henri said.

"Could you write a letter and get me out of school as well?"

Henri smiled. "If that's what it takes."

"I'm going back tomorrow, it'll be OK, Nick and Ellie will be there. It's only a few broken ribs and some bruising, seriously, I've had worse," Mitch assured him.

"It's ten stitches, a black eye, cracked ribs, concussion, bruising around your back and kidneys, two lacerations to the back of the head, a severe burn, a leg contusion, treatment for shock, that's off the top of my head," Henri said as he turned the car into the driveway of a large Georgian-style home. The gates opened and he drove in.

"Thanks for reminding me."

Henri steered into the garage and exited the car. He opened the passenger door for Mitch who, grabbing his crutches, hobbled out, swayed and steadied himself, supported by the car door.

"And balance problems," Henri added to his injury list.

Mitch sighed. "I've got to find a new place."

"You can stay in our guest wing as long as you like. Ann insists. It's separate, has its own entrance; you don't even have to see us unless you want company."

"Thanks Henri but— "

Henri interrupted him. "But if you don't stay in the main house for a few days now, you'll really upset Ann. She hasn't had anyone to fuss over since her son moved to Seattle. She's aired the room and has cooked ... I might have mentioned you've lost weight."

Mitch grinned. "I'll just have to do my part then."

————

The next morning, Ellen sat propped behind the wheel of Mitch's Audi, looking pleased with herself. "I can't believe you're letting me drive your car again. That's twice in a week." Ellen grinned. "I love this car, don't I look good behind the wheel?"

"I can't watch; I'm keeping my eyes closed, so just be careful," Mitch said, sprawled out on the backseat.

"When can we stop for coffee?" Nick asked from the front passenger seat.

"We can't," Mitch answered. "You should have had a coffee at breakfast."

"Aren't you supposed to be sleeping so that we can wake you up when we get there, grumpy? Do you need another painkiller?" Nick asked.

"As soon as we need gas, we'll get coffee," Ellen appeased Nick.

Mitch lay back, resting his head on the closed window frame; he crossed his arms and tried to keep his injured leg straight. He could see his own reflection in the car window and the outside scenery speeding by. He tuned out of Nick's and Ellen's conversation and glanced at his watch; the graduation ceremony should be taking place soon; he could call Dylan Ting after one p.m.

What am I going to do about Sam? Desk duty for now works, but long-term? Is she too reckless to have around?

It wasn't the first incident; he recalled her actions in London in the Underground and her lack of discipline in the Library of Congress.

She'll get herself—or one of us—killed. Do I keep saying that until it happens?

He woke to the smell of coffee, groaned and pulled himself upright. Two hours had passed.

"Yeah, you should have got a wagon." Nick handed him a large coffee over the backseat.

"These painkillers are great," Mitch said. "I didn't even hear you pull up."

Ellen pulled the car out of the gas station and continued on to Cape Hatteras. Mitch dialed Dylan Ting's number.

"Dylan, can you talk?" Mitch asked.

"I can," Dylan answered. "You all right?"

"Yeah, thanks. Hang on and I'll put you on speaker phone. I'm with Nick and Ellen. So what's the latest?"

"Afternoon all," Dylan said, "Well they all graduated, there was much hand shaking and many photos taken. Behind the scenes, Hai seems to be really relishing being in-charge. Since we spoke last night, Mitch, they've confirmed that Hai and Froggy will head back to the VIP house this afternoon leaving about three p.m. Ru is not coming down until Thursday."

"Do you know what they're doing?" Mitch asked.

"Not yet. I'll keep prodding. Hai is expecting to hear from Danny from Beijing I think, so we should send a text."

"Yes, thanks for that, we intended to. I'll get onto it," Mitch said. "And the VIP?"

"I overheard that William is going to collect him and they are both going to the VIP house together on Thursday really early ... and no, I don't know who it is yet. They just call him the VIP," Dylan said. "Get this, they've asked me if I would like to go with Ru to organize a drop off this afternoon. And we're going out for a bite tonight."

"This is good," Mitch said. "Are you feeling like they have accepted you, bought the frustrated with your life act?"

"Yeah, I do," Dylan said. "I've been laying it on a bit thick, but I think they believe it."

"Mm, be careful ... hang on ... for chrissake Ellie, slow down on the corners."

Ellen grinned in the front seat. "But this car grips, it's fantastic."

Mitch shook his head. "Sorry Dylan. Yeah, so timing?"

"The lift is on-schedule for this Friday."

"Phew, we're running out of time ... can we slow it down?" Mitch sighed.

"I wish," Dylan agreed. "I'm going back to the office for an hour before I meet Ru for the drop off, whatever that is. Want me to organize the text from Danny Huang's phone to Hai saying all OK and move ahead with the VIP drop?"

"That would be great, thanks Dylan. I'll call John now and let him know you'll be in and to give you access to Danny's phone. Stay in touch." Mitch hung up.

"Couldn't Sam help with that?" Nick asked.

Mitch didn't answer.

36

DYLAN TING SAT QUIETLY IN THE VAN BESIDE HIS Asian student, Ru. They waited at the dock. Dylan knew better than to speak; silence said no fear, no hesitation.

A van pulled up beside them and Ru exited the van. Dylan followed suit. Ru greeted the driver, a middle-aged Asian man, and introduced Dylan as his partner, with no names exchanged. The man indicated they should follow. He walked past half a dozen small storage areas, towards an office structure, unlocked the security screen and glass door, entered, and grabbed a folder. Inside the folder, he shuffled through the paperwork, found the one he was looking for, clipped it to the front of the folder, and gave it to Ru with a pen.

Dylan studied the young man; Ru would not

have been a day over twenty-five with his small round face and thin lips. Ru signed the paper, handed it back and nodded his thanks. The man handed over a key.

"If you want anything out of it, better get it soon. It will be sunk between seven and ten next Monday or Tuesday morning depending on our workload," the man said.

Ru smiled. "Excellent, thank you."

The man escorted Ru and Dylan out of the office and locked it. He nodded at the two men and departed.

Ru began to walk towards their vehicle with the unit key.

"Do we need to get something from the storage container?" Dylan looked back at the row of storage units and containers.

"No, this key is just for safe-keeping," Ru said, and he turned and threw it high over the dock and into the water.

Dylan gasped in surprise as he saw the key fall into the water and disappear. He turned to Ru and laughed. Ru grinned back.

"Our work here is done," Ru said. "Hai said you might like to join us to help with a project we're working on. You know we are going away for a few days. Interested?"

"Sure, count me in," Dylan said.

"Good. Let's go find ourselves a bit of action before dinner. Where's the best joint?" Ru asked in Mandarin. Dylan knew exactly what sort of joint Ru was looking to frequent.

———

Varying between sitting and lying for the past hour in the backseat of the car, Mitch moved from side to side, trying to keep his leg elevated and find a comfortable position. The compression bandage felt tight and his skin was black with bruising on both legs, fading to yellow around the edges. His arm throbbed from the burn and his ribs reminded him they were fractured with every breath.

"Are we there yet?" Mitch asked from the backseat.

"We would be if I didn't have to drive at nanny speed in your car," Ellen said.

"You're going to have to pull over, sorry Ellie," Mitch said.

"Didn't I tell you to go before we left home?" Nick rolled his eyes. He looked at Ellen. "Kids!"

Mitch chuckled. "Not a bathroom stop, I've got to stretch. Sorry; my legs are killing me. Soon, Ellie, really soon."

"Oh sure, hang on," Ellen said. She drove a little

further until she found a widening of the road and pulled over.

Nick alighted and opened the rear car door; Mitch pulled himself out of the car, grabbing one crutch from the floor of the car, and limped out.

"You want a shot?" Ellen asked. "It's your last one, then you're on the Tylenol."

Mitch nodded and hobbled away, breathing heavily. Moving away from the car, Nick lit a cigarette and stood watching him.

Ellen fetched a hypodermic needle from the chilled pack in the car boot.

"We'll be there in about an hour," Ellen said to Nick. "We should scope while he sleeps."

"He won't sleep. So don't go planning any romantic candlelit dinners either," Nick teased her.

"You wish." She grinned.

After a few minutes, Mitch hobbled over.

"Are you going to give me some cheek?" she asked.

"I don't have the energy," Mitch said.

"No I mean, butt cheek." Ellen held up the needle.

"Oh." Mitch frowned. "God no."

Ellen rolled her eyes, moved behind him, pushing Mitch up against the passenger car door, pulled his shirt up and jeans down two inches on one hip and stuck the needle in.

"Ouch, such a rough nurse," he complained. "No nice bedside manner? No small talk?"

"I'll give you small talk in a minute." She frowned at him. "That will teach you to ride me while I'm driving." She pulled the needle out.

"Yeah, you earned that." Nick nodded.

"Nice butt though," Ellen added.

"It's his best feature," Nick agreed.

Mitch smirked at the pair. "That's just great, when a guy's down, you kick him for good measure."

"Gee, now I feel bad," Ellen said.

"Me too," Nick agreed. "Group hug?"

"You two suck." Mitch tried to hide a smile as he hobbled to the rear passenger door. He threw the crutch on the floor and lowered himself in. "Come on, driver, step on it."

Ellen returned the needle to the pack and followed the men into the car. She handed two ice packs over the seat to Mitch, along with a towel.

"Put that on the bruising for a while," she instructed and then seeing his confusion added, "Well, whichever bruising is hurting the most."

Soon after they pulled into the parking lot of the Cape Hatteras hotel where the team was staying. Mitch on his crutches, followed Nick and Ellen inside.

"John's gone all out this time, four bedrooms, two bathrooms, might not go back," Nick said.

"Boy bathroom over there," Ellen pointed out, "girl bathroom here. OK boss?"

"Good idea. We don't want girl germs," Mitch agreed. He took a room nearest to the exit, entered, closed the door behind him and fell on the bed exhausted.

He heard a knock on the door.

"You alright?" Nick asked.

"Yeah be there in a minute," he answered and closed his eyes. Just need ten minutes or so to recharge ... Mitch woke two hours later when his phone rang.

37

THE VIP RUBBED HIS FACE. THE DOOR OF HIS OFFICE opened and he looked up, startled; it was early and he wasn't expecting anyone in the office just yet. It was his personal assistant. She placed a cup of tea in front of him and brought his daily mail.

"Thanks Kate." He watched her walk out, admiring her figure. He would miss the view. The VIP rose and went to the window. Sometimes he wondered if he had done the right thing, selling out, but then he recalled the treachery of his own party; he was never going to have the top job. The knives were out yet he knew he was the best man for the job. That would change when he went to China; plus his days studying in Beijing were some of the happiest of his life and he was keen to relive that feeling ... if it was not too late.

"To yesterday and tomorrow," he whispered. The VIP returned to his desk and drank the tea. *My last cup of tea in this office.* He glanced at his watch. *Time to go, meet the collectors.* He drew a deep breath and looked around the room one more time from the position of his desk and then rose. The VIP removed the sim-card from his phone, destroyed it and left the phone in the top drawer. *No use for that anymore and I don't want to be traceable.* He walked to the door, opened it, walked through and did not look back.

————

Mitch stood in front of the window looking at the beach and eating a bowl of cereal.

"What's the plan," Nick asked buttering toast.

"Nick, you need to scope the beach area as subtly as you can. Take your board, paddle out, check out the area. Ellie, can you go hire a boat for an hour and do the same? I'm going to ..." Mitch stopped mid-sentence. Nick and Ellen looked over at him.

"Mitch?" Ellen said.

"VIP," Mitch said. "No ... surely not." He slid the bowl onto the counter, grabbed his phone and rang John Windsor.

"No, everything's fine," Mitch assured him.

327

"John, hypothetical here, what are the odds that VIP is code for the Vice President? He was in office when William Ying was Chinese ambassador."

He heard John Windsor draw in a sharp breath. "We can't rule it out," he answered.

"Can you find out what the Vice President has in his diary today?" Mitch asked. "If he's got appointments we needn't worry ... assuming he shows for them. If his diary has been cleared, then we need to know exactly where he is because whoever the VIP is, supposedly he is being picked up and driven to the VIP house at Cape Hatteras today."

"I'm onto it—and Mitch, tell your team to keep this off the radar," John said. "I'll ring the Chief of Staff in the White House."

Mitch hung up.

"You can't be serious?" Nick asked.

"Worthy of a submarine departure," Mitch said. "Off the radar though, OK?"

They nodded.

"You two go, I'll keep you posted," Mitch ordered.

Nick grabbed his toast and the keys. Mitch's phone rang again.

"Dylan?"

"Hi Mitch, I've just heard that William is picking up the VIP at his home in exactly one hour's time and then they are heading down your way to the VIP house. They'll be there late this afternoon," Dylan said. "Plus I've got Danny Huang's phone. Most of the messages are just codes, a couple of words, nothing more. His old messages to William Ying are friendly, like an old pal catching up."

"Right, can you text Hai from that phone? Short and sweet. Say 'all on track, continue mission as planned'."

"No problem. Hai says Danny Huang is a loose cannon ... well he didn't say that to me, Ru told me."

"Yes, there appears to be no love lost between them."

"Interesting trip with Ru yesterday," Dylan Ting continued.

"Oh yeah the drop off, what did you do?" Mitch asked.

"We went to the dock, signed for a key, were told that if we wanted anything out of the container that the key unlocked, do it soon because it was going to be sunk early next week."

Mitch closed his eyes. "Right," he said, and sighed. "Text me through the address where the container is stored, thanks. What are you doing now?"

"I'm waiting to hear from Ru. I've been invited to work on a project with them and he's going to pick me up. They said I'd be away a couple of days."

"Sounds like a trip to Cape Hatteras, well done," Mitch said.

"Do you want me to go with him or I could come ..."

"No." Mitch opened his eyes and cut Dylan off mid-sentence. "You need to do as they tell you. You are the new guy keen to impress. Keep us posted."

———

Nick watched Ellen walk towards the boat shed to sign out a boat for the morning. She turned and nodded. There was a boat available, and he could leave now. Nick turned the car out of the harbor parking lot and drove to the beach lot.

Ellen was right, he thought, Mitch's Audi was great to drive, but he still preferred his bike. He spun it into a park, grabbed his towel, and headed to the beach.

He was about to strip off when his phone rang; it was Samantha.

"Hey, Sam," he answered.

"Nick, can you talk?" He heard the strain in her voice.

"I'm alone, just about to do a beach tour of duty," Nick answered.

Samantha sighed. "Has he said anything about me?"

Nick flicked his towel out and dropped down onto it. He looked out to sea.

"Not a word, Sam, sorry. I tried to bring you up, suggested he handball a job to you but he didn't respond."

"Should I call him?" she asked.

"I wouldn't," Nick said. "To be honest, Sam, it's not that he's avoiding you, you're just not on his radar at the moment. This is all going to go down tomorrow supposedly and you know how he works more than I do, he's got a head-full. If you push him, he'll just blow you off."

"When will you be back?" she asked.

"Probably in a couple of days." Nick looked around to make sure he was alone. "Once the swap happens we've got no reason to stay here."

There was silence on the line.

"You've known him for a hundred years. Why doesn't he appreciate a bit of initiative? Was he like that in the air force too?"

Nick flared. "Maybe if the initiative worked! He's been tortured, Sam." Nick drew a deep breath. "You know what I'd do? I would lie low. Stay out of his face and show you can be disciplined enough to understand he has other priorities. It might help. I've got to go. Are you going to be OK?"

"Yeah, thanks for the chat."

"Sure." Nick shook his head and hung up. He

rose, stripped off his shirt and ran to the water's edge.

Bloody freezing. He plunged in and swam away from the shore.

———

Mitch sighed with frustration as he watched out the window. He drummed his fingers on the windowsill, waiting for John's call. He ran through the scenario in his head; if it was the Vice President, the VIP, why? Was he a spy? Why would he turn and betray his country—and what damage could he do from one of the most powerful offices in the country? What intelligence has he already taken out of the country?

Mitch's phone rang and he grabbed for it. It wasn't John.

"Nick?"

"Hey Mitch, I've covered the area, at great personal sacrifice ... lord knows what the shrinkage damage is from that water temperature ..."

Mitch laughed. "I'll put you up for a medal."

"Yeah thanks," Nick responded. "Ellen's still out on the boat, but I've just seen one of the Asian men pull up at the supermarket across the road. Want me to trail him to see if he buys anything other than groceries?"

"Yes thanks, but don't follow him back to the VIP house."

"No. I'll call you when I'm back in the car." Nick hung up.

Mitch rang Ellen. "Ellie, when you are in the area where we spotted the midget sub last time, can you confirm the coordinates?"

"I'm there now, will do," she said.

Mitch hung up and waited.

He grabbed his iPad and logged into his work system to access his files. He read the Vice President's background and followed a hunch ... where did the VP go to school? He found the VP's high school. Now what subjects did he study? He checked the school's yearbook and ... look at that, he won the award for Modern Asian Studies. Does he speak Mandarin or Cantonese? Can't be too hard to find out if he learnt these at school. Hold up ...

Mitch looked up and took a moment. I can't believe it ... he looked back at the screen ... the VP was an exchange student for a year in Beijing. It's all coming together.

His phone rang again.

"Mitch, I'm back in the car and you won't believe what the Asian just bought," Nick said. He didn't wait for an answer. "Flippers, a beach towel, a scuba mask and snorkel."

"What?" Mitch frowned.

"Seriously," Nick confirmed. "He's headed up the highway now in the direction of the VIP house. I'm going to head to the beach and the lighthouse. Hang on ..."

Mitch waited while Nick put the phone in hands-free mode and started the car.

"Are you thinking what I'm thinking?" Nick asked.

"That the Vice President is going to go missing when swimming ... and his flippers and mask will wash up on shore," Mitch said.

"Exactly. Nothing suspicious, just another drowning at sea. Meantime, he's sold out and is out of the country," Nick said.

"Unbelievable. Got to go, John's calling."

Mitch hung up on Nick and selected John's call.

"John, tell me ..."

John lowered his voice. "The Vice President has left the White House and cancelled his appointments for the rest of the day. He's claimed a personal day for family reasons."

"Dylan said William was picking the VIP up from his home in less than an hour, it has to be him! I knew we couldn't trust William to keep us in the loop, even to save his wife and child," Mitch said. "I'm going to get Dylan to stake out the Vice President's house. If he sees him get in the car with William, I'll get him to take photos and we'll know we've got our man. John, just let me do that before you alert higher powers. If we're wrong ... well, we don't want to be wrong."

"Come back to me with a plan within thirty minutes," John ordered.

"Done and just quickly, the Vice President was an exchange student in Beijing, nice fit." Mitch hung up and called Dylan Ting.

"Dylan, can you get away? I need you to do something urgently without being seen." Mitch began his plan of action.

38

ELLEN SHIVERED AS SHE WAITED FOR NICK TO RETURN. She saw Mitch's car approaching and walked towards the parking lot. Nick pushed open the car door and Ellen slid into the front seat and turned up the heat.

"Freezing my ass off out there." She shivered. "Anything?"

"Nothing," he said.

"Me either. I guess that's a good sign. I've got the coordinates," she said.

Within minutes they were back at the hotel room. As they walked in, Mitch was on the phone, leaning on one crutch in front of the window.

Ellen went to the kitchen and set up three cups for coffee.

Mitch hung up.

"Mitch, please sit down and elevate your leg or else the doctor will blame me," Ellen begged. "And I checked the coordinates, the ones we have are correct."

"Thanks." Mitch hobbled to the couch and dropped down. He raised his leg and propped it on the edge of the coffee table. Nick disappeared into the bedroom, stripping off his wet gear and reappearing minutes later in dry attire.

"You're not going to believe it," Mitch began. "Hang on..." his phone was ringing.

"Dylan?" Mitch answered. "Great send it through." Mitch hung up. "Just got to call John. Anything?" he asked as he dialed.

"No, clear for both of us," Nick reported.

Mitch nodded. He went to rise again, glanced at Ellen and sat back down.

"John, Dylan's just confirmed the Vice President is the VIP. I have the photo and I'm sending it to you now. The Vice President has just entered the vehicle with a man Dylan identified as William Ying. Ellie and Nick are back, all clear on the beach locations. Hang on."

He put John on speaker phone and Nick and Ellen joined him on the couches.

John spoke. "You need to understand the gravity of what is happening. This cannot go any further than this room. No one you speak to must know. Understand?"

They confirmed their understanding.

"I have notified the powers above and the SEALs will take over on the beach. Give me a rundown on how you see it going so I can give them a brief," John said.

"This is how I see it being played out," Mitch started. "Pre-dawn, the Vice President will be removed by submarine. We have the coordinates. His towel, flippers, snorkel and mask—which Nick saw being purchased earlier—will be scattered on the beach or left in the shallows to wash up. Our guess is that they'll say the Vice President drowned when he went to catch up with an old friend at Cape Hatteras, a student he met when he was on exchange in Beijing."

"Is that for real?" John asked.

"It's for real he was an exchange student but I don't know if he met any of the real police officers during his time over there," Mitch continued. "In the meantime, they get the Vice President out of the country with whatever files he's sharing or has already shared and eventually, everyone believes he is dead. He gets a new life, a new face, whatever it takes; they get government secrets." Mitch stopped to let it all sink in. "John, this is my recommendation; as I see it we can play it one of two ways. The mission is shut down—using the coordinates we have, in the early hours of the morning the vessel and occupants are destroyed, evidence removed. That will eliminate the Vice President, Hai and Froggy. The media story is still spread to avoid panic and to spare retribution; let it be known that the Vice President is presumed drowned after an early morning swim. We move in to pick up Ru and William, and we already have Danny. We find out what the Vice President has given them, what they know and what information they already have that we have to get back or destroy. Once we have a grip on this, we can reveal the murder of the original police officers."

"We don't know they've been murdered," John said.

"I'm pretty sure I know where the real police officers are."

"Where?" Nick asked.

"I'm thinking they are in a container that's going to be dumped at sea next week," Mitch said.

"Do we need to intervene? Could they possibly be alive?" Ellen asked.

Mitch shook his head. "No, I suspect they died some time ago but I'll get that container relocated before the drop. We need to focus on the now."

"And the other play?" John asked.

"We reveal the murdered policemen now, arrest

the whole party and expose the Vice President, but we don't know what information has gone before him and we don't know and may never know who has the information," Mitch said. "We also expose a huge hole in our own security and there will be fear-mongering and conspiracy theories going wild if our Vice President is a spy."

"Yep," John mused. "Thank God we don't have the weapon to be concerned about."

"Assuming what Henri was told is correct," Mitch said.

"There is no doubt it is the Vice President?" John asked.

"I've just sent you Dylan's photo of the VIP as they refer to him, in the car with William Ying. I've also sent you the recommendations we just discussed. There's no doubt from the photo but can you get someone else to track the vehicle? We also need to confirm that the Vice President is definitely coming to the VIP house."

"I'll get an agent on a bike to head that way," John agreed.

"They've just left now, so we'll give it some time and then we'll also go for a drive and watch them come through," Mitch said.

"If we go with plan A, the beach will be swarming with media once the story of the missing Vice President is leaked. You will all need to be back here ASAP. Stand by, I'll contact you when I can, so wait for orders." John hung up.

Mitch called up the photo of the Vice President and showed Nick and Ellen.

"No doubt there," Nick agreed.

"And now, we wait." Mitch reached for his coffee. He sipped it, a hundred thoughts going through his head.

39

Samantha Moore sat at her desk in the FBI office watching John Windsor pace as he spoke on the phone. She heard him say Mitch's name before he closed the door and knew John was talking with him. Opposite her partition, Dylan Ting dropped down into a chair and with a quick wave in her direction, logged into the computer.

Great, even the new kid on the block is more involved than I am.

She thought about Mitchell Parker.

Maybe I should just get out of the team; I never seem to do the right thing by him anyway.

She thought about the fight at the VIP house. She shuddered as she considered what might have happened to her if Mitch hadn't been there, or what might have happened if he had not found his watch and set off the tracer. She put her head in her hands.

"Are you all right?" She looked up to see Dylan looking over the partition.

"Besides having a sore jaw and a pissed off boss, I'm good," she said.

Dylan grinned. "A normal day at the office then."

Samantha smiled. "What are you doing?"

"Just filing a report while I wait," he said. "I'm on standby for a ride, so I'd better look like I'm ready for action."

Samantha studied him. Dylan must have been between twenty-five to thirty years-of-age or there-abouts. Not her type, too pretty.

She noticed he didn't ask what she was doing.

"Well, better keep going," he said, dropping back down to his chair. "I've got to get on the road."

John Windsor came past her desk, a file under his arm, purpose written across his face.

———

"We're in position to get some extra shots of the Vice President in the car," Mitch told John. "Nick and I are on the outskirts waiting for the car to pass and Ellie's in the scrub around the VIP house or should be by now. How did it go down?"

"Shit's hit the fan," John said. "You are to continue as planned but I will call you back on a secure line and tell you how it will progress once we have that final visual identification to confirm it."

"I'll call you as soon as we eyeball him and Ellie returns." Mitch hung up. "Happy days at the top," he said to Nick beside him in the car.

"Hmm, I bet. VP ETA?"

"About twenty minutes," Mitch said.

The two men sat watching and waiting. Nick was propped with a camera in the backseat, while Mitch stretched across the front driver's and passenger's seats.

"You should have sent me in to get closer to the VIP house," Nick said.

Mitch turned to look at him. "Don't do that, Nick, I don't need it."

"Sorry, I didn't mean to question your orders, but look at the damage you copped, what if Ellie should get seen."

"Ellie is small, fast and capable. She's done a hell of a lot more stakeouts than you have, she's trained in it and I'm trying not to be sexist," Mitch snapped.

He turned to the front, his eyes watching the road and the rear view.

After a while, Nick broached the subject. "I had a call from Samantha."

Mitch continued to stare at the road.

"Clearly, you don't want to know," Nick said.

Mitch's jaw tightened. He hit the steering wheel with the flat of his hand. "I'm so angry at her that I don't want to make any decisions or say anything about her yet."

"Yeah, well I'd feel that way if I had the beating you had too," Nick said.

"It's not even that. It's all the time, every time. Our last mission she was out of control—ignoring intelligence material, throwing protocol out the window, endangering the team. You know, I can live with the consequences to me, and maybe even to her—she should know better by now. But if Ellie got hurt, or you, because of her actions, then I can't live with that."

"Was I an afterthought then?" Nick asked, breaking the mood.

Mitch grinned. "Never." He glanced up. "Here's the car, get ready to snap."

Both men lay low in the vehicle. Nick began snapping shots of the approaching vehicle.

"Windows are dark," he mumbled.

Mitch strained to see them. William Ying was in the driver's seat and beside him was the Vice President. And there was no doubt it was him. The car went past and turned into the road that led to the VIP house.

345

Mitch rang Ellen. "They're coming now. Lie low."

———

Ellen hid behind the scrub, her camera at the ready. She saw the car approaching and began to snap photos. The car was driven into the garage; the two men alighted and walked towards the house. She looked straight at the Vice President as he exited from the car and there was no doubt it was him. She snapped some shots at close range. The two men entered the house and Ellen secured the camera and began making her way through the bush back to the main road.

Fifteen minutes later she arrived and entered Mitch's car. She showed him the photos and he nodded.

"It's the VP, agree?" Mitch said to his team.

"Agreed," Ellen and Nick said in unison.

Ellen sent them straight to John as Mitch dialed him up. He answered on the first ring. "You should have the photos from Ellen and Nick any moment. It's definitely the Vice President."

"Right," John said, "thanks. Return to the apartment and I'll call you with an update in the next half-hour."

———

Mitch paced. He dialed a number and waited.

"Dylan, any news?"

"Hey Mitch," the young agent said. "I've just left work and am going to meet Ru. I'll call you back once I get an update. That alright?"

"Sure." Mitch hung up. He saw Nick smirk. "What?"

"Waiting's not your strong suit," Nick said. "I'm going to do another case of the beach, just see if there's anything unusual. I'll take the board. That all right?"

"Yeah great, thanks," Mitch said.

"I'll go with you," Ellen said, "and do some sight-seeing from the lighthouse. Just to see if there's any-thing unusual. OK boss?"

"Sure," Mitch said. "I'll just wait here for John's call ... great ..." He looked outside at the beach.

Nick hit him on the back on the way out. "Rest the leg, and arm, and head, hey?"

"Yeah." Mitch watched them depart. He hobbled to the counter, grabbed pen and paper and re-turning to the couch, gingerly sat down. He began to map out the questions that remained unanswered:

The VP was a student in Beijing in his younger years; he has now gone to the other side, why? Has a contact from that time facilitated this?

What would make him betray his country?

Who are these men who have come in to extract him?

How and when did they swap places with the four officers that were guests of the government for training?

How were they going to explain the absence of the four officers when those men never returned home?

Mitch sat back, thought for a while and then resumed writing.

What becomes of the VP when he arrives in China? What is his role there?

What secrets has he given away and can we get them back?

If we don't destroy the mission, can we get the VP back once he leaves US waters?

What are the extradition laws in the People's Republic of China?

Mitch picked up his phone and did a quick search on extradition laws. He speed-read and summarized them out loud: "Granted only when it meets a pile of conditions ... conduct indicated constitutes an offence according to the laws of both the People's Republic of China and the requesting state, hmm; the offence is punishable by a fixed term of imprisonment for one year or more or by any other heavier criminal penalty—yep, that's a given."

He read on ... "The request for extradition will be denied if it is made for a political offence, or the People's Republic of China has granted asylum to the person sought ..." Mitch stopped searching and returned to his notes.

So who are these men and is anyone else in their sights?

Mitch's phone rang and Dylan Ting's name flashed across the screen.

"Dylan?" Mitch answered.

"Mitch, Ru's on the phone, so just quickly ... the lift out of Cape Hatteras is confirmed for four a.m. tomorrow. We are to head to the VIP house now too. They've asked me again would I like to take part in something, this time they've called it something historic."

"And you said?"

"I said of course, my life is meaningless," Dylan laughed. "So they're taking me along. They've agreed I could be helpful and I guess if I'm not ..."

"But you're not being extradited in the morning too, are you?" Mitch asked.

"I don't know," Dylan said. "Do you think I should try and bide my time, tell them I've got to clean up my life before I go or something?"

"No, just go with the flow. Agree to everything and anything and do what is needed." Mitch thought about the possible plans to destroy the midget sub underwater and along with it, Dylan Ting if he was taken on board, which he couldn't let happen.

"I'll know more when I get a brief from John shortly," Mitch said.

"I'll try and call you again later."

"Dylan, there's some answers I need you to find, but do them in a way that you don't raise suspicion," Mitch said. "Ru might be green enough to spill the beans." He ran through some of the key questions on his pad. "You won't get all the information and you don't want to look like you're prodding, but if the opportunity arises to steer the conversation ... I need to know more about these men you are aligned with. I need to know what the repercussions are for the US and for the G20 in Beijing."

"I'll see what I can get," Dylan said.

"Be careful."

"I will." Dylan hung up.

Mitch called John. The call went to message bank.

"John, we've got confirmation from Dylan on the inside that the lift will happen at four a.m. tomorrow. All of their team is to be present. You understand that means all agents ..." Mitch hung up. He took a deep breath and dialed Samantha's number.

"Samantha Clarke ... Mitch," she answered.

"Sam, listen, there's a couple of things I need

you to do. Dylan sent me a text with the address of where a container is being stored. I'm sending the text on to you. The container is due to be dropped somewhere in the ocean next week ... I don't want word getting back that we've confiscated the container, but find a way to get it relocated somewhere safe and dry, and cancel the drop. Don't open it under any circumstances—the contents are highly confidential. Just store it safely and let me know where I can find it."

"Got it," she said.

"Don't open it under any circumstances, Sam," Mitch reiterated.

"I understand," she confirmed.

"Then I want you to do some background research on the Vice President. You must be covert, do you understand?"

"Yes," she answered.

"He was a student in Beijing in his younger years; find out where, who he stayed with, any connections he made or clubs he has retained membership of, any friends he may have from then ... anything. Report only to me or John if he asks. Understood?"

"I'm onto it."

Mitch hung up before Samantha had a chance to say anything more.

40

JOHN WINDSOR ENTERED HIS OFFICE AND CLOSED THE door. He dialed Mitchell Parker's number.

Mitch answered on the first ring.

"What's the latest with you?" John asked.

Mitch filled him in on the research Samantha was working on and the questions Dylan was going to try and work into conversation with Ru.

"Great, let's hope something comes of it."

"John, what's the plan?" Mitch asked.

"They'll proceed with your first option, it's really the only option," John said.

Mitch inhaled. "Tell me they are not going to blow it with Dylan possibly on board?"

John stared out of his office window to the street below. "These are your orders ..."

Mitch left the apartment and limped out to the beachfront. He had to think; there had to be a better way, there had to be a way to get Dylan Ting out of this. He rang Dylan again.

"Can you talk?" Mitch asked.

"No problem, Ru is on the phone again, he's been on and off to Beijing and the VIP house most of the day," Dylan said. "I haven't had a chance to get any info, but I'll try when we're doing the six hour drive together to Cape Hatteras. We're about to leave."

"Right," Mitch said. "You won't be getting in until very late then."

Both men were silent on the line.

"They've said I'm dispensable, haven't they?" Dylan said. "My government thinks my death is a fair trade for cleaning up the whole exercise. I guess that's how the Chinese would think too, it's just that we, I, always believed ..."

"Hold up, Dylan," Mitch said, "you're not dispensable, the government is not sacrificing you and I'm not either. I just need to manage you out of there. That's my job. Do you know any more about the plan for tomorrow?"

"No, just that we'll all be on hand and that I'm to assist Hai as directed."

"Have you been told if you will be going with the VIP or extradited some other way?" Mitch asked.

"They haven't said but Ru's not going with the VIP so I doubt I will either," Dylan said. "How are you going to close it down, Mitch? What if I'm in the way?"

"Dylan, calm down, we're in hypothetical mode here. I can pull you now and you can look like you've run scared, except they'll probably shut the mission down and assume you're a spy. So let's just work out an extraction strategy based on what we both know."

"I don't know anything yet, except ..."

Mitch stopped him. "Tell me exactly what Hai and Ru said to you."

"OK, Hai said that we had to leave ASAP because we all had to be there tonight for a full briefing and extraction tomorrow morning," Dylan said. "Ru said he would explain what the extraction meant at the briefing. We're leaving in under an hour."

"Right. Now listen up, I will get you out, but play cool and carry on until I come back to you. Continue doing the research I asked for. If for some reason you can't communicate with me or I can't reach you, we'll be there tomorrow morning watching. I will extract you Dylan, so stay focused on the job and gather as much intelligence as you can. Do you understand?" Mitch asked.

"Yes, sir," Dylan answered.

"I'll come back to you in a matter of hours. Keep your ear to the ground." Mitch hung up and shook his head.

"For crying out loud, if they're not disobeying orders, they're wet behind the ears and freaking out," he muttered. His phone rang again and Nick's name came up.

"We're back in the room, where are you?" Nick asked.

"On the beach." Mitch turned back to see the silhouette of Nick in the window. "I'll be back soon."

"You all right?" Nick asked.

"Well I'd like to have a run to help me think, but I'm having a limp instead," he said.

"No crutches, well done. Has John come back to you?" Nick asked.

"He has," Mitch answered.

"And you're not happy, that's why you're there. If it cheers you up, Ellen is cooking. Come back and we'll talk it through," Nick said.

"See you shortly." Mitch hung up. He limped to the rails around the parking lot. He sat on the timber log rail and watched the ocean, thinking through how his plan could dovetail with the orders from the top.

———

"Ha, I've rarely heard Mitch taking orders. Does he always do what you tell him?" Ellen asked from the kitchen.

"I am the eldest," Nick shrugged. "It's how we've always done it."

"He's the boss."

"I step up when he needs direction, he gives orders when we're on the job, except earlier today when I might have overstepped the mark and said he should have sent me to the VIP house and not you," Nick said.

"What?" Ellen stopped to look at him. "I bet I could out-stakeout you any day."

"Yeah, that's what he said."

Ellen looked pleased. She poured cake mixture into a tin. In the oven, a chicken was roasting.

"See, here he comes now, doing what he's told." Nick watched Mitch coming up the stairs to the apartment with a pronounced limp. "Sometimes it's good to just follow a direction, to not deal with everything. It's easier."

"I guess so. Want to lick the spoon?" Ellen asked.

"Do I look like I'm eight?" Nick asked reaching for the spoon before she had a chance to rinse it. He went to the door and opened it.

"Ha, you really are cooking!" Mitch exclaimed as

he entered the apartment and saw Ellen at work in the kitchen area.

"I picked some stuff up. I thought we could use some real sustenance before tomorrow plays out. Besides, I either cook or clean when I'm anxious." Ellen began to wash up.

"The perfect woman." Nick threw the licked-clean spoon in the sink. He flicked the kettle on and reached for three mugs. "Mitch, tell us."

Mitch sat down on a stool at the bench and sighed.

"OK, let's refer to the VP as the VIP for security reasons in all further discussions. This is what I know at the moment," he started. "I have a container sitting in a warehouse which I think has four bodies in it. The men in there have been replaced by a group from the New Red Guard."

"Communists, socialists or capitalists?" Ellen's eyes widened.

"They read like capitalist with a socialist bent if that could co-exist," Mitch continued. "The fake policemen as we know them are coming to the VIP house tonight and according to Dylan, the VIP and two of them, namely Froggy and Hai, will be extracted tomorrow morning at four. Ru and William will go back later that day with the false passports and Danny was meant to go with him. Dylan's been accepted into the party but is running scared." Mitch stopped. "With me so far?"

"Yep, carry on," Nick said. Ellen nodded.

"John's orders are for us to man the beach and lighthouse tomorrow, observe and confirm on location that all parties including the VIP are present, once we have a sighting. The SWAT team along with USERT—the underwater team—will take it from there and the ship will be destroyed in US waters. There will no information on this. The remnants will be removed there and then. The flippers, snorkel and towel that they leave on the beach or to be washed up on the beach are to remain there. Our media team will support and promote the message that the VIP was catching up with an old friend and has gone missing during an early morning swim. This won't happen until all debris is cleared, estimated time eight a.m., possibly earlier."

"Holy crap, the place will be swarming with press after that," Nick said. "So wipe out the VIP, wipe out all evidence?"

"Except for the fake police agents who remain," Ellen remind him.

"Exactly. That's where we step in. We are to capture and close down any action and agents remaining on the beach after we get the signal that the water removal has succeeded—namely William Ying, and Ru should he arrive at the beach or Hai or Froggy if they don't go with the VIP. We'll arrest Dylan Ting as well so it looks authentic and release him out of sight of William and Ru. A back-up team will do the same at the VIP house and we're to drop our cargo there, so to speak. Then we leave as soon as we have the all-clear from John who will get clearance from the other teams. But we're still no wiser as to what intel has left the US and already been delivered to China and taking out the VIP won't help in that respect."

"But we might get this information from the agents we take off the beach and from the VIP house," Ellen said.

"Maybe," Mitch agreed.

"So SWAT and USERT are arriving here tonight?" Nick asked.

"Yep, not that we'll see them if they do their job properly."

Nick said, "What about Dylan? What happens if he becomes peripheral damage ... you know, they insist he stays in the water?"

"Yeah, that's what I'm trying to work out. How do I extract him?" Mitch said. "If he stays with Ru to man the communications at the VIP house then we've got no problems. Even if he goes to the beach and stays on land, it's easier for us to extract him. We arrest him with William and fix it afterwards. If he's told to go in the sub or even in the water to help out, I'm in trouble."

"Our team know about Dylan?" Ellen asked, pointing upwards to indicate the powers above.

"Yeah, they know," Mitch said, "but they've left it to me to extract him or lose him."

"Makes you feel so valued doesn't it?" Nick said.

"I will extract him," Mitch said.

"We'll extract him," Nick said.

"But what are the odds he'll go on the sub? It is a midget," Ellen reminded them.

"Low odds I'm guessing, but we have to be prepared," Mitch said. "He'll be eliminated even if he is only immersed in the water."

"Let's look at our options. If he has to board the sub, what if when they are all just about below sea level, we open fire, shoot him in a fake shooting, he drops and we clean the rest up underwater," Nick suggested.

"OK." Mitch thought it through. "I guess we will be arresting the ones left on shore anyway ... but could they radio ahead to abort, reporting that they've been attacked? Plus we've got dead on the beach in a public space and there's bound to be a boatie, surfer or someone with a metal detector who sees it all and then reports the incident. But hey, it's only our first idea. What else?" Mitch looked out the window while he thought.

They thought in silence; accompanied by the sounds of Ellen cooking, the waves crashing and the clock ticking.

"I have an idea but we would only put it in place if it looks like Dylan is going into the water or heading to the sub," Ellen said. "What is one thing that most men are not threatened by?"

"A woman?" Nick answered.

"Exactly." Ellen glanced to the clock. "But it would involve getting Sam down here, and she'd need to hit the road now."

41

Dylan Ting rang from a gas station near Williamsburg on the way to Cape Hatteras.

"Can't talk for long," he whispered to Mitch. "We're about three hours away. Ru has given me a brief on the mission, can you believe what they're doing?" Dylan asked but didn't wait for a response. "I've enthusiastically added my support to it—like I had any option, he'd have to kill me otherwise I imagine. Anyway, he told me I'm to go out with Froggy to help in case the VIP panics. So I'm guessing that I'll be sent back to shore once the VIP is gone, but if he panics I don't know what that means for me. If you guys are going to be there closing that down, will I get caught in the crossfire?"

"There will be no firing if it goes to plan. Dylan, here's what we are going to do." Mitch explained the plan. "Just follow your part and ignore all other distractions, alright?"

"Got it. What if ..." Dylan continued.

"Just do your part," Mitch shut him down, "we'll have your covered. Remember, you want to be one of them, you want to be on their team and you are ready to make something of your life."

"Right," Dylan whispered.

"Has he told you who the VIP is?" Mitch asked.

"No, he said that would be a wonderful surprise tonight. I pretended not to know of course," Dylan said. "He'd die if he knew I was taking photos of the VIP leaving with William this morning."

"Be careful with your aliases, it can be hard to remember who knows what," Mitch said.

"Mitch, I found out something ... I overhead it."

"What?" Mitch asked.

"The four policemen ... I found out how they got rid of them," Dylan said. "The four men shared a ride to the airport, but the car that was sent for them didn't drop them to the front of the airport, it took them around the back. They were killed, packaged and put in the luggage hold and flown into the States. They were collected later and put in that container storage that's going to be dumped at sea next week."

"And Danny Huang and his team took their

places and checked in, while the police officers were below, dead in cargo," Mitch said.

"Yes," Dylan confirmed. "I've got to go."

"Dylan, will you be all right?" Mitch asked. "Because tell me right now if you can't do this and I'll pull you."

"Yeah, of course I can do it, I'm good. I've got to go, but thanks Mitch, for—you know ..." Dylan said.

"See you tomorrow after the lift." Mitch hung up.

He looked at Nick and Ellen. "He's freaked out."

"It's risky," Ellen said, "and this is way out of his league."

"Everyone has a first mission," Mitch said, "but yeah, his first one is pretty full on."

———

Dylan Ting sat in the passenger seat as Ru drove the hired sedan to Cape Hatteras. They spoke comfortably in Mandarin.

"Last time I drove down this way with Danny, he didn't say one word the whole six hours," Ru said.

Dylan laughed. "Good grief. I like my own thinking time, but that's extreme."

"Yeah. The first hour was tough and then I just fell into it. It's kind of a test with Danny—everything is. If I had spoken he would have seen it as disobedience or a sign of weakness."

"He seems so composed," Dylan agreed.

"You never really know what's going on in his head," Ru agreed. "So, no last minute regrets about wanting to join us?"

"No way, it's a rush."

"You wait until you meet the VIP, you won't believe it," Ru said.

"Yeah?" Dylan kept up the pretence. "I'm feeling kind of proud about being involved. I guess that sounds corny. But members of my family were radicals against the status quo in their day. I reckon my grandparents are looking down feeling pretty proud about now too." Dylan looked to Ru. "My life has been nothing but indulgent. I work to earn, I earn and buy, I want more. Then what?"

"You could have a family," Ru said.

Dylan shrugged. "Sure, and then a mortgage and school fees and live the great American dream. But what am I giving back? How am I changing the world? I'm just adding to it. This, your team, it is the only time I have felt motivated. I feel like I've found a purpose. Does that sound lame?"

"Not at all," Ru said with sincerity. "My family is proud of me for standing up and acting on my beliefs."

"They know?" Dylan asked.

"Of course. My father inspired me to be involved. We are a great nation, we are not just here to produce cheap goods for the Western world. Our history, our ..." Ru stopped. "Sorry, I get a bit carried away."

"I get it! It's great to actually feel passionate about something, to feel anything really," Dylan agreed, pleased that he had the chance to reinforce his commitment.

They drove for a while in silence.

"It's pretty, this part of your world," Ru said.

Dylan looked around. "Yeah, when I was a kid we came down this way a couple of times for holidays. It's packed in summer. So what did you do for holidays when you were a kid?"

Ru grinned. "I worked. Dad and Mom own a stall in the markets so I was the runner. But it's the festivals that are the best when you're a kid at home."

"Like Thanksgiving?" Dylan asked.

"Sort of." Ru merged onto the Interstate 64 West and followed the sign. "My favorite was the Lantern Festival. We'd all go out with lanterns and there was no curfew. It's a night for match-making and I had a girl in mind."

"Oh yeah?" Dylan turned to the handsome young Asian man, who looked like he was fresh from school. "Are you still with her?"

"We're engaged," Ru said. "Her name is Lan, which means orchid. She's a teacher now."

"So did you propose on lantern night?" Dylan asked.

"I proposed a lot of times, but I had to talk with her parents and my parents and arrange it and get permission. The Lantern Festival is all about finding love."

"Well congratulations. If Lan means orchid, what does the name Ru mean?" Dylan asked.

"Ru? It means scholar, more or less," Ru said. "What's Dylan mean?"

"Nothing. Mom just liked it."

The two men laughed. Dylan Ting glanced at Ru, knowing that the young man would probably never see his fiancée again—or else he'd be an old man when he did, and her life would have gone by without him.

42

JUST AFTER TEN P.M. THAT NIGHT SAMANTHA arrived. Ellen opened the door of the apartment unit and Nick rose to help her with her bag. Samantha greeted Mitch. The tension in the room was palpable. After she settled into the shared room with Ellen, Mitch called them together.

"Let's go through the plan," he said. The group settled on the two couches.

Mitch started. "At two a.m. we will take our positions. The back-up team will be at the VIP house, the SWAT and USERT teams will be ready but we won't see them, in theory. Nick and I will be in the parking lot or beach area, Ellie and Sam, you will be here, waiting for your cue. Everyone is to have their trackers on, their phone on silent, their headpiece on. I'll keep you all, and John, posted on anything I see. Nick will do the same. John will keep me posted on SWAT and USERT's movements. I expect the VIP lift team to arrive between three-thirty and four a.m."

"Who will be on the water?" Ellen asked.

"USERT will have it covered, plus there will be a SWAT contingency at the VIP house and on the beach with us," Mitch said. "And I don't want you guys anywhere near the waterfront. Our role is support and secure only. Nick, what's the light going to be like?"

"It's a waning crescent tonight, sunrise is at seven tomorrow, so we are working in the dark pretty much," Nick said.

"That's not a bad thing," Mitch said. "I'm surmising that Ru will stay at the VIP house to man the communications. Which means we have Dylan, the VIP, William, Hai and Froggy all with us on the shoreline until the moment of impact. Dylan and William are on our side, supposedly."

Ellen nodded. "Which leaves us only William to secure once the underwater mission disappears."

"And Dylan, assuming they send him back to shore or Ru if he appears but that's unlikely," Nick added.

"Yes and during this exercise I expect one of them to place the towel on the beach and swim out a bit, drop the snorkel and flippers and let the tide take them," Mitch said. "If we need to extract Dylan in case he is ordered not to return to shore, then Ellie and Sam this is where you two step in but if—and only if—you get the signal from me to do it." Mitch looked at Ellen and Samantha.

Both women nodded. Mitch continued.

"As soon as we see them nearing the waterline, we'll read the status of the VIP. If he is panicky and needs assistance, we'll know we have to act to extract Dylan or he may be required in the water. I'll signal you Ellie, and you and Sam will need to move fast to get to the beach. Once at the beach, out of sight, you two will wait until I tell you to go; I'm going to wait until Hai, the VIP and Froggy are half immersed in the water, so it is too late for them to turn back. I've told Dylan to fall behind as much as he can. The SWAT team will take care of the VIP, Hai and Froggy or anyone who enters the water, and we are to do nothing in that regard."

The girls nodded.

"Then I'll give you the go ahead, and with your shoes in your hands, I want an Academy Award performance of two intoxicated party girls who want to go for a swim," Mitch said. "If it goes to plan, Dylan will be the 'hero' who comes to distract you away from the beach area and they will have to leave without him. Understand?"

"Got it," Ellen said. "And if we're seen by anyone

other than our team, we will have to give false names and witness statements to the police saying that we were on the beach in the early hours when the VIP disappeared, but saw nothing because we were drunk but wanted a swim."

"Exactly. So Dylan will see you, he'll tell the men to keep going and that he will get rid of you both. Dylan will rush up the beach and steer you away with his charm. John will advise when we have the all-clear to leave the scene. We'll take William to the VIP house and hand him over there. Then we'll be in the car and out of the area by seven a.m., all going well. The media unit will start to leak the missing VIP story around eight a.m. Any questions?"

"Nope, got it," Nick said.

Ellen and Samantha confirmed their under-standing.

"Sam." Mitch turned to her. "Tell me your orders."

Samantha reddened and ran through what her role was in the morning.

"What will you do if Dylan pulls a gun?" Mitch asked.

"I will continue to act like a drunken party girl wanting a swim and follow Ellen's lead," Samantha said.

"Or if Dylan gets shot?"

"I will ignore it and stay in character and follow Ellen's lead ... head back to the room."

"If a meteorite falls from the sky?" Mitch asks.

Samantha smiled. "Got it."

"Good," Mitch turned away. "If Dylan does not enter the water and stays on the beach, we'll arrest him along with William—and Ru if he is there—to keep up the pretense. Let's run through scenarios," Mitch said. "One or two of the party might play renegade, shoot all the party and flee with the VIP. In which case, we step in remembering Dylan is not armed and I will call in the squad at the VIP house for back-up. Ellie, Sam, I will give you that order."

"Got it," Ellen said. "Or they might drown the VIP, let his body float and they all depart by sub, keeping any intel he's given them."

"True," Mitch said. "In which case, they'll still be destroyed and we'll arrest and clean up anything or anyone left behind on the beach."

"Do we interfere if they start to drown the VIP?" Nick asked.

"Not unless we're ordered to. So not matter what you see or what happens, don't stray from the plan unless we get instructions."

"What happens if they abort?" Ellen asked.

"We maintain our beach watch, the underwater team is called off and the VIP house squad maintain their watch," Mitch said.

"What about the missing police officers?" Ellen asked.

"Good question. I know where they are. I'm just waiting for the report from the legat in Beijing to tell me if their families know they're missing or dead. How we manage that will depend on intel we get after the lift."

"There's going to be conspiracy theories galore about the missing Vice President," Samantha said.

"VIP," Mitch reminded her. "And you bet. He'll be like Elvis. Spotted everywhere for the next twenty years. Anything else?" He looked around his team. "OK, that's it for now." Mitch looked at his phone and contacts, his finger hovering over Dylan Ting's number. *What's going on Dylan?*

"In Beijing, they'll know from their SONAR there's no sub coming." Nick interrupted his thoughts.

"They will if it is an Asian sub and not one of ours," Mitch said.

43

MITCH SHIVERED. HIS BURNS SWEATED, AND HIS BODY ran cold. He slid down low in his car seat, took a sip of water and called Nick.

"Nothing happening here," Nick said from further along the beach out of sight. "But I guess at three in the morning, you'd expect that."

"Mm," Mitch agreed looking around the dark parking lot and beach entrance from his car window.

"Don't fall asleep in the comfort of your car there," Nick said.

Mitch chuckled. "Yeah, boo hoo. You know I would have taken the beach if I could've got there and back quickly."

"Sure you would have," Nick ribbed him. "Worried about Sam?"

"All the time," Mitch answered. "Call coming in, gotta go."

Mitch hung up and answered.

"John?"

"Something strange is going on," John said. "The VIP house is empty."

"What?"

"Our team has just arrived there, got no readings and scoped the house and the perimeters. No sign of life at all," John said.

"What about in the building on the block out the back, the water reserve where I was held?" Mitch asked.

"Nothing."

"It's soundproof. Are you sure they're getting accurate readings?"

"Positive, it's empty, nothing happening at all. Our underwater team also reports there is absolutely nothing in the water, nothing on SONAR. Nothing even within a twenty-five mile radius."

"Remember the 'Song'. We were only just talking about it," Mitch said. "It quietly surfaced within nine miles of the aircraft carrier USS Kitty Hawk ... could we have something similar happening here?"

"It's always a possibility," John said. "Just hold position for now and let me know if anyone arrives at the beach. I'll come back to you in a minute."

Mitch drummed his fingers on the car wheel. He waited.

He rang Ellen. "Hey there, think this through with me," he said when she answered.

"Sure, what's happening?" Ellen asked.

"There's no sign of the sub, it's about an hour from mission time and our team is withdrawing from the VIP house, there's no sign of life there."

"What?" Ellen asked in disbelief. "Nothing in the tank reserve?"

"Nothing. The VIP and crew have moved out, but to where? I need to get out to the VIP house to see those monitors and to see if Dylan has left us a sign of any sort."

"OK, I'll come and take your post. Samantha can be the solo drunk girl."

Mitch hung up and called John.

"I'm going to the VIP house. Dylan might have left me a sign which the team wouldn't understand. Ellen will take my post," he told John.

"I'll let our people know you're coming. No call from Dylan?" John asked.

"Not a word."

"Any idea where they might have moved to before the lift?" John asked.

"No. The VIP might have got cold feet, the lift could be a smokescreen, they might have known we were onto them ... any number of scenarios but as of last night, it was all still on."

"I wonder if William Ying squealed," John contributed. "Let me know when you get to the house and I'll come back to you ASAP with any updates."

Mitch hung up, swung his car out of the parking lot and started up the road. He rang Nick.

"Nick, Ellen's taking my place, she'll be arriving in the hire car in a minute. Just keep an eye on my area until she arrives. It's up to you now to give the signal for Sam if needed," he said.

"Sure, what's happened?" Nick asked.

Mitch filled him in.

"I don't mean to state the obvious, but do you really think you should go back to that house? Why don't you hobble up here and we'll swap places?" Nick suggested.

"Geez, if I didn't go back to every place where there's been an incident, I'd have nowhere to go," Mitch said.

"What are you going to do?" Nick asked.

"Cruise in, lights off, walk through the scrub to the house, see if I can see anything, see if the crack team missed anything, go into the communications room and see if Dylan has left me a sign. That OK, boss?" Mitch asked.

"All right, but check in regularly," Nick stirred him.

"Yes, sir," Mitch hung up and shook his head.

He drove out of town, and turned off on the road that turned in to the VIP's house. Mitch cut the lights and drove into Maple Lane and parked the car out of sight. He knew the road and path to the house well enough to manage in the dark. He left the car and hobbled through the underbrush to begin the walk towards where he knew the VIP house was located. In the dark it seemed that much longer. He tripped and hit the ground hard.

Crap. His phone began to vibrate. He pulled it out and answered.

"Mitch, where are you now?" John asked.

"On the ground at the moment. I'm heading to the VIP house on foot. Ellie's in my place. Anything?"

"Nothing," John said.

Mitch hung up on John as a call from Dylan Ting came through.

"Dylan?" he whispered.

Dylan didn't answer. Mitch waited. He was hearing a conversation. Dylan Ting had called him and left the phone line open. Several voices were speaking hurriedly in Mandarin. Mitch listened, unable to make out anything but panic. Then he heard repeated several times words that sounded like "she-jong-she, she-jong-she." The line went dead.

Mitch rang John back.

"What happened? Are you all right?" John asked.

"Yeah sorry, Dylan called, can you get this translated? She-jong-she." He waited, listening as John picked up his landline and rang for a translation. He heard John hang up the landline phone.

"Shǐ-zhōngzhǐ." John spelled it out for Mitch. "Abort mission," John said. "That's the translation, abort mission. I'll manage this from my end. Where the hell are they?"

"I don't know, but I'm heading in now, I'll call Ellen." Mitch hung up.

Ellen answered. "Not a thing here," she said.

"They've aborted the mission, Dylan just rang. Ellie, follow me out here, come armed, leave your car behind mine at Maple Lane and take the scrub, they may return here. Tell Nick to stay there and call if he sees anything. Get Sam to stand by and watch the beach from the room." Mitch hung up.

———

Ellen spun the car out to the main road. She drove with her foot to the floor and called Nick on hands-free.

"He shouldn't be back there," Nick said. "I'll pass on the message to Sam, you just get there."

"Will do," she said, and hung up.

Ellen killed the lights as she found the turn off. She spotted Mitch's car around the curve in Maple Lane, out of sight from the main road, and pulled her car in behind his. She took to the bush, knowing he had a good ten minute lead on her.

———

Mitch squatted, the house in sight. No lights were on, so they were likely to be in the basement room, he thought. The white Camry was in the garage. His phone rang and Nick's name flashed on the screen.

"Nick?"

"Mitch, a car has just pulled up at the beach, and the VIP has got out along with William Ying. At least I think it's William in this light."

"Just the two of them?"

"Yep," Nick confirmed.

"What are they doing now?" Mitch asked.

"They're walking to the water's edge."

Mitch hung up and called John.

"No problem," John said calmly, "we still have the team at the beach on standby. Leave it with me."

Mitch called Nick back.

"Sam confirmed it is William Ying," Nick said, "but there's only the two of them—the VIP and William."

"John's confirmed we still have the teams underwater and on the beach, and he's alerting them. So don't move Nick, understand?"

"Yes," Nick said. "OK, they're at the water's edge."

"Stay put Nick, do you hear me?" Mitch ordered.

"Understood," Nick said.

Mitch jumped at the sound of gunshots in the house.

"Was that ..." Nick asked.

"Shit yes, but who's the shooter? No one's supposed to be here," Mitch said. "What are they doing now on the beach?" he asked as he sidled up the side of the house.

"They're both standing at the water's edge," Nick said. "They've dumped a towel, snorkel and mask on the sand. They must still be going ahead with it, but where are the others? Is Ellie there yet?"

Mitch turned and could see her approaching low through the shrubbery.

"Just arrived," he reported as she sidled up to him. "We're going in."

44

NICK MOVED TO POSITION HIMSELF TO SEE THE TWO men on the beach. William and the VIP were still at the water's edge. Nick saw Samantha coming across the road on foot. He motioned for her to go behind him and saw her slip into the shadows. He returned his gaze to the ocean.

The men were standing in knee-deep water now. They were looking to sea, waiting for a signal. The VIP dropped the snorkel and mask in the shallow water.

Waiting for a diver to emerge probably, Nick thought.

The men began to wade out further—Nick saw the black figure rising; a diver.

There's or ours?

The VIP moved towards the diver, William followed. Suddenly the VIP vanished, disappeared underwater. William looked around confused. The VIP surfaced and Nick could see the diver pulling the VIP down. The diver gripped the back of the VIP's head and with two hands held him underwater. The VIP thrashed wildly.

Nick froze, shocked. He couldn't act but he couldn't turn away.

A second diver emerged and William Ying turned. He was swimming through the water as fast as he could. He hit shallow water and began running towards the shore. Two men moved out of the shadows near Nick. He pulled back further trying to stay out of sight. As they got closer down the beach, one of them pulled a gun and shot William—a single bullet wound to the head. The only sound was the clean noise of a silencer. William Ying slumped into the water.

The VIP's body floated on the surface of the water. The diver dragged him to shore as the second diver collected William's body in the shallow waters. On the shore, the remaining two men removed body bags from a backpack and William Ying and the VIP were bundled into them. In moments, they were removed from the beach and the scene cleared.

One man stayed behind, picked up the snorkel and mask which had washed back in, waded out a distance and threw them out to sea. Nick and

Samantha watched as the man then came ashore, returned to the car and the dark SUV drove away.

Nick's phone rang and he saw John's ID come up.

"You can stand down from the beach," John confirmed.

"Those four men ..."

"They were ours," John confirmed. "Nick, back Mitch up at the house and secure it, send Sam back to clear the accommodation, then get on the road and well-clear of the area ASAP."

"Got it." Nick hung up and turned to leave. He motioned for Sam to follow him. He glanced back over the beach. It looked as though nothing had ever happened.

———

Mitch saw John's number come up on the screen.

"I'm about to go in," Mitch said.

"The beach has been cleared, William Ying and the VIP are dead and removed."

"Any sub?" Mitch asked.

"Nothing, looks like their abort mission order worked. But why call it off?" John asked.

"Why the hell would our team kill William Ying? There goes a good source of intel." Mitch ran his hand over his face. "Ellie and I are moving in. I better call Nick."

"It's taken care of it. Nick's on his way to back you up, Sam's clearing the rooms and you all need to be out of the area by 0800 hours before the media arrives."

"I've just heard several shots," Mitch whispered to him. "I'm only expecting to find the shooter alive."

John let out a low whistle. "That area is supposed to be clear. Do you want more back-up?"

"No, but I suspect it was clear when the SWAT team was here earlier. I don't know where Dylan was calling from. Got to go."

Mitch tuned to Ellen. "Ready?"

She drew her weapon and nodded.

Rising, Mitch led the way. He moved around the front of the VIP house and tried the door, which opened. With gun raised he scanned the room; it was empty. They scoped the house ... completely empty.

Mitch and Ellen moved outside to the next allotment, to the tank. They ascended the metal rail to the top; the trapdoor leading inside was gone after Nick blew it up. Mitch moved in with Ellen close behind; a small amount of light spilled out and allowed Mitch to scope the rooms. Mitch glanced down the stairs towards the basement entrance. He shivered and a wave of nausea passed over him. He inhaled. Ellen came beside him and touched his arm. He instinctively shook her off.

Crouching low, he glanced down the stairs. He indicated that she should watch the door, and he dropped to the floor. He could see the entrance to the two tiled rooms and down the hallway, the shadowed entrance to the room where he was taken. In the first tiled room, he could see a man sitting with his back to Mitch typing away at a laptop. Wearing a large jacket and knitted cap, Mitch couldn't make out who it was. He looked for a gun. It wasn't on the man's hip or on the console.

Mitch pulled back and motioned to Ellen. They moved back out and down the rail into the yard.

"We've heard gunshots so we know he's armed. I can't see the gun, but clearly he's got one."

Ellen agreed. "We can storm him, smoke him out or creep up on him."

"We don't know that he's alone and I want him alive. I think we should smoke him out and anyone else in there."

Mitch saw someone moving towards them in his peripheral vision. He pulled Ellen behind him, pulled his gun and whirled to find Nick with his hands raised.

"Can you wave next time?" Mitch rolled his eyes and holstered his gun.

"I'll come up with a unique bird whistle," Nick smirked.

"Sam all right?" Mitch asked.

"Yeah, she's clearing the rooms so we can get out of here."

Mitch nodded towards the house. "With William Ying and the VIP accounted for, we've got one in the basement here, and two missing plus Dylan. We heard a number of shots and I want to take the one downstairs alive. Now that there's three of us, let's storm him. Ellie, you take the rear in case he has support."

Mitch turned to go back in without waiting for consensus. He silently went to the basement door and squatted, waiting for Nick and Ellen to file in behind him. Looking in, he saw the chair was now empty. Mitch saw an adjoining door was half-closed. It was open before but he knew the room it led to only too well. He saw a shadow under the staircase directly below him. He turned to Nick and Ellen and indicated below him. They nodded.

In a split second Mitch dropped from the top step to the side of the stairs, gun braced as Nick and Ellen stormed down the stairs. He winced with the pain of landing on his leg. No one was there but a small steel door was closed under the stairs.

"He's gone through there," Mitch indicated the door.

Nick tugged at the door. "No go, locked on the inside."

They heard a car start and Nick and Ellen raced up the stairs as a car sped away.

Mitch hurried to the monitor room to watch the screen with the external feed; the car moved too fast —there was no way to identify the driver or if anyone else was in the car. He rifled through papers that were on the desk. There was nothing written in English and no obvious signs or alerts from Dylan on the desk or around the room.

Mitch heard a strange sound; a bird noise and looked out as the steel door under the stairs opened slowly.

Mitch returned to the stairs as Nick emerged making another bird noise.

Mitch laughed. "You're an idiot."

"It's the birdcall of the common loon," Nick grinned.

"You got that right."

"You told me to give you a signal so you didn't accidentally fire!" Nick said. "Want us to chase?"

"No, he's already got too big a lead on us. We know where that door leads now," Mitch glanced at the steel door under the stairs, "a tunnel to the garage."

Ellen emerged from the tunnel with two black leather folders.

"I found a secret stash," she said.

"Hold that thought," Mitch ordered. "We need to clear the premises. Ellie can you call the getaway car through to John for me? Let him know it was the white Camry, Asian driver, not sure if any other passengers. Nick, let's check the rooms."

Mitch and Nick split away, casing the first room. Mitch moved down the hall and pushed open the half-closed door; he entered the room that he knew too well. He felt his heart rate increase and mentally worked to get past the fear. Breathe, he told himself, focus, breathe. He reeled back. In one corner lay three bodies.

"John's onto it," he heard Ellen say as she appeared at the entrance to the room and stood beside him, observing the scene.

"Ellie, swap places with Nick."

"It's OK," she said, "I'm OK to see this."

He looked at her. His face was pale, with sweat on his forehead. He wiped his sleeve across his face.

"I know that," he said and grabbed Ellen's arm. "Just get Nick," he said.

Ellen nodded. She raced to the door and disappeared. Mitch moved towards the dead men. Nick appeared moments after.

"Sit." He pushed Mitch into sitting position on the floor and squatted next to him. "Take a deep breath."

"I'm OK, I just need a minute," Mitch panted.

"Take two," Nick said. "It's not every day you get to revisit the scene of your own crime."

Mitch nodded. "It's nothing."

"It's me," Nick said in a low voice. "Shut up for a minute and just breathe with me ... in: one-two-three, hold: one-two, out: one-two-three, in: one-two-three, hold ..."

Mitch followed suit.

"Better?" Nick asked after a couple of minutes.

Mitch nodded.

Nick rose and pulled Mitch up.

"Clear head?" Nick asked, continuing to hold his arm.

"Yeah, thanks." He broke away from Nick, took a deep breath and stood to full height.

They moved to the three bodies and pulled them off each other, laying them out on the floor.

"That's Hai and Froggy. No Dylan and no Ru," Mitch sighed with relief. "But who is this other guy?"

Nick shrugged. "A ring-in?

"Can you and Ellie scope the grounds?" Mitch asked reaching for his phone.

"Will you be OK?"

Mitch nodded, moving past Nick and out of the room into another area. He put in a call to John.

"Secure here. Three males down—Hai, Froggy

or his real name Fan Wen and the other is unknown to us. Dylan and Ru are missing. Ru may have been the shooter that just escaped but we couldn't identify him. Ellie and Nick are scoping the grounds."

"Right," John said. "No sub and no sighting of Dylan and Ru by the other teams. I'll send the squad back to the VIP house to remove the bodies."

"We'll stay until the clearing party arrives, just in case Ru or Dylan return," Mitch said.

Ellen and Nick re-entered the room. Ellen shook her head, "no one else around."

"Hang on John, Ellie and Nick are back and no sign of Dylan or Ru here," Mitch reported to John. "Any chance Dylan's turned his watch GPS on, if he's even wearing it?"

He waited while John made a call.

Nick moved into the room with the monitors and studied the screens. Ellen followed him in and gathered the paperwork left on the desk.

Mitch swore under his breath when John reported no tracer.

"Once the squad arrives, hit the road," John ordered. "We'll rethink the Dylan and Ru situation on your return."

"Understood." Mitch moved out of the room, past Ellen and Nick, up the stairs and into the back yard, drawing a deep breath and putting some distance between himself and the water reserve.

Ellen followed him out reading from the un-zipped leather folder.

"Hold up Mitch, you're not going to believe this."

Mitch sat down on the base of a sawn-off tree. Ellen stood next to him.

"Some of this is in English ... if I'm not mistaken this is a report to the Chinese Secret Intelligence Service," she looked up at him. "Guess who the agent is?"

SEARCH CONTINUES FOR MISSING VICE PRESIDENT
Associated press:
By Christopher Young

For a man who prided himself on staying fit, a quick morning swim turned into a national tragedy for Vice President Steven Turner.

Cancelling appointments the day before his disappearance, Vice President Turner told his personal assistant that he was catching up with an old friend at Cape Hatteras.

The next morning his towel was found on the beach, goggles and snorkel washed up nearby.

All searches have failed to find any sign of the Vice President. No witnesses saw him enter the water in the early hours of the morning.

As the weather is expected to worsen today, the search will continue for as long as possible, but so far there has been no trace of Vice President Turner who has now been missing for nearly 22 hours.

Seven Vice Presidents have died in office; the last was James S. Sherman in 1912.

NO SIGN OF MISSING VICE PRESIDENT AS CAPE HATTERAS SEA SEARCH ENDS

Associated press:

By Jamie Kendall

A helicopter has made a final sweep of the waters off Cape Hatteras without success, ending a three-day search for the missing Vice President, Steven Turner.

Vice President Turner failed to return from an early morning swim at Cape Hatteras beach on Friday morning.

He was in good health and a regular swimmer.

Mr. Turner told his personal assistant to cancel his appointments on Thursday, in order to allow him to visit friends staying in the Cape Hatteras region.

It is believed that he set out for a swim in the early hours of Friday morning, while still dark. Suspecting a shark attack, a surfboard rider raised the alarm shortly after seven a.m. when he found a snorkel and mask floating in the water and a towel abandoned on the beach.

In the three days of searching, no other items were recovered from the sea.

Superintendent Leo Barkley said the Vice President may have been taken by a shark but it is more likely he got into trouble swimming.

"Tides and currents kill more people at the beach than sharks," Barkley said.

The last fatal shark attack in the area was in 2001 which claimed the life of a 28-year-old man off Cape Hatteras.

Rescue boats stopped searching for the Vice President's body late Monday afternoon and the formal search was called off at the end of the day.

A private service will be held on Friday at a location determined by the Vice President's son.

The President's nominated representative, Heather Kingston, will succeed to the seat of Vice President after securing the majority vote of both Houses of Congress.

45

Mitch stood several times during the debriefing with John and his team; the injuries causing his muscles to spasm randomly after periods of sitting.

"I can't believe Ru," Mitch said, "all that time he's been with the Chinese Intelligence Service and I'm assuming Danny Huang and his team were oblivious. They've been played by the one person in charge of all their communications."

"I can't believe he is one of us, only the Chinese version and in the meantime we've got Dylan in there as well and William Ying supposedly turned," Ellen agreed.

"It's a circus," Mitch said with a look to John. "But I suspect we're the last to know."

. . .

Nick waited for John, Samantha and Ellen to leave Mitch's office before he closed the door. Mitch looked up as Nick dropped into a seat in front of his desk.

"On the beach ..." Nick began.

Mitch held up his hand for him to stop. "I know what you're going to say ..." Mitch indicated for Nick not to speak and he filled in. "Why didn't we get to finish the job ... but that's the way it works. Look on the bright side, we don't have to fill in the paperwork."

"Yeah that's a bonus," Nick agreed, following Mitch's lead. "Let's get a coffee."

"Right." Mitch stood and followed Nick out of the office. They took the steps to the cafeteria, ordered a couple of coffees and then left the building. Mitch led the way to the courtyard, lowering himself onto one of the benches. Nick sat beside him.

Mitch looked around casually. Satisfied it was safe to talk he turned to Nick.

"What's up?"

"I don't understand why they drowned him," Nick said in a hushed voice. "Why?"

"Nick, you never saw that and you can't ever speak of it again. Understand?"

Nick nodded. "But I did see it and they know that we know ..."

"Yes and no. They know that you saw the VIP

and an Asian man on the beach and that our people were there. That's all you saw, that's all you will ever see."

"Right."

"No, tell me you understand," Mitch insisted, "because if anyone knows that you are worried about it or even talking about it, your number will be up. Do you hear me?"

"I understand," Nick assured him. He reached for a cigarette and lit one. He looked around. "But why? It goes against all my training and everything I've ever done in the Air Force. While you were off flying, testing planes and causing dramas for us, our crew would celebrate our search and rescues."

Mitch sipped his coffee and explained. "If they had taken the VIP alive," Mitch referred to their agreed call sign for the Vice President, "consider the tension that would exist now between the US and China. Consider the potential public insecurity believing our intel on home security is in Chinese hands. There would be speculation—if the VIP is a traitor who else in the current government might be? Also, why keep him locked up in our jails for years? Who wants a VIP that's a traitor languishing in jail? What does that say about the office? That's just for starters. Considering the punishment for treason in some countries, he got off lightly. Are you going to be OK with this?"

"Depends. Tell me if you are OK with it?" Nick asked looking at Mitch.

Mitch went to speak and hesitated. He swallowed.

"Because if you are OK with it, then I'm not sure I'm a fit for this job," Nick added.

Mitch looked away. He thought for a moment then looked back at Nick.

"Strictly between us?"

"Yep," Nick nodded.

"I'm OK with the VIP situation. He sold his country for a power trip. I'm not OK with William Ying, I don't understand why. I bet John knows but we're going to be kept in the dark."

Nick nodded.

―――――

John Windsor summoned Mitch into his office. "Where's your phone?"

Mitch patted his jacket pocket. "On my desk."

"I was trying to reach you," John said.

"I was just outside for five minutes, sorry," Mitch conceded.

"Two things," John continued. "Our legat in Beijing has sent her report. She's been to see the immediate family of each police officer. In each and every case, a family member has received a short email saying something to the effect of 'the course is going well, we are very busy and thinking of the family'. They all believe their family member is alive and well and in training in the US."

Mitch exhaled. "So one of the fake group, probably Ru, was communicating to all the family members, so he must have the police officers' phones. Not good, for the families."

John nodded and continued. "Marcus just called. They've traced the call Dylan Ting made to you with the abort message and pinpointed it to the VIP house. He's made another call since then and he's no longer at the VIP house."

"So where is he?" Mitch asked.

"He's at sea, about fifteen miles south of the lighthouse."

"At sea?" Mitch moved to the window and look out. "Why? Is he with Ru? Is he a captive? But if Ru was the shooter, he must have shot everyone at the VIP house and then taken to the ocean ... did Dylan help?"

"We won't know until you encounter them," John said.

"Especially now that we've killed William Ying." Mitch shook his head. "Danny Huang will never talk."

"You'll have to let that go," John said. "I know you're angry about William Ying's killing."

"Angry doesn't begin to cover it. There's a bigger agenda which we're not being told," Mitch looked at John, "or maybe you're being told and I'm not."

John turned away. "You need to find your sea legs. They're on a thirty-five foot motor yacht from the intel I have to hand." He handed Mitch one piece of paper and a grainy photo showing someone who resembled Dylan Ting on the deck of a motor yacht.

Mitch flipped over the paper and the back was blank. "Terrific."

Marcus knocked on the office door and John beckoned him in.

"Gentlemen," he said. "The vessel Dylan is on is stationary at the moment. The boat belongs to John and Janet Villiers who were on board when it left the harbor a few days ago, according to the general store owner at Buxton who said they came in for supplies. If our two Asian men are on board, that makes four people—or the Villiers might have been dealt with."

"It's not a ghost boat is it?" Mitch asked.

"No, there is someone alive on board because our sources said it only recently dropped anchor in the area ... like in the last hour," Marcus confirmed. "They're not moving now but I'll keep you posted if there's any change," he said with a wave on departure.

Mitch was thinking aloud. "We need to get down there before Dylan gets taken out or they take off."

"Give me a plan ASAP and what you need," John said. "Team meeting here in thirty minutes?"

"I have to check something, so can we make it an hour?" Mitch rose. As he walked out, he issued orders. "Ellie, find out anything you can for me on Pan Ru for a briefing in an hour, Sam, check with Marcus and Justin to see if they have any translation updates or phone records from before and after the lift that we haven't seen. Nick, we've got a container to open."

––––––

"Let's get it over with." Mitch stared at the lock on the larger container.

"This is not going to be pretty is it?" Nick said, using the steel jaws of the bolt cutter. The lock snapped and Nick pulled it off.

"Maybe you should just wait over there." Mitch nodded to their vehicle.

"Job comes with the good and the bad," Nick said.

Mitch nodded and together they pulled open the iron door of the large container that had been waiting for them since Mitch had Samantha store it safely. Mitch knew what to expect; four Asian police officers. He'd seen putrid bodies before and he anticipated the stench and view would be overwhelming. His jaw locked in a reflex action and both men braced as they looked in.

Mitch gagged. Nick dropped the bolt cutter, turned, ran to the edge of the jetty and vomited into the water.

Mitch stared straight ahead into the container. He made a call to John.

"I've got four dead police officers, want to collect them?"

46

"SAM, CLOSE THE DOOR PLEASE, MITCH OBVIOUSLY lives in a tent." John rolled his eyes as Mitch entered his office to address the team, leaving the door open. The team laughed as Samantha leaned over and swung the door closed.

"I do at the moment," Mitch said.

"A tent in Henri's manor with hot and cold running service," Nick added. "They'll never get rid of you if Ann keeps that up."

Mitch smiled. "I am getting used to it." He sat down and opened the folder. "Marcus tells us that Dylan Ting is alive and well, afloat fifteen miles out from the Cape Hatteras shore line. He's on a thirty-five foot motor yacht possibly with a couple in their sixties—the owners—and we suspect Ru is with him since he remains unaccounted for," Mitch said.

"Thank God Dylan's alive," Ellen said.

"You can say that again," Mitch agreed before continuing. "Except now it raises a hundred questions: why is he alive? Is Dylan's life still at threat? Were they both involved in the killing or did they make a lucky escape? Why hasn't Dylan tried to reach us before this? Who aborted the mission and do the owners of the motor yacht know Dylan and Ru or has their boat been pirated. That's just for starters. What have you got on Ru, Ellie?"

"Very little ... Pan Ru ... he's an only child, born during China's one child policy. Nineteen years old, a party member since he was a kid—his father is a party member. Parents are workers, they own a market stall. Ru is on a Beijing government scholarship at the University of Science and Technology in Beijing. No priors, he's undertaken the mandatory military training for university freshmen and he's engaged to be married," she summed him up. "Nothing about his military life with the Secret Intelligence Service."

"I suspect that's buried to cover his alias. Has Danny Huang coughed up anything since we took him from the VIP house?" Mitch asked John.

"Not much, as you would expect," John said. "But he now thinks he's the only survivor and he knows he'll be sitting in one of our jails for a very long time. He's asking for a prisoner exchange if we want him to talk. We might get something out of him yet."

Mitch frowned, staring straight ahead.

"You alright?" John asked.

"What? Oh yeah. I was just thinking how he said to me that the only time he ever broke under torture was when he was burnt," Mitch shuddered. "You won't get much out of him."

John nodded. "You should talk to someone about that, Mitch."

Mitch looked up at him—he had been caught in an unguarded moment. "No, moving on."

"So what's the plan?" Nick asked covering Mitch's back.

"Given we don't know what the situation is with Dylan we have to treat it as though he's being held against his will," Mitch said. "I've suggested we use a research vessel and John's found us one … it's clearly marked as such so it shouldn't attract any attention."

"What sort of vessel is it?" Ellen asked.

Mitch looked at his notes. "It's a … I don't know, fifty-five foot … big boat."

John shook his head. "If you asked him about a plane he'd put you into a coma with the detail. It's a fifty-five foot custom-built fiberglass research boat designed for offshore survey work. It was built in 2005, top cruising speed of about eighteen knots with a full galley and a four berth cabin, so you can have your choice of bunks."

"Luxury, thanks Skipper," Mitch said. "So we're going to head out towards them, cut the engine, hang about a bit to look like we might be doing research and then break down. Nick and Ellen will abandon boat, so to speak, head over to them and ask for help—do your best to get onboard. Then Dylan will either out us, and Sam and I will be there as back up, or he will let you scope out the situation, which will indicate he is still on our team. You need to return to our boat for whatever reason, one or both of you, and give us an update on the situation so we can work out where to go from there."

"Why aren't you going aboard?" Nick asked, surprised.

John answered for him. "You and Ellie are better at sea, Nick, or so Mitch tells me. I'm not convinced Ru will believe Mitch is a sea-based research officer if he's clutching the side and retching overboard every minute."

"I'm not that bad," Mitch said.

"Really?" John frowned. "Remember the time when— "

"Yeah OK," Mitch cut him off. "Swimming is not Sam's strength either, so we're best in back-up here."

"Good," John said.

"It's the amplitude of the waves that makes you

seasick. I'll bring some ginger and anti-seasick meds with us," Ellen said.

"I heard you can get wrist bands that help," Samantha added.

"You can," Ellen agreed, "but I've never known anyone that they've worked on."

"I heard the trick was not to fall overboard while you are hurling," Nick added.

Mitch looked at John and shook his head. He continued, "regardless of whether Dylan is a hostage or a willing participant, we need to secure Ru and that motor yacht, close this down and see what intel he has that belongs to us. But that plan will roll out once we know the situation on board."

"Guess we're back to Cape Hatteras then," Nick said.

"Grab a car from the pool," John said.

"I'll take mine," Mitch said.

"Again?" John said. "I think you're compensating ... every time you are threatened with an ocean as-signment, you want your own car with you so you can make a quick getaway."

"Thanks Dr Phil," Mitch joked. "Clearly you haven't driven the cars in the car pool." He turned to his team. "I'll meet you all in my office in a moment so we can work out schedules." He waited for the three to leave and, rising, turned to John. "You know

I'm always the last to suggest anyone needs therapy ..." Mitch started.

"Good, Mitch." John met him at the door and placed his hand on Mitch's shoulder. "I'm pleased you've changed your mind and are putting up your hand for some help. It won't hurt you to talk to someone, even just to download."

"Not me!" Mitch frowned. "Nick needs to talk with someone. That container was a bit of shock just now; I think he's going to be seeing that image in his head for a while. I want him to talk to someone ASAP."

"I'll organize it today before he goes," John said. "And you? You're not going to be seeing it, man of steel?"

Mitch grinned. "It will have to compete with a library of other images but it might get a run."

"I think you should ..."

"Yeah thanks, John." Mitch had disappeared before John finished the sentence.

47

"FOR CHRISSAKE," MITCH MUTTERED UNDER HIS breath. He turned his back to his team, leant over the side of the vessel and threw up into the water.

"This hasn't been a great assignment for you has it?" Nick asked the obvious.

"I've had better," he agreed, wiping his mouth on his sleeve. The journey had been choppy and Mitch dropped back onto the bench portside of the research vessel. He glanced at his watch, seeing an hour had passed. Only fifteen to twenty minutes left until they would be near the Villiers' vessel with Dylan Ting and Ru on board and they could anchor. Through his binoculars, Mitch could see the motor yacht coming into view; no one could be seen above deck. He handed the binoculars to Ellen.

She gave him a sympathetic look. "You really do look green."

"Thanks. Sam, how are you?" Mitch asked.

"Fine so far," she said, smiling. "I thought I'd be a lot worse."

"Good." Mitch put his head in his hands. "Can you guys just finish this one off and pick me up when it is over?"

Nick patted him on the back.

Mitch looked up at him. "What? No one-liners?"

"I'm not going to kick you when you're down," Nick said. "No fun in that. I'll save them up for later."

A plane flew over ahead and Mitch looked up enviously. "Ah, those were the days. Come on Sam, we're getting close, so we better go below deck. If Dylan's swapped sides we don't need him to see all of us coming at him."

Samantha followed Mitch off the deck, down the stairs and out of sight.

"Lie down," she said and Mitch did so without hesitation, falling into the lower bunk.

They cruised along for a short while before Mitch heard Ellen cut the engine. The anchor rattled as it dropped. He could hear them moving around above deck.

"Mitch, are you asleep?" Samantha asked.

"Yes," he said keeping his eyes closed.

"Can we talk about— "

"No." He shut her down.

"Don't you think we should?" Samantha said.

Mitch didn't open his eyes, but he thought for a minute. "I don't ..." he stopped and tried to formulate a response that didn't include his anger and pain. "Sam, just let me lie here and be sick for now."

———

On deck, Ellen gathered her diving gear. "I'm going to go for a dive, want to come?" she asked, hoping Nick would say no. She stripped off her gear to reveal a one-piece navy swimsuit and moved to check the air in one of the onboard tanks.

Nick watched, appreciating the view. "No, I'm going to stay and be seen on deck. I'll try and look official, look at the clipboard every now and then, make a few marks with my pen, that sort of thing."

"Try to keep your shirt on and don't fish off the side, or you might give it away," Ellen teased as she lifted the tank onto her back. With a glance to her watch to note the time, Ellen lowered her mask, gave him a wave and fell back into the water.

Nick looked over the side, watching her disappear from sight.

———

Ellen shivered; the water was chilly but the view was spectacular. She glided through the water, feeling at home, appreciating the absolute quiet. She watched as a small school of fish went past, followed by a sand tiger shark lazily in pursuit. She moved lazily herself, lightly kicking as she drifted underwater, enjoying the blue around her.

Ellen turned and looked back at the hull of the research vessel; she thought about the three people —her team—on board. She liked her own company; unlike Samantha, she didn't need to be around the team all the time and if it required having to dive to have some time out, that was just a bonus.

She thought about Mitch. *He still couldn't show me he needed help after all our assignments together; he had to call for Nick to step him through the breathing exercises, and I'm the qualified medic in the team.*

Does he think I'd think less of him? Men! Always playing the hero. I'm his friend. Or maybe he doesn't think of me like that, maybe I'm just staff, one of his squad. At least he sent me on the stakeout, I guess.

She moved a little further away from the vessel, glancing back to keep it in scope and taking on board the tide, she swam underwater towards Ru and Dylan's boat. Staying a reasonable distance from it, she observed it for a while; nothing untoward. With a quick glance to her watch, she realized it was time to go back; it was so easy to lose time underwater.

She swam back to the vessel. Nick had lowered a set of iron stairs and she pulled herself up them into the boat. He appeared and took the tank from her.

"Did I miss anything?" she asked, removing her mask and tank.

"Yeah, there's a storm on its way, I've just got the forecast. Heavy rain, gale force winds. Now you're back, I'll go tell the boss. He'll be excited about that."

Ellen wrapped a towel around herself and followed Nick below deck.

Mitch swung his legs over the side of the bed and sat up. He closed his eyes and steadied himself. A sickly pallor overspread his countenance. He opened his eyes and looked at his watch. "OK, we've been stationary an hour now, long enough to do 'research'. Time to head over and tell them the vessel won't start. Confirm the orders for me again," Mitch said, gripping the side of the bed, his knuckles white.

"You are going to stay here and continue to throw up," Nick started. "Sam will man the radio, while Ellie and I head over in the dinghy and ask for help. We'll let the inhabitants know that something has gone wrong and we have no communications, we'll ask them if they are experiencing the same thing ..."

Ellen took over. "We'll get ourselves invited on board. We will know pretty quickly if Dylan has swapped sides because he'll out us and you'll hear our warning shot, otherwise we will try and get some sign from him on what is going on. Then Nick or I will come back here to get word to Sam and depending on the situation make plans to secure the boat."

Mitch nodded. "I want them both alive, but not at the risk of your lives, get it?"

They both nodded.

"And try not to create waves as you get off," Mitch said.

Ellen grinned.

"So not funny," Mitch told her.

"No." She tried to look concerned. "Sorry."

"Go away," he told them. "Sam, kill me now but take my body back to land, please."

———

By the time Ellen and Nick got back on deck, the sky had become dramatically darker.

"We better discuss this," she said and leaned

over the lower deck rail. "Mitch, you had better see this, there's a storm coming."

Mitch's head appeared at the top of the steps. He groaned. "Oh good, I was hoping it would get rougher. What are we talking?"

Nick scanned for the latest report. "According to this, lightning, pelting rain, gale force winds of up to forty knots, probable wave heights at ten to fifteen feet," he said.

Mitch lowered himself onto the step. Samantha peered past him over to Dylan's vessel where there continued to be no movement.

"Let's think this through," Mitch said. "If you go over now, you may be trapped with them and have to stay longer ... which could be good if we knew the lay of the land, but if things go sour and you're trapped there in the storm and Sam and I can't get to you, then that could be a disaster ... so let's wait for the storm to pass."

"I agree, it's coming pretty fast anyway." Ellen looked skyward. "We need to batten down everything that moves," she said, and began to secure items on deck. "Mitch, you and Sam stay out of sight, we can't risk you being seen now. Nick and I can handle this."

The boat lurched as the winds began to rise. Nick grabbed for the rails.

"One hand for yourself, and one hand for the

boat," Ellen instructed. Mitch smiled at her and she shrugged. "I worked on a research vessel for three months when I was at college."

The sky cracked with lighting and another wave slapped the vessel. Samantha fell from the middle stair, landing on the floor below and Mitch raced down to help her. Ellen lurched around the deck. She grabbed a few loose items, opened the bench seat and threw them in. Nick called to her above the rising noise. "Let's get below deck."

The storm hit quicker than they anticipated. Within minutes the winds began to howl. The vessel rocked and a huge wave slapped across the deck. Nick waited for Ellen to descend to the lower deck and followed. Lightning flashed across the sky and moments later, the rain began in torrents. Mitch steadied Samantha, who rubbed her leg.

"I'm OK, it's just a bump." She limped to the lower bunk, holding onto the top bunk frame as she went. Ellen arrived below deck, and Mitch leant up and helped Nick secure the hatch. The vessel lurched and all three tumbled, their backpacks, loose shoes and clothing hurtling across the room.

"What happens if we capsize?" Samantha asked. "Will we be trapped in here?"

"It will be a major wave that manages to capsize us," Ellen said.

In response, the vessel rolled again and thudded down as though lifted from the water and dropped from a height.

"I thought you'd be barfing," Nick yelled to Mitch as they stood together gripping the bed rails.

"I have nothing left inside, thank God," he replied.

The boat slammed on its side, reluctantly righting itself, and Mitch grabbed his shirt off the floor and threw up into it.

"OK, I found something else to barf up, my liver," he said.

Ellen laughed. "Next time we fly and I tell you I'm sick, I want you to remember this," she said.

"Please, stop with the sympathy." He leaned over again, dry retching into the shirt, and she placed her hand on his back. Mitch pulled away.

"See, you can't take sympathy," she said and dropped her hand.

Mitch frowned. "What?" The noise inside the research vessel was incredible.

As the boat lurched, Samantha slid off the bed, and hurtled towards Nick. The vessel went into darkness, creaked and tossed. Thunder roared and the waves hit the side with force.

Nick boosted Samantha up. "You all right?" he called in the dark.

"I think so." She grabbed onto him and the bunk rail.

"Ellie?" Mitch called.

"I'm all right, just waiting it out," she called from near the stairs.

A lightning crack made Samantha scream but lit the room. Mitch could make them all out.

"Oh my God that scared me," she said.

"It struck something," Nick confirmed, "hopefully not us."

Mitch retched again and this time Samantha joined him.

For the next twenty minutes the boat reeled dramatically back and forward, rolling over on its side numerous times. Lightning lit their faces and objects flew around the room.

Then it quietened down. Mitch eased out of the space between the bed and wall where he had wedged himself and helped Samantha up. Nick and Ellen moved up the stairs and pushed open the hatch. It was eerily quiet on the ocean. They stumbled out, being careful to check they weren't seen by Dylan's boat which stood still as though the storm had passed it by without issue while their research vessel was a mess. Nick tried the engine and shook his head.

"I guess we legitimately need help now," Mitch

said. He reached for a bottle of water, rinsed his mouth and spat overboard.

"Are we going to do it tonight?" Ellen asked.

"Maybe, the cover of darkness might work well for us." Mitch looked over towards the other boat where one small light came from below deck. "I just need to try and get a call through to John first, in case he has some up-to-date intel. Can you try for me, Sam?"

"Sure." Sam moved to the satellite phone. She tried a couple of times.

"Got him," she said.

Mitch joined her and took the phone. "Yeah, we're fine," Mitch assured John, "I won't say it wasn't freaky though. I think we've lost the engine, she's not kicking over and we've got no way of charging batteries to operate running lights. Anything from your end?"

Mitch listened and let out a low whistle. "Yep, I agree. Tonight."

"How's the sea legs?" John asked.

"I'm waiting for them to arrive," Mitch said.

John made a knowing sound and hung up.

"What is it?" Nick asked.

"Maybe all that noise we heard wasn't just lightning," Mitch said. "John says one of the other boats nearby called in what they thought sounded like gunshots, which initially they mistook for lightning, but decided to call it in anyway. So just to be on the safe side, we're scrapping the 'need assistance' angle and doing a covert operation instead."

"You might want to think about that; the storm is not quite done. There's more on the way. ETA thirty minutes," Nick reported.

"Damn. Sam, can you get John again for me please?" Mitch asked

Moments later Samantha handed over the phone.

"John, we've got a thirty minute window before another storm comes through. I'm thinking we should go now, in case post-storm, they're gone," Mitch said.

"Let me speak to the medic," John said.

Mitch looked at Ellen. "Why?"

"Just put her on the phone," John insisted.

Mitch called to Ellen. "Ellie, John wants to talk with you." He handed over the sat nav phone and went to help clean up.

A few minutes later, Ellen handed it back to him.

"I know what you're going to say," Mitch said to John down the line.

"Yeah, might be best you man the comms and send the three more sea-able on board, especially if you've only got a small window of time," John said.

Mitch thought about it.

"You know that part of being a good manager is to know when you're not the best person for the job," John reminded him. "You can't watch their backs every minute of the day, they'll be OK."

"Right." Mitch hung up.

48

THE DINGHY WITH NICK, SAMANTHA AND ELLEN ON board reached the side of the boat; the water now seemed amazingly still after the tumultuous storm. There was no moon and the ocean was calm, as if recovering, but Ellen could sense the lull before the next storm—there was a hum in the air.

Nick grabbed the rail down the side of the boat and tied the dinghy loosely to it. They waited. Ellen indicated for them to put their comms on so they could communicate. She checked her gun, Nick and Samantha followed suit. Rising gingerly, waiting to get her balance, Ellen climbed up the iron ladder, stealthily pausing near the top. She scanned the deck; nothing. She spotted an area where she could momentarily crouch and hide, gave the all clear signal and disappeared from their sight onto the deck. Nick gave Samantha a leg up and she followed in Ellen's footsteps.

A few minutes later Nick appeared on deck. Ellen indicated Nick to take the portside deck and Samantha to take starboard. Ellen crouched beside the rung leading to the lower level and tried to see below through the ladder. Nothing but the one light sitting on the table. She moved slowly and silently below deck. She could see thanks to the glow from the one lamp, but the boat was eerily silent. She paused, scanned the area and moved forward. Ellen stopped to listen; nothing.

Samantha's report came through her earpiece, "Clear top deck starboard."

Ellen moved quickly through each area, gun at the ready, scanning as she went.

"Nick, report," she whispered.

"All clear portside, we're coming down to you," he said.

Ellen saw Samantha and Nick working their way towards her. She tried one door which wouldn't open, put her hip into it and the door gave. The room was a storeroom and empty.

She moved out of the storeroom and turned back to Samantha. "Sam, check the engine room, and be careful," she said.

Samantha nodded and moved away.

Ellen moved quickly in the direction Nick took,

coming alongside him. She tried another closed door. This one wasn't locked and opened easily— the galley. Ellen stared at the large industrial ovens. Nick turned to look at them, two large ovens with glass panels. He took a deep breath and pulled each oven door open; empty. They both gave a sigh of relief.

"Nothing in the galley," Ellen reported through her comms for Mitch, who was listening in on the research vessel.

"That leaves four missing now," Nick said.

"Sam, report?" Ellen asked.

"Just getting there now," Samantha answered.

Ellen waited for her to go through the exercise.

"Engine room clear," she reported.

A huge crack of lightning scared Nick and Ellen and they grinned at each other sheepishly.

"Here comes the next round of weather," she said.

The boat lurched and they grabbed the table to steady themselves.

Mitch's voice came through Ellen's earpiece. "I think you're staying there riding this one out, agreed?"

"Yes boss, agreed," she answered.

Samantha rejoined them, gripping anything she could along the way.

Ellen looked around for the best place to wait it

out, and glanced upon a hatch door. She waved to get Nick's attention and pointed to it.

He moved in closer with weapon drawn as Ellen threw open the hatch door. Rolled up in fetal position was Dylan Ting.

"Show your hands," Ellen ordered drawing her gun. Dylan did not move.

"Show your hands," she ordered again and Dylan held up his hands. Nick put his gun away, pulled Dylan out of the hatch and pushed him against the wall. He frisked him and restrained his hands with plasticuffs that Samantha offered from her jacket kit.

"Not armed," Nick declared.

"Mitch, we've secured Dylan Ting, and he's alive. No sign of the missing three."

"Copy," Mitch said.

The boat reeled as a huge wave slapped the side and the three agents and Dylan fell across the floor.

Ellen looked up for loose items, but there was nothing around and the table was bolted to the floor.

Nick propped Dylan Ting against the kitchen wall and they settled securely on the floor to wait it out.

"Where's Ru? Where's the rest of the crew?" Nick asked.

"Ru ..." Dylan shrugged.

"What's going on, Dylan?" Ellen asked.

Dylan laughed. "What's going on?"

"Yes," Nick snapped.

Dylan glanced away.

"Where is Ru? Where are the other two that were onboard, Dylan? The Villiers, where are they?" Ellen asked again.

Dylan looked skyward. "They're with the VIP," he said.

"So they're dead?" Nick prodded him.

"No, they're together," he said again. "Where's Mitchell?"

"Never you mind," Ellen said. She slid forward, reached towards him and grabbed Dylan's jaw. She looked into his eyes, felt his pulse and slid back across the floor.

"Is he high?" Nick asked in a hush tone.

"If he's not, it's worse ... he's lost it." Ellen sighed.

———

Mitch had just finished cleaning up the deck and listening in on his team when a huge bolt of lightning seemed to explode around him. He quickly checked the area, grabbed a torch and got below deck. It was dark below with the lights blown and eerily quiet; he knew exactly what the term 'the calm before the storm' meant. He thought of all the times he had flown and survived without incident and now he was in a tin can on the ocean in the middle of a storm, feeling like he had no control of the situation. Within minutes he heard the sound of rain moving across the ocean and shortly after it slapped down on the deck. The wind began to pick up and he braced himself for another round.

"Ellie," he said through their shared comms, "I'm going to take the earpiece off. All OK there?"

"Other than being thrown around like a bathtub toy, we're doing just fine," she said.

Mitch removed the earpiece and moved through the research vessel, lighting each area with his torch. Everything looked intact but the rolling did not improve Mitch's seasickness as he gripped tightly to whatever he could reach. He passed through the galley which was a mess—drawers had fallen out with their contents strewn across the area. Seeing Ellen's stash of gingersnap cookies didn't help his queasiness and he turned abruptly, making his way to the cabin.

The seas began to pound against the windows. At least the other boat is clear and safe, he thought about his three operatives aboard. But where the hell are Ru and the two boat owners?

The wind began to howl, the vessel rolled and Mitch struggled to enter the cabin.

The second storm was worse than the first; the

wind screamed, and tower-sized waves pounded the side of the vessel randomly and constantly. With each hit, Mitch waited, expecting the vessel to roll. The height of the swells sent him lurching a few times. Up top, something was wrenched from its fastenings and was flogging up and down the deck. He lowered himself to the floor and braced. Turning the torch off, he wedged it between the bed's mattress and wall. A huge crack of lightning lit the room, then it returned to black.

He breathed in and out steadily; trying to keep the bile from rising. He heard the huge roar of thunder and waited for the lightning strike. It lit the room and the face of Pan Ru standing in the corner. The vessel was dark again.

———

Nick secured Dylan so he could weather the storm, but not enough that he couldn't be moved quickly if the boat went under. The three agents sat beside him, waiting it out.

"This is worse than the last one," Samantha said after the boat leveled out again.

"I hope Mitch is OK," Ellen frowned. She studied Dylan.

Is it an act or for real? He doesn't flinch with the

lightning strikes or seem to be worried about the boat rolling. Maybe he is ... gone.

"Dylan," she tried again.

He slowly turned his eyes towards her.

"Where's Ru?" She raised her voice above the roaring wind.

"Ru," he said.

"Yes, Pan Ru, you came here together. Where is he?"

"He's with Mitchell."

Nick rolled his eyes. "He was with the VIP last time we asked, now he's with Mitch."

Ellen and Nick realized something at the same time and they stared at each other.

"I'll check," Nick said. He edged himself along, stopping to brace as the boat hit the water hard, then continued.

Ellen watched him leave and turned back to Dylan.

"Where are the owners of this boat, Dylan?" Ellen asked.

"They're with whoever you believe in ... God, Allah, Buddha ..." He laughed.

Samantha and Ellen exchanged looks.

Nick stumbled back in. "One of the lifeboats is missing and it was here when we arrived. I've got to ..."

"You can't go Nick, it's too dangerous," Ellen cut him off.

"He's not expecting Ru and he's not up to it," Nick said.

"He is always expecting something and he's up to it. You can't go in the middle of this, you'll never make it." As she spoke the boat lurched dangerously on its side. Nick slipped and hit the wall.

"We have to do something," Samantha said.

"Yes," Ellen ordered. "We wait."

———

Mitch leaped to his feet; Pan Ru, on board! The vessel was pitch black as he groped for the torch and tried to listen over the sound of the storm for Ru approaching. He whirled around, sensing him near and felt the strike of the man's hand on his shoulder, Mitch hit back at throat level, making impact. The boat lurched and both men sprawled—Ru across the cabin floor, Mitch back against the iron frame of the bunk. He swore and dropped to the ground.

He felt along the edge of the bed, looking for his bunk, his backpack and the jacket with his gun in it. Lightning lit the room again and on seeing him, Ru charged towards Mitch with a large hunting knife. In the flicker of two lightning bolts, Ru was on him.

Mitch struggled with his assailant. The knife was inches from his neck.

They were matched in strength, but Mitch had a height advantage. He wrestled with Ru, using all the strength he could muster. Ru yelled like a man possessed and plunged the knife again towards Mitch. Struggling free, Mitch got his boot to Ru's abdomen and pushed him off. The pain from Mitch's leg injury shot up his spine and for a few seconds he felt himself blacking out.

Ru disappeared from sight. Mitch grabbed for his jacket and withdrew his gun. As he spun around, Ru was within inches of him.

"Don't move," the man hissed. "The blade is positioned near your artery, so you could bleed to death in minutes."

Mitch braced and hoped Ru was doing the same. If the boat lurched, he could be history. He tried to move his arm but it was pinned to his side and the gun along with it.

"What do you want?" Mitch asked.

"I want you to call off the dogs and let me slip back out of the country," Ru answered.

"So you've given this some thought," Mitch said.

Ru pushed the blade closer to Mitch's skin.

Another wave pounded the boat and Ru gripped onto Mitch tightly from behind. The boat steadied.

"Why? What went wrong?" Mitch asked.

"Nothing." He felt the young man stiffen. "It all went exactly to plan."

Mitch prepared his plan in his head and calmed himself to muster all the force he could. He waited patiently as Ru listed what he wanted and how it was to be done.

A bright, jagged streak of lighting lit the vessel and the moment it began to lurch, Mitch pushed back, grabbing Ru's arm away from his own neck. He spun around and thrust the gun against Ru's throat, pinning Ru's knife-wielding arm to the wall. He shoved his weight against the Asian man, breathing heavily with the adrenaline and pain.

"Drop the knife."

Ru held onto it.

"You don't want to push me because I've had a very bad week," Mitch said.

Ru opened his fingers and the knife rattled to the floor. Mitch spun the man around, wedging his arm up his back. After putting his gun down, Mitch reached for ties from his backpack. He secured Ru's hands, spun him round and dropped him to the floor. He grabbed more ties and secured him to the bunk bed frame.

"What if we capsize?" Ru looked alarmed.

"I'll try and remember to cut you free," Mitch said with a glance to Ru's knife which had slid under the bunk. He rubbed his neck and looked at the blood on his hands. He swore, stumbled out of the room to the vessel's head and rinsed his neck. Not deep enough to worry about, he decided. He gripped onto the basin as the boat lurched again.

"Fucking be over!" he yelled as the boat lurched again. He stumbled back to Ru and dropped down opposite him. Mitch studied the young man's face. He leaned forward, clasping his hands.

"What's going to happen to me?" Ru asked.

"Depends on your story and whether you cooperate. Start talking anytime you like; seems those English lessons have worked a treat."

Ru declined to speak. A huge boom of thunder rocked the vessel and then the rain began to pour in earnest.

Mitch lost all semblance of patience, he yelled above the noise. "For chrissake ... you're a spy, how many on the team?"

"Bravo," Ru grinned, "you found out. There's just me here, a few more behind the scenes. How many on your team?"

Mitch ignored the question. "You were never going to let that mission go ahead ... how long have you been on this?"

Ru inhaled, his chest swelling with pride. "Years, from the moment William Ying applied for the ambassadorship here. I might look young, but this has been four years of my life."

"So who exactly do you work for?" Mitch asked. He gripped the bed frame as the boat lurched again.

"It doesn't matter who I work for or who I am, it has all gone to plan."

"Except you're here and you want me to get you out of the country," Mitch said. "I've known who you are from the very start despite the cop alias. What happened to the plan?"

"It went to plan," Ru insisted.

"Yeah, then why are you here and everyone else is dead?"

"That was the plan. It's going to plan. You don't understand."

"No I don't," Mitch agreed. "Explain it to me. From day one you have been an insider, a spy on their team. They were oblivious?"

"Of course. I'm very good at what I do," Ru snapped. "I had total control of all their communications and in their eyes, I towed the line as the humble junior."

"So every message they sent, every test was a fake?"

"It was very real ... I had agents sending back confirmations," Ru said. "They were just my people, not theirs. None of Danny, William or Hai's commands were ever going to come to fruition."

The boat lurched and Ru closed his eyes and swallowed.

Mitch waited until the boat settled again.

"But we saw the sub, we saw the air bubbles at the trial," Mitch said.

Ru grinned. "The first test failed. You probably got that in your intel. It didn't fail of course, I just didn't organize it ... I'm not wasting budget on that. The second test, I hired a local sub. We, like you, have people everywhere. The sub came in, did the job, got out. Danny was happy and so was the 'Beijing office' or so I told Danny."

"You could have saved the cops ... if you knew what was going to happen to them, why couldn't you just fake their death?" Mitch asked.

"It's so hard to know who is really on your side. I couldn't risk word getting out and the mission being shut down," Ru said.

"So life is not worth much in your world?" Mitch said.

"Your people just killed your Vice President and William Ying. Couldn't you fake their deaths?"

Mitch stopped. Ru was right, Mitch couldn't take the moral high ground.

The two men sat in silence for some time as the storm calmed down.

"How were you going to let it play out?" Mitch asked.

"Much the same way as it did except they would have all been killed and disposed of at the VIP house—there's plenty of woods around there. I would have drowned the Vice President and let his body float to shore so it looked like an accident. Your people and our people would be none the wiser. Isn't that ideal?"

49

As soon as the storm abated, Nick and Ellen secured Dylan so he could not move.

"Sam, stay on watch. Once we check on the other boat, I'll come back and swap with you so can get John on the satellite phone," Ellen ordered.

"Will do," Sam said.

Ellen raced to the top deck with Nick close behind. He dropped down into their dinghy, steadied himself, and turned to help her in.

"Let's go." She turned on the small motor as Nick undid the tie. Ellen turned the boat towards the research vessel. As they sidled up to it, Nick saw it—the lifeboat tied to the other side of the vessel. He indicated to Ellen, who nodded. They drew their guns and boarded.

It was eerily quiet and dark. Ellen and Nick

quickly moved around the deck. Ellen shook her head, lowered herself to the deck floor and glanced down the iron ladder. No one was in sight and she quickly stepped on the ladder and dropped herself to the floor below, squatting, gun at the ready. She indicated to Nick it was safe to follow.

The two split up. Ellen moved down towards the cabin, Nick towards the galley. She saw a streak of blood along a wall ... Mitch's blood? As she sidled up to the first room, she saw Mitch sitting on the floor, blood on his neck. He looked up at her and she froze, scanning the room.

"Hey Ellie, it's all clear, come on in. I found Ru," he said and pointed opposite. Ellen peered around the corner and saw the young Asian man secured to the bunk's iron bed frame. She holstered her gun and called to Nick who bounded down the hall.

"We can't leave you alone for one minute." Nick shook his head.

Mitch grinned. He stretched out his legs and groaned, taking Nick's extended hand to pull himself up off the floor. He looked at his two agents. "I'm getting off the water now and I don't care if I have to swim to shore."

———

Mitch paced in the parking lot while he spoke to John.

Ellen stood outside the car and leant in to talk to Nick and Samantha.

"Do you think he'll ever get in the car?" she asked. "Or is he just enjoying walking on land?"

"We could force him in. Nick you put a bag over his head, I'll take arms, Ellie, you're on legs," Samantha suggested.

"I've wanted to bag his head for years, but I'm going for a smoke." Nick got out, walked to the back of the car and lit up just as Mitch hung up. He continued to pace, his hands on his hips, thinking before turning and walking towards Nick.

"Ready?" Mitch asked.

"No," Nick said. "Two minutes."

Samantha joined the others and alighted from the car.

"What's going to happen to Dylan?" Ellen asked.

"He'll go by ambulance back to a secure unit. John's going to oversee it and get him some help. Then we'll see if he can tell us anything," Mitch said.

"It's awful." Samantha leaned against the car.

"I just hope he's drugged and not having a breakdown, might just be something in his system," Mitch said.

He opened the car door. "Come on Nick, give it

up, it'll cut your life short and then who'll give me a hard time?"

"Fair point," Nick said as he stubbed out his cigarette and returned to the car. He lowered himself into the front passenger seat. They pulled out to begin the drive back to D.C. again, each lost in their own thoughts. After some time, Samantha spoke.

"What did Ru say to you?" she asked.

"He said it all went to plan." Mitch ran through their conversation. "I don't know what our government will do with him now."

"I want to know how two people onboard a boat go missing?" Ellen said.

"For chrissake, I didn't ask him where they were," Mitch shook his head angry at himself.

"You had a bit going on," Nick defended him. "Besides people go missing off boats more often than you would believe."

"Really?" Samantha said.

"Sure," Ellen agreed. "The Mary Celeste is one of the most famous. It was just found floating, abandoned, no crew."

"Where?" Sam asked.

"Somewhere near Portugal I think," Ellen answered. "And there was half a dozen similar ships found over the past couple of decades drifting crewless."

"Pirates probably murdered everyone on board

and the sharks cleaned up the evidence," Nick said.

"There was one in Australia not that long ago which was found with a laptop turned on and a meal on the table but the crew was missing," Mitch added.

Samantha shivered. "That's creepy."

Ellen matched Mitch with another story. "There was a Taiwanese one too, about ten years ago. It was found drifting but a few of the life rafts were missing. But there was no mayday call made and no one was ever found."

"How many were on board?" Samantha asked.

"About twenty from memory," Ellen said.

"And there was the film Pirates of the Caribbean," Nick teased, "do you think that was real?"

Mitch grinned. "Yeah I think so."

They drove in silence again. Mitch ran through all the loose ends in his head. After a few hours they stopped for a gas and coffee break.

Mitch filled up, paid with his company credit card and rejoined Nick.

"Is Ellie pissed off at me?" Mitch asked Nick as he watched Ellen and Samantha paying for coffee at the gas station counter.

"She hasn't said anything," Nick said. "Why?"

Mitch shrugged. "Nothing, just something she said."

"What?" Nick pushed.

"She had a go at me and said I couldn't take sympathy, and she's been cool with me ever since. Gave me a band-aid for the cut on my neck, when normally she'd be all over it."

"Yeah, well you can't," Nick agreed.

Mitch turned to him. "What do you mean?"

"You can't take sympathy. She was trying to console you when you were throwing up your intestines and you fobbed her off."

Mitch thought about it and said nothing.

"Chicks need to do that," Nick said. "Like Ann feeding and homing you. You know, they're nurturers by nature, we're hunters. I'd be lapping it up."

Mitch continued to think about it.

Nick looked at him. "Don't over-think it. I'm not saying get feely-touchy, you'll be up for sexual harassment. Just let them help sometimes, let them give something back to you."

Mitch frowned and looked away.

Ellen and Samantha walked towards them. Samantha handed Mitch a coffee and he thanked her as he watched Ellen ignore him and get back into the car.

Mitch shook his head and sighed.

Nick laughed and stubbed out his cigarette. "I'll drive for a while if you like?" he said taking the Audi keys from Mitch before he had time to protest.

Mitch moved around to the passenger side, lowered himself in and slid down in the seat. Nick took charge of the car, comfortable behind the wheel, while Samantha and Ellen talked in the backseat. Mitch tapped his foot and stared out the window.

Fifteen minutes later, Nick grabbed Mitch's leg.

"Enough with the tapping, you're driving me nuts!" he said. "It's over isn't it? Chill out!"

Mitch leaned forward and put his head in his hands. "No. This case is just not right—it's doing my head in. We've got a dead VIP, four dead policemen from Beijing on our soil, four imposter cops, two who are dead—Hai and Froggy—Danny won't talk and Ru thinks everything went to plan even though he's with the secret service and we don't know what intelligence he has. There's the former ambassador, William Ying, who was supposed to be dead and a trail of people who died around the time of his first death to ensure he remained dead, but then he's alive as discovered by Gunston, only to be dead again. We've got Dylan who's now not quite here, in fact I don't know where he is at in his head, and an empty boat at sea that had up to four people on it the day before and two are missing. What I'd give for a nice clean heist."

Mitch's phone rang and he looked at the screen. Charlotte! It continued to ring.

"Going to answer that?" Nick asked.

"No." He let it go to message bank out and

started tapping his foot again.

Nick rolled his eyes.

"I'm starving," Ellen said.

"I offered to get you some chips back at the gas station," Samantha said.

"I know, but I want a real meal."

"I'm with you, Ellie," Mitch agreed. "Now that the world's stopped rocking, I'm getting my appetite back. Nick, next town we go through, find a Subway or something will you?"

"If you stop tapping," Nick said.

Mitch put the window down.

"Seriously?" Nick looked at him. "The air's on. Why didn't you get a convertible if you wanted to stick your head out? Now I see why it is best that you drive."

Mitch grimaced and put the window up again. He sat still for a moment then straightened.

"We're reacting; everything we've done has just been reactionary," Mitch said, tapping his leg again. "We need to go right back to the start ... let me think," he mumbled and grabbed his iPad.

"Think out loud," Nick suggested, "so we can all add some perspective and so you don't implode."

Mitch frowned at him. "Ellie, let's revisit the people who went missing after William Ying did," he said.

Ellen reached down to her bag at her feet and

grabbed her iPad.

Mitch scanned his files on the iPad. "While you find that, let me get Dylan's report on the VIP," he said wading through files online. "Here it is, the VIP made a number of associates as an exchange student in Beijing." Mitch read aloud a list of ten names. "Mean anything to anyone?"

Nick shook his head.

"Not me," Samantha answered.

"Hmm." Mitch looked at the road ahead and frowned. Ellen interrupted his train of thought.

"So we know that three people mysteriously met their end after the cocktail party they were at when William Ying disappeared," Ellen said. "They were Rodney Lam, Jessica Wu and Joseph Kinaird."

Mitch mulled over the names. "Lam lived at what is now the vacant block of land, Jessica was dead from a hit-and-run, and Kinaird died at the wheel and his family moved away, right?"

"Correct," Ellen confirmed.

"Ellie, see what you can pull on Jessica Wu," Mitch said. "Try every known associate from her best friend to the coroner who signed off on her body. Sam, grab your iPad and start on Joseph Kinaird and I'll work on Rodney Lam. Nick, slow down and mind my car."

"You drive it faster than I do!" Nick protested.

"And that's how it should be," Mitch retorted.

50

AMY CALLAGHAN LOOKED AT HER PHONE. THE incoming call displayed Nick's name.

"Is this my M-I-A housemate?" she answered.

"Missing me?" Nick asked.

"Nick, if you had someone paying you rent and they were never there so you could have friends over, walk around the house naked, watch whatever shows you like, own the remote and the fridge, would you miss them?" she asked.

"I'm never leaving again," he said.

Amy laughed.

"I'm home tonight," he said, "just giving you the heads-up."

"Thanks. Where are you now?" She sat back, pushed strands of her blonde hair behind her ears and looked out over the Criminal Justice Information Services Division to the grounds beyond the window.

"We've just stopped at Williamsburg for a bite. So I should be back in the office later this afternoon and home the normal time," Nick said.

Amy doodled with her pen. "Who are you with?"

"The whole team," Nick answered between bites. "What's been happening there? Had any queues waiting for library service?"

Amy laughed. "You're funny, Nick, ha ha. As a matter of fact, I have been flat out; yours is not the only team I provide research for you know. Besides I had an email earlier from your boss."

"Oh yeah?" Nick looked over at Mitch. "What's he want?"

"Could be classified," Amy said.

"Information on three people who died last year in connection with the university photo gallery exhibition?" Nick asked.

"Well yes, smarty pants," she said. "How is he feeling?" Amy tried to keep her voice casual.

"He's better, limping around being his usual annoying self. He's got no sea legs though, spent the last few days throwing up his insides. You haven't asked how I'm feeling, or what I want for dinner," Nick teased.

Amy sighed dramatically. "I was thinking of

doing lasagna tonight, so I guess I could make it for two. So how are you feeling Nick, dear?"

"That's kind of you to ask," Nick said. "Well, I'm a little stiff from sleeping in hotel beds and cabin berths, but otherwise, I'm fine. But I'd be better after I had some lasagna."

"Do you want to invite Mitch to dinner tonight?" she asked.

"No, he's going back to Henri's; he rang him earlier. You'll have to fight Ann if you want to feed and care for him."

Amy scoffed, "yeah like I'm looking for that job. Anyway, gotta go, I've got a customer."

"Are they wearing glasses and a plaid shirt?" Nick teased.

"Bye Nick," she hung up and closed the internal company page featuring Mitch and his team's identification photo.

———

Ellen sat on the park bench, eating her sandwich and using her iPad to wade through the document links for Jessica Wu that Amy had just sent. Samantha sat opposite doing the same for Joseph Kinaird and Nick watched the CCTV footage again on his phone. Ellen looked up to watch Mitch. He had wandered away to listen to a phone message and she could tell by his body language he didn't want to deal with it. She softened her stance on him. I guess he is never going to be the type who'll let you support him. Probably hasn't had much experience in that area.

She returned to the files and looked at the pretty young face of Jessica Wu. She went through the police report for the second time. It was eleven p.m. when Jessica was killed; she was almost home, having been at the library with a study group. Jessica crossed the road close to her home rather than use the pedestrian crossing farther up the street. Probably no cars on the road at that hour anyway, Ellen thought.

The report said Jessica was hit side on by the car, flung onto the bonnet, hit the windscreen and flew from the car to the road all while the vehicle was doing above the speed limit. Ellen moved to the next document. An older couple walking their dog a little farther down the street and on the opposite side, didn't realize what had happened until they arrived at the body. They noted the only car on the road was a black sports car that had sped past them. They weren't able to help with registration or ID of the driver. They called the ambulance and waited with Jessica. The woman said she held Jessica's hand but Jessica was dead by the time the ambulance arrived. The driver and the vehicle were never found.

What did you see or know, Jessica? Ellen wondered.

Ellen flicked the screen to the next file ... just the autopsy ... nothing untoward there ... she thumbed through to the next page. It was the witness statement Jessica had given the police when they were investigating William Ying's disappearance. Ellen had read it earlier, but reviewed it again in light of all that had been happening. She stopped, looked up and saw Mitch walking towards them. He dropped down at the table next to Samantha, reached for his drink and glanced at his watch.

"OK?" Ellen asked.

"Yep, thanks," he said. He struggled to add more but she guessed the call was personal. Ellen smiled at him and went back to her electronic files.

"So refresh my memory on Jessica Wu," Mitch said, moving into safer territory.

"I'm just reading her statement again. Jessica Wu had seen William Ying talking with a Caucasian man and they were walking towards a black limousine parked at the rear of the gallery. She recalled William left the party in a car with number plates that looked like they were government-issued plates." Ellen confirmed the dates again. "She gave this statement the day after William disappeared and she died that same day."

"Government plates, hmm," Mitch said. "William was a foreign ambassador, so he would have a car with government plates."

"Yes," Ellen agreed. "And the Caucasian man could have been his driver, body guard, a friend ..."

"But not the VIP, people would remember that," Nick said closing the CCTV footage file.

"Anything stand out?" Mitch nodded towards Nick's phone.

"Nothing unusual," Nick said.

"Ellie, see if you can find out who William's regular driver or security person was, their name and nationality."

"Done," Ellen said.

They returned to the car, Nick taking the driver's seat before Mitch could get there. He turned the car out onto the road and continued to D.C.

"Amy's doing lasagna tonight," Nick told him.

Mitch turned to him and grinned. "I'm in the middle of a case here ..."

"Yeah, you want some, I know you do," Nick continued. "She did invite you when I mentioned you hadn't eaten for three days, but I said you were covered."

"You would have said that anyway," Mitch said.

"You're right, more for me."

"More Amy or lasagna?" Samantha asked from the back seat.

Mitch ignored Samantha's question and returned to talking work. "So nothing unusual on the CCTV footage, there's nothing new in Dylan's files that I can see. Sam, what about Kinaird?"

"You and Ellie seem to have the lowdown first time around—an accident in the wet. Nothing untoward, car in good working order and no witnesses," Samantha said.

"I think our connection with Kinaird lies in the fact that he saw William talking to one of the scientists," Mitch said.

"You think they would kill him for that?" Samantha asked.

"People have been killed for less and if they thought Kinaird had cottoned onto the fact that they were refining or making a weapon in the uni science lab, yep, I think that would do it," Mitch said. "Then there is Rodney Lam. When we went to where he used to live, not only is he gone, but the house is gone. It's an empty block of land."

"What happened to him?" Nick asked.

"Died in a fire, supposedly," Ellen said.

Mitch sighed and stared out the window. "Why would William fake his own disappearance so he could go underground and work on the weapon? Bit extreme when he was about to finish his tenure and had residency granted."

"But residency wouldn't give him the access that he had as an ambassador," Nick said.

"True," Mitch said. "So when did he get to know the VIP? Why the hell did they kill William Ying?"

Mitch began to tap his leg again, Nick rolled his eyes and Ellen grinned at him in the rearview mirror.

51

THEY WERE ALMOST FOUR HOURS INTO THEIR SIX hour journey; Mitch was staring out the window thinking, Nick was driving and Samantha was asleep when Ellen cried out.

"Mitch!"

He wheeled around. "What, what's wrong?"

"Oh my God, Nick pull over quickly," she said.

Nick pulled the car to the side of the road and Ellen jumped out. Mitch followed. She went to the car trunk, grabbed one of her folders and began shuffling through papers, handing wads of paper to Mitch to hold while she did so.

"Found it!" she exclaimed. "I can't believe it."

Nick and Samantha joined them at the back of the car.

"Remember I said to you that Dylan Ting looked

familiar to me?" Ellen said to Mitch. "When I first met him down in Marcus's area, I asked him if we had gone to the same college or school."

Mitch nodded, willing her to continue.

"He did look familiar to me." She gave a photo to Mitch. "These are the shots Amy blew up from the CCTV footage. There was someone in the car when William Ying got in it at the photo gallery exhibition. It was a fuzzy shot but Amy and I thought that might have been Rodney Lam, the person we can't find, whose address was a vacant block of land."

Mitch looked at the photo. His eyes narrowed as he squinted at the figure in the backseat and then widened in surprise.

"Holy crap," he said handing the photo to Nick.

"Precisely," Ellen agreed.

Mitch rang John. "John, you need to put Dylan Ting in high security; Ellie's just discovered that Dylan Ting is Rodney Lam who went missing when William did. I want to talk to him as soon as we get back. Don't buy the insane act, he knows exactly what he is doing."

Mitch took over the driving, his mind racing through the scenarios. He rang Amy Callaghan.

"Amy, I've got you on loud speaker," he warned her straight off. "I know you did some research on

Rodney Lam for Ellie, but can you go back further than his university years? Find his family, where he went to school, anything you can?"

"Done," she confirmed.

"Thanks, and if you find anything, can you call me back on this line?"

"Will do."

Mitch hung up.

Nick turned to look at him. "Mitch ..."

"Yeah?" Mitch glanced his way before returning his eyes to the road.

"I just thought of something since we're having a day of epiphanies."

"I'm not sure I'm up for another one ... what the heck, go ahead," Mitch said.

"I think I know where the two bodies are ... the Villiers, that couple who were onboard the boat Ru and Dylan took over."

"Where?" Mitch prompted him.

"I could be completely wrong of course," Nick said.

"Where?"

I remember walking over a plank on the boat that was a bit loose."

"Under the floorboards on board?" Mitch exclaimed.

"Just a thought; there were two people before the storm, and after the storm, there wasn't. So they've either been washed overboard or if those were shots, pushed overboard or 'stored' perhaps," Nick said.

Mitch nodded. He rang John hands free.

"This is why I should drive," Nick said, "you're always on the phone."

"Mitch?" John answered.

"John, you're on loud speaker. Nick might have discovered where the bodies of the Villiers are and if so, they're still on the boat. We're near Richmond, any chance there's a chopper heading back to Cape Hatteras that could take Nick and Ellen?"

"Mitch, you have no budget left …" John began.

"Your shout then? C'mon, John …"

"Seriously Mitch, when are you starting that finance course? I'll see what I can do. There's an emergency-only helipad at the Ocracoke Airport … but I suppose a double murder might count." John hung up.

"Pretty please," Ellen said. "A four hour drive back versus what … about ninety minutes in a chopper? No comparison."

"And no more tapping, phone calls, window down, window up, tapping again … gee I'll miss that," Nick added.

———

Dylan Ting was transferred to a high security wing in the same complex. John Windsor looked through the glass panel and watched him. Dylan was sitting in the corner, staring up at the window that was too high to see out of at ground level. He didn't move; no sign of delirium or panic, he sat perfectly still.

John Windsor entered the room and Dylan Ting turned to look at him. He was about to rise and John indicated for him to stay where he was.

"Dylan, let's drop the madness act, shall we? I assume you've been read your rights?"

"I have a contract with orders; I did what was expected of me in those orders, so why are you holding me here?" His voice had a hysterical twinge.

"Mitchell will be back in a few hours and will come and speak with you then. I just wanted you to know that I am aware you are being held here and I've authorized it," John said.

"But you can't. This is why I wanted my orders in writing, you can't ..."

John departed the room.

———

Mitch and Samantha drove away leaving Nick and Ellen at the HeloAir headquarters in Richmond, ready to board a chopper for Ocracoke Airport. They still had two hours' drive ahead of them and neither was looking forward to being together. After ten minutes of silence where Mitch silently prayed his phone would ring, Samantha cut to the chase.

"Mitch, how are you feeling now?"

"Good," he answered automatically.

"Uh huh." She rolled her eyes. "How are you feeling mentally, emotionally and physically?"

"All three?" he protested.

"We have two hours. Can't we talk about this?" Samantha asked.

Mitch sighed. "Why don't you start, tell me how you feel three ways and I'll do my best to follow suit, despite all my shortcomings in that area," he said.

Samantha turned to look at him. "Why would you say that?"

"Just the general female consensus I've heard of late." He shrugged. "So?"

"OK," Samantha began. "Mentally ..."

Mitch interrupted her. "Sam, in the interests of this discussion which we knew we couldn't avoid, let's at least both say what we mean."

She nodded. "Mentally, I feel like I don't get enough challenges. I feel like you give Ellen meatier work than me and I don't feel like you encourage initiative."

Mitch took it on the chin.

"So you know the role is largely research, surveillance and then bringing it home," he summed it up. "What mental challenges do you want?"

"I want to be given the chance to run with something like Ellen did several times during this investigation, when you got her to step up."

"Of course, but she's second-in-charge; if I'm out of action, that's her job. You'll earn that eventually. I didn't come straight into this role. I followed orders in the air force and worked my way up and I did the same in the FBI, following orders until John recruited me to lead the team. You're pretty wet behind the ears."

She looked straight ahead.

"I'll give you an example," Mitch said. "If you were in charge when I was tied up in the VIP house and you came downstairs to rescue me, what would you have done first?"

"Checked you were still alive, untied you, got medical assistance ..." she said.

"And while I appreciate that, it's not the right thing to do unless I am on fire, or obviously going to die immediately if you don't attend to me. Ellen followed protocol. She entered the room weapon at the ready, checked it was safe for herself, me and for you and Nick and then when she confirmed the men were secure and the area was clear, she approached me. If she had come straight to me and there was someone still in the room, she could have been knocked out and then I'm still in danger, not to mention you and Nick. This is the stuff you should know or be watching and learning. I know you passed your training, but you're not applying it, you've forgotten it or you're out of practice," he said. "Emotionally?"

Samantha looked out the window and avoided eye contact.

"I'm so, so sorry that you are in pain because of me. I feel so guilty and if I could take some of the pain off you, you know I would in heartbeat." She turned back to him.

Mitch nodded. "I wish you could too," he teased her and Samantha smiled.

"I am sorry, Mitch, I've been sick to the stomach since it happened and seeing you limp around and looking pale and shaky, it's been so awful. I'm sorry."

"Thanks, stop making yourself sick about it, clearly I'm OK ... or I will be now we're back on land. Physically?" he continued.

Samantha exhaled. "I'm feeling fit, fittest I've ever been and in that category, I'm feeling good. Sorry, I know you're not."

Mitch nodded. "It'll pass."

"Now you have to share and be totally honest, Mitch."

"Right." Mitch's phone rang to his relief. "John, you're on speaker."

"Where are you?" John asked.

"Just dropped Ellie and Nick off to wait for the chopper and Sam and I are heading back. Have you seen Dylan?"

"Yes, I just visited him and told him to expect you in a couple of hours. He's dropped the mad act and he's clinging onto his written orders."

"Mm, I knew that was coming."

"Nothing else?" John asked.

"Not yet. And you?" Mitch asked hopefully.

"Nope. All right, see you soon." John hung up.

Mitch took a deep breath, ready to continue his discussion with Samantha.

Nick and Ellen landed and went straight from the chopper pad at Ocracoke Airport to the boat hire and sped out towards the motor yacht formerly inhabited by Dylan Ting and Pan Ru.

They turned off the engine and drifted in beside it. Nick reached over and secured their boat to the railing of the floating yacht. Ellen grabbed her weapon and boarded the boat, going through the process again of ensuring it was clear. When they were satisfied they were alone, Nick went below deck to where he had felt the loose timber board, and Ellen followed. He tapped on it; it was still springy. He pried it up.

"Oh no." Ellen looked away.

Nick reeled back. "God, how many dead bodies do I have to see this week?"

Ellen returned her gaze to the two bodies: a mature couple, the Villiers, who had met their death in an untimely manner. Both had a single gunshot wound to the forehead.

Nick returned to deck and sat on a bench and exhaled. He pulled his shirt up and wiped his face. Ellen moved beside him and placed her hand on his shoulder.

"I was hoping you were wrong," she said.

"Me too," he said. "I've seen eight dead people this week; that must be a record. You know I wouldn't mind so much if they were all crims, but those two ..." he thought about the couple, "... this is probably their dream. I know it's my dad's to retire and sail away. And those four cops too." He shook his head.

Ellen squeezed his shoulder.

"I'll call Mitch," she said. "Why don't you get back in our boat? There's nothing more to be done here."

52

Mitch saw Ellen's number come up. He and Samantha were almost back in D.C. and a string of calls from Amy, John and Nick had delayed his conversation with Samantha.

"Ellie, are they there?" Mitch asked.

"Yep, two of them dead, single shot to the forehead. An elderly couple, the Villiers I'm guessing, but we'll need to formally identify them."

"Damn," Mitch swore. "Where are you two now?"

"Back in our boat, just drifting next to it. I think you had better chat to Nick," she said.

"Why?"

"He's freaked out. Said he's seen too many bodies this week and the older couple reminded him of his parents. He said it was his father's dream to retire and get a boat."

"Shit," Mitch said. "Are you OK?"

"Yeah, I'm fine, don't worry."

"I'll call him back on his number. Hey thanks, Ellie. I'll call John first so stay put. I'll get him to organize the lock down and call you with instructions."

Mitch rang John and updated him, handing the clean up over to him. He turned to Samantha beside him. "I know we're almost home, but I just need to pull over and call Nick."

"That's fine, stop at a gas station and I'll grab us a few Cokes," she said.

Mitch drove another few miles and finding a gas station, he pulled in. He got out of the car, walked away to a park across the road and called Nick on his phone.

"Mitch, I'm OK," he answered drily.

"Yeah, I know that."

"So why are you calling if Ellen didn't tip you off?"

"To check Ellie was all right," Mitch stretched the truth.

"She seems fine. We're back in our boat now. She's just gone down below. John rang and is organizing the extraction."

"I'm sorry I took you with me to open the container," Mitch said. "I didn't realize it would be, well, such a big week."

"You know the couple dead on the boat, the old bloke looked a bit like Dad, he was probably living the dream ..." Nick talked and Mitch let him get it out of his system.

———

Mitch returned to the car and the Samantha inquisition.

"Is he alright?" she asked.

"Yeah fine," Mitch said.

"Are you going to live up to your side of this discussion?" she asked.

"Sorry Sam, but at the moment all the other stuff coming in takes priority," he explained.

"I understand," she said. "Mentally, emotionally, physically, let's go."

"Mentally, I'm good, but I can barely concentrate on this discussion; I've got so many scenarios going through my head. I'm also aware that you, Nick and Ellie all have your own goals you want to achieve but sometimes on a job, that goes to the back burner while we solve other problems."

"Do you sleep?" Samantha asked.

"Does that fall into one of the categories?" he asked defensively.

"Let me reword it then, does all the mental activity keep you awake?"

"I'm used to the many mental tracks running in my head. When I sleep I usually crash. You learn to do that in the military."

"Emotionally?" she asked.

Mitch stiffened. He shrugged. "I'm worried about Nick, he's seen a lot of shit this week."

"But you, Mitch!" Samantha said.

"I'm too busy to think about much but work. Physically ..." he continued, not waiting to find out if she was satisfied with that answer or not, "this is the worst assignment I've had for a long time on my health. Not just because I'm black and blue, but that sea sickness, retching is such hard work." He rubbed his chest.

"I know," she agreed. "Yet we did it a lot when we were kids catching all the childhood illnesses that went around. It didn't seem so bad then." Samantha sighed.

"I know, or have we just forgotten?" Mitch mused.

"What's going to happen now, Mitch?"

Mitch glanced at her and back at the road. "I'm guessing you want to know how I feel about you on the team."

She turned to him and nodded. "Can I say first," she said, "that I hear what you're saying about earning my place in the team and abiding by my training, I can do it, I will improve, Mitch."

Mitch swallowed. "Sam, I don't think you're ready to be an agent or part of a Criminal Investigative Division team yet. You haven't got the discipline; you haven't improved in the year you have been with me. You've made the same errors multiple times and I'm not just saying this because you nearly got me killed. I'm worried you'll get yourself, Nick or Ellie killed and then I'll have to live with the fact that I should have pulled you out a long time ago. You're strong with digital media and equipment, so maybe you should think about computer forensics."

Samantha leaned back on her seat as if she had been hit and turned to look out the window.

"I'm not saying you won't make a great agent, but you haven't got the discipline for it yet. There must be other sections that interest you more or can give you the challenges that you want?"

"Are you expelling me from the team?" she turned to ask him.

Mitch felt his anxiety levels rising. "I've already asked John to find you another position."

Mitch's phone rang. Samantha turned her face to the window again. Mitch answered, not recognizing the number.

"Mitchell Parker," he said.

"Mitch, it's Amy, I'm on a secure line. Can you talk?"

"Yep, Samantha's with me and you're on speaker phone. Go ahead."

"Hi Sam, you both won't believe what I have to tell you."

"I reckon I might." He sighed.

"Dylan Ting is a registered agent with us, passed all his checks and passed all his tests with flying colors. However, the university didn't check him out very well as his student name was Rodney Lam. He was accepted on a false school certificate, disappeared as Rodney Lam and graduated as Dylan Ting," Amy said.

"How does that happen?"

"I suspect it is easier than ever today with forging documents. But it gets better ..."

"Go on, sock it to me," Mitch said.

"Rodney Lam aka Dylan Ting is related to Lam Mei, or as we say in English putting the surname last, Mei Lam. Now that might not mean anything to you but Mei Lam is the maiden name of Mei Ying, William Ying's wife."

"What the hell?" Mitch exclaimed. He pulled over and grabbed the phone, exiting the car. "Sorry, I almost ran off the road. So you're telling me that Dylan Ting is the nephew of William and Mei Ying."

"Yes, Mei Ying has a deceased brother ..."

"The gardener," Mitch said.

"Sorry?"

"Nothing, just thinking aloud. So Dylan is Mei's deceased brother's son, her nephew?"

"Yes," Amy confirmed.

"So chances are Rodney Lam/Dylan Ting has been working with Uncle William behind the scenes for some time," Mitch said.

"Yes, that's it so far. I'll let you know if I unearth anything else."

"Amy, you are brilliant," he said.

"Why thank you," she replied.

Mitch continued, "Jessica Wu is still my missing link. I can understand the death of Joseph Kinaird and now why Rodney Lam went missing—because he was reborn as Dylan Ting, but if you find anything to connect Jessica Wu, I'd love to wrap that up. And thanks."

"Sure." She hung up.

Mitch paced and noticing Samantha was still in the car, hurried over.

"Sorry I couldn't drive and take it all in at once. I'll update you as I update John, Nick and Ellie." He rang John's number and organized a conference line.

53

"THIS IS HOW IT IS GOING TO GO DOWN," JOHN Windsor said during the conference call, "and I know I don't need to stress that this information is need-to-know classified information that I am sharing with you given it is your jurisdiction, but it requires top secret security clearance. Clear?"

The group confirmed their understanding.

"Given the nature of this threat originated from the People's Republic of China, China is taking responsibility for shutting it down. A Chinese charter plane will be hired to bring home the four police officers who are in the US as our guests to train. On its return journey, that charter plane will not land. There will be a technical problem and the plane will crash and explode into the Arctic Circle. The remains of the four police officers will be identified from this crash. Photos will be doctored to show the men receiving their certificates here and departing from the airport. This will be a national tragedy for China and the United States will express our sincere sympathy and condolences to their president and the families. Any questions?"

"What about the pilot and crew?" Samantha asked.

"That's a decision for the Chinese government. If no more questions, we won't speak of this again."

———

Mitchell Parker stopped for a few moments before entering the holding cell where Dylan Ting sat on the floor staring at the window. He gathered his thoughts. John Windsor stood beside him.

"Do you want to do this later?" John asked.

"No, it's all good," Mitch assured him. "I just need to get my head in this space. I have to discard what I already know from what Ru told me on the boat and try to look at what unfolded from Dylan's perspective, so I don't trip up." He took a deep breath and entered the room.

On seeing Mitch enter, Dylan rose and went to the table and chairs in the middle of the cell. He sat at one of the chairs as Mitch sat opposite.

The two men stared at each other; Mitch waited

to see if Dylan would continue with the madness act.

"It's over then," Dylan said.

Mitch nodded. "It's over."

Dylan shook his head. "This has been years in the making, years. Why did William have to die?"

"Your uncle—I don't know, Dylan, I honestly don't and it wasn't my choice. But your aunt and her daughter, your cousin, are being returned to Beijing."

Dylan nodded. "Who's alive?"

"Danny Huang," Mitch answered.

Dylan scoffed. "Danny Huang, he's like a cockroach, you can't kill him."

"And Ru," Mitch watched for Dylan's reaction.

"He's a nice kid, just in it over his head," Dylan said.

Does he really not know that Ru is with Chinese Intelligence and has just done him over? Mitch's eyes narrowed as he studied Dylan.

"Having said that, Ru's cunning," Dylan added.

"Dylan, tell me the story from the start?" Mitch asked.

"What's in it for me?"

Same old story, Mitch thought as he leaned back. "What do you want?"

Dylan said in a low voice, "If I tell you the patriotic version, will you say I got confused, caught up in family loyalty but cooperated in the end? I want a reduced sentence."

"Depends. What's the other version?"

"The truth," Dylan said, as though it was obvious.

Mitch smirked and shook his head. "What do you think?"

"Then what can you do for me?" Dylan said.

"I'll attest that you cooperated, and that will help with your sentencing," Mitch said. "The abort plan was very clever."

Dylan squinted, his mind processing Mitch's comment.

"You told the team the mission had been compromised—what a loyal new teacher and member of their group you proved yourself to be," Mitch continued. "Really made a hero of yourself, made sure I heard the 'abort mission' message and had it translated. But you didn't tell everyone that, just the local party, then you killed them. You persuaded Ru to work with you or vice versa, and then you, Ru and William carried on with the mission with us out of the way," Mitch watched him for a reaction. "But we weren't out of the way—we didn't call the mission off, it was too late and we weren't sure if something might still go down. A bit of a win for us."

Dylan sat back and thought about it. "That's almost right."

"Well if I don't get your version, you might find a few additional charges in there ... like the murder of two people on a boat."

"We had to do that," Dylan banged his hand on the desk. He drew a deep breath, realizing what he said.

"That was a slip up wasn't it?" Mitch said.

"Your word against mine," Dylan said. "I will tell you but I'm telling this story once only, not to every Johnny who comes in wanting to hear their own version. Do you agree that you will say I cooperated?"

"Agreed," Mitch said.

"Can I have that in writing?" Dylan asked.

Mitch rolled his eyes. "Surely you know by now that your orders aren't worth the paper they are written on given your other life, which you forgot to mention. But hey, if you want it in writing ..."

"Fine, fine," Dylan said.

Mitch glanced toward the two-sided window knowing John Windsor was on the other side.

"For the record," Mitch said turning on a digital voice recorder that sat on the desk between them. He listed the date, their names and the time of the interview and sat back.

———

Nicholas Everett had his second counseling session for the week.

"Is that a record?" he asked the assigned FBI counselor, Dan Clarke.

"Hell no." Clarke laughed. "I have some staff that come to me daily. You're an amateur."

Nick relaxed. "It's just I'm new to death," he said, shrugging.

Clarke nodded. "That's not a bad thing."

———

Ellen Beetson walked in the front door of her house for the first time that week. She closed the door, breathed in deeply and inhaled the smell of fresh paint. She dropped her bag onto the bed, opened a few windows and grabbed her watering can.

———

Samantha Moore opened the letter on her desk. It was a formal notice from John Windsor advising of her transfer effective immediately to Computer Forensics. Samantha was advised to remove her desk belongings to her locker, take one week's leave and report on the date listed to her new supervisor. She was to direct any queries to her current manager, Special Agent Mitchell Parker. Samantha sat back and looked around her empty work area. She saw a yellow stick-on note on her diary from Mitch.

In interrogation room until five p.m. approx. If you want to, pack up, wait for me and I'll take you for a drink, Mitch.

She began to pack up.

———

Amy Callaghan found the link connecting Jessica Wu to the disappearance of William Ying. It was an old Facebook photo, buried deep several years back in the history pages of a deceased account that she had managed to source. She sighed, sat back and cupped her chin in her hands, looking at the photo.

In happier days, she thought, looking at the photo of Jessica Wu with her boyfriend Rodney Lam, alias Dylan Ting. That's a serious case of falling in love with the wrong man, Amy thought. Once Rodney disappeared, I guess Jessica had to as well in case she ever ran into Rodney Lam again as Dylan Ting and could out him.

54

DYLAN TING REMAINED IN THE CENTRAL DETENTION Facility awaiting transfer to the Federal Bureau of Prisons. He took a sip of water and began to tell Mitchell Parker his version of the truth.

"My uncle, William, met the Vice President when they were students in Beijing. They were close. Danny Huang was their other friend—just the three of them—and William said they got into a lot of trouble but made some great memories. My uncle said it began then, a plan to create the ultimate government party."

Mitch nodded. "Young, ambitious and all studying politics."

"Yes," Dylan agreed. "Economics and politics. They planned that this party would be the best of capitalism and socialism—a party which would ensure the country was a powerful force in the world, with a huge, loyal and willing workforce motivated by success and advancement. The standard of living would be enviable, health and education provided for all, technology would be the best in the world and China would be the most advanced culture in the world." Dylan painted their vision with his hands.

"Almost got me," Mitch said.

Dylan laughed, forgetting for a moment they were now on opposite sides. He continued. "The Vice President had his own agenda. He told William and Danny about his grandfather on his mother's side, Alfred, who was shot during the war as a deserter. Alfred was a loyal man who loved his country but he was shell shocked. He had testimonies ... well, his grandmother had spent the rest of her life gathering these from the men in Alfred's platoon attesting to this ... he wandered off, dazed, frightened and was caught and executed by his own men. For the rest of her life she worked to overturn his status as a deserter. The Vice President said it killed her, and eventually his mother succeeded where his grandmother didn't in overturning the charge."

"That bitter memory was just enough to sway the Vice President's loyalties to his country," Mitch summarized.

"So my uncle said." Dylan nodded. "The Vice

President was bitter, but he was also greedy and ambitious and the thought of being a major player in an empire was enough for him to get caught up in the plan with Danny and Uncle William."

"But this is just big dream stuff, we've all dreamed. What put the plan in action?" Mitch asked.

"I think it was big dream stuff for William, but for Danny and the Vice President it was more. After school, they went their separate ways but never lost touch. When William graduated he went into government, making his way up the ladder. He and Danny were always pushing for change; they had both been charged for rioting and inciting crowds several times while pushing for public control of industry and social services.

"It was when William got overlooked for a promotion twice that he changed. This is according to my aunty ... I was here in the States when all this was happening," Dylan clarified. "She said they regarded him as 'soft'. So Danny and William began to work on their old school plan of the ultimate party. William called in an old friend Kiang Hai, who had a network, and it became a subversive and sizeable underground party.

"The Vice President visited Beijing again when he got married. It was timely—William had recently married Mei. There was tension though because

Danny loved Mei, but Mei loved William and she would have followed him anywhere. The Vice President returned to the US and his career began to take a meteoric rise. Soon, he was suggesting to William that he should consider an ambassadorship to the US." Dylan stopped to sip his water.

Mitch watched him. "I assume the offer was not just based on friendship?"

"Oh no," Dylan confirmed. "They had plans and they were developing a weapon which would give them more power, that was actually William's pet project. With me studying at the uni, William as ambassador and the Vice President in the second highest job in the country, let's just say the university was courting us with access to some of the best scientists."

"All coming together nicely," Mitch agreed.

"Yes and Danny who remained in Beijing, began to realize this was their ticket to making a difference."

"So how did you initially get involved?" Mitch asked.

"Uncle William and Aunty Mei couldn't have children for many years and I was the first nephew. My parents travelled a lot and I became William and Mei's surrogate son; I lived with them for years. They didn't have their daughter until six years ago. Anyway, they came here, William served his year as he called it, put in for residence and got it and then disappeared so he could work underground at the university."

"But why?" Mitch asked. "Why couldn't he continue to just live here and do his work?"

Dylan hesitated and then continued speaking. "Because he had a new identity, a bit of a change of appearance and a new name and he was working as a casual in the university lab which gave him around the clock access for his research work. I saw to that through my connections and no one knew him as William."

"Really?" Mitch frowned, "hard to believe. You've got his university access cards and ID?"

Dylan nodded.

"We'll be wanting that. So no one recognized him?" Mitch asked again in disbelief.

Dylan shook his head. "Westerners think we all look alike, so it wasn't hard to pass him off as one of the scientists."

"And is that why Joseph Kinaird and Jessica Wu had to die? Because they would be able to identify you and William?"

"No. It wasn't about identification with Joseph Kinaird; he walked in on William in the science lab —we weren't sure what he heard, so we decided to play safe. Wendy ... I loved Wendy or rather Rodney Lam loved Wendy," he smiled. "But yes, she could identify me, so her death was for the good of the mission."

Mitch shook his head. "Why was the mission aborted?"

"Because I told William that the FBI were intending to destroy the sub and he might be collateral damage. He's my uncle, of course I fed him information. Did you think I'd let him die? We couldn't believe my luck when you called me in to work it ... direct access to intel that I could feed him."

"So why not abort the whole thing?" Mitch asked.

"Because William thought we could still do it under the radar if we were clever and fake the abort to get you guys off our case."

"But the abort order didn't come from William," Mitch said.

"No it didn't," Dylan agreed, "but I orchestrated it on his behalf. Having Danny's phone worked nicely for my plan, thanks. William was furious with Danny for hitting on Aunty Mei, it wasn't the first time Danny had been disrespectful. So given our death was imminent if we proceeded with the current plan, we decided to get rid of the additional party ... to fake that the mission had been aborted and get rid of everyone except the Vice President, me, Ru and William. We needed Ru with his communications skills and contacts in Beijing or I would have bumped him too."

"Lucky Ru," Mitch said. "So you told Ru the plan and he came onboard?"

"William convinced him. He respected William and I knew from spending hours in the car with Ru that he was not going to go back home and tell his family the mission failed."

Mitch nodded encouraging Dylan along. "So you didn't tell Beijing you had aborted the mission," Mitch asked testing again if Dylan knew of Ru's other life.

"No, that's why we needed Ru, he could control that. He could tell Hai he had followed his abort order but not actually do it."

"So run me through what happened on the day the VIP was to be lifted," Mitch said.

Ru nodded. "On the day of the VIP sub pick-up, I sent a text to Hai from Danny's phone saying we had been exposed. Hai panicked and aborted the mission as we expected he would. He gave Ru the orders to communicate it. That's when I rang you from the VIP house, but I couldn't talk, so I just left the phone on speaker so you could hear the abort message."

"So then you expected we would call it off and you could head to the beach, continue the mission and in theory have safe passage," Mitch said. He topped up Dylan's glass of water and poured one for himself.

"Correct," Dylan said. "But then Hai wanted to talk directly with Danny rather than just text. That was impossible, you had Danny under lock and key. So I had to tell Ru this—I told him that in my role as language trainer with the FBI, I had come across that information and had managed to steal Danny's phone."

Mitch frowned and sat back, trying to keep up with Dylan Ting's version of the truth. William and Dylan played right into Ru's hands.

Dylan straightened in his chair. "We had to act quickly now and clean up the situation."

"But I heard the shots ... you didn't kill Hai and the others until after the beach failure," Mitch frowned confused.

Dylan nodded. "That's right. William didn't want to kill them."

"He's not adverse to violence from what I re-member," Mitch rubbed his burnt arm.

"No, he just didn't want to be there when they were killed; he liked Hai. So we secured Hai and Froggy and put them in that cell room," Dylan said.

"Noble," Mitch said sarcastically. "OK, stepping back before all that ... surely the Vice President was panicking?"

"He was oblivious to all that drama. Remember

he and William were close friends, he trusted him, trusted him a lot more than he trusted Danny. Plus William removed the Vice President so he never heard the abort mission message. The Vice President believed whatever we told him ... and we told him that the other men were staying in the water reserve, that underground tank, to go over their plan. We just kept him in the house."

"Didn't he question why they weren't on the beach for the handover?" Mitch asked.

"Sure and we told him because we were minimizing numbers, keeping it safer," Dylan said. "He was so desperate for power, Ru said he would have believed anything."

"Who was the other man we found dead with Hai and Froggy?" Mitch asked.

"A stand-in. Organized to use the fourth passport so the four cops would leave the country together on the right date."

"He drew the short straw," Mitch said.

"People will do anything for money," Dylan shrugged.

"So, you, the Vice President, Ru and William continued with the plan expecting to get to the sub as normal. You and Ru stayed at the VIP house to liaise with Beijing, William and the Vice President went to the beach. Except we hadn't aborted, we were there," Mitch summed it up.

"Yes. I stayed with Ru in the communication room," Dylan confirmed. "I persuaded him to let me, but really I had to keep an eye on him even though he didn't know it. William took the Vice President to the meeting point. When Ru and I saw them killed on the beach via our screens at the VIP house, we killed the three in the cell room, took off via the tunnel and grabbed a boat to lay low for a while. We didn't think anyone would look for us at sea."

"Ah, so you were there as well at the VIP house when we arrived," Mitch said. "I thought it was just one person."

"No. Ru sent me to the car via the tunnel when he saw you in the perimeter camera. I was waiting, ready to drive us out. It was just the two of us and we had to stick together."

"But then you made a mistake, we tracked your phone. You made a call to your aunty from the boat," Mitch said.

"That was a mistake," Dylan agreed. "But if anything happened to me, I couldn't let her wonder forever what happened to William. She wasn't supposed to know he was alive and the FBI probably wouldn't have filled her in."

There was a knock on the interview room door and Mitch looked over as John stuck his head in. "Quick word?" he said.

Mitch noted the time and announced for the recording that he was pausing the interview. He rose and left the room. The security officer outside the door entered the room as Mitch left. He closed the door behind him.

"What a story," Mitch looked at John. "What's up?"

"Danny Huang is dead," John said.

"What? How did that happen? Wasn't he in solitary?"

"He was. But this afternoon he was moved from one prison to a more secure one and ..."

"You've got to be kidding. Did he top himself?" Mitch stood with his hands on his hips.

"No, he didn't kill himself. The driver of the prison transport van pulled his gun, turned the gun on Danny Huang and shot him dead before the fellow officer sitting next to him shot the driver dead. Said he had to in self-defense."

"Oh that's just great," Mitch shook his head. "So who was the driver?"

"An American citizen ..." John began.

"Whose parents were Chinese nationals," Mitch finished.

"Got it in one."

"Well that chapter's closed. For chrissake, how deep does this go? Now with Danny, Hai, William Ying and the VIP all gone, we've only got Dylan and

Ru's word for what went down." Mitch turned hurriedly back to the glass and looked through. Dylan Ting sat still. Mitch breathed a sigh of relief and turned back to John.

"Sorry, thought it might be epidemic." In the next moment he heard the gunshots. He turned to see the glass splattered with blood; Dylan Ting was collapsed on the table, blood pouring from his head onto Mitch's paperwork. In the corner of the room, slumped dead, was a dead security officer, the gun still clutched in his hand, pointed up under his own chin.

"Where's Ru?" Mitch demanded.

———

Mitch and John raced to Ru's holding cell. Mitch breathed a sigh of relief as the young man paced in his cell.

"I'll leave you to it and get back to clean up the Dylan Ting situation," John said. "I'll organize extra security for here. Don't enter until it arrives."

"I think the security was the issue," Mitch reminded him.

Mitch waited impatiently for the guard to arrive. He reached for his phone and called Henri, expecting he had already left for the day.

"Mitch, shall I tell Ann you won't be home until late tonight?" he said knowingly.

"Sorry Henri."

"Don't be. She's well-versed in our hours. Are you back?"

"Yes, but got a few dramas."

"We'll see you when we do then," Henri said.

Mitch hung up just as the guard arrived. They entered Ru's cell.

"Over your seasickness?" Ru asked in perfect English.

"I'm much better on land." Mitch said.

The young Asian man looked at Mitch and smiled. "I know why you are here," he said.

"Word travels fast, even in high security. Unless of course, you organized it." Mitch lowered himself into a chair.

Ru dropped down in a chair opposite him, across the desk. "I told you it had all gone to plan. I've even cleaned up the loose ends ... I'm assuming Dylan Ting is now dead too?"

Mitch nodded.

"Good," Ru smiled. "It would have been more successful if you hadn't pursued me. I'd be gone and there would be no connection to my work," Ru said. "You would have thought I was one of them who escaped."

"If you didn't have Dylan with you, you might have got away. You got two ambitious," Mitch said.

"He offered me access to FBI files," Ru said. "I thought I could go home with more than I came with."

"Go home a hero," Mitch said. "But you made one mistake."

Ru's eyes narrowed as he thought back over his actions.

"You left some files in the tunnel," Mitch said.

Ru's face flared with anger. He leaned forward, close to Mitch and hissed, "Do you think we would allow your Vice President to partner with a bunch of dissidents to corrupt our government?"

"Well we weren't too keen on it either," Mitch said. "So no intel from the Vice President ..."

"... ever surfaced," Ru finished the sentence.

"But you've seen it."

Ru shrugged. "I did the job your people couldn't."

"I think you'll find the job is done and you along with it."

Mitch rose and left.

VISITING CHINESE POLICE OFFICERS DIE IN FIERY CRASH
Associated press:
By Allan Warner

Preliminary investigations into a plane crash that killed four visiting Chinese police officers returning home from the United States after G20 security training, showed that the plane experienced structural failure, an aviation official said.

A specially chartered plane provided as a gift to the men from a grateful benefactor, was bound for Beijing with one crew member and six passengers aboard when it crashed near Komsomolets Island, in the Arctic Ocean 450 miles north of the Siberian coast. There was no distress call and the weather was good at the time.

Military radar revealed that the aircraft disintegrated in midair, breaking into three pieces and exploding. All bodies aboard were recovered.

An aviation officer said the plane was not properly repaired after a tail strike last year and fatigue cracks formed, which eventually led to a structural failure.

The 'black box' data recorders were recovered intact and sent to the Civil Aviation Administration of China.

The President of the United States has expressed his condolences on behalf of the people of America.

55

MITCHELL PARKER WOKE UP FEELING HEAVY. HE WAS lying flat on his stomach and he could feel his head pounding. His tongue felt like sandpaper. He swallowed, opened his eyes and tried to focus. He didn't feel in any danger, after all, he seemed to have a warm doona over him.

Mitch propped himself up; it was Nick and Amy's place and he was on a mattress on the floor; he recognized the spare room. Mitch had one almighty hangover. He remembered starting the night at the pub with Samantha, Nick and Ellen, but couldn't remember finishing it.

He began to turn when he realized someone was lying beside him.

Oh no!

He could see his clothes sprawled over the chair.

He was lying naked, under the doona with someone next to him.

Please God, don't let it be Ellie or Samantha. Christ! Don't be Ellie or Sam.

The person next to him stirred and turned the opposite way. Mitch took his cue. He raised himself and slowly turned over. Relief coursed through him; it was neither of his team. In fact, he didn't know who it was.

He moved to the chair, grabbed his shorts and pulled them on. He grabbed his T-shirt, threw it on and made for the door. He listened at the ajar door for any movement, then gauged it safe to go out. He wasn't keen on being caught by Amy, if he looked as bad as he felt.

Slipping out of the room, he glanced around; the coast was clear. He made his way to the bathroom, conscious of the smell of alcohol coming out of his pores. He stripped and climbed into the shower, gulping mouthfuls of warm water. Sometime after, Mitch heard the bathroom door open and looked over to see Nick entering. He grunted at Mitch, as he used the toilet behind the door.

"Want some breakfast?" Nick asked.

"Let's go out for something greasy," Mitch said. "I've written off my body for the weekend."

"Just like old times." Nick yawned. "Is she still in there?"

Mitch had forgotten. "Shit! Yes. Who is she? What's her name?" he whispered.

"Jane ... no ... Julie. No, that's the one in my room," Nick suggested.

"Great."

"I can't remember," Nick said. "Don't worry, they probably can't remember our names either. Let me know when you're out of the shower." Nick walked out, closing the door behind him.

Mitch stepped out of the shower and grabbed a towel.

He sighed, drying himself with as much energy as he could muster. He dressed, feeling like he was in slow motion and departed the bathroom. Mitch pushed opened Nick's bedroom door and indicated the shower was clear. He went back to the bedroom to rouse his bed friend.

———

"What time did Ellie and Sam leave?" Mitch asked between bites of scrambled eggs and bacon.

Nick shrugged. "Ellie arrived late and went early, Sam kicked on for a while."

"Do you think Sam's OK?" Mitch asked.

"I think she's hot for you," Nick said.

Mitch scoffed. "Not likely."

"Trust me, you're the only one who can't see it.

499

Since she's not on your team anymore you could ask her out. Although, I guess you could have gone out with her when she was on your team."

"Yeah, that'd be awkward, and what if she only agrees to go out with me because she wants to keep her job," Mitch shook his head. "Nuh, not interested, Sam's not my speed."

"Bet she'd be good in bed," Nick said.

"Yeah, but you've got to talk to them in the morning," Mitch said.

Nick grinned. "You always over-think things."

"Good thing one of us does."

They ate in silence for a short while.

"I think she'll be good in Computer Forensics. She's good with that techno crap," Mitch added as an afterthought.

"She'll be fine, stop worrying about her, you did what you had to do. Want another coffee?" Nick asked.

Mitch nodded and sat back. "Sunday."

Nick looked around. "Yep, all day."

"I can't tell you the last time I had a weekend off. Two days in a row."

"Good thing too; a day to recover after last night," Nick rubbed his temples.

Mitch's phone rang and John Windsor's name came up. He groaned.

"You jinxed it," Nick said.

Mitch answered.

"Mitch, got a possible new agent for your team. It would only be for a year though, a contract position. He's one of our agents located overseas with the Trans-National Crime Unit and wants to come back for a stint."

"That'd work. How soon can I get him?"

"He's here now, arrived last week, been catching up with his relatives. He's been overseas for a long time though, doesn't sound like a local. Do you want to meet him today?"

"No ... why would I?" Mitch frowned at the strange request.

"Just thought it would be good to meet him out of the office before you get caught up in the next job. By the way did I say good job on that last one?"

"Thanks, but it didn't feel like a good job, it felt out of control, like we were playing catch up the whole time."

"Who would have seen half of that unfolding as it did?" John said. "And if you hadn't cottoned on to the fact that the VIP was the VP, imagine the mess the government would be in. It allowed us to shut it down off the radar, and it finished clean at least," John added.

"I've never had so many enemies working together and against each other on one case. I'm still not convinced it's cleaned up but I'm guessing you know more than me and you're not sharing."

"Anyway, good job," John said.

"Mm," Mitch said suspiciously, "it won't feature as one of my favorites in my memoirs."

John laughed. "Where are you?"

"I'm having breakfast with Nick in 18th Street. Send the new guy down if you like. What's his name?"

"He said he knows you. See you tomorrow." John hung up without answering the question.

Mitch began on his second cup of coffee. He looked at Nick.

"Sam's replacement, the new guy, is meeting us here for coffee, now. He's home from a posting overseas. Poor Ellie is now outnumbered."

"Lucky girl," Nick said.

Mitch began to smile.

"What?" Nick asked.

"I just realized who we might have scored." He remembered the hot shot agent in the UK who joined them on their Canary Wharf job.

"Do we know him?" Nick asked.

"We know him. I bet it is Adam Forster."

"The limey?"

"He's American. He's just been working in the TCU in the UK for so long he's become one of them."

Mitch saw the car pull up before he saw Forster. The Porsche slid into a narrow park with ease and the driver alighted. He looked nearby, up and down the cafe strip, saw Mitch and Nick and grinned. He crossed the road and walked over to them.

"Did you drive it across the water?" Nick asked.

"Just leased it," he said, and shook both of the men's hands before taking a seat beside Nick, and motioning for a coffee.

"Welcome home," Mitch said.

"Thanks. I heard you needed me." Forster grinned.

"Just don't bed another one of my team," Mitch said.

Forster looked at Nick. "Not my type."

Mitch shook his head. "I was going to take some leave, the timing is looking perfect!"

"I hear there are some good cruise bargains going at the moment," Nick grinned.

THE END

Dear reader,

We hope you enjoyed reading *Graveyard of the Atlantic*. Please take a moment to leave a review, even if it's a short one. Your opinion is important to us.

Discover more books by Helen Goltz at https://www.nextchapter.pub/authors/helen-goltz

Want to know when one of our books is free or discounted for Kindle? Join the newsletter at http://eepurl.com/bqqB3H

Best regards,

Helen Goltz and the Next Chapter Team

THE STORY CONTINUES

The story continues in:
The Fourth Reich by Helen Goltz

To read the first chapter for free, head to:
https://www.nextchapter.pub/books/the-fourth-
reich

ACKNOWLEDGMENTS

My sincere thanks to:

Rachel Quilligan for her subbing prowess;

Sally Odgers and Chris Adams for proofreading and feedback;

And most importantly Atlas B. Goltz - my beloved writing partner.

ABOUT THE AUTHOR

After studying English Literature and Communications at universities in Queensland, Australia, Helen Goltz has worked as a journalist, producer and marketer in print, TV, radio and public relations. She was born in Toowoomba and has made her home in Brisbane, Queensland.

Connect with Helen
    Visit the website at: http://www.helengoltz.com/

Or Facebook at:
    https://www.facebook.com/HelenGoltz.Author/

Follow on Twitter at: @helengoltz

Made in the USA
Middletown, DE
17 April 2020